Jessica of Russ

Out of the Country

Jan Elpel

Silver Sage Studio & Press, LLC

Jessica of Russ, Out of the Country

Copyright 2020 Silver Sage Studio & Press, LLC
Cover Art and Illustrations by Jan Elpel
Cover Design and Format by GRIFFITI

Publisher's Cataloging-in-Publication Data
Elpel, Jan 1937 –

Jessica of Russ, Out of the Country / By (Author) Jan Elpel

    ISBN: 978-1-892784-47-6 $20.00 Pbk. (alk. paper)
    1. Historical Fiction. 2. Russia, 1946. 3. Mysticism
    4. Women Workers of USSR. 5. Post-WWII Attitudes
    & Culture. 6. Monastery Life 7. St. John Chrysostom.
    I. Elpel, Jan. IV Title

Silver Sage Studio & Press, LLC
[An Imprint of HOPS Press, LLC]

8215 Fowler Lane
Bozeman, MT 59718
jelpel@montanadsl.net

Jessica of Russ, Out of the Country, a novel set in Russia, 1946, explores postwar attitudes through the experiences of a 20-year-old woman and the Brothers of a monastery. The individuals seek to fit the mystical faith and spirit of the Mount Athos Greek Orthodox teachings into their lives against the daily reality of Communist atheism. JE

"Written with compelling detail, Jan Elpel's historical novel chronicles the life of a young woman and her friends to find a meaningful life in the chaos of post WWII Russia. This is a fascinating and beautifully told story of hope and friendship."

— Susan Morgan, Jungian Analyst

"Reading about Jessica's life rekindled memories of living under the controlling oppressive regime and forced labor in fields during harvest; however, staged on this potentially depressing background, Jan Elpel managed to craft an uplifting story about dreams, hope, and love."

— Zuzana Gedeon, Screen Writer and Director

"From one of Bozeman's most interesting authors is a new historical fiction based in Russia in 1946. From the amazing stories at the monastery to the incredible detail of how people were treated, you feel as if you where there along with them."

— Margie Peterson, Editor and Oral Historian

Fourteenth Century Wooden Church on Kizhi Island, Russia

Author's Notes

JESSICA OF RUSS, Out of the Country, is a fictional story of "Jessica" Svetlana Sergeevna Gilkova of Konsky, USSR, 1946, and her friends and family, as well as benefactors Abbot Konstantin, Brother Dmitri and other monks of St. Sansais Monastery. All characters, small towns, villages and monastery are imagined. The culture and attitudes of post-World War II are generally portrayed with historical authenticity.

Inspiration for the characters' search for meaning comes from the inherent mysticism best stated as the *dus'ha*, the soul of the country. For the faithful, "the heart of Russia is Orthodoxy," though diverse religions were represented in what was the Soviet Union. Central to the novel is the inner yearning of many for a sustaining belief in God at a time when religious faith was banned, and lifted only briefly during war years. Poets, writers, artists and composers were persecuted or exiled for portraying the suffering of the people under Stalin's oppression and the Communist system. Individual life became public life owned by the State. Yet the dreams of a young woman burst forth "like tulips in the spring" when Jessica turned twenty years old.

Against an historical background of Russia's unparalleled losses in WWII, I found history pays tribute to Soviet women workers, yet rarely allots even a postscript to the collateral damage they suffered in that time period. Ultimately, their stories, long buried and denied, have to be uplifting.

My life-long love of Russian literature, art and music, and the underlying mysticism continue to inspire me to turn again and again to the people's spirit of faith and survival—and spirit knows no international borders.

— Jan Elpel

Historical Perspectives

Rus refers to an ancient name for Russia, (Russ) which relates to the River Rus and the tribal people living there. Lands were unified in the Middle Ages by an extensive system of thriving trade routes north almost to the Arctic and south to the Black Sea.

1917	Russian Revolution overthrow of Tsar Nicholas II and end of the reign of Romanov dynasty. Eighty percent of the population was rural.
1920s –30s	Access to housing and consumer goods dependent upon position in society and place of work.
1930s	Famine due to severe drought and mismanagement of agricultural industry.
1939	Beginning of World War II with Germany's invasion of Poland. Women were drawn into the labor force in Russia.
1941–44	Siege of Leningrad by German and Finnish armed forces.
1945	End of European WWII with Potsdam Agreement among Allied powers and annexation of independent bordering states to Russia.
1946	Rise of industrial revolution in Soviet Union accompanied by severe drought and famine. Citizens increasingly exposed to Western culture and goods.
1953	Death of Stalin and succession of Khrushchev who increased housing in five-story concrete block state-owned apartments of low quality, nine square meters per person.
1970s	Most families lived communal style in a single room with shared kitchen and bath.
1989–90	Collapse of Soviet Union when annexed countries regained independence. Population shifted to eighty percent urban due to intensive industrialization and urbanization programs.

Russian Names

Most Russian people have three names: a first name, a patronymic, and a surname. The patronymic or middle name refers to the father's first name.

> Russian surnames usually change depending on the gender of the person.
> Men's surnames commonly end with *ich, evich, ovich*.
> Others endings are *ev, in, kov, ov, sky* and *uk*.
> Women's surnames are the same plus an *a* at the end for most surnames ending in *v* and *n*. Surnames ending in *y* change to the feminine form by replacing the ending with *aya*.

Russian nicknames, or diminutives, are short forms of the given name used between well-acquainted people, relatives, friends, and colleagues.

Sasha is a common Russian name for men and women whose given name is Alexander or Alexandra. The name may be expressed as:
> Sasha +father's name+ surname in formal use.
> Sasha in short form or casual relationships.
> Sashenka as a form of affection.

Jessica of Russ
Out of the Country

Part I

"—she sang of childhood's fun,

Russia's old glories and their gleams,

the heart and all its fragile dreams." Pushkin

I

Svetlana

Tatyana Pytrovna cried every day when she reached the sanctuary of her room, a closet large enough to sleep one small girl. Sobs penetrated a thin partition between the closet and one room that served as kitchen, dining and bedroom. And every day that "Jessica" Svetlana Sergeevna had to listen to the sobs she slammed the doors and banged the crocks and pots. This unbearable crying is not what I agreed to in the first place, Jessica often swore to herself and to anyone who would listen.

"Look at me. Not yet twenty and a nursemaid. *A pachyemoo?* But why? Quit that infernal sniffling or I will box you, do you hear?"

Muffled sounds from the tiny bedroom meant that Tatyana pulled a straw-filled duvet over her head and she would eventually fall asleep, missing supper and any chance to make amends with Jessica. Jessica sloshed water in the dishpan and washed one of her two work dresses, a thin cotton garment, and flung it over the window sill to dry.

Swiping the drips with a rag, she fumed, "My dress looks like a rag. Why do I bother?" and turned up a spurt of gas flame under a cooking pot. Warm rancid potato soup would be their supper, if Tatyana got up.

Jessica and Tatyana had made the soup on Sunday when they were rested and laughing. A village piper had come from the next town to amuse the children. The cousins, feeling free as youngsters, joined the dancing and merrymaking in the street. When the last notes of the penny whistle floated away, the piper tripped away from the wildly enthusiastic dancers and dogs. On the way home Jessica and Tatyana picked up a basket of vegetables from a woman whose garden sustained many of the residents of Konsky.

But today was Thursday and the kettle of potato soup lacked proper cooling during the past week of sunny June days. Nasty weather had merit when it preserved foods, yet food could not be wasted. Jessica frugally stretched provisions the same way her mother had done, until the next Sunday when they might restock their kitchen shelf. Cucumber medallions on bits of hard cheese served as lunches. They would finish the sliced turnip on black bread tomorrow. That would leave the squash to boil on Saturday.

Tatyana thrust herself from beneath the bulky cover and shoved her feet into stiff leather shoes to make an appearance. "*Isvinitye.* I am sorry, Jessica. I do not mean to disturb you. It is only homesickness that overtakes me when I am off work—when my mind is not forced to concentrate on stitching shoes."

"Your home is here, Tanya. By all the saints, you have been here almost a year. How long are you going to cry about it? I see no end to it."

"You have been good to me, Svetlanka. The fault is mine, not yours. It is the separation from my family and the—"

Jessica knew Tanya started to mention her old work horse, Gorgi, but didn't because she would cry again. Jessica poured soup into two heavy bowls and wondered about her own outburst—"by all the saints" echoed her mother's exasperation, not even remotely her own. She placed a bowl for Tanya, along with a spoon on a worn wooden table. Tanya often begged intimacy with her cousin by calling her Svetlanka or Lana, but it would not have mattered which diminutive she used. Svetlana had seen an American movie featuring Jessica Tandy, and the name so appealed to her that one Winter's Day in the tiny village where her parents lived, she announced, "I prefer to be called 'Jessica.'"

"*Bah*, why do you want an American name? The Americans did not win the war," Vera complained. "Mother Russia won the war, *da*!

You should be proud of your name.

"Sergey," she added, "our daughter entertains pretenses that will only bring us trouble."

Jessica later discovered 'Svetlana' meant "one of light," a common name in Russia and the name of the Great Leader's daughter. *Tak*, so what? Jessica lived away from home now, on her own in the town of Konsky, where she chose to call herself whatever she desired. There were enough restrictions and deprivations, one should be able to own a beautiful name, she argued. However, she made sure that no one at the Boot and Shoe factory knew she dared be so opinionated. Jessica frowned upon Tatyana's name, Tanya or Tatyanka when they got on, but nevertheless, one who harbored no romantic fantasies about American movies.

At a tap on the door, Jessica sprang to her feet and unbolted it to usher in Lettina, a gangly young woman in an oversize print dress, who practically bounded between Jessica's cot and the table in the cramped space. She leaned over to give Jessica and Tanya kisses on each cheek and nearly spilled their soup. Whispering and laughing below her breath all at once she regaled her friends with the latest story, while keenly aware there might be listeners on the other side of the walls.

"I went to the monastery with Katya and Greita, a new girl at the mill. We would usually be working, but we were all free because the dam broke and the stream washed away parts of the mill."

"*Podozhdite, pozhaluysta*, stop please, Lettina. Did you say you went to the monastery? And the mill washed away? I don't understand a word of what you are saying," Jessica interrupted.

Lettina's rich, hearty laugh prompted Jessica and Tanya to shush her until they all huddled cross-legged on a rag rug on the floor, dresses tucked beneath their knees.

"*Da,* a torrent of water came down the stream after the dam broke and nearly washed away the supports under the mill. It carried away one water wheel and the other may be badly damaged."

"You mean we will have no flour?"

"I mean we can no longer grind flour until the mill is repaired."

The gravity of the situation settled upon the girls, stifling their conversation. Jessica chewed her short nails. Shutdown of the mill, the mill being one certainty in generations of lives in Konsky, threatened the main source of their food supply. State promises to provide adequately after nationalization of all businesses were seldom fulfilled. And rumors of another drought in Kursk Province, as well as potential famine in Russia's breadbasket in the South, stirred a widespread sense of insecurity.

"The flood happened last week. We have been cleaning the mill since, removing equipment and supplies and mopping up. You cannot imagine—"

"I cannot imagine you traveling about midweek. Or being allowed to go to the monastery." Jessica tried to grasp the gist of the monologue.

Lettina slapped her knee and bent forward to confide. "Tomenko Barskenkovich is old, but he wants to rebuild the mill with electricity. It will take time—"

"Tell us, Lettina, did you see Pasha at the monastery?" Tanya burst in, unable to wait longer to squeeze in a few words.

"No." Lettina's voice slowed and she searched the cousins' faces. "We delivered flour to the soup kitchen in Siver, a short walk from the monastery. The most we could do at St. Sansais was ask about him for you at the gate."

"And what did you hear?" Jessica pursued.

"My friends, I am happy to report he is improving. That is what we were told. He is improving."

Silence followed the news. Cousin Pasha would live, but no doubt he would be disabled in ways the girls dared not envision. Jessica swallowed hard, not knowing if it was in relief or in fear of his condition. Dear, playful Pasha, "improving." Pasha, an older cousin she and Tanya had thought lost in the war until word recently came that the monastery had taken him in. Calmer now in the face of the reality confronting her two friends, Lettina went on.

"St. Sansais is a lovely place for your Pasha to heal and the vineyards are beautiful. I would like to stay there. As far as I could tell, the monastery sustained minimal damage during the war, not the first conflict it has endured." Her voice softened, tender and reassuring; her wide-set, light blue eyes pleaded for them to believe.

"Do you think they will keep him there if he recovers?" Tanya spoke hesitantly, as if afraid to hear that he might not recover, or that he might become a monk.

"Abbot Konstantin would not keep people there against their will. He is known for his charity, helping those suffering during and after the war." Lettina paused at Tanya's sharp intake of breath. "I did not mean to frighten you. Let us hope he will be free to do what he wants—what he is able to do when he is well."

Unburdened from the deep grief for Pasha that had permeated their days, Jessica shifted from the uncomfortable speculation, "How did it happen you were permitted to go there, Lettina? I cannot understand you and Katya and Greita having this privilege."

"St. Sansais provides one meal a day in the village to transients and peasants, those whose land had been confiscated for collectives. The kitchen is a much needed service these days. The sacks of buckwheat and rye were wet from the flood, so Tomenko sent us by horse cart with the flour before they molded. It is rare for him to spare even an ounce!"

They all laughed, finding the camaraderie an outlet for the strain of their work worlds and worry about Pasha.

"There is a bit of soup and some cucumbers," offered Jessica, knowing it was rather wretched fare for a guest, but Lettina gratefully accepted. Jessica uncrossed her long legs and rose from the rug in a studied, graceful manner, a far cry from the typical casualness of other young women. She turned up the burner ring to heat the soup and rinsed another bowl and spoon. "I wish we had a little cheese," she added, but Lettina did not seem to mind.

"How will you live while the mill is closed?"

"I have taken small jobs on the side and saved a little," Lettina said between bites.

"It is so difficult to save," Jessica said. "If the mill becomes modern with electricity, will Tomenko let some of the workers go? Does he expect the new mill to become nationalized? If it becomes widely used, who will grind Konsky's small amounts of wheat and barley for us?"

"Who is to say, we shall wait and see. We may be reassigned. In the meantime, we continue to make a pittance cleaning the mill and moving equipment while the workmen rebuild. That is all I know."

Jessica stole a look at Tanya, both thinking the same thing; they would like to invite Lettina to come over more often, though their resources were limited. Lettina licked the last of the soup off the spoon and handed it back with the bowl.

"You must come here, *pozhaluysta.* We would like to have you," Jessica urged.

Lettina nodded, her natural ebullience subdued. "I wonder if Greita and Katya have such generous friends to turn to."

The girls, rather two young women and a fifteen-year-old girl, rose from the dusty rug and smoothed the wrinkles from their dresses.

"There will be a production meeting tomorrow," Lettina said. "I hear it is about the next Five-Year Plan to compensate for wartime losses. I am alerting you, we may have to work twice as hard to meet State goals."

A blustery, early summer wind of 1946 swept the stark three-and four-story concrete buildings of the small town of Konsky. Svetlana Sergeevna Gilkova and Tatyana Pytrovna Gilkova walked home late to the minimal peoples' housing they shared. Chilly shadows cast over narrow streets lent a forbidding sense to the evening. The apartments, Benyanske's National Boot and Shoe Manufacturing where the girls worked, and the town's shops and theatre were of similar construction, that of utilitarian Soviet Russia after the Bolshevik Revolution of 1917. Each bore evidence of crossfire on the Front during World War II. People were still adjusting after last year's hard fought truce.

The girls' immediate worry had to do with the recent flood. The old flour mill, installed during the reign of the tsars on the outskirts of town, represented the flavor of rural Konsky. Unbelievably, that now appeared about to change. The water wheels on creaky beams, beloved by generations past for their faithful milling of life-sustaining grains, were finished with grinding. The main wheel had been swept downstream by a torrent of water. Jessica and Tanya, along with townsfolk, came to view the ruins. Exposed rods where the large weathered wheel had been were twisted, and damaged spokes of the remaining wheel elicited mournful grieving from old women and men alike. Frightened chatter among housewives betrayed their loss of a source of scarce flour for their bread.

Yet despite the death of the old mill, the face of the town, or rather its two faces like those of the pagan god, Janus, god of past and present, spoke more of the nature of the inhabitants. Konsky had long housed and fed traders coming and going from Moscow to the east and Kiev to the south; traders who dealt in prosaic goods of staples such as grain, or those who chanced upon a wealth of minerals, primarily gold found in Central Russia and beyond. Because of its location, Konsky was favored by Janus, also the god of gateways. Jessica had long heard stories of how her father, Sergey Fedorovich, descendent of a merchant trader, had come to ply his trade in the well-situated village and sell to the goldsmiths of Europe, perhaps lending to Jessica's fantasy of another time, another place, unaware of the two-faced god that perhaps represented several sides of herself. Her bobbed hair, turned under at the ends, and rakish way of wearing an ordinary hat betrayed her fascination with American cinema.

The day after a six-day work week, the girls woke early not to miss a moment of their only day of freedom from the factory.

"Tanya, shall we go to the monastery?" Jessica called. "If it is open to visitors on Sunday we might see Pasha."

The apartment was empty. Tanya had slipped past Jessica's cot in its only room, leaving early for services at St. Sebastians. Not that Jessica objected to Tanya's simple beliefs that tied her securely to the old ways. Tanya treasured a miniature icon hidden behind her bed. The rituals, the hopes of a better place than the one she lived in, gave her solace. This wealth of Old Tradition came from their ancestors and hardly abated through oppression of the past generation despite being banned. But the heavy mysticism, dogma, and personal sacrifice conflicted with the atheism of Lenin and Marx and the insignificance of the individual that Jessica grew up with. To her, if there were miracles at all it must be that townspeople were openly practicing their faith these days.

Thrusting aside nagging questions about religion and the role of Spirit, Jessica chose to use every precious minute for her own plans. She rushed to Lettina's apartment in another building and rapped on the door. Half awake, one of the girls who shared a mat on the floor opened it a crack and peered into the dimly lit hallway.

"Jessica," whispered Greita. They had never met, but she evidently recognized her at once as being Lettina's friend. Katya, the other girl on the mat, covered her head, signaling she did not want to be disturbed. Greita tip-toed into Lettina's room to wake her, an effort requiring a vigorous shake of her shoulders, and announcing directly in her ear that Jessica was here.

"I will wait out front," Jessica said, not wanting to stand first on one foot then the other waiting for Lettina to get up and dressed. Her Sunday shoes with a short heel and rather narrow toes were not very comfortable, though she had been drawn to the style among irregulars from Benyanske's back shelf. But she had dressed to meet Pasha, the shoes and a slim belt that nipped in at her waist her only accessories.

Lettina is not the liveliest companion in the morning, Jessica grumbled, knowing it would be noon before she was fully awake. They had both been up late at a party the night before, but Jessica decided it would be worth the wait if Lettina would go to the monastery with her. However, Lettina quickly appeared wearing the same dress she wore Thursday, now sadly rumpled and stained, and a kerchief tied over her unruly bronzed-brown hair.

"Come, Lettina, let's go to the monastery," Jessica pleaded. "I cannot wait to visit cousin Pasha. Do you suppose it would be open if we arrived early?"

Caught up in Jessica's eagerness, Lettina muttered, "I would move heaven and earth for you, Jessica, but I'd give both for a cup of coffee." Real coffee would likely not have been an issue except for its prevalence among Westerners who had passed through, and its scarcity in Russia. Even a respectable substitute was hard to come by. Having neither, they laughed and set off for the half day walk where the region's only vineyard occupied sloping foothills above vast open meadows and shimmering tributaries that formed the rivers of Kursk Oblast, one of numerous Provinces bordering the European countries.

"Anna's parents' party last night was rare. Couples seldom get to celebrate their 25th wedding anniversary."

"They have done well despite her father's breathing problem," Jessica said. "They were an upper class family, I understand, until they were forced into exile in the village. They are very faithful and quite strict, though Anna did smoke with us in the park. How often do we get to go to a party?"

"The malt beer was better than the vodka. But there were no eligible men there. Only Anna's father, a few brothers, the priest and some small boys. Do you suppose we will ever marry?" At age twenty-two Lettina made her singular goal known, to marry and have a family.

"Cousin Pasha is the only young man I have ever really known. They often spoke of him last night. The family is besieging the heavens with prayers for him, in secret of course."

"I think I'd like your cousin Pasha," Lettina grinned with a flirty waggle of her hips. "He must be handsome and charming. I am curious that this cousin has such a hold on you and Tanya."

Jessica paused to rein in a surge of irritation. "He is five years older than me. His interest is in music. He taught himself to play the violin and flute when he was only a child."

"You have been so attentive to his welfare, I cannot help—"

"I hardly knew him as an adult." Jessica withdrew a few steps, her annoyance with Lettina escalating. "He left to study at the Conservatory in Leningrad when he was still young."

"He was gifted?"

"*Da*, he was soon accepted in the Leningrad Symphony when so many musicians were drafted. Not long after, he was also called up."

"And he may spend his life in a monastery?"

"*O Bozhe*, we have no idea how we will find him or what he will do, what he will be capable of doing." The image of Pasha's large dark eyes sheltered by thick black lashes, his straight nose, curly hair and winning smile struck a pang of fear in Jessica. She looked at Lettina in near panic. "What if he is badly hurt? I am glad Tanya went to church today. I would not want her to see him terribly—terribly frightful to look at. My fears may be unreasonable, but I know she could not stand the shock. She suffers much grief already."

"Have you heard anything to justify your fears?" Lettina ventured, sobering with Jessica's real or imagined concerns. She then glanced back to see Jessica by the side of the road holding her stomach with one hand and covering her mouth with the other.

"Jessica—"

"I am so afraid—I cannot bear to see him—disfigured—his face or body, you know, blown away—." Her midsection heaved with vomit on a thicket of bushes at the roadside. Lettina grabbed a handkerchief from her pocket and thrust it toward Jessica who heaved again. The spasms subsided, but Jessica bent over, hanging limp, weak and shaken.

"Come sit here by the bridge." They had traveled a footpath part of the way, but here the path joined the road. A few old lorries rattled past team-drawn vehicles and walkers. Lettina moved Jessica with an arm around her shoulders and seated her on a grassy stream bank, where the late spring sun sparkled on the green waters. Jessica crossed her stomach with her arms in a tight embrace, until she forced recollections of good times with Pasha.

"Tanya and I used to run with him through an ancient apple orchard and climb into the loft of a rambling barn. Startled sparrows zipped past our heads and frightened us. Pasha sang folk songs and we tried to dance like the Cossacks, bouncing on one bent knee. He created games to amuse us and the other cousins. We all loved Pasha.

"My mother found the countryside dismal, but for the cousins it was an escape from supervision. I wonder at what point we ceased carefree romping. When we became Young Pioneers?"

The memories seemed as fleeting as the current in the stream. Jessica shook her head as if releasing the past and summoned her strength for the steps ahead. "I do not know if anyone in Pasha's family is able to visit him. His father passed long ago. The others may be scattered, but Tanya and I need to see for ourselves that he is all right." She pulled her tall slim body upright and followed Lettina, who was more at ease since she had visited the monastery the previous week.

They formed a solemn procession the rest of the way, finally arriving at a weathered wooden gate on the high stone fence of St. Sansais, a cloistered monastery otherwise known as the Community of Brothers. A remarkably young gatekeeper appeared from a little hut inside the walls. With his first words the women realized he was deaf. He led them along a path partly secluded between leggy sunflowers, delphiniums and phlox to a small entry room, where they were to sit on a straight wooden bench. He rang a bell on a narrow table and returned to the gate.

Lettina and Jessica noted his every action, whispering that at least he has a job and is well cared for. Yet Jessica translated the gatekeeper's loss to Pasha's potential disabilities—if Pasha were deaf, he would be unable to play his violin. Fear for his would-be losses roused resentment that again churned her stomach; she held her insides, bemoaning that such suffering happened to anyone.

Soon a monk appeared, identifying himself as Brother Anton, who inquired about their purpose. Since Jessica seemed to have lost her voice, Lettina stated they wanted to see Pasha.

"O, that would be Cousin Pavel Ivanovich Zyclov, nephew of Sergey Fedorovich Gilkov," Jessica managed to stammer.

The monk brightened. "Pavel? You must see Abbot Konstantin for permission to visit." He deferred to a large man in an uncommonly coarse robe who came up behind him. The abbot's sturdy feet were barely visible in *bast* reed sandals.

"Come," Abbot Konstantin said, already on his way down an outside corridor. "It is a fine day to walk and you have come far," he said, noting Jessica's limp in the ill-fitting shoes. "It is kind of you to visit Pavel Ivanovich."

Jessica choked down sobs and nausea again, hoping the abbot would help them get through the initial meeting. Seeing Pasha in an unknown condition loomed as a foreboding trial, but she hid her fears and followed him. They crossed a secluded courtyard and ducked through a low arbor to suddenly come upon Pasha sitting on a raised cot in a sunny garden. A wool blanket was drawn up to his chest, his attention miles away or on times past, Jessica could not tell from his faraway gaze. The three stood still and waited for him to acknowledge their presence. Brother Anton drifted toward the garden and selected early vegetables, placing them in a small cloth bag.

Gradually Pasha's head turned to face them. The shadow of his wide straw hat hid his eyes. Jessica saw his lips moving, but no sound came forth. He barely nodded in a nonspecific direction. Jessica rushed forward to fall at the foot of the cot and bury her head in the rough blanket, babbling and pleading; all the tears she had tried so hard to contain poured forth at once.

"*Mne tak zhal'. Pozhaluylsta, bud'te zdorovy.* I am so sorry. Please be well."

Lettina settled her unwieldy frame on the grass behind Jessica, no hint of the earlier flirty interest in her gaze. They sat with Pasha for a long time, breathing in little gasps when his toes wriggled under the blanket.

"A sign he is not completely paralyzed," Jessica exclaimed. Any hope at all felt encouraging.

At last curtailing further outbursts, Jessica ventured, "Pasha, dear cousin Pasha, I am your cousin Svetlana. Do you remember me?" He was so distant she wanted to shake his hands, his shoulders, even his feet or legs under the blanket to get an answer.

His lips, reddish in an almost white face, moved again and Jessica leaned nearer his cheek. Here she could see into his eyes, still bright and round and brown, while appearing to be the eyes of a stranger. She gently folded back the blanket and reached for his hand—but shrank from it. The hand lacked fingertips. It lay limp on the cot. Blunt ends of his fingers remained with the ugly scarring of frostbite.

Jessica's deepest hopes thudded and fell—"O, I am so sorry."

The missing fingertips had drawn infinite subtleties from the strings of his violin, strains like no other, strains familiar and enchanting in Jessica's childhood. She could almost hear refrains through a bewildering cascade of disbelief, pain and anger. War, the world had cruelly robbed this gentle young man, her precious cousin. Grief registered on every feature of her wide pale face. Nearly as stricken, Lettina shifted to her side. Jessica glanced up at the abbot.

"*Da,* you see he had frostbite, probably from last winter on the Front. A farmer found him in a field nearby and brought him to us," the abbot said, "but I regret to say, we find it is his mind that is more wounded."

"He is a musician, *ser*. Frostbite of his fingers is a devastating loss. He would not be Pasha without his music, without being able to play his violin. It is his gift. He performed in the Leningrad Symphony. Now what will become of him?" Jessica stoutly defended the immensity of Pasha's wounds, forgetting the proprieties of addressing the abbot.

Abbot Konstantin's substantial frame stood tall and authoritative, even in the frayed brown tunic similar to those worn by the monks. His rich, deep voice rolled from beneath a dense gray beard, and blue eyes crinkled among deep lines in his face.

"Of course, any wounds inside or out are grievous, yet I have the greatest faith in this young man's recovery. His mind is improving, and when he chooses to rejoin the world, I suspect his mind will clear."

"'Chooses,' Father? You mean he has blanked out like this on purpose?" Jessica's reply was edged with impatience, upset with the presumptions of the holy man, offended by his good humor, most of all overwhelmed with long-harbored fears. Instead, she felt he was making light of Pasha's injuries and the girls' concerns.

"It is common in war for the mind to escape. If this young man is a musician, I believe he may have been extraordinarily sensitive to the horrors he encountered." Abbot Konstantin bowed deeply and backed away when Jessica cringed, his demeanor entirely somber. "I beg your pardon. I did not mean to expose you to such details. You must come now."

He could not have helped but notice the skin was rubbed raw on Jessica's inflamed heels as she knelt by Pasha's cot. "You must have come a great distance to visit your cousin Pavel Ivanovich," he said, acknowledging the sacrifice, and glanced at his own comfortably worn sandals woven by monks at the monastery.

Jessica gently squeezed Pasha's unresisting hand and promised over and over she would return, each time hoping his eyes would light up, but that was not to be during this visit.

Abbot Konstantin walked them to the gate. Bowing again, he handed them the tote bag of vegetables Brother Anton had picked. Two blue violet plants wrapped in moist leaves were tucked into the top of the bag.

Abbot Konstantin remained in the garden absently stroking his beard and staring at the toes of his sandals protruding beneath his habit, lost in reflections on the young women's visit—and his own response. They had not seen Pavel Ivanovich Zyclov as he had seen him the night his body was brought to the monastery, and Konstantin surely did not want to tell them. Nor did he want to hide his delight in providing a sanctuary for the young man, filthy as he had been when he was left at the door. The Community of Brothers, sheltered within the Vineyard, had opened its doors and arms to many other lost or wounded souls who had nowhere else to go. The abbot readily recognized that Pavel had a special radiance about him. His improvement was celebrated daily at the monastery. Konstantin smiled again, a merry, almost mischievous look that had so perplexed and offended cousin Svetlana Gilkova. To the abbot, the monastery's Brothers, vineyards, gardens and guests were all gifts of God, and of these, the guest the cousin called Pasha quickly became a favorite.

Eventually he motioned that Pavel be moved inside. Konstantin followed Brothers Anton and Vessaly who lifted the cot, a very light weight because its occupant was so thin, and carried him to a small, sunny chamber reserved for guests. Here, beyond the long covered corridors, light entered the narrow windows from both east and west. Anton refilled a pitcher with fresh water, poured a glass, and held it to their patient's lips while he drank without hesitation. The Brothers, including Konstantin who considered himself one among the Brothers, smiled at each other, pleased with Pavel's progress. Pavel had been near death when the farmer, alerted by foxes stealthily crossing his field, had found him lying face down in his barley field. Emaciated, dehydrated, exhausted and glassy-eyed, only a deranged babble indicated a life force within him, but that tenuous spirit convinced the farmer the young man might live if he received care.

"You must take him." The farmer had removed the body from a small cart behind his tractor at the monastery gate. "My wife is over-burdened and we need her help in the fields."

The abbot and gatekeeper accepted the limp form in a tattered Red Army uniform who was thrust into their arms, along with identification papers found on his person. The garbled words the farmer had heard were the last Pavel Ivanovich Zyclov uttered for three weeks after he slipped into a world of his own where neither light nor dark, sun nor chill, good nor evil could reach him. His attendant, Brother Anton, had washed him and prayed, coaxed soup into his mouth with a spoon and prayed, chanted softly to him and prayed. Eventually a hint of strength returned to Pasha's spent body, allowing him to hold up his head and sit if propped in bed.

After seeing the attachment of his cousin, Abbot Konstantin and the young monks prayed even more fervently that awareness break through the chasm separating Pavel from others, that they and the cousin could reach the person behind the vacant eyes. Inspired by the individual at whose bedside they sat, the abbot, and Anton with Pavel's half empty water glass in his hand, fell into deep contemplation, as deep as any derived from Matins or Gregorian chants or solitary time in their cells. In the heightened awareness of a meditation on the Spirit of each and every soul, they sensed the mystery, the life blood that made each earthly, and even more miraculously, godly.

"Indeed, the Lord moves in mysterious ways," Brother Anton said. So it was that the visitors had found Pasha improved.

II

Pasha

Jessica and Lettina left the monastery awed by their encounter with the young man who existed in the in-between sphere of one's choosing, if and when unthinkable cruelties of the real world became too much. At a distance away from the scene their withheld responses erupted.

"Do you believe he allowed himself to fall into unconsciousness weeks ago from which he is yet unable to awaken?" Lettina queried.

"I wanted with all my heart to escape the shelling, you remember, the terrible roar of guns and mortars outside Konsky. Smoke so dense day was like night and night was without stars. It smelled rank of--of--I don't want to think of it, death. *Da*, I, too, wished to become numb to it."

"'Choosing' is a strange notion. I wonder how Pasha became lost in the field," Lettina said.

"Surely he must have been aware and thinking until then, which means oblivion overtook him when he approached the vicinity of his home. Does that mean he felt safe enough to let himself go, to become unconscious?"

"Jessica, my friend, such deep questions. I am not one to entertain thoughts of a mystical nature, let alone those outside the functions of milling grain. Maybe someone dumped him in the field."

Knowing pursuit of this line of logic was purposeless with Lettina,

Jessica let it go. Not far into the long walk home she realized her heels were bloody and painful—but she had felt no pain while she was preoccupied with thoughts of Pasha. *I can go away in my mind. I was thinking of Pasha in his pain and my pain ceased to hurt. Is it a matter of choosing or a matter of one's beliefs, which I already find mystifying?* Her mind became fuzzy trying to make sense of the strange notion. Dropping theoretical abstractions, she needed to deal with the immediate crisis, the abrasiveness of the once stylish shoes that caused her suffering.

"Lettinyevna, I cannot walk another step." She removed her shoes to go barefoot until a remedy could be found. The cool grass and roadside weeds felt good on her burning feet; the firm ground a contrast to the mystical. Mullein grew randomly along the winding lane, producing thick furry leaves that Jessica picked to line the shoes, a peasant remedy her mother learned when she moved to a village.

"What do you think will happen to Pasha?" Lettina asked, restless with a discussion she did not understand, and what appeared to be his unsolvable problem.

"We must take him a violin."

"A violin?"

"*Da, da*!, He will recognize it! He is sure to recognize a violin, and it will bring him back to us."

Lettina blinked. "Jessica, sometimes I do not understand the leaps you take in your thinking."

"I am positive he will recover if we try hard enough to find one. It can't hurt to try." Jessica wadded the padding into the heels of her shoes.

"But how can we get a violin? Obtaining a banned recording of music is difficult enough. We might as well wish for a grand piano."

"We will find a violin," Jessica declared. The remaining miles evaporated unnoticed beneath her feet while the idea took shape in her mind.

After the war ended in September 1945, survivors continued to pass through Konsky, known far and wide as the gateway town on the Western Front of the motherland. Among the returning Red Army veterans were the thrice beaten refugees, displaced persons who survived both Nazi and Soviet invasions and subsequent nonselective forced repatriation across formerly contested borders. Sending foreign-born Russians back to Russia and Germans or Finns born in Russia back to their countries amounted to de facto post-war ethnic cleansing, which two World Wars had failed to accomplish. At the same time, Radio Moscow proclaimed the country was rising on powerful new terms after its Army liberated neighboring countries— once independent nations now within the Soviet fold.

The cousins often witnessed the gaunt frames of these survivors, men and women, whose wretched clothing hung like rags from wire coat hangers. Even young men made their way haltingly past the Benyanske Boot and Shoe factory, their limbs often bandaged or missing, shuffling like old men in tattered footwear or feet bound in dirty rags. Against this scenario, Jessica realized Pasha's condition could be viewed as being either better or worse.

Returning from the trip to the monastery, Jessica quietly let herself into their third floor apartment in case Tanya might be napping, but Tanya had gone, leaving a basket of fresh bread and cheese on the kitchen shelf. Pleased with the opportunity to change clothes and mull over her trip, Jessica slowly removed her dress and set it aside to be washed. The bloody shoes appeared unsalvageable until she swiped the stains with cold water and salt. At least I learned something.

"I want to remember to think of something else if it relieves suffering. Is that a religious idea? It may be risky to inquire." The whiplash of banned religious traditions and institutions in *Rossiya* and their eventual reinstatement led Jessica to distance herself from the pious as well as secular loyalists. Her father scoffed at the reprieve permitting religious practices as being a transparent ploy to gain people's loyalty during and immediately after the war. In the meantime, Believers of traditional Orthodoxy sustained their beliefs while nonbelievers felt allowed to question. Impatient with both the faithful and faithless, Jessica ripped a button off her remaining dress.

"*O, Boshe moy,* I can't be bothered. What I really want is to get out of here—there has to be more than sewing ugly shoes alongside women who seem to accept striving for production goals day after day."

Somewhat contrite, she fished in a bowl for a needle and thread, acknowledging that all workers feared being reported if they were lax, all feared a return to pre-war religious persecutions and even more stringent austerities than existed at present.

Tanya came in later, her piping young voice anxiously asking, "Jessica, where have you been? To St. Sansais? O, I wanted to go with you. What did you find out?"

"He will live," Jessica said. "That is all I know." She avoided giving Tanya unrealistic hopes before she brought up the idea of finding a violin. Relaying what she could of the abbot's explanation for the blackout, she said, "We were so near but he remained so distant. He did not appear to see or hear us. It was most painful."

Tanya threw herself into a chair that sagged to the side. "Please, you must take me with you next time. I pray for him at St. Sebastians, but I cannot visualize his face as a grown-up. He has been away for so many years."

"Of course we'll go together next time. The boyish look we remember from our times at Uncle Ivan's is still youthful and kind, but it is a man's face now, pale with strong features. You would expect that after the war."

"I am so relieved and happy for Pasha that he lives. Now if we could only take him something."

"Tanechka, I was thinking the same thing. Only I hesitated to say so. It may be unrealistic for a man who is unaware and cannot feed or change himself."

Tanya waited, lips parted to protest, yet dissuaded by the possibilities and impossibilities implied in her cousin's outburst.

"No, it would be foolhardy to rush in with high hopes. The monks know best. You cannot imagine, Tanya, how kind the abbot is—did you see the lovely fresh vegetables and sweet little plants? One for you, one for me."

Jessica jumped up to fetch the wild violets that grew profusely in the shady undergrowth of the monastery's extensive gardens. A wide leaf bound each hardy little plant in a rich, mossy bundle of earth from its hiding place. She handed one to Tanya. They planted them in cracked pots for display on a shelf that received a ray of light. Lettina had accepted half the produce from the tote bag but insisted Tanya have the violet, knowing she would be upset that they had not included her on the trip.

Invigorated by the excitement of taking Pasha into the center of their lives, Jessica shook the heaviness of worry and war from her shoulders, and flipped her bobbed hair until it naturally curled under. She slung a red woven bag with a long strap over her shoulder, and picked up the stylish shoes from under her cot. She would leave the shoes on a ledge outside the building for someone else and go uptown with Anna. They would meet the other girls at the theater.

"Come to the movies, Tanya," she invited. "Meet us there after Anna and I see if there is anything, even rationed bread to buy."

Fingering a few kopeks in her pocket, Tanya declined the invitation. "Go with your friends. I have other things to do."

Jessica knew Tanya was frugal, foregoing shopping and movies. She would buy candles at the church to light for her parents and the animals, and also for Pasha whose body lived but his mind was lost.

O Bozhe, Jessica privately responded to Tanya's piety. She makes me feel uncaring and frivolous—Tanya may be a saint, but I am saving for something special when I turn twenty.

The marquee was uninspiring, offering yet again a reprise of Alexander Nevsky's 13th century victory over Teutonic Knights who invaded the motherland, a censor-free film encouraged by the regime.

"I have seen this four times, and I loved it every time." Katya said. "I am waiting for another film produced by Sergei Eisenstein."

Jessica snubbed the film's bloody battle on the ice. "After *The Seventh Cross*," with Jessica Tandy, I find an invasion by Teutonic Knights dreary."

"O, Jessica, ever the romanticist!" Lettina teased.

"A realist. Spencer Tracy reveals his true feelings."

"That cinema was allowed in *Rossiya*?" Greita queried.

"Not only that one but Humphrey Bogart in *Casablanca* with Ingrid Bergman."

"We were not allowed to expose our students to fantasy or romance when I taught Youth Academy in Sochi," Greita said. "They were permitted to see only movies like "*The Foundling*," a family comedy.

"Father was astounded by the sudden openness to the West, but he said the Americans supplied us with tractors and trucks during the war. That's why *Amerikanskiye* films were allowed here," Jessica replied.

"Come, let's go to the park. I have a surprise." Lettina slyly sidestepped an increasingly sensitive topic among them, a subject paralleled by the public at large, cautious that young people would be influenced by the West. She led the sprint along a stream and broke into a clearing. Anna, smaller and more delicate, was last to catch up.

Greita bent over laughing, trying to catch her breath. A newcomer, she was unfamiliar with the antics of this crowd—"*besshabashnaya kucha*, a rollicking bunch, *da*!" she breathed aloud, and set the others laughing, too.

"We cannot suppress ourselves—grinding flour all day kills one's instincts for merriment." Lettina said. "We plot our own course from time to time," which prompted cheers. Lettina pulled a pack of Lucky Strikes from inside her blouse and displayed it around the circle. The girls stared in awe. Smoking was not a novel experience; they frequently feigned window shopping until they left the last block in town if they had a few cheap, distasteful Russian cigarettes, a roll of cardboard with a plug of tobacco at the end. But a full pack of *Amerikanskiye cigareti*?

"How did you manage this?" Anna breathed, "From the black market?"

"Fear not, I came by this legitimately. I cleaned house after work for a woman who lost her husband in the war. When she finally gathered his belongings she found this pack of Luckies and gave it to me. Let's smoke to the poor soul who left it behind."

The 'poor soul' was a bit of a damper on the merriment, and so was the notion of burning through what was used as Russian currency.

United States' C-ration smokes bought a few ounces of bread during and after the war. Only in Konsky with its own flour mill and elderly bakers willing to bake would they dare to squander the cigarettes. Besides, working girls were expected to refrain from publicly revealing bad habits. Smoking was one the girls did in the forest, not in Konsky.

"Are you sure, Lettina? On the Black Market you can trade—"

"Greita, join in the fun. How often do we have a better opportunity for a fling! I wish we had '*Hit Parade*' music on a radio to go with these!" Lettina stripped the seal and handed the pack around with characteristic abandonment. The ritual was solemnly embraced by her friends. They spread their hand-knit sweaters for cushions and settled on logs and stumps for the evening or the end of the pack, whichever came first. To ease the mood, Lettina said, "Greita, you can run! Were you one of the pampered few in competitive sports?"

"The legs come from my parents. They skied in the Urals and even the French Alps a long time ago. I used to teach track sports at a school in Sochi, but working here at the mill I am too exhausted to think of sports. How about you, Katya?" Uncomfortable with girls she did not know well, Greita shifted attention from herself. She had been housed in Lettina's apartment since it had the cubic feet permitted for three persons.

"I probably have the physic for throwing discus," Katya laughed, "but now I wield a hammer at the mill. Tomenko Barskenkovich assigned me to help rebuild the exterior wall where your beloved water wheels had hung. "Maybe I will grow into carpenter's shoes and an apron," she joked, puffing heartily on a rapidly diminishing Lucky. "and be able to afford *Amerikanskiye cigareti*!"

"Men seem to acquire cigarettes regularly if not easily," Jessica said. "Seriously, I wish I could be assigned elsewhere, anywhere other than the boot and shoe factory." She examined a gash on her finger that had escaped being severed by a razor-sharp leather cutting tool.

"The pace, the pressure, it is so tiring. All of us are ready for something better." Anna lapsed into silence as if she had momentarily stepped out, leaving the other girls waiting. Uncertainty crept into the space, inviting festering resentment as sundown settled over the woods. Linden trees cast wavering lines across the meadow beyond the forest edge.

Jessica's glance lifted, resting on the glow of her expiring cigarette. Anna had captured her unrest exactly. "My birthday will be—"

The words failed to thrive, as if they had nowhere to go or nothing to do. They sounded foreign, even to Jessica. How long since she or anyone had talked of birthdays? Comrades did not celebrate birthdays. The faithful privately preserved the rituals of Name Day if a birthday fell on a saint's day. Yet expectations circled among the girls facing Jessica, a cheer here, a query there, on another a look of dismay.

"It will be my twentieth birthday. I have to work that day," Jessica added, opening her heart to her friends, not through words, but from the depths of her dark eyes pleading for a bright future, even a glimmer, even a wisp as ephemeral as the cigarette smoke that dissipated almost as quickly as she exhaled.

An unaccustomed tension hovered over the group, allowing rustling birch leaves overhead to sound their raspy, uncertain tunes. This time the group went away, minds turned inwardly, not to possibilities but to the improbability of experiencing anything better, of making any changes at all. Twenty might as well be thirty. Beyond that was unimaginable. Few lived past fifty. Or forty-five. Many were lost before they were twenty during the Sieges and crossfire, deprivation and famine. Jessica shuffled her feet, now encased in sturdy leather oxfords like those Tanya wore, shoes made in the local factory.

The pack of Lucky Strikes made one last round, only slightly dizzying the girls who'd experienced much stronger homeland smokes. Only Greita passed, saying she felt sick.

Lettina soon crumpled the cigarette package and tossed it, as if Jessica's loss confirmed her convictions—they needed to plot their own course.

"I think I'll go back." She stubbed out the American-made butts with a devil-may-care attitude, and extended a hand to Jessica on one side and Greita on the other. Too quickly they followed suit, though at other times and places butts were at a premium. This was Lettina's show, and at that moment, Lettina defied austerity, rebelled against privation that embedded itself into the very fabric of their beings.

The girls brushed mossy daubs from their skirts and strode toward town. Behind the mauves and purples of evening lay the outlines of concrete buildings with Benyanske's sign in the center as if to mock Jessica's lack of allegiance.

"I—I am sorry to spoil the fun," Jessica broke in to relieve the discomfort. "Now my job serves me well. I am able to visit Pasha on my day off. Which reminds me, I need to locate a violin for sale."

"All I ask for is a carpenter apron and she wants a violin," moaned Katya. "Apparently I am not much of a dreamer."

"I told you, she was a romantic, enamored by anything modern and of the West," Lettina said.

"*Nyet,* I did not get the notion from the movies, though I did appreciate the score Prokofiev composed for *Alexander Nevsky.* No, the violin would not be for me but for my cousin taken in at the monastery. I thought it might aid in his recovery. He used to be a wonderful musician and played in concerts in Leningrad and Novgorod."

"I have been trying to find a way to acquire one, but so far I have not cleaned for anyone with a violin," Lettina laughed, inspiring a round of giggles. "I am not a dreamer either if it makes you feel better, but I do have hopes. Is it too much to ask for a boyfriend, a husband, a man, or even an occasional date? Chances of them coming true are like *writing with a pitchfork on flowing water.*"

"An apt proverb for all of us," Jessica said. The toll of war left the country with few able-bodied men. Women occupied the greater part of the labor force in the factories, in the fields, and industries building planes and trains.

"I'd like to marry," the big girl said simply, laying bare yearnings, if not her heart, again shifting the tone of the gathering. Lettina, who should have been the first son in her family, looked ungainly in ill-fitting dresses that appeared to complain of draping over such angularity. But the admission resonated with the nods and tight lips of her friends.

"That is where I am a realist," Katya said. "That dream will more than likely never become a reality for most of us."

"It is easier to come by a violin," quipped Anna, always the cheerleader for Jessica. The tension vanished in a spurt of laughter, while they picked fir needles from their sweaters. With a last glance back, they left the now shadowy woods dampened by early evening dew.

Benyanske National Boot and Shoe Manufacturing enjoyed a rather celebrated if misleading name given that production was generally hand-crafted, and that primarily by women. The three-story factory situated on Lenin Street in central Konsky rimmed an enclosed courtyard for brief lunches and respite of the workers. On the right and in the rear of the factory were four blocks of worker housing, also gray concrete three-story structures not much different in appearance than the factory. Each state-owned block offered small apartments at nominal rents, such as the one occupied by Jessica and Tanya. Two of the blocks featured *kommunalkas*, communal living, a basic tenet of the Party. Four to six families shared a kitchen and bathroom, while entire families each occupied one of several bedrooms that angled off from the central shared space.

Jessica hurried past the long Cultural Hall common to all cities, towns and villages of the Union of Soviet Socialist Republics, its purpose to promote the socialist way of life. On the front of the building facing the street a weathered slogan, *LAND, BREAD, PEACE, All Power to the Soviets* in large letters, summed Lenin's reach into Konsky. Broken promises only aggravated Jessica's already gloomy outlook. Benyanske's had boosted production of boots to meet wartime demands, though footwear was made of increasingly inferior leather, often thin or crackly as cardboard. Post-war production was even worse with supplies scarce or substituted. Popular *kirza* boots, primarily layers of fabrics covered with waterproofing, came from industrialized centers farther north.

The moods persisted over the following days. Jessica's impatience with the shabbiness rose tenfold after the demoralizing experience of walking to the monastery in dress shoes that blistered her feet. While her hands were occupied with the clanking old leather-stitching machine, tides of restlessness swept her mind. Irritated with cheap products and her obligations to the factory, she jammed the machine even harder and faster—her twentieth birthday, would come and go and nothing would change. The thrill she enjoyed counting the days had changed to a dismal outlook for her future.

Yet her mind skipped from one fantasy to the next—I could design and sew beautiful dresses like those American women wear for elegant parties. Even their day dresses have fashionable shapes and accessories. I would travel like father did years ago as a merchant trader to select the best materials, Paris or New York or even Milan! Becoming more excited but equally despairing of realizing any of the dreams, she concluded at least I could plan for a nice birthday party with my friends.

There would be no such yearnings had her mother, Vera, not vaguely alluded to her own privileged childhood of ruffled dresses, knee-high silk stockings and dainty shoes. Birthday parties at the time of the tsars were apparently lavish celebrations attended by all the relatives, as well as local clergy. But Vera came from the generation later stripped of titles, position and property after the Revolution turned *Rossiya* into a classless society. Subsequently, the Gilkovs endured the hardships of farm work on the collectives outside Konsky, where Svetlana spent her early years. When her mother's health declined, the family was sent to live in an *izba,* a timber-sided cottage on a dirt street in the countryside. Jessica grew up in serviceable cotton or muslin if yardage for a dress were to be found.

When the Germans swept across their 1,400-mile Eastern Front in their advance toward Moscow, the family had splintered in self-defense. The crossroads of Konsky were inevitably in the path of the invading Axis Army. Nothing was spared; forests, farms and villages were destroyed either in their advance or during several inglorious retreats. Sergey Fedorovich had withdrawn his only daughter from Ten-Year School, and sent her to work in Benyanske's Boot and Shoe factory because, it was rumored, workers would be safe making boots for the defending Russians, and in a worst case scenario, supplying footwear for the invading Germans. His trader's instinct served him well before, and it had this time: Svetlana toiled unharmed in the factory for four years, where her cousin Tatyana eventually came for the same reason.

Factory bells punctuated Jessica's dreams. Boris Mikhailovich Ivchenko, the floor supervisor, strode past, barking at the girls to hurry up and meet their quotas. When he was at the other end of the immense room filled with dozens of sewing machines and cutting tables, Jessica turned to the woman on her right who sewed the double-leather heels of work boots.

"Agata Illyinicha, *pozhaluysta,* please may I ask, how do you manage to be calm every day under constant pressure in this noise?" They had a passing acquaintance after years together in this third floor warehouse-like room, but Agata generally sought the older women for companionship, just as Jessica joined the younger crowd after work.

"Ah, Svetlanka, if I appear calm, I do not always know it. It comes from the inside I suppose." Clearly Agata was pleased to hear the comment and to talk openly with Svetlana.

Jessica thought about calmness radiating from the inside, an unfamiliar concept though recognizable in the monks and in the mysterious beam in the abbot's eyes when she questioned what there was to be merry about. An inner serenity explained how women like Agata could live with beauty inside when sorrows of war, starvation, persecution, and an endless means of suffering drowned the outside; how her own aged parents gathered strength from their faith to carry on; how Anna's mother and her dying husband were able to celebrate their wedding anniversary.

"I wish I were able to be more accepting like other comrades. It seems my mind challenges why things have to be so," Jessica said.

"It is normal to question, though certainly not encouraged." Agata's half smile and sly wink told Jessica she understood. They both laughed, paying special attention to the stitching lest the needle of the electric machines pierce their fingers.

Bent far over her work, Agata Illyinicha spoke in a low voice, "We could talk at my flat on Thursday after work if you would like to join several of us."

Boris Ivchenko again passed by, randomly inspecting cut pieces of shoes and boots in all stages of assembly. "You will not sew the right upper onto the left sole," he once ridiculed a girl in front of the others by holding the contorted piece aloft. Older women had paled and younger ones suppressed giggles, though mishaps from fatigue, illness, or inexperience were not isolated incidents. Each factory worker could attest to that.

Jessica later whispered to Agata, "I would like to come next week, *spasibo*, thank you. You must tell me more." Without another opportunity to talk, Jessica left after work on her own pursuits. Undefined yearnings carried her far from the oppressive gray of the town center, where a breeze blew freely through her coal black bobbed hair.

Mulling over her birthday, she wondered, "What will it mean for me? Nothing, I suppose." Yet buoyed by fresh air and a sense of expansiveness outside the factory, one thought became clear. "I must first consider Pasha and what I can do about the violin."

Still the prospect of finding a sense of calm, the maturity that Agata Illyinicha represented, teased around the edges of her consciousness. She shrugged and swung her empty lunch bag, now like a school girl free of classes, then like a woman denied, and flung the bag into a nearby tree in disgust.

"Lettina is right. All of our problems are unsolvable. Nothing is possible from the confines of the factory and the mill," words lost in a rush of wind and tumbling water that beckoned her off the road. Her footsteps led to a path along the swollen stream below the dam that had burst, destroying the water wheels of the old mill. She followed the stream down to the site of destruction and found Katya out in front sawing a board for siding. She waited while Katya nailed the board into place where the large water wheel had been for as long as anyone could remember.

"Lettina is cleaning up from the flood," Katya mumbled around a nail clamped between her lips. Jessica approached the aged wooden building until she caught a glimpse beyond the novice carpenter through an open door into the mill's back room. Lettina stood full front in rays of the sun, her blouse open and down around her waist. The old miller, Tomenko Barskenkovich, was fondling her breasts.

Jessica stared, slowly convinced her eyes were not deceiving her—this was Lettina, *da*, and Tomenko was lowering his face toward her nipples.

"*O, Chort, nyet, nyet*! Why, she's no better than the girls in the munitions factories," Jessica breathed. She waved vaguely in Katya's direction and fled.

III

Konstantin

St. Sansais Monastery and Vineyards ranged across the foothills above state-owned grain fields, gardens and a few private plots, all benefiting from many tributaries and rivers, notably the Seym and Tuskar rivers. Like Benyanske's Boot and Shoe factory, the vineyards were strategically situated near the ancient trading roads leading through Konsky. Both the factory and vineyards were deemed of wartime significance for loyal as well as insurgent troops moving into and out of western Russia. The saving grace for the monastery lay in the quality of wines the cloistered vintners had perfected over three hundred years; the factory's salvation came from the desperate need for footwear by either side when in control of it. Abbot Konstantin, a menial monk at the time of the Revolution, endured that upheaval and two world wars, while marauders escaped with shoes, boots, wine, and produce.

Many lesser souls had fled despite their pledges to maintain a cloistered presence in Russia, but Konstantin proved to be too *Russki* to abdicate and too excellent a vintner to persecute, or so it seemed. Only a few knew that Konstantin was, in fact, a soldier in monk's cowl, the better to serve God and man. One of the few was Brother Anton who shadowed the abbot's every move, action and spiritual inclination, and became acutely aware of his Superior's true nature.

Claims that the abbot was too accommodating bore merit, however. As a young aspirant, Konstantin had unwittingly wandered into the monastic fold like a lamb among the lions of the Russian Orthodox Church. Raised on tradition before the Revolution, he did not realize his aspirations were different. It was not until middle age that he awoke to the politics, hierarchies, and rules of a succession of Russian adaptations of Greek Orthodox orders. Chafing from expectations of the order, Konstantin found that he was born akin to the community-spirited monks of Mount Athos. By then it was too late to leave St. Sansais, which he rechristened Community of Brothers, so there he remained bent upon his spiritual journey.

"It is a little joke the universe played upon me," he remarked pleasantly to his superiors, who prodded him from time to time to be more stern, disciplined, and obedient to the tenets of Russian Orthodoxy, as well as more demanding of the novitiates.

"Brother Anton," he said, "your dedication without hesitation or limitation to the Community reflects the true nature of service we are bound to by the Almighty."

Anton's young face beamed while he bent with even greater vigor to hoe a row of beans in the monastery's extensive gardens. As usual, without self-elevation or consideration, Anton's fervor spoke of willingness to carry out every task, including carrying out the slop pot from the guest room occupied by Pavel Ivanovich.

In this curious manner, the discipline of the 7th century Benedictines evolved to live 1,300 years in the middle of Russia's Western Front, where Konstantin left the original order's rule-making to the past. However, this holy but relaxed discipleship had been hardened by the earlier German invasion of World War I. He had not forgotten for one minute the lost generation of young Russian soldiers, including many of the resolute Brothers, who either joined the defenders or became martyrs of the faith. It was during this tragic period that Brother Konstantin acceded to the position of abbot when his predecessor, the elderly Abbot Petrorskil of the Indomitable Spirit, could prevail no more and died of pneumonia, according to the records, when everyone knew he had died after repeated interrogations.

Konstantin bitterly recalled the German army's plunder of wealth found in ancient churches along their march inland, as well as the abundantly stocked monasteries which had been reserved for Russian use in such a crisis. All of this led to Abbot Konstantin's first sacrilege, which was to lie about the whereabouts of much of the stores, secreted away by the same monks who had worked so hard to reap them. In addition, *Kommandeures* had ordered the monks, who for one reason or another had not fled, been rousted, beaten and robbed of all but their spirit, to resupply their troops for an expected easy conquest of Moscow. Axis troops therefore moved rapidly inward unburdened by sufficient winter clothing or supplies, a fatal error in judgment which ultimately saved Moscow.

Konstantin took that experience as a reminder to speak with the present-day Brothers Anton and Vessaly. "We have reason to believe that hardships are increasingly widespread, despite our previous out-look for war's end. I suggest you take every caution when you cart vegetables to neighboring villages of Siver and Thor."

The current threat from his own countrymen did not lie idly with Abbot Konstantin, but his mission followed a higher order: that of serving his fellow man without regard to race, religion, or lack of it. The inhabitants of the monastery had suffered not only the crushing invasion but deprivation when they shared remaining secreted supplies with their starving countrymen. Eking out what they could to tide the homeland over until better times, they had learned valuable lessons from the Civil War of 1917 and the first World War, which seemed only just past before another began in 1941.

Among the charitable acts for which St. Sansais became revered was that of saving the lives of young men, who through no fault of their own were caught up in the brutality and all too often deserted by the regiments to which they had pledged their loyalty. However, few knew that the guest who previously occupied the sunny room where Pavel now resided had been a young German soldier, a boy really, found starving along the road and brought to the monastery in much the same way and condition that Pavel arrived. When he was sent on his way disguised in peasant clothing that replaced the scandalously inadequate combat uniform with its swastika, he was well fed and carried within an altered attitude.

"St. Sansais is open to those in need," the abbot quietly professed to monks and civilians alike. At the height of the invasions a steady stream of needy heeded the words, so much so that the corridors, halls and cells of the monastery became a hospital. Vows of a cloistered life of contemplation for the novitiates were temporarily suspended for the greater good. Yet the needs were so lasting and widespread that the monastery maintained contributions to the soup kitchen in Siver, where food was augmented by the generosity of those like the miller, Tomenko, who thought of others in hard times.

Konstantin savored a small satisfaction knowing that through waves of war and persecution, St. Sansais had been saved from ruin. The blessed ancient institution now benefited old and young monks as well as guest, Pavel Ivanovich Zyclov, and his dedicated cousin, not to mention those privileged to indulge in the piquant St. Sansais label Cabernet Sauvignon which the vineyard produced.

The day Jessica chanced upon the mill along the swollen creek and witnessed Lettina with the old miller she had stopped, stunned, and fled like a slinky coyote back into the woods. Lettina? With Tomenko, an old married man? Jessica had choked down gag and run home.

Where have I been? We talk about having affairs but I never saw such a thing happening, she scoffed at her naivety in the hours since. I might have expected it of Lettina. The American cigarettes probably came from him—he must have paid her. I'm nearly twenty years old. *Lah*, I need more than learning to be calm—I need to know how to live, but my mind is going crazy. I have to quit thinking of Lettina and him together, or I will stitch my thumb to the leather.

"I need to talk with you, *pozhaluysta*, if you have time," Jessica confided to Agata Illyinicha early the next day after their usual brief acknowledgments.

Agata appeared surprised but rebounded quickly after a glance at Svetlana's troubled face. "Please come with me at lunch time," she managed to convey above the noise. "I gather with a few other women outside. We may be able to talk then."

The two moved slowly out with the crowd of mostly older women and a few men from the third floor into the small courtyard off the general dining and meeting room of the factory, where a trace of sun bounced off sheer concrete walls to warm the benches. Tanya and her friends generally gathered on the streets to gossip, ogle passersby, and eat their hard bread while standing on the corner. Anticipation mixed with dread emboldened Jessica, or she would never have taken the first step into what looked like an insufferable world of older women characterized by dowdy dresses on sturdy figures, thinning hair caught up in combs or covered with kerchiefs.

A sense of style is so lacking in Russia, Jessica lamented. The dresses are far too long, the shoes flat and shapeless, the loose waists shift up and down at will. She glanced down at her dress that had little class itself with its faded fabric and quaint puff sleeves. I'm not sure why I came here. Its not like me ever wanting to become one of them. O, *khorosho,* have I nothing to look forward to, never a chance to create fashion, not even have an affair like Lettina?

Agata led her to a corner where she gathered with a few of her friends. Caught in a pouty attitude of resentment and despair, Jessica slipped onto a bench apart from her coworker so as not to appear dependent. Agata casually introduced her and the conversations went on as before. None of the women were really strangers since all worked in the same factory, aware of each other's presence, but involved in separate worlds.

Here I am literally in their inner circle. Older, to Jessica, meant late twenties, maybe thirties, certainly a number in their forties and early fifties. She tried to relate to those who might be her mother's age, though her parents had always seemed old to her. Jessica lumped all mature women into a category occupied by adults who could teach her little, a notion shared by her girlfriends, with the exception of Anna who seemed to be close to her family.

Jessica glanced around the larger group milling in the courtyard in an attempt to identify anyone who might be a *shpion*, a spy, yet knew Agata would have warned her in advance. Jessica shook off a sense of unease and focused on how these older women conducted themselves. They chatted as they ate meager lunches of cheese and bread, then stretched to relieve tense shoulders and backs, strained from bending over the stitching machines or standing at high tables where they cut leather from patterns with sharp knives or cutting machines. A few walked about flexing cramped legs laced with raised blue veins. They appeared to be at ease, even congenial, their faces patient: so Russian, Jessica thought, compared to those of American women where emotions flared at will on the movie screen.

A large woman with a bulbous nose captured the attention of those nearby when she related last night's dream. "I was in a long, rectangular hall of a palace decorated with fine tapestries, gold, red and blue murals, and fine woven rugs over marble floors. Of course, I did not recognize the hall. I have never been out of Konsky. Other women and children lined the room. I have forgotten most of the dream, but I saw myself looking up and a great tiger leapt from the ceiling near one corner of the hall. All the people fell back. It was all quick and silent. I reared up in bed to scream, but I woke up."

Jessica had never heard a grown woman speak so candidly of what sounded like a childish night terror. She searched Agata's face for her reaction, for some context for this casual disclosure, for a reason why an older woman dared bring it up in a group. Jessica's friends might mention dreams, but dreams were dismissed outright since an inner life was considered unfit for comrades. Here she heard the murmurs of others gathering in tempo, some adding their dreams or nightmares, some trying to comfort the woman with benign explanations of the terrifying images.

"Did you eat cabbage before going to bed, Ludmila?" one asked, which sounded like something Lettina would say.

O, I forgot about Lettina, Jessica realized, while she had been immersed in the worlds of those around her—I forgot her completely and Lettina and Tomenko are the reason I was so upset that I came here today. She tensed, dark eyes wide and chin high, determined to take in everything while she had the opportunity.

"My mind is racing all the time, about nonsense of course. It is all irrelevant but I have been unable to attend to my inner life," said the woman whose thick blonde hair trailed over her shoulders.

"Contemplation can take place in the recesses of our lives, Sasha," Agata quietly assured her and turned to whisper to Jessica and others nearby, "We must find ways to keep the Spirit alive among us."

The sharp discordant ring of the bell brought them all to the doorway of the courtyard and the stairs leading back to work. Agata smiled at Jessica who managed to confide, "My mind has been racing, too," but she had not broached the subject of her concern, or anything confidential to the one woman at the factory to whom she was drawn, Agata Illyinicha.

"If our informal gathering would help, it is impersonal if you wish it to be."

"You mean keeping the Spirit alive is your secret to being so calm?"

Agata laughed. "I find it helpful."

The days flew by for Jessica who glanced furtively at the woman working next to her. Agata, who bent steadfastly over her work, had a mysterious hold on her that intrigued Jessica but also disturbed her. Agata was complacent and friendly in the distant manner of the other women, yet Jessica felt spooked since meetings were forbidden. Jessica rejoined her friends when they stood outside the next day at lunchtime.

"Why are you so serious?" they asked.

"I am so unsettled," Jessica admitted. The restlessness in her long slim legs seemed contrary to contemplation of any kind. Not knowing what that entailed, she dared not take a chance. "I feel so distracted, I will probably stitch boots front to back and Boris Mikhailovich will make a mockery of my work and I will have to work extra hours tonight."

The girls laughed, relatively comfortable that they would not be fired and plotted means of acquiring black market coffee and cigarettes.

At home in the cousins' apartment, Tanya pleaded with Jessica to take her to the monastery on Sunday. "I will light a candle every night until then so I feel free from services on Sunday. You have spoken with the abbot and talked to Pasha. You can tell me what to do and say. Should I buy an extra candle for Pasha?" She spilled the queries in a monologue unusual for her, an apparent means of releasing excitement mixed with anxiety. Jessica nodded agreement to all her pleas and agreed they would go together, her mind preoccupied with how to break the news to Lettina that she had seen her with Tomenko. Jessica waved off her cousin to deal with her own problems.

"I will be late Thursday evening," she told Tanya at last. "Agata invited me to visit. She works next to me."

"Why Agata? O, please, don't go. Don't get involved in an uprising or anything." Tanya mouthed her panic, "What should I do if you are detained? We wouldn't be able to go to the monastery."

Meetings were tacitly forbidden. The current reprieve from enforcement allowed religious freedom, yet everyone was alert to the gradual crackdown on subversive elements that were supposedly plotted in gatherings of any kind. Announcements, posters tacked on walls, and ubiquitous signs appeared daily throughout the country, both for and against hardline policies, though no one explicitly talked about comrade loyalty or protests—it was more a gut sense, a scent in the air, a hollow echo of what had been.

Jessica chuckled at Tanya's fears, imagining the authorities storming an apartment to arrest adult women, most *babushkas* who gathered for tea. "Tanechka, you make a mountain of a mole hill," she said, tossing her a shriveled orange she had bought on the black market. "I am sure Agata Illyinicha is a mother and grandmother. We have never talked about personal matters. One woman did tell about a tiger that leapt from the ceiling—"

Tanya shrank in her chair, eyes instantly alarmed as if her worst fears were confirmed.

"No, no, it was a dream. Ludmila, a friend of Agata's, described her dream. The woman looked like she should be home peeling onions, and there she was sharing a dream about a tiger leaping from a high corner of a beautiful palace hall upon the—"

Tanya had already covered her ears and eyes with a shawl.

"*O Bozhe moy*, Tanya, you would have to have been there."

Sometimes I think she is as dense as Lettina, Jessica fumed, before a vision of Lettina's ready compliance with Tomenko's salaciousness at the old mill reminded her some things were worse than a dream.

The block where Agata lived on an enviable side of town next to the forest made the invitation more agreeable, yet the plain gray concrete three-story apartments were not too different from one another. Agata's family occupied a one bedroom unit that Jessica found spacious compared to her one room and closet. The two women Jessica had seen before, Ludmila, who had dreamed of the tiger, and Sasha, the restless woman from the courtyard, arrived about the same time, sweeping Jessica inside in a flurry of exclamations, "nice to see you again." The smell of freshly baked *pechen'ye* rushed to greet them. Jessica noticed the guests each carried a tote bag of crocheting, knitting, or sewing, and wondered if she should have done the same. As quickly, she privately rejected the notion as being at odds with her nerves. Unsure if she wanted to be part of this gathering, she tried to keep increasing apprehension from showing on her face.

Since invitations were rare, Jessica had changed from her faded work dress into a knee length navy skirt and tunic top caught with her one patent leather belt and freshly polished black oxfords. The women looked brighter, cleaner, fresher than they appeared at the factory. Alive. Away from their worktables, they looked alive. Unlike Jessica's outfit, their casual wear lacked a hint of fashion, but something lent a sparkle to their eyes. They laughed and joked while Agata explained the children were at a Marxist study camp. The women seated themselves around the table. Slanting rays of sunset warmed the drab walls in a soft orange glow.

"We focus inwardly to find inner peace and preserve our faith," Agata explained to Jessica.

Questions toppled one over the other in Jessica's mind. Was it a prayer group? No icon was visible. Was it associated with St. Sebastions? Was it Orthodox like her parents' faith? Jessica's youthful resistance to ritual and dogma roiled in her chest and shortened her breath. Young Pioneers had instilled the ideals of atheism with every bowl of kasha, and denounced the delusions wrought by religion with every salute to the Party. Older people and their beliefs had not yet made the world a peaceful place and apparently never would.

So why am I here? And Sasha? I cannot relate to women with closed eyes who appear to be praying but call it something else. With rising impatience came a sense of uneasiness. Tanya's warning should have alerted me. If this is a meeting of dissenters, we might be detained—but there was nothing to do but sit, as if she were in the midst of worshipers and had to go to the *taulet*. An evening out of the closeness of her flat seemed like a great idea earlier, before she became trapped in an impossible situation. Half-thoughts skittered here and there, aggravated by tension of not knowing, until she fell into the even breathing of other women.

"I am not Tanya. I am not hysterical. I can do this." Jessica gradually calmed herself without thinking about the strange words "focusing inwardly."

Quiet settled over the room now warmed by the bodies of those present, though they did not seem present at all. The abbot was more present than these women, Jessica observed. She had felt the same in the monastery garden as she felt here—a sense of being suspended, a nameless spell that was the same. She peeked at Sasha, and saw a half smile lingering on her lips, reminding Jessica of Boris Pasternak's poetry with its allusions to a better world ahead, a world with unapologetic steadfastness to true values—he meant spirituality in all the old ways.

She wanted to say, *Bah*, my mother clings to the old ways, the icons and rituals of her faith and what good does it do her? She is so unhappy. I don't know if this is a traditional or very ancient form of worship, but—but I think it would help her.

Surprised that she linked a practice she had no name for to her mother, indeed was unclear about the faith it represented, Jessica remained mystified about what was happening and why. Time quietly passed; she shifted her feet into a more comfortable position, relaxed her spine, and her mind drifted to a bright dreamy morning when the scent of bursting aspen buds and moist, steamy undergrowth meant one was rooted on the earth.

> *It seems a primal happiness was setting,*
> *It seems the wood was sunk in sunlit dream…*
> *Happy folk don't spend time clock-watching,*

Happy folk don't spend time clock-watching—again Pasternak spoke in what some called his homely way—certainly he spoke to the people in our villages, Jessica mused, though he was reportedly out of favor in higher circles. A rush of uneasiness brought her back to the room. She had strayed from the meditation, as if she had stepped too far out on a precipice. The memory of Ludmila's vivid description of the tiger jumping from the ceiling jolted her from further contemplation.

Eventually, stirrings in the room meant the sitting was over. Jessica glimpsed the women crossing themselves with two fingers from right to left, confirming the signature practice of the *Raskolniki*, the Old Believers. Agata served tea and small slices of rye bread with berry jam and the cookies. The women spoke very little, seeming to savor the gathering so they could take it with them. Jessica's mind felt subdued, as if tumult she had recently experienced had fizzled away, leaving a sense of welcome quiet behind. To Agata's kind, inquiring eyes, she nodded assent.

"*Spasibo*, I am fine and I would like to come again."

That night Jessica slowly removed the only dressy outfit she owned, a hand-me-down, feeling that somehow she had entered upon a threshold of change—and that the circle of women, at once threatening yet potentially reassuring, represented something significant in her life.

IV

Chrysostom

Early one morning Brother Dmitri, head vintner and eldest monk at St. Sansais Monastery, heard a summons by the tiny bell that hung from a cord in the corner of his cell. He gently replaced his frayed devotional book inspired by a fourth century theologian, St. John Chrysostom, on the bedside table, and reported to the guest room, where it was as he suspected. Pavel Ivanovich Zyclov was giving Brother Anton a bad time.

Pavel's thrashing arms had delivered a large purple bruise over Brother Anton's eye before they both tumbled to the stone floor, inciting more bruises. Responding to the altercation, Brother Dmitri caught the patient under the armpits and held him from behind, this time forestalling further damage to either. A wash pan for Pavel's bath had been overturned, spilling soapy water on what appeared to be a clean set of clothes. This may have been fortunate, otherwise an upturned candle might have lit the whole of it on fire. The monks stood looking at each other as Pavel's body became limp, and his eyes wandered the room in a daze.

At six-foot-two with more straight, graying hair on his bushy eyebrows, mustache and beard than he had on his tonsured head, Brother Dmitri's presence had been required more than once lately to stabilize the young man. The monk privately thanked his Swedish mother for his tall frame and strength, though he credited his Polish father for his dark features, and dubiously, for his intensity.

"I do not want to impose upon Father Konstantin," Brother Anton said, "if we can find a way to get Pavel dressed and outside. Here, I will wrap him in a blanket and go to the laundry room for a dry tunic if you would kindly sit with him."

Dmitri set the now decently covered patient on the cot and held him firmly by the shoulders as Anton sped down the outside corridor. Plenty of good nutrition had transformed Pavel's skeleton to that of a slim young man of about twenty-five. Dmitri wished Pavel's mind would show similar improvement. His impatience escalated with the relatively slow progress. Physical recuperation he could understand, mental rehabilitation he could not. He really wanted to shake the cobwebs from the patient's clouded mind, but as he well knew, his great strength could easily be misused—and misconstrued as well.

He and Anton managed to dress Pavel and with one on each side, walk him up and down the corridor. At first Pavel explored the stone walk with a tentative toe as if he were blind, gradually placing each sandal-clad foot properly as they moved about. With each step Pavel seemed to connect the movement with growing confidence. Brother Anton nearly burst into shouts of joy. His eyes darted from Dmitri to Pavel's feet, then down the hall to see if the abbot might be coming.

For Brother Dmitri, the prospect of their patient walking without an intact mind was less than appealing. "Now he will walk *and* thrash about," he predicted sourly. "How will we manage him then?"

Brother Anton's glee was not to be dissuaded. "Perhaps it is a breakthrough. My mother, bless her, often said babies who walk early can talk early." But he made a mental note to lock the guest room from the outside thereafter. The short walk soon tired Pavel, so they placed him on a cot in the garden. The patient fell asleep almost immediately.

Brother Dmitri continued on to the vineyard to supervise the newest novitiates in tilling more land for planting rootstalk. He pulled a makeshift plow while they loosened the soil. Plowing was not his favorite occupation, though he supposed he should not question it.

"I committed to monastic life in search of solitude and prayer," he often lamented to anyone who would listen, "but I find myself in this noisy circus instead, where a guest thrashes about and a monk runs down the corridor to the laundry room."

To compound the insult to his simple aspirations, Brother Dmitri was reading St. John Chrysostom, not because he earnestly sought the spiritual teacher, but because Abbot Konstantin had recently acquired this particular devotional volume from a grateful beneficiary of the monastery. In fact, it was one of the last sole possessions the man owned to his name, but he had given it whole-heartedly in good faith that it was meant for St. Sansais Monastery.

The text Dmitri had been studying, *"No good of any sort, however trifling it may be, will be scorned by the righteous Judge"* remained in Dmitri's thoughts as he went about his work preparing the soil with the novitiates. 'Trifling good? What good is a trifling good? And if the righteous Judge is scornful of things presumably bad, then how can He be a loving God who is not scornful of trifling good?' The first part represented a benign and loving God; the second part a judging and wrathful God, as he saw it. He thought how confusing this sounded when all he wanted was straight-forward teaching and discipline consistent with his humble Polish origins.

Abbot Konstantin insists I must acknowledge and embrace the first part, but Eastern Orthodox emphasizes the latter. Dmitri's ruminations became tinged with irritation when he recalled the abbot had implied he was confusing himself; that he must go back and study the good book of St. John of Chrysostom again, though Dmitri knew from experience it would further confuse him.

Polar positions on the nature of God that Chrysostom so passionately defended were equally as mystifying. Was God the "incomprehensible," thereby beyond the realms of inquiry and the expressible, or comprehendible by the mind of man? Or was God known in human encounters as being unfathomable because one was stricken to prostration by the wondrous, awesome and transcendent nature of the deity? A memory of an experience with the overpowering presence of the Spirit when Dmitri was a young shepherd shook him from the entanglement of concepts—he was certain of one thing and that was how he felt in the presence of the holy as a young person.

"I must speak to the abbot again," he said aloud, startling the other monks who worked in silence with him in the vineyard, raising fears that the head vintner might speak to Father Konstantin about them or their work, though it was not in his character to do so.

Jessica felt as though the summer days were passing by without her. Borscht? Leek or cabbage soup? Wash and hang my clothes. Clean the apartment. *Bah*, Lettina has her own life. Anna is out of town to assist her parents. I have nothing planned with my friends. But, I did promise Tanya we would go to the monastery on Sunday.

Tanya retreated to her room whenever Jessica was in a bad mood. This time she claimed to be sewing, but Jessica thought she was probably moping. Tanya's room was oppressive, wide enough only for a small cot and space for feet on the floor. Her belongings were stored overhead. A draft of air seeped under the shabby door. Fortunately for Tanya's health, the door was often ajar.

"You may come out, cousin," Jessica fairly shouted, though an audible whisper might have conveyed the message. "We must plan for tomorrow—to go see Pasha."

The fifteen-year-old appeared halfway from her room as if ready to spring back inside. She glanced at Jessica with damp solemn eyes set in dark hollows, and stood uncomfortably as if a stranger in her adopted home.

She is suffering, she has suffered, too. Unexpectedly, Jessica saw her cousin as if for the first time—really looked at her. Surprise stopped her in mid-sentence when she tried to discuss arrangements. When does a twenty-year-old wonder what a fifteen-year-old thinks? she breathed, excusing her oversight. They are annoying relatives put upon one for the sake of their mutual families.

Embarrassed by the stare, Tanya slipped into the broken chair.

When does a twenty-year-old look at older women in their peasant scarves? I stared like a lost cat at them at Agata's. I saw something in them that I—I want, but what is it? Their serenity? Jessica's silent discourse rattled her composure. She jerked out a tote bag and began packing it with bread and cheese, her mind still groping for answers.

"Tatiyanka, I am sorry. I must be losing my mind. Maybe Pasha will come visit me in the sanitarium." Shifting her tone, she pleaded, "Please, let's be cheerful and make it a nice day tomorrow."

Jessica knew she must settle down, even bring her cousin into her confidence. She had revealed that she met a few women at Agata's but failed to disclose the nature of the meeting. Afterwards, the meditation group struck her as being foreign, weird, even subversive. Jessica told herself she had attended it by accident, not unlike stumbling upon Lettina having an affair. There was no way upon pain of death would she tell Tanya about that experience or about Lettina. In fact, she could think of no one to tell to unburden her mind.

The next day the girls left the apartment to walk to the monastery. Tanya wished to avoid the few people she knew who attended Sunday services. Unsure what lay ahead with Pasha, she did not want anyone to inquire where she was going.

"Will Lettina be coming?" she asked to allay fears of her first encounter with Pasha since she was eight years old.

"No, just us," Jessica answered too sharply. "We will hurry along and get there early afternoon. Last time we found Pasha and the monks in the garden."

That last visit seemed long ago. A time when I was blind and dumb and innocent, she chastised herself. I was a child who foolishly walked in dress shoes. Now I'm a great deal more sensible about what a woman is and wants. I hadn't really listened when Lettina said she wanted a man, though she made it known repeatedly. I am sure I wasn't mistaken—Lettina's open blouse betrayed her willingness, her consent. *Tak*, so it is.

Jessica's distractions carried her along the dirt roads while Tanya's excitement grew. She had tucked the candle she bought for Pasha into the bag they took turns carrying the considerable distance. The ugliness of Konsky receded and farmland opened ahead with fields of lavender-blue lupin tucked between shaggy rows of willows. Overhanging trees hid *izbas,* quaint peasant houses built in the days of the tsars. A few cows grazed in pastures, and an infrequent sun burnished everything green and gold, relieving the pitiful chimneys standing above burnt homes, the twisted bed frames upended in tall grass.

Tanya threw back her head to inhale the fresh cool air that hinted of the wandering tributaries that fed Kursk Province's myriad rivers. She turned to Jessica. "I feel so good out of doors! No wonder Pasha is improving in the countryside. *Spasibo! Spasibo!* Thank you for bringing me."

Jessica nodded. Whatever Tanya said seemed to irritate her. If she feels good in the country, it means she is miserable in town. Jessica experienced her usual helpless feeling around her cousin.

"*Da*, hopefully he continues to improve. We will see. I wonder what will become of him. Surely the abbot is aware of his family's reduced circumstances, hardly able to care for themselves, I understand."

"If only Pasha recovers his mind, he may be able to work, but that may be too much to ask. I am sure God has a plan for him in either case," Tanya finished, looking helpless as well.

At St. Sansais, the gatekeeper took them around back of the sprawling stone building to the garden. A huge, bristly monk supported Pasha with an arm around his slight shoulders, and a young monk held Pasha's elbow on the other side. The girls stopped in awe.

"Pasha is walking?" Tanya looked at Pasha then at Jessica, questioning whether what she witnessed could be true.

"O, I am so happy and so surprised," Jessica managed to say, partly to Tanya, partly to the older monk who introduced himself as Brother Dmitri. Dmitri appeared to be Pasha's primary attendant. Brother Anton was nowhere in sight.

The monks released their charge on the cot, and withdrew in consideration of the family gathering, though Brother Dmitri remained close to leap to their aid if Pavel began thrashing about. The girls were unaware of theatricals that had taken place. They only knew that Pasha had gained weight and his recovery appeared promising.

"Pasha, cousin," they both exclaimed, their faces glowing, hands touching his feet, hands, and finally smoothing his brow. Jessica moved a small stool to his side, and Tanya perched at the foot of the cot.

"We came to see you. We are so happy you are walking. Please, tell us you know your cousins. I am Jessica—I mean Svetlana Sergeevna Gilkova, and this is your younger cousin, Tatyana.

Deep brown eyes lined with thick black lashes widened and ran over their faces without recognition. Dismay momentarily swept over the girls, but Jessica noticed his mouth seemed controlled rather than hanging loosely as before. Pasha ran his tongue over dry lips and shifted his body into a more comfortable position.

"Water. He is thirsty, I think," Tanya cried, looking to Brother Dmitri who produced a tin cup of water from a pitcher nearby. The stumps of Pasha's fingertips on the right hand were clearly visible as his wandering hand attempted to connect with the cup. Jessica had warned Tanya of the frostbite, both choking with tears at the loss for a musician.

"He knows," Tanya cried. "He knows about the cup, about walking, about feeling thirsty." In her delight, she saw no deficits.

Jessica stroked his pale soft palms that she guessed had been rough and grimy before he came here, raising images of the war that she immediately banished. She had learned to shut out those ghastly times, unlike her mother who dwelled on misfortune every day, until Vera's fine features sagged with worry lines and a pallor unbefitting one once so robust.

Abruptly Jessica called to Brother Dmitri. "Pasha is a musician. A violin would help him move on from the past." Jessica sensed that she, too, strived to do anything to avoid becoming like her mother.

Perplexed, the monk bowed politely. "Ah, in my youth in Poland, long before I took vows, I attended the National Concert Hall in Warsaw. *Taka radosé!*" His eyes misted with a joyous feeling. Such an indulgence was now permanently forsaken by his vows. Scowling at the girls as if he had shown a weakness, he said, "We must have a violin in the monastery, *czy my,* do we? And next we must have a concert hall for Matins and Vespers." His voice became deep and grumpy.

Jessica hardly dared ask, "Should I approach the abbot? If I managed to find a violin, even one with one or two strings or one with a broken bow would the Brothers cleverly fix it?"

Brother Dmitri shook his gray head, a sign the girls most assuredly understood as "*nyet.*"

"God will provide if it is to be," Tanya whispered to Jessica. She reached into the tote bag for the short, fat candle she brought, engraved with Созерцайте я - с Вами всегда, '*Behold, I am with you always.*'

"May I leave this for Pasha?" she asked, handing it to Brother Dmitri.

He accepted the candle and the girls took their cue to leave, remembering the monastery's usual vow of silence. They each kissed Pasha, first on one cheek then on the other, and squeezed his hands that lay at ease in his lap. He looked limp and forlorn in the loose, undyed nightshirt supplied by the monastery, a picture they took away with them on their quiet trek home.

Still grimacing that evening about the notion of a violin in the uncertain, if not reckless, hands of his patient, Pavel Ivanovich Zyclov, Brother Dmitri decided to read aloud to him from St. John Chrysostom for his own edification, if not for the patient's, since he had to sit with him anyway. Dmitri suspected that Pasha could hear. Whether he made any sense of the sounds was yet to be determined. In his low sonorous voice, the monk slowly read, *"God who has predestined the salvation of man has, of course, not laid commandments upon him with the intention of making him an offender because of their impracticability. No; but that by their holiness and the necessity of them for a virtuous life they may be a blessing to us, as in this life so in eternity."*

Knowing he himself did not have the most nimble mind, he read the passage again. Meditating upon the contents, he thought first that it implied that rules must govern one's life. Indeed it says, in effect, commandments are necessary for a virtuous life. This was so consistent with Dmitri's own thinking that he read the passage aloud again.

But what if one fails to uphold the holiness of the commandments and becomes an offender? Dmitri often thought that at best he failed to uphold them, and at worst, he was an offender despite the admonishments of Abbot Konstantin that he was being unduly hard upon himself. The abbot cited the statement *"God...had not laid commandments upon him with the intention of making him an offender"* as being the critical message, the remainder in support of the *"predestinated salvation."*

So let there be no more worry about it, Dmitri concluded, adding, "Truly, I find myself *like a fish out of water*," a Russian proverb the monk regularly declared to himself. He lit another candle and hastily read passages of the theologian again to keep his mind on the *"virtuous life"* and the *"blessings"* to come. He became drowsier with each reading. It had the same effect upon Pavel who was soon sound asleep. Dmitri quietly withdrew from the room and locked the door behind him.

V

Mme. Marsolet

The Benyanske factory whirred with the usual workday clamor. The long roomful of needles chomping through heavy leather felt like an assortment of discordant hammers pounding in Jessica's brain. Ten-hour shifts became interminably long and robbed her of incentives to enjoy the late spring evenings, the nicest time of year in Konsky. Ancient trees that gave the town its only beauty hung leafy, low-hanging boughs as if they alone cared enough to hold its citizens in their arms. A slight breeze snooped up and down through the corridors of concrete apartments, cleansing the residue of the day. Slinky dogs on the street chose to stretch out on the warm earth rather than beg from passersby.

That morning Jessica had methodically sorted her meager wardrobe. She selected the navy skirt, the tunic-length blouse and a much repaired coat to wear. She dropped two work dresses into a pile for rags. On second thought, she shoved the faded garments under her bed. She rummaged in a hidden slit in her straw mattress to retrieve her savings—her life savings, which she placed in a drab handbag with several half-formed plans in mind. Her motions reminded her of the butcher slicing a sturgeon, the fillets here, soup scraps there, inedible-by-humans parts elsewhere.

"All my things are discards," she muttered, "I don't want any of them, and I don't want to be here, and I don't want to think of Lettina and Tomenko." The admission set off another stormy sense of confusion and defeat. Unable to face her closest friend, Jessica had been avoiding Lettina and the other girls from the mill.

"Let Lettina be," she told herself. "She got what she wanted. It's not my business. Old Tomenko, a married man. *Pshaw*."

But fantasies sprang forth anew. Why can't I have a real lover— like Ingrid Bergman or Susan Hayward had. The images appeared to Jessica as naturally as breathing, their romances burned into her soul, their waist and bodice-clinging dresses the ideals for her fantasies. Her heart echoed in recognition, yet when she witnessed Lettina and Tomenko in the dirty old mill, the revulsion she felt drowned her hopes.

Jessica's sleep-deprived monologue drifted into a refrain familiar throughout the Republic: it's not fair; the war took the best and maimed all the rest. She heard the mournful words of the soldiers' song *"Wait for Me,"* with the even more painful sense that she had no one to wait for, nor a soldier to wait for her.

Yet longings rose like tulips in spring from roots deep in the ground, seeking the surface by a universal prompting—it is time, it is time; innocence responding through the ages, thwarted only by lack of an object of desire. The mallard hen mates for life to the dazzling, emerald-collared drake. When she finds him crushed by the roadside, she worries at his prostrate side until she, too, is finished. For Jessica, rushes of excitement became intense, unnamed longings that were similarly crushed. She flushed in embarrassment for having accidently eavesdropped on Lettina, and now for feeling possessed by unfamiliar urges, for being robbed, not of Tomenko, but of having someone to love, someone who might love her.

Tanya manages better these days than I, she moaned, knowing her cousin left the factory laughing with a group of her friends. At nearly twenty years of age, the unbidden hopes sought their way to the sun, regardless. With undefined promptings she was determined to go shopping. That evening she slipped down side streets on her solitary mission. Her reflection in a window showed her usually buoyant dark hair hung straight and disheveled. A spot of grease from the machines shadowed one side of her nose. The white collar of her plain white blouse was smudged with sweat, all infractions on her appearance she tried to fix before anyone saw her. "I couldn't be more plain," escaped her lips.

A few shops, all nationalized, remained open downtown in the midst of empty store fronts, their shelves bearing only tins of mackerel here, caviar there, the first too common and latter too exotic; both were for show, but neither affordable for citizens of Konsky. Jessica raised her chin to shake the sour mood, picked up her steps and began to smile. Since the factory workers began early in the day, businesses were open for a brief time after hours. Jessica knew exactly the shop she was looking for located near the theatre where she, Anna, Lettina and Greita checked out women's wear in its window displays, generally gray uniforms and the same formless day wear on moth-eaten manikins.

She no sooner pushed in the unpainted door than it was opened with a flourish by a tall thin gentleman who bowed slightly, murmuring pleasantries in heavily accented Russian. Almost as immediately, a soft-voiced woman in black wearing high heels such as those Jessica had seen in the movies, came forward and extended her hand.

"Bonsoir, mademoiselle."

Jessica straightened to her full height and tucked in her stomach, struck by the sensation of having wandered onto a runway in Paris. She took a deep breath, exhaling in relief that she had detached the sweaty collar and put it in her bag.

"The navy you are wearing becomes you," said the woman in Russian, eyeing Jessica's figure and the way the skirt fitted trimly at the waist. The hem came to the bottom of her kneecap, shorter than hems worn by factory girls.

"Thank you." Jessica swallowed hard, relieved she had not come in a shapeless cotton work dress.

"I am Madame Marsolette. Please meet my husband, Monsieur Marsolette. We see few people this time of day. Do us the honor, *s'il vous plaît*, and join us for tea."

"O, how nice, but I have so little time. I want to say I often pass by your windows. My--my curiosity got the better of me today." She did not want to say 'when she went to the movies.' It sounded so tawdry. Or that she had dodged her equally tawdry friends to come here.

"We are pleased to meet you, *Mademoiselle*."

"Jessica, my name is Jessica."

At this disclosure the woman turned and closely examined her visitor in the dim interior. "Jessica" was not a name heard in Konsky. It implied a lineage, perhaps an American one—or higher aspirations.

Jessica stood uncomfortably enduring the scrutiny, disconcerted by the sudden close attention. "I beg your pardon. I am Svetlana Sergeevna Gilkova. Lana for short, if you care to know. I named myself Jessica. I often forget it sounds foreign."

"Ah, from the movies, I imagine!"

"*Oui*, Madame. You know me as well as I know myself!" Committed now to revealing more, she added, "I work at Benyanske Boot and Shoe Manufacturing, but I want so much to become a fashion designer," she blurted, alert to Madame's frank and insightful response. She was also keenly aware she would be unable to hide anything from Madame Marsolette. Blushing, she added, "I might as well have told you the whole truth in the beginning. American movies are the only thing that inspires me to become the person I want to be."

Except Pasha and his sad condition, of course, but that was not relevant to her love of fashion. She had not told another soul her dreams of studying fashion design since her parents, Tanya, and girlfriends collectively denounced the notion as being bourgeoisie, as well as an impossibility. Who would allow such a thing, they all said; end of conversation. But beyond the flurry of doubts in her mind she heard Mme. Masolette's soothing remarks.

"So, the movies have brought you here, and you are attracted to fashion design."

Jessica nodded, trembling from her audacity to reveal herself to a stranger.

"I imagine you can do anything you set your mind to. Now let us see what fashions might appeal to you. *Venez par ici , mademoiselle* Jessica." Madame shared a glance with her husband and they escorted

Jessica into a wide room behind the front shop, quietly closing the door behind them. Racks and shelves of apparel spread to the corners and up the walls.

"We display what is permitted in the shop windows so as not to draw attention of authorities. We maintain this special selection for women like you who occasionally venture here seeking more pleasing fashions."

Jessica gasped at the world beyond her known world, except that she recognized an inventory that could only have been traded from far and near and likely surreptitiously sneaked into hiding in Konsky. Struck by the risk the French boutique owners were taking, she wanted to back out and forget about shopping. But Monsieur came with a tape measure to measure her height, length of skirt, and finally her waist, and her initial alarm gave way to a decision to stay, to follow through with her plan. She held her breath and nearly died thinking he might measure her bust, and he did ever so unobtrusively, though surely he felt her heart racing. Images of lecherous old Tomenko came and went through her mind. She hoped she did not embarrass herself by turning beet red.

"*Oui*, so lovely a figure. And what does Mademoiselle Jessica have a desire to see today?" he asked, as if she frequently shopped here.

"I—I don't want to look like the other factory women, though I do not mean to be disrespectful. I will have my twentieth birthday in two weeks. I, uh, I want to feel nicely dressed, to feel better about myself." The words spilled breathlessly on their own accord. She had not been sure exactly why she had saved what roubles she could spare with the intention of coming in until after she said it.

"Naturally. We all want to feel good about ourselves, and how we dress has a great deal to do with that. Twenty years old. That is a fine time to think of fashion," Madame exclaimed.

"O, I have been thinking about lovely dresses since I can remember. My mother tells stories of wearing ruffles and lace when she was a child." Jessica smiled, grateful there were no lectures or moral condemnations of her most cherished desires.

"Ah, you have a radiant smile like the American film stars! As well as a perfect figure and lovely legs. I hear American women exercise their independence since they have the vote. They have apparently become much more self-reliant than the flappers of the '20s, likely due to their wartime service. Loosening their bonds is true of French women as well."

"I am not sure *Russki* women have loosened their bonds, though we contributed heavily to the war effort," Jessica admitted below her breath, glancing at the tell-tale callouses on her hands and her broken fingernails. "O, how I wish I had been born in America, or even under the tsars. My parents refuse to talk about those days, but I suspect they were accepted in social circles."

Jessica's rare disclosures seemed daring, even to her; immediately she regretted the remarks which if overheard she could be sent away on charges of plotting with foreigners. Yet the hidden room behind the store felt safe, and the discreet French shopkeepers had enough at stake to be trustworthy. She ran on as if she could no longer contain herself. The older woman snapped clothes hangers along metal racks without responding to Jessica's comments.

"We must find something suitable. *Non,* more than suitable." Madame examined and rejected item after item in search of the perfect outfit that would fulfill a young woman's dream. Monsieur did the same, critically scanning various combinations, which he handed to Mme. Marsolet, while he off-handedly mentioned they had converted a room of their apartment to this boutique and stocked it with styles they purchased over the years from various fashion houses. The Oriental rugs that originally graced their home now gave a rich, colorful décor to the unauthorized premises.

Jessica marveled at the contrast of the shop with her impoverished apartment. Deep down it felt like a betrayal to her comrades to enjoy it, and a betrayal to her parents who endured poverty in a country village *izba.* According to whispered tales likely not meant for Jessica's ears, her mother had dressed elegantly under the reign of Tsar Nicholas II. Now she chopped wood with her thin, age-spotted arms to heat one room she and Sergey lived in. The other room had been closed off long ago and valuable, inherited furnishings had been sold for necessities.

Jessica choked down the reflections mixed with fears that caught her in the unsolvable problems of the present. Worse than betrayal, it was likely a crime to spend her savings here. Yet Madame hurried back with several garments that roused a protest.

"I cannot imagine these with the shoes I am wearing," Jessica laughed. Both realized the stout leather oxfords would be the next to go. Madame moved her behind a curtain and stayed to slip a burgundy velvet dress with simple lines over Jessica's head as fast as Jessica could remove the navy skirt and blouse. A scooped neck flattered Jessica's wide shoulders. Tiny tucks at the waist fitted perfectly. Long slim sleeves caressed the back of her hands.

Jessica stepped out past the curtain in bare feet. Her eyes first sought Monsieur for approval. His noncommittal face was disappointing. A sense of being rebuffed momentarily irritated her, but she bit her lip and turned about in front of a mirror, affirming her resolve; she was going through with this notion, even if no one else approved. Madame helped her slip on one dress, skirt, and blouse after another, adding a snap-on collar here, a scarf there, or a belt to accentuate her waist.

"You are delightful, *cherie*. Thank you for coming into our boutique. You are like our daughter, so lovely," she murmured around a mouthful of pins.

Jessica sensed there was more to her story, but she had no time; indeed, it would be presumptuous of her to ask about it.

"I must go. Surely your shop would be closed by now. It is far overtime and my cousin will worry. Let me see, I prefer this crimson red silk blouse and plain black skirt, if you please. I may be able to find dressy shoes later." In the mirror, she saw that the red highlighted her smooth complexion, rosy with excitement, and enhanced her dark eyes. The rich gabardine skirt was a classy complement to her swingy black hair. Again she first glanced at Monsieur, seeking his opinion, an involuntary motion that distressed her.

"You have the discriminating taste of a beautiful young woman," Madame replied. "I am sure you will find many occasions to wear such a sensible but fashionable outfit. I congratulate you on your selection, and on your twentieth birthday!"

"It is your doing, *spasibo,*" Jessica told her, genuinely thrilled with the accomplishment, but now anxious about paying for it. "How much is it? And may I have you hold it if I am unable to pay all of it today?"

"Tres bein, tres bein. We will make arrangements and hold the garments for you if necessary." Monsieur took over the transaction. Jessica opened her small coin purse and pulled out a handful of roubles amounting to about one-third of the price. Undaunted, she asked that they hold her purchase and she would pay a little each payday.

She left softly singing "this is me, this is me," her head high and feet tripping back to the apartment.

"I knew what I wanted—just as Lettina did—and our wishes came true. If saying so out loud makes it happen, I may have a chance to make my own way."

The roar of sewing machines receded into the background the next day while Jessica bent over her work. She was barely aware of Agata Illyinicha, who invited her to gather with the women again on Thursday evening. Jessica declined a bit too evasively while she worked fast and efficiently with a smile on her face, encouraged by knowing a crimson red silk blouse was being held for her at the boutique. It represented the first important transaction of her life on her own behalf. And most important of all, Madame had said she was "lovely," even "beautiful." Jessica could not remember when she had ever received such a compliment. Since then she checked her reflection at every opportunity to confirm the statement. For all the anger and despair that led up to the spree, Jessica credited Lettina for the advice to go shopping to lift her spirits—her other half-formulated plan had been to run away, to board a night train to somewhere, anywhere.

At noon she rushed down the street to the edge of town to meet the girls from the mill. Lettina was there with Greita and Katya.

"Where on earth have you been?" Lettina questioned. "We've looked for you for days."

Greita and Katya nodded agreement. Jessica welcomed the warm reception without divulging her recent adventures.

"It must be Pasha," Lettina said.

"Yes, Tanya and I visited him last Sunday. You would be surprised at his progress. He is walking with assistance, though he still suffers from amnesia and did not recognize us. He requires such a lot of care. I wonder that they don't send him to some of the relatives and be done with him."

"O yes, a relative to care for in your apartment is all you need," Lettina laughed. Before Jessica could object to the jibe, the conversation drifted to ordinary trifles of their lives.

"I must see you after work," Jessica whispered to Lettina before they went back to their separate jobs. "I will meet you here," she added firmly, making sure she did not wander into any more scenes at the mill.

Lettina showed up as expected and the girls walked toward the *kofeynyy magazine,* where locals gathered for tea. "I saw you and Tomenko in the back room at the mill." Jessica abruptly got the message off her mind that had weighed so heavily for several weeks.

Their steps sounded loud on the sidewalk before Lettina replied. "So you know. Well, it seems everyone knows, so there it is. I am not trying to hide anything."

Her reply caught Jessica off guard. "I don't understand. You admit it?"

"Look, I admit someone cares about me. If Katya saw us and told Greita, and you found out, so what? Are we to wish away our lives for nothing?" Lettina hovered over Jessica, her voice defensive.

"I'm sorry, Lettina. I am not sorry you found someone, but that we intrude upon your life. I did not mean to upset you." The conversation had not gone at all the way Jessica expected, that of releasing all her pent up indignation, probably tinged with moral superiority and charges of faithlessness to her friends, among the many resentments that had grown in Jessica's mind over the past days. But she hoped she had not sounded envious.

They neared the tea shop after jostling among other workers on the street. Jessica had no further desire to confront her friend. Nor did she want to share her own escapades, one having met with older women for a strange meditation she had yet to understand. And certainly she would not tell Lettina she was buying an expensive outfit on time. Lettina sometimes belittled Jessica's "fashion quirks," as she called them. Madame and Monsieur Marsolet would remain her secret. Their dreams were very different in many ways. Jessica clung tightly to hers, sensing she had better be careful what she wished for. In any event, there were no loving masculine arms to distract her from her singular purpose.

The shop served hot tea brewed in a small teapot at the girls' table. Even the honey sweetener failed to revive their familiar chats. Finally, Jessica asked, "Lettina, do you know of any cleaning jobs I could do on Sundays?"

Lettina looked sharply at her, but did not probe. "I will be working for a family that is moving out of Konsky. They may need extra help. I could find out and let you know." Jessica shrank back in her chair in relief, alerting Lettina that Jessica had not told her everything.

"Are you buying a violin?" she queried.

Jessica nearly spewed tea from her lips when she burst out laughing. "I should have, but not knowing where to find one, that was impossible!"

Lettina knew her better than that and remained unappeased. An uneasy distance remained between them when they left the shop. Self-consciously they gathered their small bags and parted as if they were acquaintances who by chance happened to run across each other and have tea.

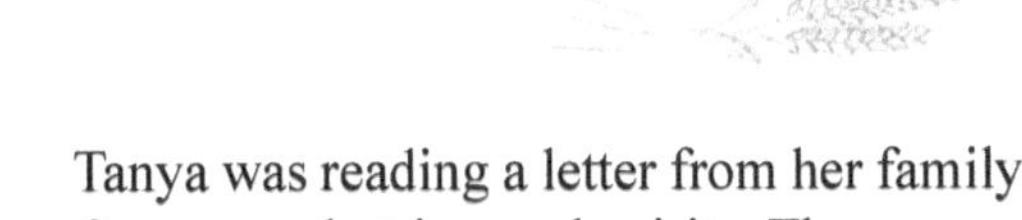

Tanya was reading a letter from her family when Jessica appeared late for supper but in good spirits. The room smelled like onions and cabbage, the same stale odors that clung day and night to the narrow stairwells between the flats. Tanya had boiled their usual supper and waited for her cousin. They ate bowls of soup on good terms. Jessica realized Tanya no longer cried at night and she took more responsibility to make things better between herself and Jessica.

"I'm sorry for my bad moods lately, Tanechka. I know you have suffered."

Tanya gave her a quick, surprised glance and flushed. "O, that is nice, Jessica, *spasibo,*" she mumbled, and stared into her soup bowl.

Jessica reddened. It was the second time she'd had to apologize today. But she looked at Tanya with a certain understanding, not seeing the annoying child she had involuntarily accepted in her apartment. A momentary reflection struck her that she was acting in an uncharacteristic manner, and it felt good, as if the world were kinder, more habitable. But Jessica had to disappoint Tanya again.

"We will not be able to see Pasha this weekend. I may be working with Lettina on a part-time job."

"O, he will miss us—rather, I will miss him. I have a letter from my parents I wanted to share with him. I had written, telling them of Pasha's progress. Everyone is pleased to hear he is recovering."

"Yes, but it will take time," Jessica said, distracted by the sight of her old leather oxfords beside the door. A private smile threatened to become a permanent fixture on her face while she mused about finding a pair of dressy black shoes to go with the red silk blouse and black skirt.

"We must be patient, I know."

Jessica did not want to hear Tanya's note of disappointment again. She disliked a particular state that Tanya slipped into at moments like this, her long sighs spoke what her fifteen-year-old self was unable to say. She suffered when others had more control over their lives than she had over her own, whereas Jessica felt uplifted by her decision to shop. She was struck by the difference a few years can make.

Her twentieth birthday took on new significance for her budding maturity as if tulips bobbed above the earth with radiant femininity and a sense of abandonment.

VI

☩nton

In a nation characterized by centuries of florid court gossip under the tsars, rumors of bad tidings shadowed even the most optimistic Soviet citizens. The stone walls of the Community of Brothers were likewise remarkably porous, a necessary but perhaps unholy leniency the abbot permitted after the Revolution. The state's denunciation of the Russian Orthodox Church, the bans on practices of the faithful including folk traditions, and the persecutions that followed had winnowed his cadre of cloistered monks to a team of outwardly secular vintners.

Rumors that currently drifted inside the walls suggested authorities had begun to extend nationalization *programmes* to less populated regions of the country. The disturbing news revived suspicions that privately owned small businesses and farms in Kursk Province that had previously escaped collectivization would be converted in the interest of strengthening the Party's internal hold. In addition, religious affiliations that had, mercifully, been given a reprieve during the war would likely be curtailed at the same time. Concurrent with nationalization, Konstantin expected controls on religious freedom would again be tightened and bans on Orthodoxy reinstated.

As a man, Abbot Konstantin had vowed to defend his countrymen and the Church against threats, yet he had been forced to fall back on what he believed to be a greater duty, which was to trust in the Almighty

Lord and Savior to handle the affairs of all mankind. This trust had been sorely tested. Up to now, Konstantin credited the quasi-secular nature of St. Sansais Monastery and Vineyard and its production of strategic goods and staples, in this case, rather delectable wines. Yet ever since the agreements of Yalta, VE Day, and Potsdam settled the affairs of two continents, Konstantin privately railed against his own impotence to protect the bodies and souls of his people.

Summer deepened in the heartland as worrisome news came of extreme droughts from the Crimea to the Baltics. Lesser but still damaging dry seasons occurred in northern provinces as well, threatening the country's already exhausted food supplies. Konstantin vividly recalled famines of the early 1930s, which had been followed by subsequent years of crop failures that decimated the population and brought harsh austerity, rationing, and restrictions. Belts had already been tightened since the overthrow of the Romanovs, two World Wars, and the well-intended though experimental Soviet collectivization *programmes*. Reserves distributed to the masses ultimately drained the country of food storages. In addition, low yields under successive Five-Year Plans meant greater hardship and suffering.

But calamities had not yet hit the vineyards, where Abbot Konstantin's infectious good spirits and trust in the Almighty prevailed. Midsummer's sunny days brought out the deepest purplish reds of the grapes, while teasing out an unusually remarkable fruity flavor of the Cabernet Sauvignons, a taste hinting of the warmer Southern regions from hence the roots stalk had come.

"Bien, bien," he said to his chief grower in the vineyard, and *"Gutten"* to the master of crushing and blending the grapes, wishing to please these able members of community life who had come from throughout Europe. The abbot reserved special praise for Brothers Anton and Dmitri. Young Anton, with an engaging personality and strong physical condition, became the monastery's intermediary with the outside world when he trundled carts of produce to market in Thor, a neighboring village. The abbot recognized Dmitri, in his fifties, as head vintner and the "Lord's Polish laborer." Dmitri added "nursemaid" to his title as a consequence of serving the poor and

wretched of the world that the abbot took in as if he ran a charitable hostel. Both monks lost or found traditional prayer time, depending upon their natures, while working in the gardens and vineyard, and tending to their guest, Pavel Ivanovich Zyclov.

Konstantin observed how Brother Anton took simple delight in sitting with Pavel, sinking into deep contemplation with one whose luminous spirit, he claimed, transcended consciousness. On the other hand, Brother Dmitri clearly experienced it as a lesson in piety, even of suffering, both of which he endured with a good bit of grousing, yet always a steadfast commitment to fulfill his duties. Accordingly, Abbot Konstantin directed his spiritual guidance toward the monks' individual differences and spiritual needs. The abbot's serenity and joyful presence harbored an inner fire as if he had a secret pipeline to heaven, or more likely, that he rested in the favor of the Holy Spirit for he did not often rest in the Holy Church.

One day Brother Anton found a moment to approach the abbot in his office.

"My beloved *Starets*, I have a most earnest desire for unceasing interior prayer according to the teachings in the Gospels."

Konstantin smiled. Brother Anton implored the same thing every time he met with him. Anton, along with many others, had been attracted to the famed, ancient St. Sansais Monastery by the abbot's gifted, positive, and insightful spiritual teachings, most derived from centuries-long teachings of the monks of Mount Athos, an island off the eastern side of Greece.

"And what have you found most helpful?" the abbot inquired, noting the slight frown on the otherwise smooth, upturned face of the monastery's youngest member. "I understand your time with the patient has been most beneficial for quieting his soul and yours."

"Indeed, Father, indeed, I would have it no other way. I am sure that in Pavel's distant world his interior prayer surpasses that of most who diligently work day and night for such an elevation of Spirit. I am quite humbled by his goodness and purity."

"And how have you practiced that excited your soul for such fervor?" Konstantin pursued.

Brother Anton bowed to the floor of the abbot's small office and pronounced in a small voice, "Father, as you taught me, I say the Jesus Prayer, 'Lord Jesus Christ, have mercy on me' continuously with my lips, my mind, and my heart until it says itself and gives me great joy." He stood up, his eyes shining with a special radiance as he crossed himself from right to left and again bowed low, his hands behind his back.

"The prayer is saying itself so much it has become a part of you, and now you wish to further perfect this interior prayer."

"*Da*, O yes, Father, that is my one desire."

The abbot drew a deep breath, absorbed in the openness to Spirit by one so young, who appeared to have a limitless capacity for seeking the Gospel's admonition to pray without ceasing.

"First, be thankful to God that this desire has been manifested in you and for the gift of the prayer that says itself within you and gives you such joy. St. Simeon, the Theologian teaches us that the joy of unceasing prayer comes from the simplicity of a loving heart. And truly, your love and devotion has brought great blessings upon yourself, our patient, and the monastery. Now continue as before until you fully become the prayer. You will find in the becoming a great peace and contentment."

Overcome by the abbot's validation, his throat choked by grateful sobs, the young monk clasped his hands at his chest as if in prayer, bowed deeply and backed out of the abbot's office. Outside, his feet pattered down the corridors as if he could barely restrain himself from jumping for joy.

Abbot Konstantin smiled again and stroked his beard. He sat down and stared into the small candle, unaware that it dripped wax on an exquisitely embroidered cloth on the little table. Seeing himself at an early age with similar aspirations, he marveled at the wondrous nature of the human being God had created in His likeness. Then his gaze lifted to a gold-gilt icon of St. Benedict that hung on the stone wall above the table, and his smile hung around the corners of his lips. The saint's compassionate face with a slight frown conveyed several messages at once; gather the brotherhood in community and live strictly therein. How? Konstantin questioned periodically. How to live and make it worthy of our lives? We must reconcile human nature's *bon vivant* with the discipline of the Order, he reminded himself without too much conviction; surely the monastery must remain cloistered enough for contemplation, while allowing the soul to spread its wings and soar.

Feeling that he could not cope with Brother Dmitri's dour outlook after sharing such a thrilling moment with his youngest novitiate, Konstantin slipped out a side door to sit alone in his private garden and attune his heart to the equally compelling mysteries of bees gathering honeysuckle pollen, toads seeking coolness against the stone walls, caterpillars chewing lacey patterns in round leaves of serviceberry bushes, and sparrows dropping seeds from the wilds that would become underbrush in next year's garden.

In the Benyanske Boot and Shoe factory, Agata Illyinicha began noticing Jessica's cousin, Tatyana, after Jessica's visit to Agata's apartment. Jessica had since abruptly terminated her tentative outreach to the older woman, and now hunched over her work at the workbench, keeping her eyes to herself. Absorbed in her own affairs, she spoke only if spoken to. The younger cousin often appears more mature than Svetlana, Agata noted, but as a mother she sensed Tatyana's thinly veiled vulnerability and the hurt feelings she was unable to hide. Agata turned her attention to her hoping to maintain a connection to the girls in the absence of observable family support.

Tanya worked below on the second floor of the factory, where shoes were made of softer leather that required more exacting treatment than the stout leather boots and oxfords that were produced upstairs. Deerskin occasionally arrived with other leather supplies, as well as expensive calf skin, both tanned and rubbed to a buttery texture occasionally sought for women's dress shoes. Marketed with appropriate Soviet braggadocio, the finished products were meant to convey the economic well-being of the Republic and increase its stature in the world of trade.

Agata viewed the shift from wartime marching boots of composition materials to peacetime ballerina shoes and loafers with detached skepticism. Shoemakers were first to notice that living standards for those in power was in keeping with the history and culture under the tsars regardless of stringent postwar austerity. Most citizens were as poor as serfs had been under the tsars.

She paused at the second floor workroom and observed Tanya at work for some minutes after the noon bell rang. Tanya's small hands manipulated the leather into intricate forms beneath the whirring needle, her dexterity evident by the lack of mishaps or serious damage to her slim fingers. A few older women with years of experience cut the valuable hides according to layouts of patterns for various styles and sizes. Crowded worktables jammed the room, leaving only space for the small army of younger women workers. Agata had noticed Tanya among friends that dawdled in the hallways and that she attended St. Sebastians. Today, after the others left for lunch, Tanya remained, head in her hands as she sat by herself, a picture of youthful loneliness. Agata hesitated a moment before walking up to her.

"May I introduce myself? I work near Svetlana upstairs. She may have told you about me."

Tanya tensed and sat upright when the woman came over; a woman who was familiar as dozens of other similarly dressed factory workers and as much a stranger.

"*Zdravstvuyte*. I am Tatyana Pytrovna Gilkova. Please, do tell me your name. I don't think Jessica mentioned anyone—I mean Svetlana Sergeevna did not say anything."

Overlooking the slip of the tongue, Agata introduced herself and sat down when Tanya patted the chair beside her. She noticed the girl's thin arms and legs. Her feet were poorly shod for one who labored making exquisite new shoes for others. Hollows formed under her wide hazel eyes.

"I have a daughter about your age," Agata said, addressing the core of her visit. At Tanya's puzzled look, she added, "She does not work at the factory. She cares for children of parents who work in another building, and lives with their family in that communal block. Now tell me about yourself."

"I live with Svetlana. Our parents sent us to work in the factory during the war. I find it difficult to come from a small farm to work in a factory, but we both must until something changes."

The bleak reality for youth across the country and for her own children made Agata want to slump with her head in her hands, too. "I am sorry to bring up situations we cannot change. Surely we can improve our lot by brightening our days among ourselves. Would you like to meet Adriana on your rare time off?"

"O, *spasibo*! I would be so happy to meet her, but on Sundays we visit our cousin Pasha, that is Pavel Ivanovich Zyclov, who is recovering from the war at St. Sansais. We go except this coming Sunday when Jessica is cleaning house for someone, and the next week is her birthday. I do not know if we will go to the monastery then or not." Tanya betrayed the anxiety and stress that prompted her present sense of despair, hence her lapse in using Jessica's chosen rather than given name.

"You must care for Pavel a great deal," Agata said, placing a reassuring hand on Tanya's arm.

Tanya's eyes filled with tears. She swallowed, stopping short of sobs when the bell rang for them to go back to work. She nodded without looking at Agata, took a few bites from a bit of cheese and rye bread, and turned back to work. Agata assumed the monotonous routine of the factory felt safe and predictable to her.

That night a courier came to the apartment complex in a block known as cheap people's housing for factory workers where cramped rooms often harbored twice or three times as many workers as designated by housing allotments. The young man inquired of tenants where he could find Jessica. No one seemed to know anyone by that name.

"An American? *Nyet, nyet*. Not here," they laughed. "Why would an American live here in Konsky? They are too rich to live in *Rossiya*!"

Unable to find her, yet undaunted, the courier ran back to the shop to ask if she had another name. Madame Marsolet had promised a generous gratuity when the parcel was safely delivered into Jessica's hands.

"*Oui*, she did say Svetlana Sergeevna Gilkova, pardon my oversight. You may locate her more readily with a proper name."

The courier ran through the concrete maze of buildings. He was there when Jessica left her friends laughing on the corner, and met him face-to-face at the main entrance. At once, the courier recognized the "modern" girl Madame had instructed him to find.

"Please, ma'am, I am looking for Svetlana Jessica—." His badly cut, straggly hair stuck out from beneath a flat wool cap.

Jessica peered at him and at the parcel, reaching for the rectangular box without saying a word.

"Are you—?" The courier gripped the box more firmly.

"*Da*, here is a kopek for your troubles. *Spasibo*. Thank you." Jessica's breath came in short bursts. "I know what is in the box, but why it is delivered to me just now?"

She instantly feared something had happened to the Marsolets and their boutique hidden behind the women's wear storefront, and practically tore the package from the boy's hands. He gladly relinquished it, but stammered he knew nothing.

She waved him away and rushed upstairs three steps at a time, let herself into her apartment and checked to see if Tanya was there. Finding she was alone, she dropped into the lopsided chair and tore open the double-wrapped package. Beneath the brown wrapper she found a small envelope tucked in carnival-colored gift paper tied with purple and maroon ribbons. Jessica gasped at the stunning wrappings as her trembling fingers opened the envelope and slid out a note.

In an elegant script in pen and ink on vellum, Madame Marsolet had written,

> *Jessica, we must leave the country. Consider your purchase paid in full. You are so beautiful—as was my daughter. If I can ever be of help to you—   Mme.*

The note and parcel slowly slipped to the floor from Jessica's weakened fingers. "We *must leave—we must leave—we must leave the country—*," the terrifying words reverberated in her mind, a numbing experience at a preschool age when her parents' merchant trading business was appropriated and they were sent to labor in the fields, words laden with real or imagined threats of prison or death from powerful unseen forces.

"They must leave," Jessica said vacantly; her jaw dropped and the package lay unopened beneath her glassy stare when Tanya came in.

Shocked and puzzled, Tanya bolted the door and sat down without knowing what to say. Afraid the news pertained to their families, her lips puckered. She dared not look at Jessica, but her stare was drawn to the mysterious box. Waiting, nearly blind with fear when Jessica didn't speak, her hands flew to her ears, expecting the worst.

Grappling for something to say, she whispered, "Who sent the box, Jessica?"

Pulled back to awareness, Jessica fumbled for it under the brown wrapper and lifted a splendidly bright, gaily tied gift box.

"I bought some new clothes. I--I spent my savings. *Da,* it appears reckless. Now I am heartbroken because the people at the boutique must leave."

Tanya visibly wilted in her chair from relief.

"Here, let me show you. I want to see for myself. Perhaps I dreamed all this." Jessica gently untied the ribbon without damaging it, and carefully unfolded the ends of the gift wrap, a thin tissue that looked and felt foreign to her. At last she carefully lifted the lid, a moment she would have liked to savor alone.

The soft folds of the silk blouse spilled over onto her bare knees like a caress, a shimmering drape reflecting light in variations from bluish red to an almost transparent crimson red. Unmoving, Jessica let it lie there. Her damp eyes met her cousin's equally moist gaze.

"O, these are more beautiful than I remembered. I left a down payment on the fashions awhile back, but they sent them to me anyway." Jessica eased out the smooth black gabardine skirt. "I feel like this is my birthday! What more could I want?"

"It is purely like you, Jessica," Tanya murmured, squinting at the cascade of color so out of place among gray overtones of their studio apartment.

"I do feel like it is me," Jessica agreed, smiling broadly at Tanya whose understanding gave her pause. "I'm glad you are here to share this moment with me. Now I must get shoes."

"I wish I could make a dressy pair for you." Tanya mentally shifted gears from dread to happiness for Jessica. They both managed to laugh, a little like two people in a glass cage, but for now life bestowed its graces, a limitless sense of abundance in the young women's hearts.

VII

Dmitri

The warm, nose-tickling scent of blushing grapes seductively wisped over the foothills above the grassy meadows and croplands of the river bottoms of Kursk Province. Hustling of workers marked the spurt to gather harvests at St. Sansais and across the motherland. Brother Dmitri tramped through the vineyard and calculated how many barrels were needed to receive juice from the ripening grapes. Preoccupation with endless demands of the winery meant Dmitri had suppressed his own needs until they burst forth in the presence of his *starets,* a man younger than he, but a mentor he sought time and again with his innermost yearnings and spiritual struggles. Today, in need of spiritual uplifting, he had trudged to the office for his weekly meeting with the abbot. Left outside the door were their frequent discussions regarding the gardens, marketable produce, and winter stores for the monastery.

"I beg your pardon, Father, but I do not understand the meaning of suffering. Everywhere there is suffering and pain. I have yet to reconcile it with belief in a benevolent God." Dmitri's naturally defiant eyes spoke of an inner rebellion that surfaced more frequently these days, primarily since Pavel Ivanovich Zyclov had become a resident in the guest room.

"I wonder, Brother Dmitri, if you might be speaking of Pavel

Ivanovich, as well as the human condition," ventured the abbot in his gentle, curious manner that was capable of unsettling even a man as large as the Polish monk.

Brother Dmitri lowered his eyes. His head sank into the cowl of his robe. A tinge of red crept from his burly neck to his cheeks, betraying the subject of his distress. The abbot had rightly exposed the monk's ambivalence towards their actively recovering guest. Pavel's progress was daily credited to the efforts of the Community of Brothers as a whole, and to Brother Anton's round-the-clock attentiveness and prayers that brought the patient back from near death. But in no one's mind did anyone contribute as much as Brother Dmitri to facilitate the rehabilitation. That subtle acknowledgment contributed to Dmitri's present discomfort, and it clashed with his private assertion that the monastery was a place for contemplation and not for 'nurse-maiding' a mental patient.

"Pavel suffers more than before because he relives the war. Night terrors punish him at all hours and he cannot sleep. I confess, the strain dims my own belief. But I am most guilty of having neither patience for his outbursts nor for the intrusion of the world's suffering from outside the monastery."

Abbot Konstantin silently viewed the monk standing in front of him who wrestled heroically with his own questioning nature and sense of personal shortcomings. "It appears that the strength of your faith is not tested as much as your will, Brother Dmitri."

Dmitri was accustomed to rigorous reflection on his faith, but his will? After weeks of tending to the baths and chamber pot and drools, his willingness was questioned. His willingness? He grimaced.

Yet Konstantin smiled. "As I understand it, you would like to close the walls to the suffering that enters from outside—"

"*Tak, tak, Ojcze.* Yes, yes, Father," Dmitri burst out in Polish, unaware he rudely interrupted his superior. "I had hoped to leave all that behind in Gdansk. My brother and his wife had ten children. Such noise and confusion and too many mouths to feed. Two of the youngest died of starvation early in the war. The poor and elderly survived on garbage from the streets. I could do nothing except pick up a gun and join the Army where I would create more suffering. Forgive me, Father, but I could bear no more. I fled the country. I found my way here, old as I am, to become a novitiate."

"You have not found the relief you sought." It was a statement of fact and a question. Konstantin had heard the monk's pain over those years, and it was unclear what guidance would help him.

"I have found relief, Father, in the vineyard, in the stillness when I can work hard with my hands and enter a place of oneness with the vines. My prayer feels like an extension of the vines and myself and I experience a sense of peace and quiet."

"And Pavel is no longer quiet?"

Brother Dmitri's brows raised in surprise, startled that the abbot was so ill informed.

"My apologies, Father, but Pasha—the patient—recites the teachings word for word without thought for his audience or appropriateness of place. Believe me, he has been most receptive to the same passages you advised me to read. I read those to him night after night to comfort him and to calm myself."

Abbot Konstantin threw back his head, releasing a huge, spontaneous belly laugh. His sturdy old chair creaked in protest as his shaking body upset the decorum of the office. The outburst shattered previous concepts Dmitri had about the solemnity of his sessions with his *starets* as well as the time he spent reading to the young man he had come to call Pasha. Eyes wide for a moment, unwittingly flashing in defense, Dmitri's lips parted to say something then closed. His rough hands fiddled behind his back. Not knowing what else to do, he bowed his head and waited.

"My good man," Konstantin said, leaping from the chair and clutching the taller monk's shoulder. "I must commend you. Truly, you are teaching me as well as Pavel Ivanovich. Now please sit down and tell me what is going on in the guest wing of the monastery."

Dmitri gratefully allowed his weak knees to let him sink into the sole chair opposite the abbot. Uncertain of his status in this atmosphere of unaccustomed familiarity with his spiritual guide, he piously folded his hands in his lap, and began a story that felt neither spiritual nor lofty to him.

"You are aware that Pavel Ivanovich regained his mobility. With assistance he is able to walk in the gardens. He takes meals in the kitchen with the Brothers who work there, all of which he does very normally. He even makes comments from time to time about the food or weather or 'the very nice place' here."

"And this is disturbing to you, to lose your patient?"

"Unfortunately, Father, I—we—may not lose him. I do not mean that disrespectfully. I mean his mind is far from well, though he has a gift for reciting Scriptures and readings by heart. But memory of his prior life has not returned. Only the nightmares reveal previous incidents. I doubt he would recognize his cousins."

Konstantin sank into his chair in a state of stunned realization. "A miraculous healing it seems. A manifestation of the Almighty in one man's suffering." He pondered this mystery that had occurred precisely because the monastery accepted an outsider. "And a credit to you, Brother Dmitri. I am hesitant to make assumptions, but it appears we have a rare, divinely inspired believer in our midst. What could it mean? Surely Pavel's conscious mind had been erased, *tabla rasa*, so to speak, leaving it as impressionable as that of a newborn babe."

The abbot's unfettered pronouncements struck Dmitri as too much to contemplate at once. If he had filled Pavel's head with the Holy Word, where would that lead indeed? He dared not imagine. A manifestation of the Almighty? He twisted his palms together in his lap, concentrating on a purplish grape stain that reminded him that the grapes were also manifestations.

"*Izvinite*, excuse me, but I must hurry back to the vineyards."

But Abbot Konstantin was not finished with their meeting. "I understand you find these recitations by the patient distract you from your time for devotions and meditation."

"Indeed, Father. I would like to return to the vineyard and be able to reflect on my own thoughts. I find it difficult to do so when the patient requires constant supervision."

"Ah, I have imposed upon you to the detriment of your well-being. Forgive me. I will take over the supervision myself to free you. Let me see. If the young man is truly gifted, and you have provided for him not only bodily but spiritually in these months of his recovery, you have served in a higher capacity in the Lord's eyes than that of a vintner. Can you accept that to be true?"

Dimtri's head bowed low, his hands clasped and unclasped in an expression of humility. "I was aware only of my service as a Brother." His voice faltered, muffled by his cowl. "I ask forgiveness for grumbling about my duties." His jaw twitched and he could say no more.

The abbot turned his attention to a worn copy of *The Philokalia,* a collection of mystic and spiritual writings by Schema monks of the Eastern Orthodox Church that shed enlightenment on various aspects of the Gospels. He tenderly smoothed the frayed cover and opened threadbare pages to a well-marked passage.

"Macarius the Great of Egypt writes that the inward contemplative 'burns with so great a love that if it were possible he would have everyone to dwell within him, making no difference between good and bad.' You may find solace, too, in Mark, the Podvizhnik, who writes, 'The soul which is inwardly united to God becomes, in the greatness of its joy, like a good-natured, simple-hearted child—and wants everyone to find joy in the world and praise God.'" A sliver of sunlight through a tall, narrow window tinged the icon hanging above the abbot's head with a golden glow as if called by the mystical teaching into the tiny office.

"'Burns with so great a love,' Brother Dmitri. As either vintner or 'nursemaid,' one whose soul is inwardly united to God is carrying on the interior prayer and contemplation that you so earnestly desire. I hope you will find this a confirmation of spiritual practices which you are already doing."

Silence crept around the room as if baffled by so heady yet lowly teachings.

"I wonder if Macarius the Great addresses your spiritual needs, Brother Dmitri?" the abbot pursued at last in an effort to relieve the monk's pain.

"Much more so than I deserve or expected, Father." Dmitri rose and backed towards the door, nearly doubled over in gratitude for the insight and wisdom of the abbot, but most of all for his compassion.

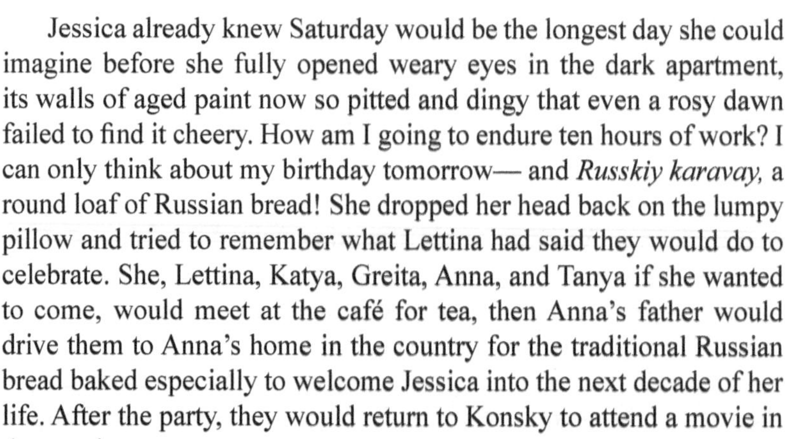

Jessica already knew Saturday would be the longest day she could imagine before she fully opened weary eyes in the dark apartment, its walls of aged paint now so pitted and dingy that even a rosy dawn failed to find it cheery. *How am I going to endure ten hours of work? I can only think about my birthday tomorrow— and Russkiy karavay, a round loaf of Russian bread!* She dropped her head back on the lumpy pillow and tried to remember what Lettina had said they would do to celebrate. She, Lettina, Katya, Greita, Anna, and Tanya if she wanted to come, would meet at the café for tea, then Anna's father would drive them to Anna's home in the country for the traditional Russian bread baked especially to welcome Jessica into the next decade of her life. After the party, they would return to Konsky to attend a movie in the evening.

Twenty! Jessica reached under her cot and withdrew the rectangular box bearing the red blouse and black skirt that she had carefully rewrapped. Kneading her fingers inside, she stroked the silk as if it were a kitten while dreamy moments passed unnoticed. Finally, she sat up and gently shook the folds of the gabardine skirt, leaving a wrinkle-free sheen on the richly woven garment, a panoply of elegance unknown in her life. A little gasp escaped her lips, indulging a fantasy of slipping into the outfit, the soft fabrics gently outlining her slender form, an image she recalled from seeing herself in the mirror at the boutique where she turned about with the natural flair of a star of cinema. Startled, she had looked again, hardly recognizing the woman who stood in bare feet modeling unheard of fashionable apparel in Konsky—even a full-length mirror such as that was unlikely in the region, as far as Jessica knew.

But she quickly reminded herself she needed to get up and confront the consequences of her purchase. Where could she wear such a fine outfit without attracting notice of the authorities? They would question her about the black market or her commitment to the working class, or her deviation from expected austerities; certainly they would say she flaunted symbols of dissonance. Yet a wave of resolve swept away second thoughts. The purchase was a gift to herself—after all, one should have beautiful clothing as well as a beautiful name. Her image at the boutique had been a revelation—she wished she'd had time to examine what felt like her newfound self. A womanly face featuring a rather dark complexion framed in black hair had looked back at her. Defense of her purchase came automatically. An inner strength resisted conventions just as her mother had, a disconcerting link that she now dashed, and self-consciously replaced the box under her cot.

Jessica's feet hit the cold floor as she called Tanya to heat their beetroot brew, a substitute for coffee. She threw a loose chemise over her head and nearly tumbled over leftover laundry in the middle of the floor.

"We must hurry and pick up in case the girls come over here tomorrow," she said to Tanya. "And we can barely make it to work on time as it is." They sipped the hot drink then Tanya shoved the woven reed clothes basket into her room and closed the door. They used this time for brief talks and walked to work together. Jessica outlined the birthday plans for Sunday. Tanya agreed to go to Anna's but declined the movie.

"I have a surprise for you. Maybe I should give it to you tonight if you are going out early tomorrow morning." Tanya hesitated. "But I do want to go to the monastery. We have not heard of Pasha's progress for awhile. Might we go next Sunday?"

Jessica sensed that if it were Tanya's birthday, she would prefer visiting Pasha. "Perhaps next Sunday," she said.

The factory soon swallowed the throngs of workers into its plain concrete walls, the windows as blank inside as out, the smell of warmed horse-hoof glue and cigarette smoke stifling. Jessica floated down the crowded aisle to her station at the heavy duty sewing machine, the world beaming at her and she at it. Even Boris Mikhailovich's stern visage softened, his footsteps lighter when he patrolled the work rooms. Whirling machines soon overpowered attempts to socialize, but Jessica noticed that her tablemate, Agata, seemed happier and the other women more friendly, perhaps a reflection of her own outlook.

Tomorrow, tomorrow, sang in Jessica's heart. She resolutely refused to think of anything after tomorrow. In fact, she could think of nothing other than coming back to the same position in the factory. Nothing would be different when she was twenty rather than nineteen. How could it be? Quotas must be filled. The coming autumn would turn to winter. Her mother, Vera, would sink lower into her crushing disillusionment with life. Pasha may or may not recover. Lettina had a private life she did not talk about. Tanya may live with her for years.

O well, *Nu chto zh*. Jessica grimly decided a week ago that she would not allow circumstances to rob her of her birthday. Tomorrow I will wear the red silk blouse and modern skirt from the boutique. I will have a birthday party with my friends—that is enough to ask for.

Anticipation kept rhythm with her sewing machine, a cycle of pleasure mixed with gratitude for the Marsolets. Mme. Marsolet, so gracious, so understanding. "If only I could be like her," escaped under her breath. She flopped recalcitrant pieces of leather in place to stitch the uppers of work boots as she had done for much of the last four years. Madame's graceful hands had slipped rich fabrics ever so elegantly over Jessica's head. She moaned softly at thoughts of the velveteen on her skin. As tough as her own fingers were, this particular leather felt coarser; it burned her fingertips. She shoved it aside, disgusted. The nagging worry about the Marsolets filled an empty place. Why did they need to flee the country? I have only just met them and now they are gone.

A short toot of the noon bell meant respite. She leaned back in her chair with a sigh. But the bell continued to blast persistently and louder than before. Women rose unsteadily from cramped positions at their stations. She caught Agata's eye. Questions shot from one to another. The continuous ring conveyed a sense of urgency. Jessica rubbed goose bumps from her arms. It was similar to a fire alarm or air raid signal. Whirring of machines ceased. The ring persisted, resounding louder now in the rapidly vacated workroom. Women queued at the stairwells; men offered them first passage. Narrow stairways became jammed with those exiting upper floors. Jessica stumbled along in the crowd, peering over heads in an effort to spot Anna or Tanya.

Outside, Boris Mikhailovich appeared shocked and pale. He roared through a megaphone, "Assemble in the Cultural Hall. Move along now and remain there until given further instructions."

Jessica shuddered, dread of frequent burdensome announcements such as Five-Year Plans a common experience. Or demands for further austerities, perhaps already spare rations reduced to wartime levels. Or an attack somewhere, a bombing? But nothing can happen to upset things, not after I have made plans, not after I have dreamed of my birthday for so long.

The concrete Cultural Hall bore the tired connotations of her youth. Weekly classes for Young Pioneers had grounded students of all ages in the glories of socialism. Giant posters of Lenin and Marx represented their mentors, their heroes, their gods. The inspiring ideals had caught fire with their spirits, the slogans they spoke in unison became their guiding principles. The educational program wrapped in service to country provided direction for their futures. Walls draped with red flags bearing hammer and sickle barely registered with Jessica, so common were they, but Jessica sensed the sacrifices required in service to the country had something to do with today's assembly.

The crowd of workers from the three floors of Benyanske's clutched unopened lunch bags and pressed inside the Hall. Jessica was forced to the back of the room, still searching for Tanya. Women shuffled and whispered among themselves, their eyes sharp as if to determine their fate. A wave of rumors of what sounded like "mass deportation" again jolted Jessica—*da*, Monsieur and Madame Marsolet had to leave the country suddenly for unknown reasons. Had they been deported? What had befallen them, not arrested and sentenced, she cried to herself—a sense of loss clashed with a surge of anger. What are they going to do with us now? Deep, unspoken feelings seemed to emanate from the crowd of mostly women.

Several unknown men, one in uniform, gathered at the front of the Hall, framed by the authority vested in wall-size portraits of the Supreme Ruler. The long, flowing red flags alternated with banners of Workers of the World featuring Lenin and Marx proclaiming "UNITE."

The crowd silenced, overcome by an ominous sense of impending bad news. Jessica wished she and Tanya were able to bear it together.

Boris stepped up on a bench, cleared his throat and straightened his tie. "There will be a few brief announcements then you may resume your lunch break. You will reconvene at your stations in thirty minutes."

A tall middle-aged gentleman dressed in a plain brown suit took the supervisor's place on the bench, and introduced himself, though Jessica could not hear his name. She heard only that he was in charge of recruiting in Kursk Oblast. A collective groan arose among the women. He paused until the reaction and uneasy rustling stilled. Jessica strained to hear how many, what for, why, where. All she could determine was that it was about a drought.

"*O, Bozhe nyet*. I've heard that one before. My parents had been recruited like this. Tanya, where is my cousin Tatyana?" she blurted to the woman she recognized as Sasha. They both turned to hear the intoned words.

"The *programme* goals of production have exceeded expectation in a few provinces while others have not been so fortunate. You are aware that workers everywhere are obligated to work for the common good on the *kolkhoz,* the farm collectives. This is an opportunity to serve your fellow comrades and the Republic simultaneously. Your efforts will enable the country to not only recover from the war, but to become a world power under our Supreme Leader."

The words sounded to Jessica as if they had been clipped from slogans posted on the walls of the Cultural Hall. Murmurings among the women muffled the short speech further extolling citizen responsibilities. Yet the workers' unrest amounted to an expression of disbelief of the laudatory remarks, scripts typical of government men when they wanted something of them.

"Harvesters are needed on the *kolkhoz* up north," Sasha whispered as Jessica tried to stand on tiptoe to hear.

"As you leave the Hall, those selected will be given a card with their name on it, and where they will report," the speaker said. A sudden outburst of voices with questions and statements of alarm prompted the uniformed officer to step to the speaker's side. Raising his arms for silence, he repeated," You will be given a card at the door. It will tell you where to report. That is final." Both men stepped down from the bench.

This time silence hung over the crowd, knifing hearts raw from last year's sacrifices, the pangs of empty bellies. Any last gasps dissipated in the suffocating air. Only the slight click of cards drawn from a packet broke the stillness.

"You may resume your lunch break," Boris assured the crowd. "Workers will be brought in to take the places of those who are transferred. Benyanske's will continue to meet production goals."

The factory. The transfers. Her birthday. All dead to Jessica with the few words, "those who are transferred." Her body rebelled as much as her mind. She was shoved along with the crowd to pass the table by the door where she would receive her card. She refused to look at it until she found Tanya.

Astoundingly, Tanya's face was bright, even eager, her eyes alive.

"Tanya, I have been looking for you. Were you in the Cultural Hall? Did you hear them? Why are you so happy?" Then she realized that for Tanya this transfer meant freedom. She wanted to slap her. Tanya the *ferma rebenok,* the farm child. O, I hate her, Jessica fumed, turning away. But she knew she had to find out her own fate, and it was too frightening to do alone. Slowly she turned over her card and read "*Report to Konsky Railway Station 6:00 A.M. Monday.*"

"Not that! Not Monday!" Her knees nearly buckled. She found a bench and slumped, holding her head in her hands. At last the magnitude of the recruitment set in.

"I will be ruined like my mother. She never recovered from the shame, the forced labor. How can I bear it?" she wailed.

Tanya sat down beside her, whimpering in sympathy, knowing from experience that whatever she might say would sound hurtful to Jessica, but she tried. "Your birthday party, Jessica. We will still have your party."

The clang of the bell called them back to work. Jessica whisked away tears that did little to disguise cheeks flushed with inner fury.

They climbed the stairs, neither having had breakfast or lunch.

Saturday dragged on for Jessica, the bright hopes of morning shattered; in their place the specter of work on a *kolkhoz*. Her mother's ceaseless complaints rang in her ears, grinding toil and deprivation under inexperienced overseers on the farms. Vera's deeply lined face still registered her time on a collective in hollow cheeks, sagging eyelids and jowls. Jessica bitterly dashed the image. I will be like poor *Mat*. She lost everything. I don't want to be beaten down and poor and ugly. I should have run away before the recruiters came.

Officials in the Cultural Hall had claimed the current drought in the Black Belt would cause even more hardship and death than the drought of 1932 and 1933 that decimated the nation's breadbasket, tales of which were still spoken in low tones if at all.

Our obligation, Jessica fumed to herself. Our local collectives are already stripped of their hard-earned yield. We shall have no grain for the mill in Konsky this winter. She stitched faster on pace with her thoughts, the projections grim and desperate. Pausing to change needles, she noticed other women were essentially stalling, waiting for the time to leave the factory, maybe forever. They had apparently quit, their minds turned to wrapping up this part of their lives before six o'clock Monday morning. Boris alternately begged and threatened, his voice a bit sheepish through tight-pressed lips. His manner was distant as if he had never before seen these workers. Apparently he had been ordered to meet quotas for the afternoon or face consequences.

Many workers shrugged. It was always like this. The older women had no illusions about how *programmes* were implemented; the production of boots and shoes ranked behind petrol, industry, and food in importance. Agata shook her head almost imperceptibly when Jessica's inquiring eyes met hers. She had not been recruited. Jessica wondered why. Too old, too valuable a worker, too many children? Ah, probably the children, she decided, and let herself sink into the numbness of not knowing her fate. Not knowing much of anything except that for a few their lives would go on as before. Exhausted with the mental discipline required to complete her work that day, Jessica followed others out to the street and looked for a familiar face. Lettina and Katya soon rushed from the direction of the mill, flashing identical cards before they reached Jessica.

"It's true, it's true. We have to report, too," Lettina said between breaths. "Are we going to the same place? What will happen to us?" They matched cards, finding they would all meet at the train station for departure at the same time. Katya and Greita clung to each other, Anna wept into her handkerchief. Lettina grasped Jessica in a bear hug in relief that they were not split up.

"Did we not understand this when we were in Young Pioneers? We asked how we could best serve our country. I thought they could not do without factory workers. Silly me," Jessica said, forgetting she had earlier considered running away from her job.

"We are expected to celebrate this opportunity," Katya said. "My parents served with fervor to express their loyalty. Of course, that was years ago during the initial burst of patriotism."

Jessica interrupted, "I didn't see women cheering."

"I thought mill workers might be spared as they were during the war, but it is not so. Even Tomenko is being transferred." Lettina tried to maintain a brave face.

Jessica flinched at her mention of Tomenko. She crossed her fingers that he would not appear at the railway station, or worse, be on their train. Would Lettina sit with him instead of her?

Katya added, "He tried to protest that the mill must run or the people will have no bread, but the government men said if there are no harvests there will be no flour for the mills. Even Tomenko, as strong as he is, cannot resist even after rebuilding the mill for electricity."

"We have only one day to prepare," Jessica conceded.

"Your birthday—I am so sorry. It is too cruel." Lettina said what many were thinking. The girls fell silent and absently turned their feet toward the outskirts of town where they found their comforting hollow among the trees. No one had cigarettes, but Jessica remembered her lunch. She withdrew a flattened piece of rye bread and broke it into five pieces.

"The Last Supper!" declared Lettina, and the craziness of their upside down world now became anchored in time by hysterical shrieks of laughter and breaking bread together. They munched a few pickles, a bit of hard cheese, and nibbled a slice of stale summer sausage shared among them.

That night Jessica's thoughts shot like fireworks in a celebration of the country's Patriotic War of 1812 victory over Napoleon's forces. In an effort to speak with reason and restraint to Tanya about Sunday, her birthday, she needed to make up for postponing a visit to Pasha. Jessica glanced at her, not want to see her looking too happy. That would taunt Jessica for clinging to the factory work they had complained incessantly about.

"I want to go to Anna's home for my birthday party," Jessica began. "Her parents have been so kind. I think it would help us to spend time with them. And I know you would like to see Pasha, perhaps our only chance for awhile."

"*Spasibo*, Jessica. I've been thinking the same thing. I do so want to go."

"If we went to the monastery early, we could stop at Anna's on the way back."

"O, we must. I would worry so about him if we left without seeing him." Tanya's voice squeaked high and thin, betraying tension she had yet to acknowledge. Jessica nodded agreement, suspecting she had caused much of Tanya's strained emotions. They packed the small tote bag they would take on the long walk, ate little for supper and went to bed, dozing on and off through the night. Hours later Jessica got up and drew aside the curtain, but it was early and dawn not yet committed to the day. A day she dreaded facing, her plans ripped from her at the last minute.

"I feel much, much older than twenty," she muttered to Tanya.

A glance in their tiny mirror confirmed dark circles under her eyes. Unwashed hair hung straight over her ears. She plunked herself for what she believed to be the last time in the broken chair and stared, trying to imagine a future but no images came. The harder she tried, the more blurred her vision became. At dawn Tanya poured her a cup of real coffee, steaming hot.

"For your birthday! Jessica."

"O, Tanechka! Coffee!"

Tanya beamed.

Jessica clasped the cup with both hands and inhaled the smell—"Oh, Cousin, I will make this last forever. Please have a cup! How did you ever come by this?"

Tanya was curiously evasive about the source. They laughed and poured coffee, lounged in nightwear, and finished the pot down to the dregs, which they would boil again later.

"We have money," Tanya said. "We'll not need it in the fields. They might even take it away from us. We could pay bus fare to go to the monastery then we would be back in time for the party."

Jessica looked at her cousin, surprised at her ability to think straight, to sound so mature. "Yes, I have a little. That is a good idea. I don't want those officials to have it."

"We could give the remainder to Pasha. Or to the abbot for Pasha's keeping."

Jessica agreed so readily that Tanya appeared taken aback.

"They might buy a violin for him," she added hopefully.

"Tanya, you are such a child after all," Jessica teased her. "Old Father Frost will surely come to the monastery and bring Pasha a violin if you believe hard enough!"

But the idea boosted their energy. Jessica warmed enough water to wash her hair before they left. "I will wear my new clothes and make a day of it. Who knows, it may be our last chance to do as we choose for a while." Undercurrents of fear crept in beneath her brave remarks. While she towel-dried her hair, she thought of the Last Supper the girls had celebrated in the park.

Tanya disappeared into her room and rummaged under her bed, pulling out the hastily wrapped gift she had secretly prepared and handed it to Jessica.

"Happy Birthday, Lana."

With her hair clean and bouncy, Jessica was in better spirits. "I can guess. You made it."

Tanya looked pleased while Jessica unfolded the plain paper and held up an embroidered white blouse with a low drawstring neck and small puff sleeves. Intricate chains of red, blue, and yellow flowers with green leaves followed the curving neckline among all the gathers, an exact replica of a peasant blouse.

"O, it is so well done, Tanya. You are true to our country folk traditions." She held the blouse against her chest wondering why she felt like a modern girl while Tanya remained blissfully tied to the past.

Tanya's small oval face broke into crinkly pleasure knowing that Jessica was impressed. "It is no match for the red silk blouse you chose for yourself, but I nearly had it finished when I saw your purchase."

"*Spasibo*, little one of many talents. You know I love beautiful clothes, and I see beauty in every stitch. Now we better hurry to catch a bus that goes toward the monastery."

VIII

Kolkhoz

Konsky's railway station bore the imprint of history. Situated on ancient trails where Mongols once invaded from the east, the railroad struck through vast stretches of taiga to accommodate heavy trading. Routes planned ostensibly for trade purposes were primarily used for strategic military transport in defense of the homeland or attacks against neighboring nations. Consequently, the Revolution and two world wars later magnified the significance of the gateway town of Konsky. Tracks stretched in every direction. Red banners draped the station's entrance and official portraits of the Ruler dominated dark walls inside. A dearth of flag waving among the crowd set the tone in the pre-dawn darkness of a Monday morning in August.

"They said we would be sent north," Jessica reminded Tanya, gripping her cousin's hand and steering her toward a cluster of people near one of the trains. Dozens of women, young and middle aged, gathered in two's and three's in subdued conversations. Each carried a single cloth or canvas bag, some with short handles like a suitcase. The girls slipped around the outer edges of the crowd, intently searching for their friends among those who had been called up.

"Ya ne mogu v eto poverit' You will not believe this. Most of the women from my floor are here," Jessica murmured. "Except Agata. She may not have been recruited since she has young children."

Lettina clinched Jessica's shoulder in a grasp that made Jessica wince. "It will take a generation of children, especially boys, to replace those lost in the war."

"Lettina, I'm so happy you're here. And Anna?"

Tanya stepped behind the older girls who chatted in nervous excitement until all eyes swung to the far end of the track. A train had just pulled in and discharged its passengers.

"*Chto ya vizhu?* What am I seeing? Is that a trainload of men coming from the rail cars?" Lettina voiced the shock of the other girls. The men straggled towards the women, most wearing tattered parts of uniforms, long gray coats here, trousers there, holey boots on others. Among them were amputees leaning on stout canes. Others limped alongside the track.

"Veterans will likely take our places," Lettina whispered, catching on quickly that the men were too disabled to work the fields, but they could sit at the work tables in the factories. "Yet none can do the heavy work of running the mill for the people of Konsky."

Speechless, the girls watched the men approach under the dim yellow lights of the railway station. Heaviness hung over the travelers as if life were a greater burden than their duffle bags, their weary bodies hauled forward by will. Jessica saw little relief, let alone joy, in those who would get a job, accommodations, and a steady if paltry paycheck.

"Men arrive when we are leaving," Lettina hissed, throwing up her hands, until Jessica shushed her. The whistle blew on the train nearest the girls. The comrade who spoke to them on Saturday waved at them to board.

"*Udostovereniye lichnosti, pozhaluysta.* Personal identification, please." He took their cards, his sharp eye looking them over.

Jessica tightened her jaw in resistance to becoming a commodity sent to market. She found a seat and sat by herself in a sullen rage while the others boarded. Yesterday had been markedly different, promising. She and Tanya had taken a small public bus to St. Sansais Monastery. Jessica had worn the red silk blouse and straight black skirt, exercising a last fling in retaliation for being robbed of celebrating her birthday.

On the way the bus had picked up the uniformed official, one of the authorities at the Cultural Hall. Jessica could not help but notice him; he seemed to be staring at her. He was fair-skinned with dark blond hair combed straight back, and a rather good looking mouth. Tanya had shrunk in fear. Taking her cue, Jessica turned away but not before her gaze met his. She was aware she was dressed in her best, actually the only nice clothing she had ever possessed. He had openly admired her and her smart outfit. His calm, unhurried appraisal left Jessica flustered. She had dodged behind a sturdy passenger and avoided him when the bus stopped.

Anna boarded the train and slipped into a seat beside Jessica. She moved with a lady-like grace that matched her delicate features and shy personality. How will she survive in the fields, Jessica wondered. She is modern in a sense of being well-dressed, but old-world in a genteel sophistication resembling Anna's mother. Mothers! Old world, traditional, and outdated. Jessica compulsively fingered the box in her bag containing her fashionable apparel and smiled. If only I had my fingernails painted—bright red would be perfect.

At last Tanya boarded and Jessica signaled that she take the seat in front of her. Lettina, Katya and Greita found seats across the aisle. With a shower of sparks and the stench of hot wheels on rails, the electric train shot from the protective arms of Konsky's little station. Tanya poked her small tearful face between the tall upright seats to catch Jessica's eye.

"Remember Pasha," Jessica whispered, seeing the transfer was also overwhelming for Tanya. Yesterday, on Sunday, they had been thrilled to find Pasha at work in the garden watering rows of carrots and peas. He looked more like the cousin they had known, his face bronzed by the sun, his brown hair curled down to his shoulders. He talked easily with the Brothers about the bountiful plants. Brother Anton brought the girls to meet him and Pasha was excited to make their acquaintance as if for the first time in his life, then continued watering on the other side of the garden. Uncertain what to do next, the girls talked with Brother Anton until the abbot could see them.

"Your cousin has been a great blessing to the monastery," Brother

Anton said. "He is truly a saint, I do believe. He takes the teachings to heart in no time and inspires us to tend to our learning as well."

"It cannot be," Jessica protested. "He was as rebellious as we were in our youth. We would hide or take a long walk and be much too late coming back for devotions or liturgy that our parents maintained in secret. They were forever distressed with us, saying we would come to no good if we shirked our faith."

"I was much the same," laughed Brother Anton. "Now I cannot wait to resume my studies, and I keep a prayer going in my heart and mind continuously, as surely as I breathe. In fact, I have dedicated my breath to prayer as the only way I know to pray unceasingly. You understand?" he asked, in the manner of Abbot Konstantin.

"Not really," Tanya had quietly admitted, unsure if this was supposed to be a lesson in spirituality.

"Blessed child," Brother Anton said fervently, "If my breath is the first thing I draw at birth and the last thing I do when I die, prayer shall have become unceasing during my lifetime, only I did not consciously start praying at birth." He laughed again, the mirth drawing dimples in his cheeks, "but now I have made that choice."

"What is this merry crowd?" inquired Abbot Konstantin when he walked into the garden. Jessica and Tanya were laughing, too, finding the young monk irresistible.

"My apologies. I cannot stop thinking of the joy of constant interior prayer. I may be boring the young ladies," Brother Anton said.

"We are so surprised and delighted to find Pasha so well," Jessica exclaimed. "Thank you, all of you. It is a truly a miracle. He did not recognize us, but I think with time he will. Perhaps he needs to make a connection with his past."

"With a violin as you suggested?"

"*Da ser,* I mean Father. You remembered!"

Konstantin's face had lit up with delight in keeping with that of the girls. "I am becoming acquainted with your Pasha myself, and finding in him a remarkable young man. One of the Brothers, if you please."

"O, *ser*, do you think so?" Jessica did not know whether to be alarmed or grateful.

"Only he will decide if he feels called," added the abbot, "but you have come to visit with him, not me."

Jessica inhaled and drew herself up with enough courage to relate the news. "Tatyana and I have been recruited to work in one of the farm *programmes*. We are being transferred north to help with the harvest." Her voice faltered and she clasped her hand over her trembling lips.

Tanya finished. "We leave tomorrow. We've come to say goodbye to Pasha and give him a little money we have saved."

Abbot Konstantin stiffened, the merriment fading from his face at once. "So recruiters for the farm *programme* have come to this area. It is possible our men in the monastery will be called up." His voice sounded hollow and distant. Sighing deeply, he turned back to the girls who stood quietly, Jessica, so modern and well dressed, and Tanya, only five feet tall, neither appeared hardly capable of the demands of harvesting.

"But that is not your worry. The city to farm worker *programmes* are most challenging. However, I find your family quite strong and adaptable." Mumbling, he added, "For all my learning and spiritual practice, I am unable to find comforting words for so great an upheaval in your young lives." He held out his hand to accept the small pile of roubles and kopeks the girls offered.

"We will be away only for the harvest. A terrible drought has stricken the South. The grain will help feed the people." Jessica shrugged as if the matter remained a remote concept rather than present reality.

"You are both blessings to the monastery and to Pavel as well. We shall pray for your safety." The abbot had bowed low, a disconcerting sign of humbleness to Jessica and puzzling for Tanya.

"We have so little time—the train leaves early tomorrow." Jessica had reached for Tanya's hand and practically pulled her out of the monastery before sobs overtook them both.

Abbot Konstantin had waved, a slight motion with a huge hand, and said as if to himself, "Sometimes I have found only the human heart can reach out, one to another." Pavel had unconcernedly watered the primroses and columbines by the walkway.

Startled by a jolt of the train, Jessica tried to take in the strange surroundings they were passing through, a northwest part of the country she had never visited. Dawn's slanting, cool pink and silver rays hung somewhere over the Ural Mountains far to the east beyond the forested, hilly land through which they passed. Its glow backlit the girls' profiles in the seats across the aisle. Jessica peeked to see if they were dozing, or motionless like she was in stunned assessment of their fate.

In these few quiet moments Jessica reflected on the letter she had hastily scribbled to her parents. On her own, she had been herded into a *programme* without her father's support. He couldn't arrange a protective cocoon around her this time, nor spare her from a recruitment that he and Vera had endured years before. How could she complain, or unduly worry him? Jessica wrote platitudes that sounded like Soviet slogans, and posted the letter before she unwittingly poured out her mounting anxiety. Apparently Tanya did not wish to be spared; she appeared to find it quite an adventure. Excitement yet uncertainty bounced within her like a giant bubble. Jessica's only certainty came from her mother's stories—Vera had bequeathed a legacy of dissidence, though Jessica had essentially absorbed the Party line as she grew up.

Jessica wrenched herself into different positions in her seat, disturbing Anna next to her. Anna had removed her cotton headscarf and twisted it until her hands were damp and red. Pained to see her agitation, Jessica's fury flamed again, but she knew exploding now would upset everyone and attract the recruiter.

"Anechka," she whispered. "Thank you for the beautiful birthday party. Did I properly thank your parents for hosting us?"

Anna lifted puffy, tear stained eyes to meet Jessica's. They had cried so much at the party about the transfer that she had almost forgotten it was a celebration for Jessica's twentieth birthday.

"O, *da,* Jessica. My parents wanted to invite you, and it makes them happy, only—"

"It's not their fault it became a going away party. Whatever would we have done by ourselves? Drink tea at the café and cry?"

With wry smiles they settled against each other, comforted that two could surmount whatever was to come.

After the girls left the monastery, Abbot Konstantin tucked his hands inside his robe and retraced his steps to the office along the herb garden path and onto the worn flagstones of the long corridors of the monastery. St. Sansais was in danger; he could feel it in his bones. Other than rumors, he knew little of day-to-day happenings in the outside world. News had come to the monastery by way of an influx of novitiates, men young and old, who fled one jump ahead of recruitment into the army, fields or factories, depending upon needs—or whims—of the governing agencies. Saints be gone and their claptrap churches with them, according to 1917 mandates of the insurgents who had overthrown the Tsars. And the Red Terror only ten years ago still burned in the abbot's memory, his powerlessness to stop waves of persecutions, even of monks and parishioners who had been charged as dissenters. By a recent quirk of fate, those bans on religious practices had been lifted during the war years. Prelates who had not fled, been reprogrammed or killed were allowed to resume services. The abbot knew the indulgence would not be lasting.

Konstantin fought down fury rising in his gorge. The Soviet takeover of neighboring autonomous countries last year, sanctioned by the Potsdam Agreement and tradeoffs by far away Allies, invited crackdowns within Homeland borders despite Allied awareness that the atheistic ideology remained a goal of the regime. Konstantin knew the stone walls of the monastery and the generally high esteem accorded him and the Vineyards were as nothing in the face of a renewed takeover. His mind instantly registered concern for his Polish monk. Citizens of Poland suffered forced repatriation at that very moment.

"Dmitri's conscience drove him from his homeland. He should never be called up again." Konstantin's aggrieved mutterings dogged him all the way to his office. Now fifty-four years old, Dmitri was a sustaining member of the monastery, who not only preserved but enhanced the rows of vines sweeping over the hillsides beyond Konsky. The Vineyard's redoubtable reds glowed with the full body of Loire River Valley rootstalk grafted onto hardy Russian vines, the heritage tenderly nurtured century after century. The vineyard may survive, but the workers?

Konstantin paced six long steps across his office and back, until what he experienced as testing of the soul drove him into the private side garden. Finding no peace there, he ventured into the chapel and knelt in the shadows by the iconostasis, a wall of gilded icons edging the sanctuary. Thoughts raced through his otherwise disciplined mind like roe deer fleeing wolves in a forest. Fears rampaged unchecked, raising his blood pressure that hammered in surface veins at his temples.

"The recruiters are coming to St. Sansais, I know it as sure as if a message were writ in the heavens," he murmured aloud, pounding his chest with his fist. His efforts to focus on habitual prayers and eloquent words of the spiritual masters failed to overcome the foreboding prescience that the recruiters were coming. At last, faint rustlings of footsteps of novitiates filing in caught his attention. Kontstantin hastily withdrew a small copy of the Gospels from his pocket and discovered the money the girls had left for Pavel. Hoping he would not create a sound, he moved to his accustomed position in the chapel and fell again upon his knees, the words of the ancient *starets* soothing his soul.

"Trust that everything is under the all-knowing providence of *Bog*, our God." He did not hear the others leave for their daily tasks.

Several days passed before Konstantin resolved to alert residents of the monastery that Soviet *programmes* were being revived. Recruitment of civilians for harvesting in the north had occurred in the region.

"I have personally heard nothing to indicate that the *programme* would affect St. Sansais," he added in a short speech to the residents assembled in the dining hall. His firm strong presence silenced the few audible moans. Eyes, usually downturned and focusing inward, raised at once, searching the abbot's face. Konstantin took a deep breath and continued in his rich, full voice, softening the blow as best he could.

"We will maintain confidence in the renown of the vineyards, which was been accorded special protection before. We will conduct ourselves as our Community requires, relying upon the indwelling God in whom we have been so fortunate to find our spiritual path. The One who provides for ourselves and for the produce market.

"It is therefore advisable to prepare for market tomorrow as usual. Townspeople in the village depend upon the vineyards to supply them with food on Wednesdays. We shall not disappoint them."

Assigning them an immediate task proved to be a stroke of genius. They carried on with much digging and washing of vegetables until dusk. At four o'clock in the morning, they packed their late summer harvest into a small pushcart for the trip to Thor, several miles distant.

Brother Dmitri lingered in hopes of speaking privately with the abbot before starting off with the cart and Brothers Anton and Vessaly. The wide night sky above the motherland had lightened by a degree or two when Konstantin came from his early devotions in the chapel to bless the deliverymen and produce. After the usual ritual, Dmitri hastened to the abbot's side. In a low voice so as not to alarm the young monks, he suggested, "I would be willing to wear civilian clothing and go alone to market to avoid bringing undue attention to St. Sansais."

Konstantin peered at the troubled face of the elder monk, his heart warming in a burst of love for this gentle soul who sought to spare the monastery and protect his fellow Brothers from harm.

"We will stand together regardless what might befall us," the abbot assured him, voicing confidence while bracing for unknown malign forces. "In my experience, the officials are thorough, and if they want to find us they will. Go with my blessing and that of the Almighty." He placed a hand on the shoulder of his favorite monk, so like himself in dedication to the wider Brotherhood, hoping fervently that the short trip would go pleasantly as usual.

Brother Dmitri felt like the donkey he had used on his family's farm outside Gdansk, Poland's principal port. By habit his gaze swept the skies for weather as if he prepared to herd sheep or work the land that day. He grew up as bound to the farm as he was currently bound to the gardens and vineyards of the monastery, a natural occupation which he welcomed rather than renounced from his former life. Therefore, with ease and familiarity, he slung the harness of the cart over his shoulders and cinched it at his waist. With Anton's last adjustment of the bundled red chard to prevent crisp leaves from falling from the cart, the trio creaked slowly down the rutted trail toward the main road.

Anton and Vessaly threw their weight behind the heavy load as they had done on Market Day for the past year. Heavy dew soaked their bare feet exposed in woven reed sandals, and the morning chill sneaked well past their knees under their flowing robes. Dmitri knew that the challenge heightened Brother Anton's desire to focus only on the Jesus Prayer, rising from within and resonating with each of his warm breaths to bubble forth in the form of steam. Anton sought every hardship that led him into a deeper, more profound oneness with God, which in turn, increased his evolution towards self sacrifice. Not that Abbot Konstantin would have asked Anton to endure more than the weekly early morning trip to market and the usual rules and obligations of their community life, including harboring unexpected guests. Extreme asceticism was not in the abbot's nature, nor was it within the original Benedictine Orders from which the monastery had sprung centuries ago.

"I choose to deny myself," Brother Anton had once confessed to the abbot and Dmitri when pleading to skip certain meals, "so I can focus more fully on interior prayer."

"Your calling is great and your response is admirable. You need only remember that as a faithful servant, your health and welfare is a greater gift that must be honored," said the abbot. Brother Anton knew that his dear *starets* forbid self-flagellation and extreme prostrations.

"Then what shall I renounce?" queried the young monk, assuming that little remained within his realm to sacrifice.

"Rather the question is, to what shall you open up?" asked the abbot, unconsciously patting his rather rotund midsection.

"Open up, Father? Why I shall open my mind and my heart for the glory of God and give thankfulness for His Providence," Anton replied at once. Abbot Konstantin had bowed slightly, his lips betraying a quiet smile, amid Dmitri's gruff, "Amen."

Today, as dawn unfolded over stands of lindens and aspens, Brother Dmitri threw his shoulders into the harness more determinedly than ever. He failed to notice that Brother Vessally motioned them to stop long enough so he could pull the hood over his tonsured head. He and Anton were oblivious of the cold and Vessaly's discomfort.

The quaint village of Thor, a 'mostly forgotten' village the inhabitants claimed, lay at the forest's edge in one of the many ravines of western Kursk Province. Small plots of land held rustic *izbas*, many with thatched roofs and tiny gardens among rocky outcroppings. The clamor of Market Day reached the monks first. Jostling of carts and cries of greetings among vendors represented often life-long friendships of peasants and small business owners. On the outskirts of the village Dmitri shed the harness, and grasped the cart's handholds to steer it into their familiar stall, all the while nodding to male vendors and avoiding admiring women whose remarks were purposely loud enough for him to hear. He artfully arranged the vineyard's produce on and around the cart. Squash in front of baskets of carrots and beets, bunches of parsley and chives among them for accent, the inevitable onions and cabbages heaped on burlap bags on the ground. Busy with the display, he had to admit that the village thrilled him. Its name, Thor, connected him to Scandinavian roots on his mother's side of the family.

The village is a bit of poetic whimsy in the Russian countryside if nothing more, Dmitri admitted with a half-smile, marveling that it had escaped a reactive name change after Soviet Russification banned any association with the Norse God of Thunder and Lightning, especially since the swastika inexplicitly copied a bolt of Thor's lightning. Any semblance of pagan beliefs had been systematically rooted out since the early days of the Revolution. With imposition of a secular dictatorship, Orthodoxy had been outlawed as well.

Dmitri sighed, O, well, *khorosho*. By any name I will not change my affection for Thor or its villagers. The pagan gods with all their whims, vanities and uninhibited behaviors may have been more forgiving than Orthodoxy—but my mind is wandering.

Early shoppers interrupted his ongoing self-inventory. By ten o'clock the produce cart stood empty except for a few wilted cabbage leaves and traces of loamy black soil that had clung to the vegetables. Chernozyom, the black soil in the fields of Kursk Oblast, was a welcome anomaly, the abbot had explained. The Province grew barley, rye and livestock feed, while the soil of neighboring Ober Oblast lacked fertility. The longevity of the monastery and industry of the monks had further built up and preserved the soil's richness until it was said to rival even the Black Belt in Southern Russia. To maintain this reputation and the quality of their gardens, the novices scraped the bits of soil into a corner of the cart to take back to the vineyards, while the villagers bemoaned the poor, eroded soil in the ravines where they lived.

Many hours had slipped by since early breakfast at the monastery. The Brothers hastened to leave while only Brother Anton relished a growling stomach. At that moment a faded green Army truck roared into the village and blocked the road. Three officials stepped out to halt the stream of customers and vendors.

"Ostanovka, Stop," cried one of the three, who sprinted toward the far end of the village, intercepting those who were going home that way. An official in uniform motioned that the crowd gather around the truck, while a third turned the vehicle to face away from Thor, evidently ready for a quick departure in case of unrest by the villagers.

The merriment of the Market shifted to an ominous silence. In small clusters, the people shuffled into a nervous group at the outskirts of the town. Dmitri remained alert with hands respectfully behind his back, an attitude the young monks adopted in lieu of another response.

The official did not need a stentorian voice to reach the small gathering, but he employed it as an extension of his authority.

"I am Captain Yuri Stanislov, in charge of our visit to this Province. I see that your gardens were plentiful and the produce generously distributed among you." He gestured toward individuals who held overflowing shopping bags, but his attempt at levity failed to elicit a corresponding response. Footsteps shuffled backwards, a mixed *nyet* swept over the shoppers.

"The harvest is precisely why you see the three of us here today." A muted groan expressed fears that what little they had would be appropriated, leaving their families to suffer.

"Wait. You must hear the announcement."

Again a murmur of alarm spread from woman to woman, child to mother or father. Dmitri, Anton and Vessaly maintained their steady gaze at the ground, seeking inner strength at this moment of uncertainty.

The Captain continued. "All northern Provinces from Leningrad east to the Urals have produced moderate crops of wheat, rye, and barley this year, despite semi-drought conditions reaching this far north. Comrades, this attests to our ability to rebound after the devastation of the Axis invasion. *Vy menya ponimayete?* You understand me?" He paced back and forth in the worn Red Army uniform and cheap dust-covered shoes. The other officials kept a watchful eye on those gathered there, not over one hundred at most, counting the dogs.

The long pause further unnerved the assembled peasants. They glanced warily at one another and slapped at occasional flies. Bags were warily slipped behind them, out of view except for wispy carrot tops. A few men removed their caps as if that would relieve the strain.

"You may not be aware this year's drought destroyed crops in the Central District of the South all the way to the Black Sea. The drought has done what the Germans failed to do, that is threaten to conquer the mother country through mass starvation. So you see," he said, cajoling the crowd with a voice of compassion and concern, "it is our patriotic duty to come to the aid of our southern comrades and their families."

He pulled himself to his full height measuring less than six feet and fully confronted the uplifted faces. Young and old village men, three monks, mothers, grandmothers, and children awaited his words.

"Therefore, many of you will be recruited to harvest northern crops to ward off the coming winter famine in the South."

With a flick of his finger, Captain Stanislov indicated that the other officials hand out cards. He gestured for able-bodied men to step forward. Many appeared frozen in place. It was only with further prompting that they gave their names to be inscribed on cards which were placed in outstretched hands. They were required to report to the railroad station in forty-eight hours. They and their loved ones turned away and headed for home to hide the wails of their children. A few elders, the disabled and older women with heavily lined faces lingered.

Dmitri was aware his pulse throbbed in his neck. Hoping the officials would not see his alarm, he drew a long breath and shifted his body in front of Anton and Vessaly.

"You. Come," Captain Stanislov ordered, noticing the movement. Dmitri stepped forward immediately, his hands remaining clasped behind him. "Where are you from?"

"From the vineyard, *ser,*" Dmitri answered evasively. St. Sansais Vineyards was barely recovering from ravages of the recent war. He dare not embroil it in the recruitment. The grapes were bursting with flavor, the barrels clean and ready to receive the juice.

"A vineyard? And you think a vineyard is more important than harvesting for the purpose of feeding your fellow comrades?" demanded the Captain.

"Our Order is aware of the need to feed the people," Dmitri said, nodding at the cart. "That is the reason for our presence at Market today."

"So you grow food as well as grapes?" The query mocked the monks and prompted guffaws from the officials.

"*Da, ser,* for centuries, *ser,* " knowing that St. Sansais had been spared before.

"Then I must visit the vineyard when I have an opportunity, but I am on a tight schedule throughout this Province." He motioned impatiently for Anton and Vessaly to step forward.

"*Pozhaluysta ser*, take me in their place. Their labor is required in the gardens at the monastery," Brother Dmitri persisted. The Pole made an impressive figure, chin thrust forward, his large dark eyes calm and still under bushy brows. Brothers Anton and Vessaly outwardly appeared resolute but pale.

The recruiter holding the cards looked uncertainly at the Captain and back at the monks.

"Then you shall have your wish, Brother. Write his name on a card," Captain Stanislov growled, dismissing the young monks with "Be gone and be sure to labor twice as hard in the gardens for your country, *Vy menya ponimayete?*"

Dmitri inclined his head, the others nodded that they understood. Dmitri made his way through the remnants of the crowd ahead of the cart pushed by the younger monks. Open weeping from every quarter accompanied their passage.

IX

Captain

The train transporting recruited workers rumbled through dark conifers and even darker, chillier ravines of the vast northern provinces. Jessica shook Tatyana's lightly clothed body. "Tanya, you are shivering."

"I heard wolves howling, Jessica. Bears are lurking in the forest and there are poachers. I heard gun shots. I think they are shooting the bears that are catching fish or eating carcasses."

"Shush, you are imagining things, and do not call me Jessica. They will take me away." Jessica returned to her seat beside Anna, and Tanya peered between the seats at them, seeking forgiveness as well as security. Her eyes bulged, wide awake and scared. Jessica knew she feared being left alone. "You were happy about being sent for harvesting. Remember how much you loved your old farm," Jessica whispered back to Tanya. "You may find animals to feed and horses to care for," but the mention of horses set off Tanya's tears for the loss of old Gorgi.

"*Bah*, you have to brace up like the rest of us." Jessica made it clear she had enough of the fifteen-year-old. Tanya turned away, her sobs in tune with the throbbing and clattering of iron wheels on the rails.

Jessica and Anna slept intermittently. Jessica roused in panic that her chosen name might raise suspicion she was an American spy infiltrating the farm *programme*. From movies to spying, *da!* she snorted, but the matter was too serious to discuss with her friends, and Tanya would feel endlessly at fault if I were to be charged.

By morning the train pulled into a station. Officials accompanying the farm laborers required passengers to show their identification cards, checking that recruits did not escape enroute. Greita and Lettina crumpled back in their seats across the aisle while other girls moved about. Older women traipsed past heading to the station latrines or tending to other affairs. Jessica opened the window half way, allowing a soft warm breeze into the stuffy car, a distinctly more humid air than they had in Konsky. Soon the train was in motion again; the cars jerked in protest, and wheels ground on a gradual uphill pull in highland country, a contrast with the vast steppes to the east. The track later leveled out, and the sweet scent of autumn heralded the ripening of grains and sunflowers of the open fields of Smolensk Oblast.

Lettina, her usual kerchief askew over her bronze hair, looked questioningly at Jessica who sat numbly in her seat. "We must be nearly there. I smell fresh wheat and barley just like at the mill."

Jessica stared as if she heard but chose to disbelieve that Lettina was embracing the harvesting. The proximity to the farms revived faint memories of her early years when her parents had been recruited, years that left a lasting bitterness in the family.

"The familiar smell is comforting," Lettina continued, "yet I have little actual experience as a farm laborer. Harvesting will be easy for Tomenko Barskenkovich. He was recruited also. He is strong from lifting heavy bags at the mill--but--but he was so humiliated by the recruiters." She paused as if testing Jessica's willingness to listen.

Jessica slunk into her seat, the travel bag hugged to her chest, but Lettina told the story, whether Jessica wanted to hear about Tomenko or not, given her initial shock at seeing him with Lettina at the mill.

"He told the recruiters he was needed at the mill to feed the people in Konsky. One mean official, the blond one, put his hand on his revolver right in front of us, and asked, 'So you think you are important?' Tomenko smiled and said, '*Da, ser*, important to the townspeople.' Then they handcuffed him, and the blond official pointed to old Olga Vors. 'This woman will run the mill,' he said, and they dragged Tomenko out and put him in a van. To be replaced by a woman, and especially by an old one, a *staraya zhenshchina*, shamed Tomenko. Olga was there only to purchase a small sack of flour. Her rheumatism barely permits her to walk." Lettina shuddered and clamped her lips, her story criticizing the authorities having escaped unbidden.

Caught between Tanya's fears and Lettina's tale of the heavy hand the Army exercised over the civilian workforce, Jessica became increasingly shaky and sleepless the remainder of the way. They traveled in silence for most of the day through miles of farms, the foreboding prospect of the harvesting ever more worrisome. Arriving at a depot in the vicinity of Smolensk Victory *Kolkhoz*, they were herded into the backs of covered farm trucks. Older women crowded onto long benches along each side, while younger ones sat on the truck bed, their dresses tucked beneath their knees. A soldier ground the clutch of the snub-nosed GAZ, a counterpart of USA's Ford truck, and drove the last leg of the farm workers' journey to the labor camp.

Jessica first glimpsed outlines of old military wall tents when she peered under the tarpaulin that covered the truck back. Worn canvas was strung over corner and ridge poles in a compound at the edge of fields a short distance from what appeared to be a manor house.

"It is a military camp," she whispered, "ah, that is bad." Encampments as far as the eye could see near Konsky during the Red Army's advances along the Front flashed in her mind, as well as those of invading forces from Eastern Europe over the past four years. Her knees became so unsteady she could barely stand when they climbed from the truck. Tanya bore the look of one overwhelmed by past war trauma, a feeling that soon proved prophetic.

Behind the three-story frame manor house, a fine stable and barns spread beyond a circular driveway to a forest of linden and aspen trees. Farm workers that included the women, a dozen or so veterans, and a number of youthful girls and young men, were briefed on what would become their routine for the next few weeks: supper at nine, go to bed early dormitory style, and rise at four a.m. for breakfast. In a trance-like state, Jessica picked up her bag and followed the other women to their designated tents.

The next morning, she croaked through glands swollen from allergies, "I feel like a *zek*, a prisoner without a choice about being here."

Tanya was already up and dressed, a hopeful attitude replacing her earlier dismal outlook. Lettina, Katya and Greita, in threadbare work clothing they had worn at the mill, appeared tired and sluggish. They joined the others for breakfast in a makeshift Cultural Hall, a former farm warehouse that now served as a mess hall. Walls were lined with slogans, red banners, and tables of Communist Party literature. Workers ate under a single light bulb before they spilled out onto the grounds for duty.

A burly manager in a loose fitting tunic and cummerbund strutted in front of the assembled harvesters and barked orders for the day, already alienating the girls by trailing a tantalizing smell of good Turkish coffee. The farm workers' coffee had been brewed from roasted malt barley and rye. Most chose the weak tea.

"You, you, and you, form teams of four," he bellowed, pointing at various women. He snapped his fingers to hurry them up. With a wave of his arm, he motioned half the group to one side. "You stack the bundles," and to the other half, "You load the wagons." He selected a team of stronger men and women who would operate the threshing machine while others re-formed into groups of four.

"And you and you," he pointed to Tatyana and several of the disabled men, "*Vyberite iz zerna rozh i ukladyvayut otdel'no.* Cut the rye left behind with scythes and stack it separately."

He bounded toward each team to hammer home his orders, a daunting presence emulating the hard-driving Cossacks. Jessica's heart plummeted with fear of failure and a wave of physical illness in the face of such hard labor. Wagons pulled by sturdy horses arrived to transport the laborers to distant fields. Again, the women tucked the skirts of their dresses under their knees when they crawled into the wagon beds, or sat on the wobbly wooden sides, clinging to each other or the wagon on the ride over uneven ground.

Familiar faces from the factory now became more real to Jessica, a team of comrades exercising their patriotism, though it felt more like cohorts in suffering. They seemed to accept the harvest *programme* as a duty, or at least as one more inevitability in their lives. In the field one of the older women tutored Jessica in handling tied bundles which they would pitch into wagons that collected the stacks for threshing.

"To save the grain heads, carefully stack bundles with all the heads in the same direction like this." She placed them together in the nearest upright stack called shocks. "Work fast and efficiently. We are the Army of harvesters for the glory of *Rossiya*," she laughed.

The stubble caught around Jessica's shoe soles and scratched her bare ankles until they bled. Stalks raked the tender skin of her arms. Aware she was neither efficient nor inspired by the glory, she carried only one bundle at a time to the stacks. Jessica's feet dragged while time dragged—harvesting was far from the romantic notion of Tolstoy's Levin, whose rhythmic sweep of the scythe was in harmony with that of the peasants. In fact, it brought into startling clarity the suffering her parents must have endured in their downfall from life as merchant traders to that of farm workers.

"It left them lifeless," she muttered, inwardly vowing that would never happen to her. Images of her father's spent form and her mother's weary sadness were stamped on faces everywhere she looked.

By noon the girls hardly recognized each other under the dust and sweat. The fabric of their dresses clung to their chests, and stockings they had dared to wear were shredded. Words hardly summed up their initiation into harvesting: they were city girls while farm women and peasants recruited from villages adjusted more easily with cheering and joking.

"My hands," groaned Jessica, still choking through swollen glands. She showed Lettina her blistered palms and broken nails, munched a few bites of hard cheese on rye bread, and fell over in the stubble to nap the balance of lunch break.

"You must eat better or you will be sick," Katya warned in passing. Her team of four girls placed the stacks of bundles in wagons for transport to a stationary threshing machine. Hand labor by a few men and a hundred or so other women moved methodically over the fields as far as the eye could see, some following a rickety binder that cut and bound the bundles, others scything around rocks and bushes.

A warm, earthy smell enveloped the workers, a scent inhaled with dust and chaff of the crop.

The thresher, an unwieldy, galvanized metal-sided machine powered by a petrol-fueled tractor, featured a hopper on top that received bundles and sent them to separators, beating the barley from its stalks. Chaff, the chopped residue, blew from a stack on the other side of the thresher.

"Petrol is expensive and scarce. If you are not working, you are wasting time and petrol," bellowed the manager, who patrolled on horseback. "Remember your calling. Save your comrades in the Black Belt from starvation this winter."

Lettina, long accustomed to Tomenko's yelling, tensed each time she heard the manager. Jessica noticed she kept an eye out for her former employer among the laborers, and at meal time Lettina diverted her path among the wall tents to reach the mess hall in hopes of running into him.

"He must have been sent to another camp," Lettina concluded, though Jessica had little time to talk with her. But she sensed Lettina's loss, a loss her friend never admitted, and one Jessica failed to understand without seeing her as a victim of Tomenko's advances.

Moderate temperatures of late summer prevailed most of the mid-August *Medovyi Spas*, days marking the harvest of crops. Ancient harvest festivals went uncelebrated on the collective, though small farmers would surely continue the traditions. To peasants and those close to nature, blessing of crops and gathering of honey would be especially important to enable the motherland to rebound after the war, but the festive apple day, *Yablochny Spas*, August 19, also came and went without recognition. Orchards, having long ago turned wild, dropped their overripe fruit unattended, while citizens toiled to fulfill quotas of grain calculated in distant offices of the Kremlin for distribution to distant comrades.

To Jessica, accustomed to the dim interior of the boot and shoe factory, afternoons in the field felt sweltering. Occasional thunderstorms and light rain raised the humidity, yet under the relentless haranguing of the overseer, the farm workers maintained a formidable pace of cutting, threshing and loading of what were considered adequate crops, as if Nature made up for the killing drought in the South by modestly favoring the North.

Jessica alternately moaned and cursed, despising the inhumanity cloaked in service to humanity, and the system of collective farming idealized by the socialists. Her experience here markedly contrasted with her prior encounters with St. Sansais Monastery. Its quiet purpose worked towards the same end, a deeper sense of commitment to the welfare of others, while it preserved a sense of oneself. Ten days of stooping and lifting, stooping and lifting, sapped the remaining strength in her arms. In desperation, Jessica recalled the day she walked in her dress shoes with Lettina all the way from Konsky to St. Sansais. She had gained relief from the painful blisters on her heels when her thoughts remained on poor Cousin Pasha, wounded and nearly lost in the war. She forced her mind to again dwell on Pasha, to envision him healthy and whole in body and mind, to remember him standing tall, his curly brown hair tousled over his brow. She saw him being playful with two little girls, she and Tanya, ages five and ten years old, both idolizing their fifteen-year-old cousin, who sang spirited folk songs and teased them with puzzles and treasure hunts.

"O, we had enchanting times when we were young!" Jessica breathed, feeling softer, subdued, and less in pain than before. But the lengthy daylight hours of late summer allowed work to continue till dusk, when dew moistened the ripened seed heads. Harvesting ceased until crops dried the next day. By the time the crews returned to camp and swept the wagons, cleaned up after the horses, and loaded the grain into decrepit trucks, shadows from the single overhead light made strange figures on the shed walls when the workers sat down to supper.

Jessica's place at the table remained empty, her meager meal of bread, boiled potatoes and carrots with a sliver of baked fish untouched. Anna said Jessica worked all day and probably went to bed without supper. Tanya slipped from the mess hall with bread and a potato in her pocket.

Jessica lay on her cot, her hip forming a bony protrusion under the blanket.

"Jessica, Jessica," she whispered, careful that the American name was not overheard. "Are you sick?" She shook Jessica's shoulder and found it to be a skeleton beneath her palm. *O, Bozhe*, dear God, nothing can happen to you, Jessica," she cried.

Jessica opened leathery lids, scaly from sunburn. Her long dark lashes were matted with dust and salty tears. "My arms—" she managed to say in a voice Tanya did not recognize.

"I am afraid for you, Svetlanka." Tanya edged onto the cot next to her cousin and sneaked out the food she had secreted from the Hall. "You must eat, *pozhaluysta*, Jessica. Do it for me. You are starving, I think."

"I wish," Jessica said, then realized how Tanya was hurt by her condition. "You must not worry. I will live. Do as the abbot would want you to do, believe in the Providence of God. Did He not bring Pasha to the monastery?" She lifted herself on one elbow and nibbled on the dry bread and cold potato.

"You must be strong in body as well as spirit, Jessica," Tanya admonished, bossing like her older cousin. "I will fetch water. Don't get up." She rushed with Jessica's container to the barrel of drinking water in the compound and hurried back, her arms and legs athletic from working in the fields.

"It takes time to build yourself up Jessica, but you can do it. Didn't your friends, the shopkeepers, say you could do anything you set your mind to?"

"I am trying, but it is the tiger leaping from the corner of the ceiling, seizing the women and children. I can feel it." Jessica's voice trailed off.

"You frighten me, Jessica!" Tanya bolted upright holding her hands to her throbbing temples upon hearing the bizarre words. Her mouth formulated the words "Jessica, don't go away like Pasha, *nyet*, don't leave us—" soundless cries that choked in Tanya's throat. She adjusted the Army blanket over the wasted form and staggered out of the tent when the other girls entered.

"*Bozhe moy*, my god, what is the matter with you?" Lettina asked, seeing Tanya wild-eyed and stricken.

"*Nyet, nyet, nyet*, she can't go away in her mind like Pasha," Tanya uttered, pointing to Jessica. "She says it is the tiger—"

Thoroughly confused, Lettina led the others to Jessica's bedside, a canvas camp cot covered with thin Army blankets. She slipped back the covers. Jessica had surrendered to sleep, a half-eaten potato in her hand.

"It is best she sleeps." Anna motioned the others away. "We will check on her in the night and in the morning. This about a tiger might be a nightmare."

Jessica rose before the cowbells were rung at four a.m. She sat on the side of her cot and attempted to brush tangles from her matted hair.

"You must eat this morning," Lettina said. "We missed you at supper. You will get in trouble if they find out."

Jessica nodded, her lips too cracked to wryly reply that not eating was only one of many charges she may face. She threw on two layers of loose garments to hide her thinness and went to the mess hall, her steps wobbly but resolute. Gruel of freshly rolled oatmeal tasted palatable enough. She soon felt able to work, however, the gaunt cheeks and hollow eyes caught the attention of a staff person, who motioned her away from the mess hall. Shrugging her indifference toward the girls, Jessica followed him into a hay barn converted to house supplies.

"Wait here," he said, and left her standing alone.

From the supply shed, she had a view of the manor house, formerly a handsome three-story structure. She knew food was prepared there in extensive kitchens, and the officials quartered in its many bedrooms. Now overgrown with hops vines, it had settled into years of accumulated rotting leaves. Apparently, an estate of a noble or wealthy landowner, it was one of many vast landholdings nationalized and placed under the Soviet's eager collectivization *programmes* resulting in famine in the 1930s.

"Your name?" demanded a voice behind her. Jessica startled and turned to find the blond-haired official pulling out a notepad and pencil.

"Svetlana," she remembered to say.

"Svetlana, ah, so many Svetlanas."

"Svetlana Sergeevna Gilkova," she said.

Puzzled, he looked up from the pad, at first not recognizing her. "From Konsky?" he ventured.

"*Da, ser.*"

Captain Yuri Stanislov slowly replaced the pencil and notepad in his pocket while he scrutinized Jessica. His eyes roamed over her swollen lips and appraised her long, straight legs as if he recognized a certain familiar look. She knew he had seen her on the bus with Tanya the day they visited the monastery.

"I have been looking for you," he said, low and under his breath.

Color flushed Jessica's already burned cheeks, and her eyes, red and swollen, dropped to examine her fleshless hands twisting in front of her. Unsure what he meant, but sensing a vague danger, she waited knowing he was one of the recruiters at Benyanske's Boot and Shoe factory. The Captain led her into a smaller supply room away from eavesdropping of the workers, and sat her down on a wooden crate.

"I brought you here to say I can help you."

Jessica startled with a quick glance, but she could not look at him or conceive of a reply. Withdrawing into herself, her knees visibly shook beneath her clothing.

"I remember you wearing a fashionable red silk blouse, Svetlana." The words were surprisingly gentle. "You were very beautiful."

The silence in the dimly lit room became sodden with humidity and smell of moldy cellar. A light flared beyond the open door, inviting a line of escape which Jessica's shaken frame had no willpower to pursue.

"Svetlana Sergeevna, I know and you know that field work is against your nature—"

"*O nyet ser*, I am perfectly capable. My parents worked on a *kolkhoz* when I was a child. Please give me another chance—I will—"

"Enough. Listen to me. You are here for better or worse." He rose on his heels and hissed through his teeth, "You can make it much better for yourself if you choose to listen to me."

Jessica stared as if struck dumb, the tone, the insinuation, the Captain towering over her.

The Captain hesitated, unnerved by lack of a response. Breathing unevenly, he paced back and forth and pulled his hat forward on his brow. The hat's Red star loomed above Jessica, commanding and intimidating.

"I can help you," Captain Stanislov repeated, attempting to be conciliatory, "but shirking your duties by starving yourself will be met with harsh consequences. Now go help in the kitchen and laundry."

He strode out of the building before Jessica could question what this proposition was about. The prospect of making it better invited a means of escaping her present hardship. Yet the veiled threat "for better or worse" curdled her veins. Worse? How could it be worse? she cursed. His kindness, his very presence, inspired contradictions. Captain Stanislov's offer to help felt couched in threats—Jessica glimpsed the fleeting form of a tiger in the peripheral of her vision.

X

Tatyana

Harvesting at Victory *Kolkhoz* in Smolensk Oblast was coming to an end. Tatanya left on a wagon for the farthest field with three young women and a couple middle-aged veterans. They tended to pleasantries and sang sad old ballads, but did not disclose much about themselves. The field yielded the hardy rye that flourished in the northern climate, competing with the province's winter wheat or barley. Her fingers, strong and dexterous after years of sewing shoe leather took naturally to the repetitious chore of harvesting the tasseled stalks. The fields were quiet, the sense of timelessness of the harvest inducing meditation. The errant crop Tatyana was gathering would be used for making bread and for horse feed over the winter, a fact that encouraged her to scrounge industriously to salvage stalks from among the thistles, low lying brush, and wild sunflowers. She welcomed the natural world that calmed her youthful, uncertain being, especially after the fright she had experienced with Jessica. She stifled recurring fears and did not confide in anyone.

Instead she remarked to a girl next to her, "I wanted to go home when I first came here. We had an old horse named Gorgi." Her voice quavered, betraying her shyness. The girl glanced uncertainly at her.

"But I quite like working on such an enormous farm," Tanya

continued. "I always dreamed of living on a farm with horses and cows." She paused, admitting harvesting on a *kolkhoz* was nothing like a small farm.

"I don't know what my dreams are. I never had a dream." The girl's statement was flat, as if aspirations were not something one harbored in their youth, or indeed in their lifetime.

Though conversations were not always heartening, Tanya found gleaning proved to be entirely worthwhile, even satisfying as the last of the rye was later stacked inside the far end of the long building. Already some of the laborers had been transferred to another site when Tanya came in late in the evening and recognized Brother Dmitri leaning under the hood of a grain truck with another man she recognized as Tomenko, the miller. She stopped, peering through the shadows to be sure—the man she saw could be no one else—the tall, wide shouldered Pole with the bushy hair escaping from under a workman's cap was unmistakable, even as a mechanic rather than a monk in a flowing robe with a cowl. At once she decided to engage his help with Jessica, who continued to worry Tanya with her starved appearance and wretched mental state.

After washing her hands and face, Tanya lurked about the area waiting for the two men to come in for supper, hoping fervently that they would not drive off before she could contact Brother Dmitri. Finally, she could bear the tension no longer and ran across the road to the pasture where the trucks, tractors and the thresher were parked.

"We need to get a new carburetor and some hoses for this one."

She overheard Dmitri's familiar long-suffering voice, low and muffled under the hood.

"I already stripped any usable parts from those old ones," answered Tomenko, indicating a couple of derelicts behind the shed. "I can tape the hoses to make them usable, but new parts are just about impossible to come by. It takes nothing less than weeks or months if then to get parts. She may have to sit."

"Brother Dmitri, it is me, Tatyana, Pasha's cousin." She reached the monstrous truck as the men closed the hood and looked her way. She slipped behind the truck to avoid attracting the attention of those at the buildings and tents.

"Pavel's cousin, so it 'tis," Brother Dmitri said. His thick graying eyebrows raised with delight. "I suspected you might be with the laborers somewhere here in the north. I am glad to see you. How is your cousin, Svetlana?"

"That is why I need to talk with you, kind *ser*. She is not well nor fit for this kind of work. She is in such a state, talking about a tiger. I am so afraid she will go away in her mind like Pasha." The words tumbled out all at once. To Tanya it seemed like weeks since she found Jessica raving in her cot.

"Child, calm yourself, please. We shall see what we can do. You may know Tomenko Barskenkovich who also comes from Konsky."

Unable to endure any distractions, Tanya curtsied briefly in Tomenko's direction. Brother Dmitri assured the miller that he, too, had been recruited and returned to civilian duty. Tomenko's jaw dropped when he learned he had been working under the truck's hood with a monk.

"Svetlana works in the kitchen and laundry," Tanya said to Dmitri, pleading with her eyes that he follow up as she ducked out of sight among the machinery and fled back to the mess hall.

"I saw Tomenko," she told Lettina first thing as they filed in to supper. Lettina's chin came up in a curious manner, her eagerness to hear the news betraying more than a passing interest.

"He was working on a truck's engine with Brother Dmitri. Imagine Brother Dmitri as a greasy mechanic! I barely recognized him."

"We only need old Olga from the mill, Brother Anton from the monastery, and Boris Mikhailovich from the factory to have Konsky well represented here," Lettina said as if dismissing the subject.

The truck drivers dined with the civilian staff in another building, so neither Tanya or Lettina expected to see the mechanics at supper.

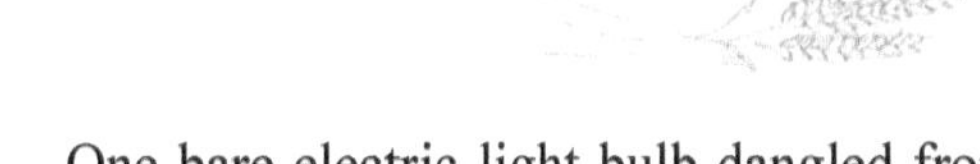

One bare electric light bulb dangled from its cord over the long table reserved for the staff, including the manager and field supervisors in the shed. Flashes of orange and purple sunset crept through the tall trees surrounding the manor house and glinted off the windows of the makeshift dining hall. Shadows claimed the corners, rafters and side rooms in an eerie haze. As a newcomer, Dmitri could not determine whether the staff normally ate without talking or did so because of his presence. He had worked as a laborer for the previous weeks on an adjacent property until he was called over here to assist with repairs on the truck. Unaccustomed to table discussion from his experience in the monastery, he was perfectly comfortable with the silence. He tended to his inner prayers, while keeping an eye out for Pavel's cousin, Svetlana, whom he hoped to encounter.

Women scurried about serving platters of food cooked in the manor kitchen to members of the staff; roast venison, pork, and steamed sweet potatoes, all fare that he had not enjoyed for many years and certainly did not receive as a laborer at the adjacent farm. Soon the meal was over and the men dispersed, though Dmitri, hyper-alert to the welfare of the cousins, noticed that four young women were pulled aside to accompany several officials to the house. He suspected this was not an unusual event. His lips closed firmly in a grim assessment of their fate.

Preoccupied, Dmitri started to walk around the compound containing the labor camp, but he was soon accosted by an attendant who suggested he take this opportunity to retire since tomorrow would be a busy day with the move. Accordingly, the monk strode directly to the tent where he had been assigned and found an empty cot next to Tomenko who was already snoring.

The night wore on for Dmitri who was flung back into the world of human suffering and chaos—chaotic to him who had chosen to leave all this and live a cloistered life. The carburetor entered his mind on the heels of images of Tatyana's brave face; the commitment to help feed starving people in the south of Russia clashed with his sense of injustice of forced labor; his intense desire for peace and contemplation was drowned by snoring inside the tent and the roar of responsibility in his own ears to find the young woman, Svetlana. Hiding his identity that he might not bring attention to the monastery of St. Sansais dogged his every thought.

In addition, it was time for the two week fast prior to the Feast of the Assumption that those at St. Sansais would be strictly observing. The Dormition of the Virgin of the Great Forest, the death of Mary, Mother of Jesus, the *Theotokos*, was close to his heart since his youthful vision that he attributed to the Holy Mother of God.

I am falling away here, unable to keep the sacred days. Why, why do I find myself wavering, confused? Holy Mary—he threw himself over and over on the cot, swatted annoying insects, and sat for hours with his head in his hands trying to focus on simple prayers. His nose ran continuously from the day's accumulation of chaff which he wiped on his sleeve. His soul quieted and his breathing slowed, yet events of the past week revolved in his restless mind.

"You, there with the pitchfork, you know anything about a threshing machine?" One of the officials had ridden a horse out to the field that day to find laborers who might have mechanical skills.

Dmitri had paused, fork in mid-air as he tossed a bundle into the wagon, and wondered if he was the one spoken to. He preferred to maintain his anonymity.

"*Da*, you, come over here." The official halted the horse a short distance behind the wagon so the other workers could continue filling it. "I understand you know something about mechanics. Where are you from originally?" the official asked, his glance noting Dmitri's tall frame and substantial strength.

"Gdansk."

"Farm?"

"Some."

"Good. Come with me. They are having trouble with the gears on a thresher, the ones that keep the belts moving, and we need to finish up on this collective."

Without waiting for an affirmation regarding experience, availability or inclination, the official had ridden off in the direction of the broken down machine, expecting the newly discovered mechanic to follow him. The short walk of three-quarters of a mile gave Dmitri time to pull his thoughts together about the intricacies of farm equipment, though his family and others at the time did most of their work by hand or with horses. It was only when he hired out as a young lad that he'd had the opportunity to drive a tractor and operate a seeder, mower, buckrake and stacker. A thresher was generally afforded only on big operations in Poland, or one was shared by a cooperative of small farmers. He was left to rely on his schooling in physics: ratios, leverage, blocks and tackles, fly wheels.

Several apparently inexperienced mechanics had been working on the mammoth machine for a couple of blistering hours in heat reflected from its sides.

"What went wrong and how did it happen?" Dmitri asked.

"A belt flew off. It was frayed and thin as paper. Parts of the belt got stuck in the gears. Before we could shut the machine down, the gears became jammed. I think it is seriously damaged." The mechanic seemed to be the spokesperson since the official was evidently not knowledgeable about the multiple problems. "We tried to tow it into camp for repairs, but moving it forward completely hung up the gears."

"Are there replacement parts if we can identify what is needed?" Dmitri asked the official, a young man, who was eager to contribute in some way.

"We would be lucky to get anything new, but they must have planned for this kind of contingency. One threshing machine to serve such a large parcel ought to have back up parts. I will check though I don't know exactly what we need."

The men removed the huge sheets of metal screwed to each side of the machine so they could examine the working mechanisms inside. Indeed, one of the conveyor belts had gone its last round and the pieces were chewed up like confetti. Whatever else the machine was, it wasn't terribly complicated. A brief study proved to be enough to prompt a suggestion.

"Maybe we can try towing it a few feet backward in case the gears would reverse and spew out the debris," Dmitri ventured. "Then we could set everything in neutral and tow it into camp as you suggest."

The mechanic ducked behind the tractor to unhitch it before the words were barely out of Dmitri's mouth. Grinning ear to ear, he roared the tractor to life and turned its unwieldy iron wheels around to position it behind the thresher. He jumped down to attach a log chain to a stout axle underneath and without hesitation slowly tightened up the chain to inch the bound-up machine in reverse. The hulk wobbled and clanked until enough immobilized gears rotated backwards to free them. From there on it was a matter of preparing the outfit for towing forward as usual. The official met them halfway back, his report unsurprising with no apologies or alternatives offered by the supervisors. They would have to make one thresher out of two similar ancient hulks.

Dmitri shook his head. His rapid promotion from monk to fieldhand to mechanic had been a dizzying complement and setback at the same time. Robbed of his inner calling, he was now obliged to keep the Ford grain truck, a Lend-Lease acquisition from the Americans, running so no time would be lost with breakdowns. Trucks were expected to deliver grain to the rail cars tomorrow for shipment south.

Now it was four in the morning of moving day. Dmitri stiffly lifted his head from where it rested on his hands. He had sat on the edge of the cot most of the night. The sound of shuffling outside the tents meant camp attendants came to heat water for breakfast and rouse the laborers.

Dmitri had not slept, not uncommon for him. Many nights in his life he had deliberately stayed awake in prayer and contemplation, sometimes in a joyous exaltation with a hallowed sense of Oneness. At other times he tried to force his thoughts as he had this past night. Today he had a sense of foreboding, a feeling he tried to shake by sloshing cold well water over his face again and again, then plunging the top of his head where the hair was growing back into cold water in a wash pan. Drizzles followed the line of what was now a short beard and dripped on his shirtfront.

An official came around the corner with a small torch obviously seeking the mechanics. "We have a truck loaded with grain and it will not start. We need you men to get out there before breakfast and work on it," he said.

Dmitri could not see his face in the dark; the torch caught only the shine of his eyes and the bright insignia on the official's hat. He handed the torch to Dmitri and was gone before Dmitri recognized him as Captain Stanislov, the officer at the village of Thor who had ordered that he be recruited.

Tanya had alerted Jessica that Brother Dmitri was in camp. Jessica went to the managers' shed early to prepare breakfast in hopes of setting out the serving dishes so she could make contact with him. Excited, but not nearly as thrilled as Tanya, Jessica had brushed her black hair and put on a slim cotton dress. Her frame had filled out some these past days since she no longer worked in the fields, but gray strands of dawn threw shadows that accentuated the transparent skin over her high cheek bones and jaw line.

The meal came and went, and the crew began packing pots and pans, eating implements, everything for the move to another site. Orders were curt and hurried. Pressure the officials must have felt was relayed to the workers: dismantle the camp, set up at the next *kolkhoz* and resume work at your stations.

"We are here for the harvesting. Waste no time clearing out of here," barked one attendant after another. Jessica packed foodstuffs in tubs and crates and placed them outside to be loaded on wagons in a mindless routine. Once outside, she heard furious wrangling across the yard near the trucks. Arms were waving amid shouts. Later, as a convoy of heavily laden trucks moved slowly out of the camp, she heard that their group of farm workers was under goal. Therefore, only one truckload of grain would be left here for local consumption, affording subsistence food where the generally adequate harvest had been stripped away. Not only were local farmers shorted, but whispers spread that grain was being secreted to occupied border states as part of a campaign to woo starving people to Communism.

"Under goal?" Jessica whispered to one of the older women. "What does that mean? After all this work and all those tons and tons of barley, how can we be under goal? Will we be punished for something that was not our fault?"

With a furtive glance around, the woman stated shortly, "It means we get the blame for their stupidity, and we will have to work harder in the next field." She and Jessica shared knowing grimaces and sped up their packing before the anger was directed at them.

The happenstance of the location of St. Sansais Vineyard in Kursk Oblast was due mostly to the fortuitous confluence of the East-West, North-South trading routes rather than the favorableness of the climate or the incongruity of growing grapes among buckwheat and dairy farms. This far north one would wonder about any crop less hardy than a turnip, according to the local wags, when winter storms sent sub zero temperatures and the growing season was often bookended by Arctic storms. But the region's black soil had attracted growers centuries ago. Over time the ingenuity of vintners passionate about Russian grown vines developed those whose very fragrance was heady. The wine itself embodied an intensely concentrated blend of mountain air and the juicy organic wildness of the land.

Abbot Konstantin knew that in the absence of his head vintner, Brother Dmitri, he would be wise to remind the other monks to begin mounding the roots with earth in preparation for the unpredictable timing of winter. A covering of the precious loose soil would serve as a warming blanket for any fragile characteristics remaining in the prized vine stalks. The abbot encountered Brother Anton and Pavel in the now dry and ragged looking garden where they were beating a pile of dried beans from their stalks with sticks.

A rosy flush played over Pavel's cheeks when he merrily greeted the abbot then swung even more ambitiously at the pile. Sweat burst across his brow under long curly brown hair that had not been trimmed in months. His was the only full head of hair in the monastery signifying his status as a visitor, but Pavel acted as though he belonged there as surely as the laurel trees and the rabbits in the bushes and the ancient stones making up the monastery walls and winery. In fact, he seemed to have awakened to find all was new and exciting, while little of his past was real. Apparently war had become a distant, if not forgotten, experience.

Brother Anton was more subdued, focused inwardly on continuous prayer which came to him effortlessly at times, "Lord Jesus Christ, have mercy on me." At other times it eluded him completely, and he would fall back upon the reliability of his breath, "Lord have mercy, Christ have mercy." Today he beat the beans particularly vigorously expressing an unspecified anxiety that Abbot Konstantin perceived and addressed at once.

"I wonder if you are worried about Brother Dmitri?"

"O, *da,* Father. Day and night, I wonder what has befallen him. Why would fate take the man who desired escape from the outer world into that very world under most unhappy circumstances?"

"Tis fate, yes, but I believe a Fate of a higher order. Would you not agree that Brother Dmitri would be the first to accept responsibility for his fellow man?"

"As he did for me," interrupted Pavel, stopping his work and standing humbly before the imposing figure of the abbot. "Day and night he and Anton cared for me, much of which I knew nothing about until I began to understand the healing here at St. Sansais. No greater man is he than one who gives up the peace of his soul for his brothers." He dared to raise his eyes to the abbot as the corners of his mouth quivered with emotion.

"Peace of *dus'ha,* the soul," echoed Konstantin. "And what did you come to understand of the healing?" Peace of the soul, was central to his teaching, in fact suffering and the soul were the heart of Orthodoxy.

Words flowed at once surprising even Pavel Ivanovich Zyclov. "I came to understand matters which I had never before thought of when kind Brother Dmitri read the words of the saints. I learned to search my heart as taught by St. Simeon the Theologian, and I found in this a great joy for which I was so thankful that even the room seemed light in the darkness and my soul felt healed." Unconsciously, he turned his palms upward and gazed at the stubs of fingertips lost to frostbite during the war.

"This is nothing, nor the loss of my toes, in compensation for what I have found in the presence of God—that I now find everywhere," he hastened to add, in an apologetic boyish tone.

As often happened in the presence of the novitiates, Konstantin felt his heart expand as if it would break. He, too, felt the Spirit that moved the young people to such reverence and devotion. In response he could say nothing, only tip his head and remain standing in the garden. Experiencing an astounding inner sense of certainty of the nearness of God and His love, he released some of his anxiety and grief. He fell into being with the One who had prayed in the Garden, and had led him to the ancient monastery of St. Sansais.

Dried bean stalks made scratchy noises as their vines relaxed into the forgotten heap. These past weeks since Brother Dmitri had volunteered for harvesting on the collectives had shaken the abbot's belief in the Spirit as well as the secular worlds. Flashbacks haunted his waking and sleeping moments: the Revolution when he was not yet a man, the White insurgency doomed to failure; the suffering of his people and persecutions of Jews, Muslims and pagans, the sense of powerlessness of the clergy during plundering and wanton desecration by the sadly alienated forces of atheism. Lost to generations was their faith, their only solace.

Knowing he was getting old having had too much history penetrating his consciousness, he swallowed hard and solemnly raised his chin to confront the patient novitiates.

"Brother Dmitri would want us to continue his work just as he undertakes work outside the walls," the abbot said. "We shall begin covering the rootstalk in the vineyard with deep soil after the last of the grapes have been gathered."

Abbot Konstantin's brown homespun robe swirled with each stride back to his office, his flat *bast* sandals slapping the stones. The pure and simple manifestation of the Spirit when he heard Brother Anton and Pavel Ivanovich accept their suffering with joy and thankfulness prompted an urgency to take his own inventory. He had shielded the young men from knowing the toll that waves of persecutions and *programmes* had taken on him. Perhaps he had unduly shielded himself from memories of the physical, mental, and spiritual tolls he had endured. After all, suffering came like deluges of rain during the Revolution, preceded and followed by bitter civil wars and purges, and again through two world wars. Spiritual suffering felt the most crushing of all. He gratefully let himself inside his office and closed the heavy wooden door against those unspeakable times.

At St. Sansais, the obligation to take one's spiritual inventory formed the heart of the Community of Brothers, a revived and simplified adaptation of ancient Greek Orthodoxy, reduced from its rituals and dogma. Derived from the Lord's Word, and matching his own teaching exactly, Konstantin found no other way to truly guide and develop one's faith than by examining one's conscience; certainly not by discipline, deprivation, or self-inflicted suffering. Only by intense and honest self-examination, coupled with willingness to be open to the Spirit did one's soul blossom and become joyful in its presence. How marvelously Brother Anton and Pavel radiated this elemental teaching!

With hands forward as if to catch himself from falling, Konstantin grasped a small oak table, one fleshy palm at each end, and propped himself there above the unlit candle and delicately tatted lace cloth. Reddish hairs stood up on the backs of his hands that faded from flesh-colored to white then purplish with the pressure of his weight.

"Lord," he gasped, "Your healing, Lord." A great breath overtook the words and he fell into soundless communion, one way though it may be. With all the power of his convictions and that derived from Russia's heritage of monasteries and the Holy Orthodox Church, Brother Konstantin prayed, nay implored, that his people be spared suffering, that they enjoy the gladness of heart that is their rightful gift, and *pozhaluysta*, Lord, that they need not lose minds and fingers, such as occurred to Pavel Ivanovich, to feel the gladness. Your healing, Lord, of the oppressed and those suffering injustices, and the young who suffer the loss of their future, their hopes and well-being. And if rulers pronounce scourges upon us, let us at least hold in our arms all that is precious to us.

His head fell upon his chest and he crumpled to his knees, a humble supplicant at the small table beneath beneficent miens on icons of the saints. Childhood feelings arose, sweeping him back to the memory of a favorite toy, a small wand that he waved over his toy horses and commanded them to arise and walk, yet the toy horses remained as impervious to his commands as the God of this moment. Bitterness sprinkled with salty tears brought him back to his contemplation.

"I am powerless, joyless, and fearful, Most Holy *Theotokos*, Lord Jesus Christ, and all the Saints," he managed to utter, striking his heaving chest with a fist. "How can I be an instrument of thy peace? How but by some miracle can those in the monastery rely upon me, or upon Thou through me, with my weakness and blasphemy? Forgive me, but I do not see improvement in the outer world, only in the inner—"

Perhaps that is enough, came back the reply.

For a long time Father Konstantin remained kneeling at the small table, his legs stiffened and cold; his palms long past tingling were numb. "And I shall dwell in the house of the Lord forever, amen," he murmured aloud. A faint tap at the door removed his attention from one world to awareness of another. Brother Vessaly appeared with a covered bowl of hot garden vegetable soup. Only then did the abbot realize that several hours had passed.

Part II

"All the working people must enjoy fruits of their common labor." Vladimir Lenin

XI

Anna

The laundry staff were the last to leave Victory *Kolkhoz* and move to one of the next collectives. The irregular sputting and chugging of the gasoline motor on the washing machine reminded Jessica of the heavy-duty electric stitching machines in the Benyanske Boot and Shoe factory, the needles crunching through cowhide, a maddening chop, chopping until one became accustomed to it. Any attempt to talk had to be several decibels above the roar.

"This might as well be an engine from the grain trucks. I'll be deaf before we are done," she groaned to Evangelina, another laborer assigned to laundry duty. They were last to leave camp since blankets needed to be washed to prevent lice before being reissued at the next camp.

"It is to kill bed bugs and prevent nausea from sleeping in someone's foul, sweat-soaked bedding." Jessica insisted. She never stopped wishing for her old apartment with its relative quiet, though it had thin walls and she hated it at the time.

"Didn't I smell real coffee?"

"Of course. Do you think they drink boiled root in the main house?" Evangelina was not only well informed about practices of the officials, she endured their authority with contempt.

"Have you been in the manor house?"

"*Da. Nyet.* Not because I wanted to," she said evasively. "Not for a long time and not here." She had the dried sun-bleached hair of a farm woman, and knotty fingers to suggest middle age. Her face, rounded into soft folds, might have been attractive years ago.

"I think all the officials are gone with the laborers and machinery. I'd like to slip in to get a cup of coffee."

"With your looks, my dear, you could have anything you want," Evangelina said. She turned back to plunge the scrubbed blankets into a rinse water tub after Jessica fed them through the wringer by hand. Evangelina wasted no time in throwing the still dripping wash over the fence after the clotheslines were full.

Jessica shrugged. "If we're lucky these will dry fast. We may be in time for supper at the next camp. If not we'll go hungry, punishment for *potrachennoye vremya*, wasting time, though this washer is pitifully slow."

Risking bodily injury, she steeled herself with the last of her strength to pull the heavy wet blankets faster from the hot water of the washer and thread them through the wringer "without mangling your fingers or arm," as the attendant warned before he left. Failing to find other places to hang the remainder of the blankets, she snapped them briskly in the air and let them alight on the crisp grass at the edge of the field. She did not see Captain Stanislov until he had apparently watched her for awhile.

Startled, she said, "That was a close call, Evangelina," thankful she had not tried to sneak into the house and steal coffee. She winced again when he turned on his heel and left. Unsure whether he had overheard them or not, she sagged against the wildly vibrating empty washing machine and wished desperately for a cigarette.

"You will work in my office." Captain Stanislov caught up with Jessica late that night at the next collective, a group of nationalized small farms that made up Red Bounty *Kolkhoz*. She was unloading the truck that had transported the laundry crew from Victory *Kolkhoz*.

"Go to the main house," he commanded before passing on, issuing orders as he went from group to group.

"Evangelina, I had no opportunity to ask when, why, or specifically where I should go."

"You will find out why soon enough." Evangelina huffed something about a fatted calf, or was it a sacrificial lamb?

Jessica stared after her. She felt herself hardening as events unfolded on the collective, but Evangelina had become much harder. She left a grim outlook for Jessica without a trace of pity. Unable to sort out her feelings, Jessica avoided the house. She joined a dozen men and women who erected the long tents and set up cots inside in the close quarters. Wagons had hauled personal belongings over from the last camp, but she gave up searching for her small bag and looked for Tanya. The laborers were still spread out in all directions in the fields, bending and lifting to bring in the harvest until the last rays of light.

I'm unable to give her a message to find my bag and I'm afraid to go alone to the house. I dare not fall under the Captain's command—he looks at me in a creepy way. A moment of panic seized her. Being disoriented and exhausted, she could only mutter, "Tanya must be exhausted, as well." The heaviness of fatigue sank into her bones. Her arms sagged against her sides from hoisting wet blankets, leaving her with a sense of being small and intimidated at this new camp. Anything more challenging than lifting a fork to her mouth for supper would be too much. She forced her feet to move toward a cluster of sycamores interspersed with spruce. A two-story, stone farm house, obviously the home of a wealthy landowner prior to nationalization, rose beyond the trees. Jessica skirted the untended herb garden and flowerbeds to reach the servants' entrance at the rear of a long wing on the side of the house. It would seem pretentious to appear at the front door in her ragged dress.

"Annetta," she cried, finding her friend weeping inside the door.

"You, too?" Anna's look of surprise and dismay registered at the same time.

"I'm so glad to see you!" Jessica moved to embrace her longtime friend, but Anna shrank from her. "Are you all right? What is happening?"

"We can't talk here." Anna beckoned to Jessica to follow her into a side hallway. In the dim light of a kerosene lantern, Jessica saw Anna's altered face, her refined features distorted by anguish.

"Anna—"

"My parents—I'll never tell them what happens here—they will be so crushed."

Jessica shook her gently by the shoulders, directing Anna's eyes to her own. "Let me see you."

"We—I—some of us are being used—the filthy officials, don't you know?" Her voice revealed the wretched truth. Jessica's heart dropped, sensing what she was walking into. Her limited knowledge of men using women came from seeing old Tomenko ravishing Lettina. Yet Lettina had been willing. Maybe she had invited him. Clearly, even to Jessica, that was not the same as what Anna was forced to endure.

"I didn't know," she blubbered, bile rising in her empty stomach, further debilitating her weakened condition. "It is not your fault, Anna, please believe me. You would do everything in your power to honor your parents. You are so good, Anna—"

"I feel used, used like a serf or the lowest peasant girl."

"No, Anna, no, don't say that," Jessica's pleas came out a whimper.

"I am ruined, Jessica. I cannot face myself—"

Jessica grasped her in her arms in an effort to comfort the shaking girl who was once the poised and ladylike one among them. Anna fought like a cat, even with Jessica, as if there was nothing more to lose, her person so violated she struck out in aimless fury. Jessica's legs nearly let her slide down on the floor, pulling Anna down with her, until a door opened somewhere in the main house. Alerted, the girls struggled to regain their balance and composure and grimaced "We'll live," and moved toward the sound. A short round older woman shuffled down the hallway to meet them.

"You are guests?" she asked.

"Of Comrade—," Anna whispered, muffling the words so Jessica did not hear the name. The woman nodded and pressed Anna's arm reassuringly.

"I am to work in the office of Captain Stanislov, if you please, ma'am," Jessica said, her voice sounding artificially assertive to her ears.

The woman, apparently a housekeeper holdover from collectivization of the farms, led them towards the library and front parlour. "Wait here," she said, indicating a room for each.

In the library, Jessica stood for a long time on the woven wool rug, sensing its softness beneath her feet in stunning contrast to the wrenching encounter with Anna moments before. "We were taught to chase the 'bluebird of happiness,'" she moaned. "Devotion to Lenin, Marx and Engels, *bah*! It is a coverup. I feel betrayed. What do I know of real life? Where is the romance of American films?"

Wounded sounds escaped her constricted throat until she caught her breath. There is no God, there is no mercy, there is only suffering, she cursed, and stamped her disgust into the soft rug, a quiet Middle Eastern receptor that held all her secrets.

Eventually Jessica sniffled and attempted to reorient herself to the library. She scanned the floor-to-ceiling shelves of books of every size and binding imaginable. A smile escaped despite the recent trauma and her acute self-consciousness. Here I am standing in a landowner's home. He must have been educated and free to explore, she marveled. Favorite volumes of Aleksandr Pushkin occupied center shelves within easy reach from a reading chair.

"O, my, these others—who reads Milosz Czelaw on philosophy? Goethe and Heine? I was withdrawn from Ten-Year School too soon."

Distracted from her plight and the perils Anna experienced, Jessica quickly traced other leather-bound books on philosophy and religion, including 18th century works of Immanuel Kant, worlds she had never even hoped to explore. Next to two icons were foreign language novels, works of Shakespeare, Dickens, and Cervantes in French. Tolstoy's familiar novels in Russian claimed a position with what Jessica recognized were classic and contemporary works though she had never read them.

This is how the upper class lived, Jessica breathed, until they lost the property and manor house to the collective. Taken aback, she recalled her education centered upon history and economics with upbeat treatises on Five-Year Plans, essentially Socialist themes. But her studies ended at age sixteen due to the invasions. She calculated what she missed with what she viewed in this library. She wondered if the field laborers whose fingers now bled from harvesting had read these authors at one time.

A peculiar fascination with an insight into how the noble men and women lived drew her around the room, past a low fire in the grate of a tiled *Russki* stove that occupied much of the wall opposite the door. Two deep, sienna leather chairs with high carved arms and sculptured backs faced the fire. Bronze fireplace tongs, poker and brush unexpectedly remained after the probable looting of homes such as these by the idealists of Lenin's equalization *programmes*. Several smoke-clouded portraits hung awry in dark corners, vestiges that triggered stories Jessica's mother used to tell of her family. Or did I imagine the stories and give myself a noble family? Jessica wondered. These days her mother barely spoke, even of wildflowers in spring or plump wild hens they bagged in the fall.

From Jessica's perspective in the library at Red Bounty *Kolkhoz*, it became clear that Konsky had offered little other than a strictly enforced egalitarian culture throughout her upbringing. But she also sensed that little things like the fireplace poker felt familiar, also the array of family mementos on the desk. The scent of old wool and aged leather in this dark, cavernous home that kept the hot sun at bay on summer days roused a vague memory of another place, another time.

"The wealthy indulged their profligate ways and decadent culture, while intellectuals flaunted their education, both gained at the expense of others." Captain Stanislov strode into the room and caught a glimpse of her admiring the surroundings. "We do them a favor by sending them into the fields. They need conditioning in the reality of the common man. You will get no romantic ideas, Svetlana." His voice dropped to a sneer, tinged with hate.

"Landowners earn no distinction in our society." His clipped accent matched the way he habitually walked, as if he were under orders at all times. His small mustache neatly matched the exact corners of his wide mouth and lips.

Precise, she guessed. The military is so ingrained in him. "What will I be doing in the office?" Jessica tried to speak confidently, though she was quivering from his abrupt appearance and scorching condemnation of comrades, some better off, others less well off than himself.

"What I tell you. You will start at dawn tomorrow here in the library. Now have the old woman show you to your room."

Jessica nearly ran with relief to find the housekeeper, passing one of the officials in the hallway. Jessica cringed at his arrogant suggestive smile, glad that her matted dingy hair and bony frame hid her normal appearance. Her stomach revolted at the thought that this slick, cocksure, middle-aged veteran of the Red Army might be Anna's assailant. The housekeeper led her to the servants' quarters.

"Anywhere," the woman said, her rough hands directing Jessica to choose one of several small, unadorned rooms. "The *taulet* is down the hall."

Left alone at last, Jessica plopped on the nearest cot, but immediately visions of Anna's wasted face and form forced her to bound up and peep down the hall. Anna was doubtless somewhere in the house, but she neither saw nor heard anyone in the servants' wing. A draft came from a cracked window or unclosed door, merging with Anna's haunting declaration that "we are being used." She dared not venture forth—Anna had more experience within staff quarters than she did. She threw herself about the servant's room, wanting at once to charge to Anna's side and then, in fear of reprisal, held herself back. The chill of the unused room, shaded by overgrown trees, urged her to wash quickly at the small vanity and forget about her bag lost in the move. She again fell into bed in her clothes, her pillow soon wet with tears. Wind brought the chatter of night birds to mingle with the rumblings from the main part of the house. Under this cover of sounds she pounded the dense straw-stuffed mattress in an agony of aloneness in the servant's quarters.

"Why had I complained about the factory? At least it was safe—safer. I want to get out of here." A myriad of fears mixed with fragments of hope that her fortune might change muddled Jessica's mind until morning.

The first thing Jessica noticed when she awoke was the smell of good coffee. She peered out the window and determined it was very early, still not fully light. Lacking even her small travel bag to refresh herself, she combed her hair with her fingertips, put on her shoes, and slipped into the main house where the kitchen crew served breakfast to the officials in the formal dining room. The opulence of the dining room and the hearty smells of good food struck her as being offensive. The officials' crude laughter hung over the china, ceramic goblets, and silverware as if they were guests at the manor house.

Crude, yes, Jessica observed, before she crept behind the huge masonry stove to warm up and dared to pour a cup of coffee from the pot on the warming oven. A delicate rose pattern rimmed the china cup and a petite streak of gold embellished the ornate handle. She held the cup under her nose, the steam hinting of Arabic grounds flavored with a bit of cardamom. Maybe I am crude, too. Jessica smiled and touched the cup to her lips, but I could drink this whole pot. No, I would share half with Lettina if only she were here. And I haven't seen Anna.

Her indulgence was interrupted by the stamping of boots when a number of officials crossed the dining room and left. Jessica hastily concealed the cup and waited until they passed before she hurried into the library, taking a few wrong turns from hallways on the way.

Captain Stanislov had not yet arrived, but the desk had been cleared of the previous family's mementos. With an effort to control her nerves, Jessica approached the chair behind a stack of papers and what appeared to be bills and receipts. She felt much too uncomfortable to sit in the Captain's chair, and she had never before done clerical work of any kind, despite the school's efforts to train a workforce. Sewing tough boot leather hardly constituted preparation for a secretarial position. She twisted her strong and capable hands that now felt incompetent and waited.

"I will sit there and you will sit here," Captain Stanislov said, bringing in a straight wooden chair from the hall. He placed it across the desk from his chair. "Do you type?"

Again startled by his abrupt appearance, Jessica leapt from behind the desk. "*Nyet*—"

"Can you do billing? Do you understand the system of accounting in ledgers?"

"*Nyet*. I may be able to help with billing."

"What did you do in Konsky, Comrade Svetlana? Surely you must be trained in some capacity. To each is given as—"

"I stitched boots. I had to leave the Academy early and work in the factory." Bristling under the grilling, Jessica refused to let him denigrate her war effort, yet her staunch defense of it felt risky.

"O, *da*, I remember the boot and shoe factory. Unfortunately, manual labor does not prepare you for more intellectual endeavors. You shall write."

For the next few hours, Captain Stanislov dictated messages at a furious pace, required her to deliver them to other officials in the house, and sent her for lists of food and supplies to be procured for the camp. He made no personal overtures, indeed seldom held eye contact, and Jessica began to relax. Later, in a fleeting moment, she compared this position with that of laboring in the field with the least bit of satisfaction.

The office work halted for dinner when the cook struck a resounding triangular bell outdoors with an iron bar. Jessica ate in the kitchen, famished for having missed breakfast as well as supper the evening before. Her hands automatically ran over her hips, bony to the point of emaciation after the laundry sweatshop yesterday and the overnight fast. She acknowledged that even the fatty pork and too-sweet applesauce, if her stomach tolerated them, would take time to make her presentable again.

"Eat" she remembered Tanya and Katya saying. Tanya, she might not know where I am—she will be frantic, though Anna may have returned to the tent and told her. Pulled toward both the tent and library, she determined to brave out the office duties and find the girls after work.

O, Bozhe moy, Tanya must not know even a hint that women are being used, forced, *da*, like serfs. She would be hysterical worrying about me and my fate, perhaps a fate like Annetta's. It is the officials and—and the Captain may be one of them. But he is in charge here, he cannot be one of them. I wish I were back in the field.

Grimly assessing the situation for the last time, she muttered, "I must get on with it. I can do nothing to save myself—or Anna."

The afternoon proceeded much the same as the morning. Jessica sorted boxes of papers and addressed envelopes, this time with trembling hands and acute awareness that each official who came and went without so much as an introduction may have assaulted Anna. Utter disgust roiled her stomach and settled into her boney frame. Yet the gawky girl with matted hair interested no one, except perhaps Captain Stanislov, and if so, he kept it to himself.

Harvesting continued without missing a beat at Red Bounty *Kolkhoz*. Broken machinery was miraculously replaced by another machine, often "borrowed" from another farm. The weather cooperated, and the harvesters melded into teams of formidable competence and spirit. Hearty cheers, often led by Lettina, accompanied a wagon filled with bundles that was dispatched to the thresher. Hurrahs erupted again when one of the mammoth dump trucks, filled with grain from the thresher's long chute, left the farm for the local railroad depot, the grain on its way to ease the drought-stricken South.

Gradually folksongs of the *muzhiks* arose to celebrate bringing in the harvest. The singular humor in their *khorovods*, fun songs, intermingled with the rumbling of ancient tractors and creaking old wagons. *O Sparrow* lamented the lazy man.

Is the sparrow home?
He's at home, at home.

What's he doing home?
He's lying sick.

The *muzhiks* of old, former serfs who became landowners when freed in 1861, became the *kulaks* of today. They not only harvested their own small plots, but lands of their former lords as well, securing their posterity in the contemporary novels of Leo Tolstoy. Reapers timed the tempo of their scythes to folk tunes handed down over generations; those with pitchforks heaved bundles to the rhythm.

Lettina quickly picked up previously unfamiliar songs and joined in lively dance steps in the fresh-cut barley field with the spontaneous exuberance of the *kolkhozniki*, the women farm workers. Factory women who had been heavy were now svelte and chipper; those who had been pale and drawn were robust and daunting. The young sang of days until harvesting would be finished and they could go home. The elderly sang, rubbed alcohol into their rheumy joints, and drank the remaining contents of the bottle.

In the long, light evenings, soft crooning sometimes lilted from bed to bed when women sang lullabies they had nearly forgotten. Or a bawdy tale arose from the men's dormitory tents, followed by low, embarrassed laughter. Less often, but a Russian treasure all the same, a Cossack's fine baritone carried the song on the day's-end breeze, a stirring reminder to patriotic souls that the best of the homeland remained in the hearts of her people.

On an exquisite morning in the field when the sun tinged the surrounding dense forest with a dewy golden hue, a tune began *"Rejoice, rejoice,"* as if life could not help but respond in harmony. Voices joined, one after another, raising the volume of praise, until a watchful eye noticed an official riding towards their crew. The hymn faded away as imperceptibly and unconsciously as it had arisen.

"Lettina, you are smiling," accused Katya. "Do you know something we don't? Will it snow and we can all go home?" The two served on the same team that pitched bundles into the thresher because of their strength and endurance for the overhead work. They had taken a break for a few sips of cold coffee from a vodka bottle that Jessica had liberated from the kitchen.

"We can all go home when it is done, that is all I know," Lettina said, but she maintained her secret until Katya managed to pry it out of her.

"Tomenko worked here for a few days after the workers arrived, but I believe he has been transferred."

"But you saw him?"

"I did."

"And you were together–like at the mill?"

"We—were."

"Well, who cares who is with whom here—it is no shame and no secret," Katya brushed it off.

"Yours has never been a well-kept secret, Katya, so why are you bragging? How could a secret be kept in the tents?"

"True, and I for one do not care. Don't be a fool, Lettina. We are women with feelings, with needs and desires—can we not live like human beings?"

"I am sure other women understand. They, too, suffer the longings. We all do. Only Tomenko is married. It is a sin, I think."

"You think it is a sin when churches have been discredited and banned? What is morality other than working? Forgive me, please, but who is talking about sin these days?"

The silence hung indifferently as if there were no case to argue, as if Katya's blatantly obvious conclusion summed the Soviet lapse from the Orthodoxy of the tsars. Lettina shifted her weight on the hard ground, and Katya picked at a soil-embedded scab on her elbow. Born after the Revolution and between two world wars, both acknowledged their schooling had consisted of Lenin-Marxist doctrine in lieu of what was termed the soulless emptiness of religion.

Still, they sat in the stubble of the field and grappled with principles which might apply in these tumultuous times after the cessation of war. If killing is a sin, God help the Russians who bloodied and beat the Germans back with their own emaciated hands. If loving the wrong person is a sin, God help the women of Russia whose fathers, husbands, brothers, sons, uncles all died in the battles of Leningrad, Stalingrad, Moscow, and on the conqueror's march from the Black

Sea to the Baltic. If adultery is a sin, who is to say so when families are ripped apart and half have been disabled or connived to flee the country over the past ten years of continual oppression, famine and war.

"Alas, we inherited God with our mother's milk," Lettina admitted, in support of moral values.

Baffled, the girls looked at each other and laughed.

"It is all confusing. Ideals of morality are contrary to ordinary life," Lettina said, "but what is ordinary life? Meet goals of Five-Year Plans, give away grain grown by those who need it? This is the way of Rossiya now. *Vse normalno.*"

"You were born in this ordinary life—the way of comrades is to be poor, single, atheist, and half dead from work. Do we have to also be bigoted about sexual mores? It is not going to be different for any of us, don't you see?" Katya spit out. "You are being stupid, Lettina, for hiding something nice and beautiful with Tomenko."

"And you suppose that you and Greita acting against nature is acceptable?" Lettina stood and threw down the charge, while slapping stubble that was clinging to her dress.

"That is between Greita and me. Besides, in Youth Camps we girls were expected to grow out of it. If not, women attracted to women is not condemned."

"I didn't mean you have to grow out of it, but men are severely punished if found degraded, even executed or exiled to Siberia if caught in compromising relations with other men. Differences are not valued so don't get caught."

"*Pravda, ne suschestvuet.* "Unnatural" women do not exist in *Rossiya,* " Katya chided.

"Yet only workers and party members are valued." Lettina tried to maintain her better judgment despite Katya's persuasive arguments.

"*Da,* and we better get to work or we'll be arrested for resistance and hooliganism," Katya laughed, lithely bounding back on the wagon and reaching down to pull Lettina up.

XII

Emilia

If the days held bursts of the joyous, indomitable spirit of working men and women in the fields, the nights held ears listening for any disturbance, any upheaval that would potentially make their jobs harder. Not entirely unexpected, scuffling at the manor roused the women in the military tent nearest the house. Officials cursed. Women's low voices protested without giving away the cause of the scuffling. Lettina bolted barefoot to peer past the tent flap in that direction. Shadowy figures in semi-darkness beyond a thicket of wild roses and berry bushes shifted around three women. Unable to indentify anyone other than officials, Lettina bounded to Anna's cot and found it cold and empty. She had not come in.

Terrified for Anna after the disturbing conversation she'd had with Katya that afternoon, Lettina burst past men and women laborers in tunic nightshirts, who had also heard and leapt from their beds.

"*Nyet, nyet*. Let me go, let me go—you dare not—." Anna's gritty, clinched-teeth utterances and the commotion outside the manor house carried to the tents.

Harsh male voices and laughter followed the tight, desperate outburst. Lettina ran past linden trees and shrubs sheltering the house, arriving in time to see several officials force the resisting Anna and two other girls inside the back of the manor house, and swiftly close the door.

Greita, Katya and Tanya were close behind Lettina, breathing hard and shivering from fear and the chill of night. Nudging each other to be quiet, they choked down oaths, unable to speak, forbidden to speak. Men who had harnessed stubborn teams, swung scythes all day, and labored in the fields also became mute behind haunted looks betraying war trauma. Women with sweaters thrown over their shoulders formed small silent groups along the side yard. Their fury came at last in short bursts of female rage.

"They can't do this."

"We are unprotected here."

"We don't have to allow them to assault women." Katya clenched and unclenched her fists, almost daring Lettina to storm the house.

"Leave this up to the officials," Ludmila admonished.

"The girls are harvesters like us. They came in good faith," someone objected.

Yet the chilled group did nothing but mill about.

"Jessica—I am afraid for Cousin Jessica if she is with these—these—," wailed Tatyana over the curses and threats.

The men and women all turned towards the fifteen-year-old who had called out an American name. Tanya slumped, fist in her mouth and whimpered how sorry she was. Lettina swooped Tanya up in her arms and strode unsteadily back to the tents, passing the women who remained outside while their questioning yet sympathetic eyes followed the procession.

Men with downcast faces hid their shame, their impotence to stop the officials writ large upon the wind stirring across the now joyless farmland. For some, the bulge beneath their nightshirts betrayed excitement by the sexual conquests that were not theirs. The young girls' pleas had apparently penetrated the consciences of others, perhaps for their own rapes in Germany and border countries. For a few, a jut of the chin, a quick dart back to their cots meant consciences had been dulled over the years by endless indignities and suffering, by lack of a hero's welcome after their victories spanning the breadth of the continent, by an aftermath of purges that decimated those of rank as well as foot soldiers of the impervious Red Army. Their current loss of self in fields that were also not their own was hardly new. In their Cossack garb of loose tunic and baggy trousers, they had been conscripted for the harvest just as the women had. They had left families, professions and education behind. Knowing glances to each other, frowns and guttural oaths betrayed that they, too, felt raped.

"Beasts, *da*, foul beasts. We are held and used like captives in the camps," one woman seethed, her bitterness obviously shared by others, some younger, some older.

"Shush, you will frighten the little one. They are grown women. They will survive," Ludmila interrupted. Her sternness momentarily quieted the reactions, as if a voice, a guide, a motherly presence such as Ludmila's dared contain the rage.

In the lengthening shadows, women silently watched the bedraggled men troop back to bed, extinguishing the flames in their kerosene lanterns. The darkness made the men seem even more inaccessible, less liable for happenings outside the enclosure of their small world this night.

"They forced me, not here but in the first camp," a shy young woman said. "I did not, could not fight like Anna. I was so ashamed I had not told anyone until now. Anna was brave, but foolish. Who is to help any of us? There is no law on the *kolkhoz*—we can do nothing. Men would be shot or sentenced if they intervened. We women would suffer the same abuse or worse." Heads nodded in agreement, the tension threatening to escalate.

"I wouldn't complain," Ludmila whispered, "or you may find yourself in worse trouble than the girls. Pretend you did not see or hear anything tonight."

"Ludmila is right. We must not draw undo attention to ourselves. Many men experienced much worse in--in the war." The wavering voice belonged to Sasha, known for her strong views secretly expressed among women at Benyanske's Boot and Shoe factory. "Whatever happens we women, young and old, possess uncommon strength of spirit," though the tremor revealed she was badly shaken by events taking place. "We must break up this meeting and go to our tents before someone sees us."

Inside the tent at Tanya's bedside, Lettina sensed that any pure elements of the Russian psyche had been buried with the past, alive only in blazing nationalistic, revisionist history in the newspapers and heard on radio stations. She recognized the rancor in faces of comrades who experienced the high hand of the authorities, the double message of equality of the masses. Their grim outlook reinforced her feeling of loss, loss of one's entitlement to a hopeful destiny, loss of respect for their persons as workers.

"We have all been loyal workers, Tanecha. I am sorry." To herself Lettina swore, we have been betrayed. There would be no redress of grievances in the camp. The futility of protesting prompted her to further assure Tanya, "I will find Jessica for you, never fear. I'm sure she is all right."

Instead of dispersing outside, a group of younger women crowded into Lettina and Tatyana's tent. Lettina waved both hands in the air to quell the chatter.

"Svetlana may be safe in the servant's quarters. Anna and the others will likely come in later. We must wait," she demanded, her tone dense with constrained power, unspoken words. Still, no one dared question who "Jessica" was. Tatyana toppled into a heap on the cot, still covering her mouth for exposing her cousin. Lettina pulled a blanket over her, yet the women did not leave. Instead they stood or sat in a silent vigil, tiny movements exaggerated in the quiet, their unease gradually giving way to comfort within the confines of their kind, women now chastened and older than they were hours ago.

A similar vigil occurred outside the tent. Lettina stepped out to find many women had remained, some barefoot, others without heads covered in the chill, all exhausted from the demands of the day, but gathering in moonlit shadows of tall leafy sycamores and lindens that blocked light from the manor and outbuildings. Low voices protested that to which they had born witness, some in outrage.

"We are the labor force in factory and fields, yet we lack power to resist assaults. Did we expect it would be different after the war?"

"Different or worse? *Bah*, it has always been this way. But we must carry on for our families, for our old parents, and for our Church." The elder woman's heavy lids drooped as she crossed herself with two fingers, clearly a holdover of the Old Believers who must have been recruited from their settlements, those purposely dispersed among the *programmes* in an effort to dismantle their secret religious services.

"You say that," interrupted another voice. "You've lived under nothing but deprivation and sacrifice all your life, yet must the young whose idealism is—?"

"Suffering is our *zavtra*, our destiny," the woman's cracked voice interrupted. "You fancy there will be a better life? We cannot secure it for ourselves or for them. You better go to bed or you will be reported." She tightened a wool shawl around her thin shoulders and summoned the effort to march back to her tent.

"*Nyet*, it does not have to be our destiny," Lettina objected under her breath, reluctant to join the discussion. Strained murmuring followed her remarks.

"Why are you complaining? We are here because it is our duty. *'In work is honor,'*" quoted a slim woman whose flaxen hair was wet from rinsing out the chaff in the tanks behind the tent. She had the peeling sunburn of the *kolkhoznitsa*. "We are celebrated as workers. *Russki* women have strength to withstand suffering. Besides, the girls may get privileges and not have to work so hard."

A woman who appeared to be forty-five or so signaled for quiet. Despite her short stature and face lined with hints of humor she carried a sense of authority. Lettina imagined her portrait on a Soviet stamp representing workers of the Peoples' Republic. The woman slipped into prayer as she often did with the devout.

"We pray, O Lord, for the souls of the officials who cannot know Thy ways, and for the women among us who suffer hardships, cruelty, and abominations. Keep us in Your comfort, Lord, for we have nowhere to turn but to Thee," she whispered. A few heads nodded in agreement. Most turned away.

Midnight neared and women who had been too angry and upset to sleep began to retire when they heard cautious footsteps. Glancing beyond their circle they wondered if an eavesdropper had betrayed them. There would be reprisals because meetings were banned. But the abducted girls appeared from behind the bushes, finding their way to the darkened tents. Surprised, the trio paused at the outskirts of the gathering.

"O, why you are up?" A small voice ventured to speak.

"Is that you, Anna and Svetlana?" Lettina cried.

"Anna, yes. We did not see Svetlana."

Lettina stammered, but failed to intervene to question Anna. They had not seen Jessica. Perhaps she had been spared—Lettina also pressed her fist in her mouth, not knowing what to say or think.

The girls, now vaulted into maintaining the impassive dignity of womanhood, slipped through the gathering. Their hurt, their humiliation and shame intuitively honored by those present, was beyond tears or consolation. Those waiting at the vigil hid their faces in their hands and disappeared into their separate tents, pulling tent flaps closed behind them.

The rapes continued for three more nights that first week at Red Bounty *Kolkhoz*. Officials came and went under the direction of Captain Yuri Stanislov, assigned to supervise the *programme* after his commendable role in the Army's western campaign through Germany and north through the Baltics. Gone were the songs of the workers in the field. Men pulled sun hats of hastily woven rushes over their brows and bent aching backs to gather the harvest. Women formed subdued clusters of small groups, speaking in low voices among themselves. Anna's friends surrounded her at every opportunity. Masha, another of the girls forced into servicing the officials, bore a flat mask of bitter stoicism. The third girl remained unidentified, able to keep her disappearances a secret, except among her tent mates who did not expose her.

"What if it happens to us?" Katya whispered in Greita's ear.

"It won't. They pick the pretty, modern looking women."

"I never expected to appeal to men. I prefer the roles of men, field and carpenter work," Katya laughed, kissing Greita's short blondish hair with its sweet smell of the barley crop.

At dawn one morning following a series of assaults, a thin body shrouded only in a light cotton dress was found swaying from a cottonwood branch behind one of the farm buildings. A horrified pall settled over those first hearing the whispered news. The whispers spread, each more aghast, more disbelieving— denying the gossip was true. Who had found the body? Who had seen the ghostly form in the darkness beneath the trees? The authorities wouldn't have done this. It would spark a riot. Dread and speculation ran rampant one woman to the next. Men shrank from hearing or knowing, ducking back into the tents or clustering around a water barrel. Before anyone discovered who it was, the girls tried to shield Tatyana from wild rumors that swept through the camp, but she heard.

"Lana, Lana, Lana—" she screamed, the shrieks echoing through the compound. Her sharp fingernails dug into restraining arms. Small feet struck out. Older girls whisked her back into their tent and forced stolen vodka down her throat to calm her.

"Quiet! We will find Svetlana. *O Bozhe,* we feel the same, but it is too dangerous right now. You must wait, Tatiyanka. We don't know what happened." The girls huddled together pinning Tanya among them, their voices trembling. The tentacles of dawn felt as if a death sentence would descend upon them as well. Unknowns hung in the air, infiltrating every breath, every speculation.

"The officials will blame us," one said. "They won't admit fault."

"All the good we have done is undone. We are the enemy now. We will be punished."

"Why, why won't someone tell us who it was and why. Not Anna, O dear God—"

"No, she is too strong. She fights back," Lettina insisted, based on little evidence and too many occurrences to the contrary. One after another the women tried to reassure themselves and each other.

Tatyana struggled for release, her small arms throwing off those encircling her. "What more can they do to us? Let me go!" She ran out of the tent. The others followed, listening to commotion around the compound.

Shuffling sounds from the manor house meant cooks attempted to set out breakfast, though the workers were quickly dispersed. Rapid footsteps of the military to and from the house meant a charged response to the death. Women with lips pressed thin and tight, draped shawls over their shoulders. In the confusion Jessica escaped to find Tanya. They fell babbling incoherently into each other's arms, stealing precious moments before Jessica had to sneak back to the servants' quarters.

"Tanya, are you all right? It is not for you to worry. Let them take care of this."

Unabated fears rolled across Tanya's distorted face. "Do you hear me, Tanya? It is terrible, I know, but we couldn't have helped her, none of us, do you understand?" With huge gulps of air, Tanya tried to curtail hiccupping sobs and compose her face.

"I'm afraid for you, Lanenka." She stuffed the ends of her scarf into her mouth.

"*Nyet, nyet,* calm yourself. I am treated well. Please, Tanya, believe that," Jessica insisted, kissing her on both cheeks, surprising her cousin so much she was quiet in time to hear Masha confide that Emilia had been one of the abducted girls.

"Emilia? Emilia who? The shy one who served in the kitchen?" Heads nodded among the group. Jessica panicked and whispered to Tanya, "I don't work in the kitchen, don't worry. I didn't know who she was." Yet Tanya threatened to wail again in fear for Jessica.

"Hear me, I do paperwork. No one even looks at me, I promise, Cousin," Jessica pleaded. "Come, I'll bring tea to you at the back door."

A hushed inquiry continued, drawing in the other women. "You saw them take her, Masha?" asked one of the women. "Did you hear anything?"

"They dragged us upstairs to separate rooms. I cannot tell you any more, except she is—she was very pretty and cheerful." Masha's voice barely carried to those around her, her eyes on dewy grass beneath her feet.

"She didn't want it to be known. It was not my fault no one knew," Masha shot back as if being interrogated. "I only know what happened to me." She pulled down her collar to reveal red finger marks remaining on her throat.

"I am so sorry," Sasha murmured, offering an arm that Masha swept away.

"How would I know Emilia would take her life? She didn't seem to talk to anybody. I should have guessed when she did not return to our tent." Masha's reserve tumbled and she fled from the group. The women stalled going for breakfast or receiving orders for the day. They stayed in the sideyard, observing movements of the authorities at the house.

"If the girl, Emilia, were religious, she probably felt it was her fault. Maybe she couldn't take the shame," said one of her tent mates.

"Virtue after the war? There is no honor in virtue." A story of having been assaulted was etched in deep lines traced in the older woman's brow and set of her jaw. "She would have been alive today had she accepted that coarseness is the nature of men. It is human nature.

"*Nyet*, it was violence against her—she'd not want to repeat that experience, yet where else could she go? We are all trapped on the *kolkholz*." A young girl's fury ignited that of others her age. "*Chyart voz'mi*. I hate them!"

"Emilia was young. Youth camps taught us to be noble workers. She was a noble comrade. Her idealism was betrayed along with her person," Sasha said. "Being preyed upon was too heavy a burden. My heart is breaking for her and her family."

The mess hall bell clanged. The crowd moved in that direction.

"It is too late for Emilia. What can we expect from the officials now?" Sorrow enveloped them in shared experiences, for some the ravages of themselves as spoils of war just past, for others a crushing blow to their willingness to serve in a farm *programme* managed by the military.

"We did not really know Emilia or anything of her family that might have helped us understand her before this happened. It is not uncommon."

The convoy of empty trucks pulled into the farmyard at breakfast time that morning. Dmitri and Tomenko, along with other drivers, had made the night delivery of grain to the rail station without mechanical breakdowns. They returned to reload, believing that every shipment of the harvest to drought-stricken provinces represented life-saving measures for those regions, yet less food security for northern regions.

The drivers in the same dust-caked tunics and trousers they had worn for days arrived in time to see the body bag loaded into one of the official's vehicles. Tomenko lurched forward, tripping on the uneven parking area, hands reaching for the still form, choking aloud, "No, no—not Lett—" before Dmitri stopped him.

"Let it go," he said, grasping the miller's broad shoulder. "We cannot change this—whoever it is. Come." Dmitri shook the miller while his own deep hazel-grey eyes darted about.

"Leave it," he said again, this time harshly, sensing Tomenko's rash actions foolishly betrayed his involvement with one of the girls. "Christ have mercy," breathed the monk. "Lord have mercy, Christ have mercy," while he practically dragged the stumbling Tomenko after him into the mess hall. Conversation between two officers abruptly ceased when the truck drivers entered.

An older official, distinguished by an array of medals, confronted them. "You have orders to report to the field immediately. We are shorthanded. Comrade Tomenko, you pitch bundles. Comrade Dmitri, keep machines running and bring in the trucks when they are filled."

Any hopes the drivers had of breakfast or catching a few winks of sleep while their trucks were parked under the loading chute were short lived, though they had been on the road since two in the morning. Dmitri recognized the ruse immediately and it was soon confirmed by the mechanics. The cooks had notified Captain Stanislov of the grotesque sight when they set tables to serve breakfast. He had sent the workers into the fields before dawn, many without breakfast, to distract from the hanging that had stunned even the officials. Stringent regulations required him to promptly report a death in the camp. The former landowner well understood subsequent procedures. Considered a risk by officials that he would undermine harvesting efforts, he was more than willing to divulge what he knew to Dmitri, a trustworthy monk in disguise.

"The Chief of Collectivization and deputy of the current Five-Year Plan will investigate. Captain Stanislov's superiors in Leningrad who administer the drought relief will be interrogated along with other officials involved in the farm *programmes*. The Captain is already spreading rumors they will find nothing—only that 'the individual who died had been mentally unstable.'" His bitter statements revealed the education of a former representative in the Duma and the experience of having been in the inner workings of the Party. He had no illusions about how the death of a worker by hanging would be covered up. The outcome of the event also appeared quite clear in his view.

"Regardless, this unsavory affair has brought undesired attention to the Captain's management of his detachment of laborers," the man added. "The Captain has often hinted he'd like a promotion to a post other than on the collectives. Something seems to be working on him, besides this morning's incident."

Dmitri joined the others in the parking area. Drivers, mechanics, and workers all bore the brunt of orders Captain Stanislov handed down at dawn prior to his driving off to report a death on the *kolkhoz*.

"Get that thresher started. Don't stand around wasting a day," a field supervisor ordered, glancing at the new officials for approval. "Move the wagons out!" He flourished a stick at slow teams of horses before lashing their frightened haunches.

Dmitri walked past an official's car leaving with the lifeless body. Another official sped away as messenger to Novgorod with orders to telegraph Captain Stanislov's superiors in the Agriculture Management office in Moscow.

XIII

Sasha

Harvesting continued at Red Bounty *Kolkholz,* the weight of tragedy reflected in slumping shoulders and methodical steps that carried workers to the fields. They numbly toiled all day under fear of reprisals, as well as a heavy September sun that indiscriminately baked the laborers while it dried the crop. Diarrhea struck several who made frequent stops behind brambles at the edge of the field.

"I felt something bad was going to happen," one woman admitted. "I always get premonitions, but I fail to trust my feelings. Not that it would have helped."

Tanya vomited several times during the first few hours, becoming so weak she could barely lift her arms to stack bundles. A young man, his face scared from burns, came to help. Alarmed by her desperate expression, he managed to share a bit of his own experience.

"*Mne ochen'zhal', malyshka.* I am sorry, Tatyana. I wanted to die once like the young girl, but I am glad I am alive."

Tanya took his proffered hand and felt the warmth of his compassion. He reminded her of gentle cousin Pasha, a tender soul thrust unwittingly into a brutal world of conquer or be conquered. She eagerly embraced the comfort, anxious to spill her fears for cousin Svetlana. Most of all, she wanted to plead to be sent home or be dead, too, if Lana were injured in any way.

Sensing her despair, the young man spoke gently. "You must go on living, *ne vazhno chto,* no matter what."

His words were lost to Tatyana whose eyes flashed with an awakening attraction to a man, this kind man whose attentiveness aroused a latent desire, an unfamiliar rush that swept like rivulets through her blood, tempting her to fold herself into his protective arms. Flushing with embarrassment, she dashed strange feelings and ducked away. At noon, she wilted on the field grass at the edge of the women's circle, privately nursing the few moments of tenderness with the young man, yet overhearing a conversation that was far less heartening.

"Work is the best antidote," cautioned a psychologist, who claimed to have worked in the trenches of mental health in Moscow hospitals serving veterans during the war, until she was recruited for the harvest. She conveyed a sense of authority with her experience and her graying yet stylish upswept hair. "I witnessed innumerable cases of soldier's mind and suicidal depression in our clinics. Some patients recover, some do not."

Sasha confronted the statement that sounded callous. "We fail poor Emilia who was exploited," her candid remarks breaking an unwritten rule of speaking in indirect terms if at all. Tanya shifted her position on the grass to Sasha's side, seeking elusive comfort.

"Depression is endemic in Russia," the psychologist said. "Half the population hardly knows otherwise. How could we fail others when we are the same as they? At the clinic we do the best we can." She invoked the war, lack of food and goods, and now drought in support of her observations. Her forceful tone quieted the conversation for a time, her audience knowing that a staunch party professional would laud success over adversity regardless.

Dismissing the risk of being reported, Sasha pursued her thoughts. "But the senseless loss of a young life? I cannot reconcile that with comrade ideals. What a terrible thing if the poor girl feared she was to blame. One's faith in the Republic and in the Church should feel supportive in times of crises, not punishing."

When the psychologist left to relieve herself behind the trees, the others talked more freely. "What faith? An empty story we no longer accept. Do you not realize it rings hollow at times like this?"

Tanya shuddered, her lips moving frantically in prayer for Jessica, her own faith alternately supported and denigrated by these women.

Sasha took the opportunity to share her views with those who might be open to further discussion. "Sacrifice and suffering must have meaning. That purpose is for healing, rather than earning a reward in heaven. I believe it has to do with the way we view suffering and oppression."

"That is blasphemous, Sasha," interrupted a woman who glanced about to be sure the psychologist had not returned. Who would believe that suffering is not for salvation? The Orthodox would be the first to condemn that kind of thinking."

"I have been steeped in Orthodoxy also," Sasha persisted, "but the ancient *starets* teach we are born divine and have no need of salvation. These are the early teachings of the monks of the Amalfon Monastery on Mount Athos."

Tanya did not know if Sasha's reproachful look at the other woman indicated she did not agree with her or whether she frowned upon the stated teaching of the Church. "In these times of atheism and nihilism, it is good to question everything, to separate the wheat from chaff as we are doing here every day."

"It is heresy to question," said another.

Tanya cringed and pulled her short dress over her knees. The charges back and forth felt like physical blows to her traditional beliefs, once the province of Russian peasants. Her simple faith seemed assailed and dismantled in front of her, yet also deepened by Sasha's searching. Tanya's spiritual life had existed in safe-keeping of the underground religious and alive only in St. Sebastian's Church in Konsky these past few years. She had threaded her discipleship between that of her parish priest and Jessica's disavowal of affiliation.

Sensing Tatyana's fragility, Sasha added, "There must be voluntary submission to have sacrifice."

"Submitting to tyranny is martyrdom," interjected the skeptic.

"I mean sacrificing for others, not sacrificing for oneself," Sasha clarified. "There is power in giving, not that we want power but that it creates miracles, *da*." She released a long breath and looked down. "I know from my own experience. That belief led me to study medicine as a graduate student before I was sent to a factory then here to the farm. But right now I am speaking of spiritual healing."

"Tell us, where is God in the healing?" another woman said. "He was not here last night."

"Talk, talk, talk. *'Na miru i smert' krasna. With company even death loses its sting'*," Ludmila said. "We are not addressing our grief nor the anguish and suffering that led to the girl, Emilia, to take her life."

Yet talk continued as if it might absolve everyone of guilt; as if there were a reason for one hanging oneself; as if it might undo the unthinkable—talk as if it would make sense of their insecure world and make it a safer place.

"It is we who must do the healing," Sasha insisted, signaling they needed to listen.

"*Pshaw*," spit out the critic. "You are wasting your time, Sasha. This nonsense will be reported and get us all in trouble."

Theology aside, cursing and anger split the quietude of the field for the remainder of the day. Both men and women rehashed happenings leading up to the hanging, as if to explain how one could die an isolated death in the midst of so many harvest workers, their labors in unity if not their individual loyalties. The tragedy drew the laborers back to the image of the lifeless body suspended from the tree, whether they had witnessed it with their own eyes or were told of the occurrence. Sasha's higher purposes were dismissed as being too unrealistic to contemplate right now.

At dusk, fatigued to the point of illness and weeping, Tanya followed the field workers to the mess hall, washed, and sat down for supper. Captain Stanislov did not appear. The official bedecked with medals, a stranger in camp, made a brief announcement.

"The family of the young woman who died has been notified. We will resume harvesting with greater diligence to fulfill our obligations to our comrades residing in the South."

That night a lantern was left in the rear seat of a private car belonging to one of the officials. Kerosene spilled inches from the flame. A kerosene-soaked rag on a stick fed into the tank of petrol. The explosion at three a.m. woke the camp, all except for Katya who had not slept.

At the blast, Jessica's bare feet hit the floor running as did others in the manor house. She grabbed a dishtowel on her way through the kitchen to disguise herself, tying it low over her brow and covering her hair. Again she took the opportunity of a crisis to flee to Tanya's side. They met a crowd gathering in the dark at a blackened hulk. Leaping flames still shot over crumpled, disintegrating parts of a vehicle.

"Tanechka, you must be brave. *O, chort* we will all be blamed. Now hear me, this may be my last chance to speak with you for awhile—no, no, don't cry." She loosened Tanya's grip from her arms.

"I am so afraid for you, Jessica—." Tanya's teeth rattled. The predawn autumn chill crept inside the girls' nightwear.

"Believe me, the – uh—Captain has been kind to me—"

A howl escaped Tanya's lips. "Not the Captain—*nyet*! Not with him. He forced us to come to this terrible place."

"Listen, I am in no danger. Now shush before we are reported."

Tanya could only nod, her eye sockets sunken in deep hollows.

"I will be all right, whatever comes of this. Do you hear me?" Jessica's voice conveyed the authority she had used over her cousin at their apartment. "I think Captain Stanislov is in trouble. With the death of a farmworker there are sure to be consequences. *Da*, poor Emilia."

Searching for a means of comfort to leave with Tanya, she said, "I don't know what the orders are for next week, but whatever happens, you must remember Pasha. You must get back to him. Remember the violin. He still needs your help."

The words conveyed the truth to the extent Svetlana could reveal it. She sensed Tanya stiffening as if she struggled with an inner battle of nerves and emerged stronger. Hardened before her sixteenth birthday, she reflected the distant, battered-by-circumstances resignation of elderly women in the camp.

Jessica patted her back, relieved to have given her another focus, another outlet for her steadfast but often hysterical devotion. A flood light came on and swept over the pale faces of the crowd, prompting women to duck under cover of the tents. Jessica retraced her steps to the back door of the servants' quarters.

Men who had worked in the fields rushed forward with shovels to contain the fire. They threw dirt on flames that flickered and spread along the perimeter of dry grass. Swift glances among them queried each other about the cause of the explosion, eliciting almost imperceptible shakes of their heads denying they were involved.

"Beware the grain trucks. Keep back," shouted the older official, not knowing if the trucks were rigged to explode as well. In military fashion, the authorities prepared for the worst. Armed guards circled the compound, searching with torches for anyone lurking about. They ordered a water tank to be filled and hauled by horse-drawn wagons to the parking area for other emergencies. The flood light remained on for the remainder of the night. Acting aggressively, the supervisors sought to rectify the present situation and forestall further damage, knowing that sabotage and fire would lead to someone's demotion, if not a sentence to Leningrad's Kresty prison or to the Butyrskaya in Moscow.

Captain Stanislov had not yet returned by the next morning. Lacking an office assignment, Jessica threw herself into work in the kitchen, plunging bare arms into the great tub of hot water for washing dishes, pots and pans. The suds tickled their way inside the sleeves of her light dress, and made her laugh, an inexplicable bizarre humor after a mostly sleepless night and series of mind-numbing events.

"I sound as hysterical as Tanya, but I can do this—as well as what comes next, and next after that. You'll not see me hanging from a tree," she vowed half aloud. Hastily avoiding the imagery, she turned to two dark Tartar women who spoke a mysterious tongue-twisting language of Eastern countries under the Soviet Republic. But words spilled from Jessica's mouth as if they could understand, as if she could no longer contain them.

"We must have it nice and clean for Captain Stanislov. Clean." She swiped a cloth over tubs used as a sink. "And good food prepared, the best in the house. We must not fail now. You hear?"

Their curious eyes met her outburst, recognizing only the word "Captain." They nodded and smiled, and resumed their methodical pace as before, while Jessica whirled about like a sparrow caught inside a screened porch. Morning cleanup was barely finished when it was time to begin cooking the evening meal. Five-and ten-gallon Red Army kettles heated water on low gas burners, while Jessica, the kitchen women, and half a dozen others from the field peeled potatoes and diced onions for soup. Always, the pot of cabbage simmered on the back of a woodstove. They made dozens of loaves of coffee-laced black bread, its fresh-baked smell drifting from the stove's enormous oven. Aroma of fennel, caraway seeds, and vinegar enhanced the baking according to the whims of the bakers and ingredients left in the former landowner's pantry.

At last Jessica sank into a kitchen chair, releasing a long pent up breath. "I was scared to death last night, but today I'm more in charge of myself, at least at this moment." A new sense of competence emerged, bolstered by coffee and adrenalin. Her fingers flew over the paperwork, compiling freight lists and bills from local businesses, according to previous instructions. Yet images persisted of the body hanging from the tree, a scene that she had not actually witnessed. The car's charred undercarriage, still smoking tires, and shattered glass remained out front for all to see. Her mind reeled with the staggering recent events.

Harvesting will surely end soon. Tanya and I, Lettina and all of us will be sent back home. Prayers streamed automatically, the only way she could reach them now despite a deep down, persistent voice denigrating divine intervention. To Vladimir Lenin, "there is nothing more abominable than religion." The men may attack us, but they cannot crush us. If there is a God, *pozhaluysta* help us before something else happens. Biting her ragged nails to the quick, she found her new confidence besieged by old doubts.

Captain Stanislov came in late after she had fallen asleep at the kitchen table, her head on her arm over the neatly organized paperwork. The cooks had retired to the assigned servants' quarters.

"I need you," Captain Stanislov said waking her, his exhausted voice low, husky.

Jolted to her feet, Jessica shifted from one world of nightmares to another of unknowns.

"Svetlana, come," he ordered firmly, motioning her to follow him up narrow stairs strung with ragged tapestry-like carpeting held over from better times. The newfound pool of resolve gave her enough strength to rise and her legs to act independently of herself.

A few days later skies became overcast with ragged blue-black clouds chasing the last of open skies over low distant ridges. The sharp voices of the officials betrayed the tension behind plans to transfer to other harvest sites.

"Prepare to move to four different farms. Due to circumstances, we are late in completing the harvest here," bawled the superintendent, a citizen underling who imitated the military by insinuating workers were responsible for the delay. "A storm may set in, comrades. Report to your stations."

Previous chatter among field workers became hushed conversations; seasoned bodies bent to their tasks. Stubble left in the fields formed harsh yellow stems that etched bare legs and ankles while workers made a final sweep to clear the crop.

As predicted, blame had already been placed squarely upon the laborers. These maneuvers by the officials had origins that Svetlana recognized, their fear as palpable as her own when Captain Stanislov forced himself upon her, the gut-wrenching fear of the powerless. Ashamed, she vowed like Anna that she would never, ever tell her parents what happened to her on the *kolkholz*, and sealed the vow with hot tears. The chipped green paint on the ceiling of his bedroom had strayed in and out of her vision. At once she re-experienced the feeling of being a captive recruit, unable to alter her fate. Except this personal violation drowned her senses until she collapsed into a foggy consciousness where rationality gave way to sensuality; a horror of passion and instinctual responses told her this was adulthood.

She had pleaded, "*Pozhaulstra*, I want to go home."

Captain Stanislov laughed, a short grunt. She wanted to bite him and hated herself for small whimpers that would not stop. He'd see her as a child. That part of her rebelled. She was not a shrinking baby this soldier took to bed.

He doesn't know me. Not his kitchen maid or street woman or war conquest. No way is Yuri going to steal my dreams. Yet the next day she had become violently sick washing the ruined sheets of the virgin's bed; he'd already stolen that.

Battles waged in her mind, abhorrence with private dignity, revulsion with concession, both a woman's kaleidoscope of awakened responses. Mired in a daytime delirium, Svetlana suppressed both in an angry, fitful denial of "not me." Yet at night she succumbed to "a woman's place," the Captain's words, according to his whims, a place where nothing made sense, not the Captain's gentle entreaties, not the strange virile male odor, not the astoundingly soft down bedding that would have thrilled her in other circumstances. But the forces of nature, his nature, were against her that night and the following three days and nights during which he exercised authority over the laborers in public, and became a predator in private.

When he had taken her to bed for the fourth time the previous night, Captain Stanislov confronted her anger and resistance. "You are wasting your time rejecting me, Svetlana. I am the supervisor here. No one need know about us, and if so, to whom would they report?" A hint of pride and superiority softened his low, throaty voice. "But I would be grateful if you could find it in yourself to be willing. Would that be so difficult? Surely you want more of life than what you had at the factory or what we have now in camp."

His smooth pale face had been quiet, his light blue eyes honestly concerned. He half turned, resting his bare shoulders and blond-haired chest on one elbow. Twisting a cigarette stub between his thumb and forefinger, he appeared open, even eager for her to share the intimacy.

"*Nyet, nyet*—," echoes of Anna's resistance strained Svetlana's voice, distanced her even more from him, from the actual assaults that bruised her body inside and out, a horrific first time experience that erased any shred of romantic love stories. *Nyet, nyet*, it wouldn't happen to her, but it did, and the loss of innocence hardly balanced her entry into womanhood, all forced by a fit young man who now pleaded for her to be receptive.

O, Bozhe moy, he will hurt me if I refuse or worse if I report it. Ensnared in a twisting double life herself, wanting and not wanting, gagging and being repulsed, resisting and being transformed in the resisting; she was too exhausted to perceive it for what it was. His overtures and implied promises drew her to him; his arrogance and underlying threats scared her. Her nerves were stressed to breaking, verging on an outbreak of eczema she had experienced before. The constant shifts destroyed her appetite and reduced the little weight she had gained. Again her hips showed bony outlines through her thin print dress. After his initial demands, Captain Stanislov tried to be patient, soothing her by charm and flattery. Yet his understanding and consideration soon alternated with impatient demands.

Svetlana bore his alternating personas with gritted teeth; one, her supervisor at the *kolkhoz*, the other a willful lover attempting to engage on his own terms, both exercising superiority over her. He acted as if nothing had changed between them since they worked in the library before the tragedy and explosion, yet he took advantage of her every night.

Unable to face the field workers, Svetlana took quick meals with tea in the kitchen and slipped back to the library to process the stacks of work Yuri left for her. But her mind replayed images of a recent release, *Duel in the Sun*, with Gregory Peck as Lewt, a film she had seen with Lettina and Anna in Konsky—Lewt's aggression, Yuri's commands; Lewt's compelling manner, Yuri's manipulations—

"Da, I cannot sort it out, I am so upset," Jessica plowed through each succeeding day that fueled an unquenchable rage tempered by forbidden fantasies. From the library, she fled to the kitchen to wash dishes and clean until late at night, experiencing for the first time what it felt like to be unleashed from the solidity and relative safety of home, factory, even the Church that she cared little about. Cast away from all that was known, she found herself pleading in desperate litanies like her mother's, then chaffed at her own disbelief.

"It's not my fault," she maintained. "Not the woman I wanted to be. Lettina, Anna and I learned of the good life from American movies! Now look at us. We can't undo what has happened to us. We are trapped, *my okazalis' v lovushke. Posmotri na nas*—our dreams of the future now desolate fantasies in a pointless vacuum. But I do not want to go back to Konsky or the factory."

While Svetlana kept records in order inside, Captain Stanislov commanded the farm workers without mercy, forcing them to knuckle down and complete the harvesting. "We must meet grain quotas. I have orders from Moscow," he announced at every meal, an unstated threat that hovered over the weary heads of the laborers who kept their eyes on their plates.

Svetlana overheard officials saying in private conversations. ""Break up the mob. There could be more explosions. Send them to separate farms or there will be mob rule."

The officials are scared, and I am glad, she thought. That is the double life Yuri lives—taking me at will, but subject to higher authorities himself. *Bah*, this whole farm *programme* stinks!

Yet Yuri persisted. This morning he had stroked her hair, his fingers gently lifting the curling ends and caressed the side of her neck. "You are beautiful," he breathed, his eyes searching hers, asking almost apologetically for acceptance, while he trailed his palms over her breasts, her blood pulsing beneath his hands. Svetlana wrenched herself away, puzzled by his contradictions.

"You want finery and nice clothes. I know you, Svetlana. I saw you in the red silk blouse, remember? With me, you could have anything you want," he whispered in her ear.

Had she not heard those words from the sarcastic housekeeper, Evangelina? These thoughts hammered her brain and made her temples ache. Against her will, against portraying herself as a child, she uttered, "O, I am so afraid." She had tried to rise from the bed and leave the room, but he had pulled her back.

"Think about it, Svetlana," he had challenged. "Do you think I want to spend my life on the cursed farms? I have plans. You and I, we want the same things. You have no idea what the future could hold for us, if no one gets in my way." Distracted, his faraway look told her that he had turned to his own dreams, or worries, she did not know which.

Thwarted dreams? The Captain has dreams which the rest of us are not allowed to have? Not dreams of riches, that's not possible now or ever in Russia. And plans? He is trying to trick me, yet it is true, we want something better. She gulped down feeble hopes, hiding any hint of the ambivalence his entreaties aroused in her.

I cannot give in, not for myself, not for Anna, not for Emilia. If I give in even a little, he will take me away, I know it—and I want to, but I don't want to—truly, we are used like serfs. Yet she shuddered at what felt like her own greed, desire, and rebellion, all raising their ugly heads beyond constraints of her past, her parents, the Church, her own sensibility when she saw Lettina with Tomenko. And now I am no different, *da*. She could feel the hollows of her stomach draw in as if in condemnation.

Her strength was still sapped hours later when she dismantled the pantry and packed supplies belonging to the government as well as those of the landowners according to orders. Sinking deeply into what felt like the wreckage of her soul, Jessica was barely aware of whole hams being secreted out the back door. Local farmers sent surrogates to lift their property before it was lifted by someone else. Jessica had seen previous landholders also raid kitchens when the harvesting crews were moving out. At last, to avoid any accusation of collusion with the thieves, she attached herself to the laundry detail outside.

"Run cotton blankets through the wringer two or three times so they will dry faster," a woman there told her.

Empty grain trucks, notably missing the cantankerous Ford, edged in to transport laborers and supplies to four separate harvesting camps. Jessica's anxiety soared knowing she would likely be separated from Tanya. Stone-faced women went through the motions of moving, discovering friends would be sent to other farms, their newly minted emotional and spiritual support lost to the indifferent, over-arching strategy of "break up the mobs."

At noon, a towering bald official new to the camp, ordered all work crews to appear in a group. "We will move east beyond Novgorod to four farms. You will be assigned to new teams. Everything here must be dismantled for hauling, even the wagons, and loaded onto trucks *nemedlenno*, immediately. We are short a truck due to mechanical problems, therefore compact everything and pile it high on the other trucks. Beware of theft. The *kulaks* are stealing food and grain, and hoarding supplies we need to meet production goals."

He left nothing to chance. Jessica heard rumors that the official came directly from the Farm Program Agency in Moscow. He commanded Captain Stanislov, who oversaw every detail of preparations for the move. The Captain had left the bedchamber before dawn that morning, and Svetlana had not seen him until now. When he had a moment, he appeared at her elbow while she hung sheets on the clothesline.

"I will take you away from this today. Now is your chance, Svetlana." His voice sounded tender, and a glint of excitement sparked his eyes. A half smile she had not seen before softened his lips. "You will wear the red blouse I saw you wearing on the bus from Konsky."

"Where—where are you—?" a warble emerged from Jessica's constricted throat, unable to respond to what sounded like an invitation veiled in authority.

"To Leningrad. You will enjoy the advantages. Go now. You will find the baths in the manor house. And nicely scented soap."

Blood pooled in Jessica's body, leaving her head spinning, her face ashen. Instantly, in what seemed madness, she knew he was right. *I do want more. This may be my chance, a chance to be myself, to be* who I want to be. It cannot be all bad if it is my dream, too. The red blouse. A dream she'd had for fashions had come true. A talisman she determined to hang on to. It meant a way out of here.

Moments later, however, the question of unknowns, risks, and betrayal intervened. She grabbed a washboard and rubbed stained work pants with her bare knuckles, as if she could fend off the whole world and do as she pleased; fend off the feeling she would betray Anna and Emilia and herself. She scrubbed harder; madness clouded her vision like steam boiling from the tub of laundry. She choked back what felt like chunks of dreams, muttering, "I cannot be weak and stupid and let him own me. What would my friends think?"

The haze began to clear. She found her senses and admonished herself for letting her frail hopes gain a foothold. After all we witnessed? After the offhand exploitation of the girls night after night? After Emelia hung herself, her situation no less than mine? After the arson? Why am I even thinking these things? *Bah*! Lettina is right. I have seen too many romantic movies. Movies with happy endings. Ugh, whichever I chose will not have a happy ending. He will be furious and hurt me some way. Or I will hurt everyone I care about. I will not be able to face myself.

But her worn oxford shoes heavily protested each step into the house toward the baths. She poured quantities of hot water in the cast iron bathtub and soaked, salving the inner twenty-year-old with lathers of soap, an almost unknown commodity, until the water turned cold.

"I don't know what is happening to me—I cannot help myself anyway—." The crimson-red silk blouse and slim black gabardine skirt lay folded in their original box as if they were new, still lovingly enveloped in the carnival-colored wrapping paper, all long protected in the bottom of Jessica's travel bag. But now, after what had been alternately sordid, reprehensible, and yes, semi-consensual nights when she learned she was desirable, she felt she was putting the clothing on someone else.

This other person could not resist envisioning the trim athletic male, comfortable in his body, confident in his relations with her. The Captain's authority told her one thing, his need told her another.

Dashing the thoughts, she fought down an involuntary surge of longing for an ideal love of her own, for the fantasy she and her friends shared for years when they smoked in the park, when men their age were at the Front. Later when most were lost or crippled in long campaigns their hopes had plummeted. "Will we be old women in shopping queues who have no one and wait for nothing?" they had asked, appalled they would even think such a thing.

"I do not know where this is going, where I am going," she breathed as if she were talking with friends. To herself she confessed, I am a fool, but I am a woman like Lettina with Tomenko. I want what I want, and I want to be pleased with how I look. *O, chyort voz'mi!* These buttons will not button. With a yank she nearly ripped the silk-covered, pearl-shaped buttons from the silk blouse.

On impulse, she rifled the bureau drawers for clip-on earrings belonging to the former owner's wife, routed from her belongings by collectivization. Finding none, she picked up a small mirror with a quaint, carved ivory handle and, after a glimpse of herself, flung it against the far wall. Shattered with it was a sense of who she had been before her birthday, before the farms, before the rapes. She knew her reflection would forever betray traces of bitterness that she now saw in Anna's face.

Quiet reigned outside the farmhouse when Svetlana emerged, preoccupied with thoughts of the past, not of her immediate future. It had all begun with Madame Marsolet and her reserved, gentlemanly husband, Monsieur Marsolet, whom she had met at their boutique in Konsky. Again she felt Madame's immediate understanding, as a mother of a daughter, how important Jessica's twentieth birthday was to her; that Jessica needed a measure for attaining womanhood. She recalled looking no further than Monsieur's obvious approval for confirmation. As a calloused-handed boot maker in a wretched factory dominated by male supervisors, he lit in her a touching sense of preciousness she thought lost in childhood, a time when her mother smiled at her and her father beamed his approval. Tears formed under her lids; she had never expected to regain that warm feeling of well being.

The tall and elegant proprietors of the boutique remained her sole benefactors, privately sustaining her throughout the months on the collectives, while she worked her fingers raw and sold her soul for a vision. As Svetlana, she since claimed them in her heart, drew on the complements that she was beautiful, and found they unwittingly encouraged or even crystallized her desire to become a fashion designer. That image took possession of herself wearing the crimson red blouse and black gabardine skirt, and not by choice, the heavy leather shoes made in Benyanske's. The view influenced a studied runway stroll toward the waiting car.

Captain Stanislov brightened at her approach until he noticed the footwear. "We will have to do something about those. I cannot say much for national footwear if this is an indication." His smile softened his cheeks above a clean shaven jaw accented by the small mustache. With a hint of boyishness yet maintaining a formal manner, he opened the passenger side door of the pre-war blue Opal two-door coup, its prominent headlights projecting from either side of a small rounded chrome radiator. To him, and to anyone who might have observed, Captain Yuri Stanislov had caged his pigeon.

In the car Svetlana's lips went white, her spirit of moments ago taking flight as surely as they drove toward the improbable destination of Leningrad. Not knowing where else to look, she stared at her hands in her lap, hands peeled by harsh lye soaps and puckered by the almost boiling hot water of the kitchen and laundry. Her fingernails were clean but ragged, too short for comfort, in contrast to her finery. She was aware her companion turned to admire her, rather than keeping an eye on the road.

"Appearances are nothing, *ser*," she whispered in self-defense.

"Appearances are everything in Leningrad, *ma bien-aimee bella.*"

Without replying, Svetlana forced herself to think of good people in her life who would not agree with so bland a belief. Abbot Konstantin, Brother Dmitri and Agata Illyinicha, even Mme. Marsolet who sensed her deep down yearnings fueled by American movies, would not likely rate appearance as a most salient feature, though at this moment Jessica felt they were the most beautiful humans alive. Given her position, she could not argue, but citing them was a means of rejecting Captain Stanislov and his appraisal. She felt very much like the shoemaker she had been or a miller's daughter or a peasant's daughter, though she knew these last were not her story. Now I understand how *Mat* might have felt, Jessica mused, startled that Vera likely had romantic ideas before she became the displaced, disillusioned woman whose loyalties clung to Old Russia.

"Wait and you will see I am right about appearances," Captain Stanislov persisted, intruding upon her reflections. "I think you will be pleased. *La ville est grand avec l'art et la museque*," he said.

"Museums? I know so little about culture—I—I would feel very out of place." The allure of the former capital, Leningrad, seemed overwhelming and the prospect of strange social settings daunting. Besides, his French felt like an affectation compared to the charming authenticity of Madame and Monsieur Marsolet.

"Perhaps you should take me back."

"You want to go back to that dead end work. It will never change in *Rossiya*. Do not complain if you do not like it." The Captain's neck reddened above the starched collar of his uniform. "You set yourself up as a modern girl, a woman, now act like one. This is what you wanted, Svetlana."

Who is this man I am with? Jessica asked, turning her face away, words frozen in her throat. His words and impatience pierced Jessica's reserve; he saw in her the person she aspired to be. How could he, a government tool, know her heart? Or have identified her in peasant-style dresses on the farm after she lost so much weight? Alarmed at his insight, she feared he could see into her mind and force himself into her dreams, raising an even more revolting assault than being raped.

Why am I am letting myself do this? This is a terrible mistake. Tense moments passed. Yuri's lips pouted, trying to curtail further outbursts. With rising terror, she put her hand on the car door, envisioning Anna screaming and fighting to free herself, but she did not pull the handle. The collision of worlds, inside and out, drained her body and destroyed any resolve she had to resist.

Unseen was the golden countryside interspersed amid fading tank treads and evidence of troop movements of recent years over open land and in forests of northwestern Russia. Unnoticed was the throbbing pulse in the Captain's jaw. The little four-cylinder auto crunched its way over rough two-track dirt roads until it hit the thoroughfare to Novgorod and took the pock-marked Moskva-Leningrad highway north. Jessica picked at her hangnails until they bled, withdrawn for the remainder of the trip to Leningrad.

"Is this the way it is going to be, Svetlana?" the Captain demanded.

XIV

Oleg

Newly implemented rules at Red Bounty *Kolkhoz* required dispersal of small gatherings of workers. Guards on twenty-four hour duty effectively locked down the collective.

Orders, supposedly delivered privately to officials and attendants in the manor house spread to truck driver, Brother Dmitri, and field workers within minutes. They knew authorities were running scared, not knowing how or where the next hostile act by the laborers might come. Trucks loaded with machinery, tractors, tents and supplies, in addition to crews, sped from the scene of death and arson, headed toward the main highway beyond Novgorod, where they would diverge to harvest sites on four different farms.

"Break up the mob! Break up the mob!" became the driving force behind the strategy to prevent suspected subversive activities.

The constant pressure to hurry jangled Dmitri's nerves, but he managed to leverage the ancient binder and thresher onto low trailers and secure them with sturdy iron J-bolts scavenged from bombed out railroads. He determined the awkward binder, used to cut and tie sheaves of grain, was securely strapped on before pulling out of the country lane into traffic. On the road his mind flashed back to the early '40s. The shock of seeing the body bag had stirred vivid scenes of the Germans overrunning hometowns, his own and neighbors. The loss of innocent life drowned his senses until he saw only past atrocities, not the blurred passing of slow lorries, swift military vans, or wavering farm vehicles around him. His palm swiped under his stuffy nose, the chaff a constant irritant, emotions draining from eyes and throat.

Flashbacks left him fleeing at the beginning of the war, still raising bile in his stomach. He feared for his own descent into insanity if he remained in Poland and fled to the monastery, his conscience forbidding him to participate in the killing. Prone to anxiety, he now forced his thoughts back to the sweet serenity of the monastery, the protective stone enclosure lying along the foothills. Surely he had been privileged to find solace there, even if for so short a time. Its sense of timelessness and calm eased his breathing now.

Ahead of him, the truck driven by Tomenko lurched and swayed under its load in a disconcerting manner. The disturbing elements around "breaking up the mob" were compounded by loss of opportunity to see the girls or ascertain the reason for the explosion, though he guessed it might have been in retaliation for the rapes. The long days of labor he could handle, but given these incidents, he found it impossible to feel even the remotest spirit of God the Father, Jesus the Christ, or the Holy Spirit. Stripped of this armor, he had a foreboding feeling about workers being separated from the group and the heightened security that prevailed. Depression settled into the sagging folds of his leathery face and pulled the corners of his mouth into hiding amid his shaggy gray, chaff-filled beard.

At the first small farm, Dmitri was directed to unload the binder at the edge of the oat field in preparation for an early start the next morning. He had released the tie-downs when a Universal tractor with giant iron wheels arrived to tow the binder off the trailer. He recognized the tractor as one made in Kharkiv, Ukraine, a familiar model on Eastern European farms for over fifteen years. The driver, a youthful lad with a jaunty air had driven the tractor much too fast across the field. He swung the tractor around in place behind the trailer, grinding the gears and squealing the clutch. With engine running, he propped his arm over the steering wheel and sat waiting for the older man to attach the tow bar.

He would give me a hand if he had been raised on a farm like I had, Dmitri growled, but they get neophytes from the city. In no mood for the young man's self-satisfied, unconcerned attitude, Dmitri stepped between the tractor and trailer to handle the job himself. With no signal given to move, the lad leaned hard on the throttle. He jumped at the roar of power, his foot slipping from the clutch. Still in reverse, the tractor lurched backwards. To self-correct the lad floored the accelerator instead of hitting the brake. Ribbed tracks on the wheels designed for driving in mud ground up the earth, hurling dirt higher than the men and crashed the tractor into the trailer. The clash of iron on iron split the air, drowning Dmitri's cries.

"*Mishot! Piristot*! Stop! *Aaaaaaahhhhhh* ,"the big man keeled instantly with a monstrous groan, his right leg caught in the vise between tractor wheel and the end of the trailer. Panicking, the youth figured out his mistake and tugged at gears. The tractor weaved forward as if uncertain of its function, and stood idling, prepared to reverse its course again. The lad leapt from the seat and ran back. The truck driver lay on the ground folded into a fetal position, writhing in pain.

Abandoning the tractor and Dmitri, the youth ran across the field calling for help. Minutes passed before he convinced anyone there had been a serious accident, and that they must come at once. By the time one of the attendants contacted an official and the official car arrived on the scene, Dmitri had slipped in and out of consciousness. A rush of endorphins had flooded his prone body, numbing his knee and leg.

"*Izvinite*, sorry, *ser*. Sorry, I didn't mean…I didn't know the tractor was in reverse…" blurted the young man, nervously thrusting his hands in and out of his pockets. "Truthfully, I did not know he was going to step behind the tractor," he added in self-defense to anyone who would listen.

"Shut off the damn tractor," the medic ordered, "and let me examine the man."

Reviving Dmitri with a dash of cold water, the official, whom Dmitri had seen at the temporary camp infirmary, examined the angle of the leg and asked questions, both Dmitri and the lad competing to answer, neither having the presence of mind to be credible. Dmitri minimized the extent of the injury, while the lad, jabbering incoherently in fear of being disciplined, protested that this was the first farm he had worked on and that he had been an architecture student before he was recruited for the farm program.

The doctor found damage primarily in and around the knee with tendons and ligaments crushed and leg bones forced out of alignment. The kneecap appeared to be shattered, news Dmitri accepted with a grimace, as well as the prognosis of a lengthy, if ever, recovery.

"I do not know how we are going to manage here without you," the official finally said, "but I am sending you to Moscow for medical treatment."

Quickly ordering evacuation on a stained military stretcher, an official dispatched a government van with orders to "get him back here as soon as possible, even if he is on crutches."

The oblique compliment was not lost on Dmitri, but he held a firm belief that even as the outside world went on as before without him when he joined a cloistered community, it would continue on here without him as well.

Peasant life in the small village of Thor maintained traditions a great deal older than the village itself. One cherished tradition was the market that occurred just before the first frost blackened the gardens, coinciding with early pagan festivals honoring Poludnitsa, goddess of the harvest, a time when peasants put a few stems of rye behind the icons in their homes. Brother Anton organized preparations at St. Sansais Monastery and Vineyards for Thor's last market of the season. With their cart, formerly towed by Dmitri, they joined the increased numbers of vendors, shoppers, and pilgrims who filled the roads leading to the village. Among them were gypsy wagons piled high with handmade or traded wares, and bearing musicians and dancers for their once-a-year participation in the market. Their trademark *chastushka*, simple rhyming songs, and tin flutes were heard long before the wagons came into sight.

The children of Thor climbed gnarled limbs of oaks to get a first glimpse of the gypsy parade, while thin mongrels ran in circles, barking at any excuse to join the excitement. The clattering of tin pans and silver bells heralded the arrival of small, lively horses, shaking their long shaggy manes and prancing in the swirling dust on the outskirts of the village. The gypsies hastily set up camp in an open meadow long used by their ancestors and generally avoided by superstitious local people. They had carried baskets of smartly crafted tinware and beaded jewelry across the road to the market by the time the cart from St. Sansais trundled into town.

Brother Anton, Brother Vessaly and Pavel Ivanovich applied their shoulders to the rear of the obstinate two-wheeled outfit, turning it into a corner of the marketplace. Hounds immediately sounded a chorus of "owww-ooos" at the flowing robes of the two monks, the howls joining the merry bedlam of the gypsies.

Pavel laughed, guarding his lightly clad heels against dog bites, though he wore the conventional loose pants and tunic of his countrymen. "What a welcome! Is it always like this?"

"Not quite, Brother. The gypsies set the dogs on edge." Vessaly made sure everyone knew he was not enjoying the meleé as much as Pavel.

"Look, a rainbow," Pavel exclaimed, indicating bouquets of sunflowers, zinnias, daisies, brown-eyed Susans and coneflowers that reflected their brilliance over bins of scrubbed potatoes, carrots and cabbage of the vendors.

All of the region from Konsky on north past the monastery appeared to be represented in the streets of Thor, as well as from enclaves known only to the gypsies who traveled far to the east, south, and often over borders to their countries of origins to the west. Bright flames of vendors' braziers sent pork-scented smoke over the market, alerting townspeople that sausages would soon be sold along with liverwurst and spears of fish, the burly cooks reveling in the biggest event of the year.

No sooner was the cart from the monastery in its place, the baskets and burlap bags of garden produce displayed, than Pavel drifted away from the stall, first to one vendor then the next, admiring the goods, cheerily greeting the women, and doffing his small cap to the men.

Brother Anton looked askance toward his charge. "I wonder if it was wise to bring Pavel to market today of all days. The stimulation may be too much for his mind."

"If he wanders off, we may not find him. In any event, I do not want to upset Father Konstantin," replied Brother Vessally, visibly shaken by the prospect.

"One of us should mind the cart and one of us accompany him," suggested Anton. He handed a pocketful of change to Vessaly for tending the sales. Anton trailed after Pavel, now at the farthest end of the market shaking hands with a tall sober-looking gentleman whose wife stood quietly behind him.

"Brother Anton, meet an acquaintance of my father," Pavel said, introducing Oleg Yakovlev. "He recognized me at once."

"Indeed, I could not mistake that curly brown hair. 'It is our dear friend's son, Pavel, come home from the war' I said to my wife." Oleg smiled happily, the lines breaking up those of sadness ingrained in his firm features. He seemed reluctant to release Pavel's hand, "the lost, who has now been found. You will be coming home, will you not, Pasha?" he inquired.

Clearly, this intimacy and expectation after Pavel's long confinement in the monastery became a jumble in Pavel's mind, just as Anton had feared. "His family understands that he will stay at the monastery for awhile," Anton replied for him. He did not want to refer to 'healing' in front of Pavel, who conducted himself very much like a normal person, except when he easily became overwhelmed as he was at the moment.

Oleg's wife stepped forward. "Your parents had grand parties when they lived in Novgorod. You were a remarkable musician, even before school age. I recall you performed in the Leningrad Symphony. Your lovely cousins, Svetlana and Tatyana, must be grown women by now."

"*Da, da,* ma'am, they are grown. And lovely," interjected Brother Anton, immediately blushing by confirming their loveliness, but he was nervous that Pavel's loss of memory might create an uncomfortable silence. "We must get back to our cart. Pavel Ivanovich has been of invaluable assistance to St. Sansais."

The monk bowed and gently propelled Pavel by the shoulders through the market, though he felt unstrung by the longest speech he had made in years to civilians, those outside the monastery. Equally astounding was discovery that Pavel had performed in the Leningrad Symphony, which heightened Anton's responsibility for his charge.

Unaware of Anton's efforts to monitor him, Pavel became distracted by the heightened excitement of a trio of gypsy musicians who passed by. At once his arms extended toward the violinist. A wayward step made the trio a foursome as Pavel fell in with the group, his frost-bitten fingertips seeking chords in the air, an imaginary bow tripping over the strings to an enchanted tune only he perceived, until Anton hurried to pull him away by the sleeve.

People gathered three deep in front of the monastery's display, and Brother Vessaly sold produce as fast as he placed it in outstretched hands and accepted payment. "Good black soil, ma'am," he said to a young woman who inquired how they grew such sizeable cabbages. He relinquished the sales job with relief to Brother Anton and Pavel, murmuring that it had been nearly four hours since they awoke and he'd like a bite of bread and cheese. Anton knew fasting did not appeal to Vessaly as it did to himself.

Soon the musicians with pipes and fiddle, and dancers twirling in wildly patterned skirts, paraded back up the street, their wares having been sold or traded. They were followed by merry children and youth who joined in the familiar folk songs. At their arrival in front of the cart, Pavel loudly burst into song. His alto voice carried well over the tambourines and tin whistles. A roar of encouragement rose from the crowd and the gyspy train halted to launch another tune. Pavel threw his head back and sang with the gypsies and children, a marked departure from the low chanting at the monastery.

Vessaly stopped chewing, paling with the inappropriateness of his companion, until he realized that Pavel was not a novitiate like himself and therefore not encumbered by vows. He sought reassurance regarding the behavior from Brother Anton, who was likewise astounded, but for a different reason.

"He remembers, he remembers," shouted Anton in joy.

Pavel's arms waved like those of a symphony conductor, responding to the sea of eyes upon him, his feet automatically tapping the rhythm that threatened to carry him away with the other dancers until Anton grabbed his shirttail. The commotion died down when the caravan entered the clearing, and Pasha, his cheeks flushed with color, resumed his obedient role of helping Brothers Anton and Vessaly.

As usual at the market, Anton had not failed to notice the pilgrims whose lips moved in continuous prayer or fingers ran nimbly over their rosaries. In or out of the relative few monasteries still remaining in Russia, the Old Believers were not to be denied their faith. Conscious that his own inner contemplation had been forgotten in what seemed like circus festivities in Thor, Anton abruptly announced, "We must depart," motioning that the cart be filled with the broken chard and carrot tops left over from the sale. With a burst of energy he threw his weight against the cart before he succumbed to the smell of spicy sausages from the popular grill.

The monks' cart rattled over the dirt road out of Thor, destined for the quiet but potentially boring harbor of St. Sansais while Anton rehearsed the story of Pavel's untoward antics and his breakthrough in recalling folksongs, a report sure to elicit a smile from the abbot.

A week or so later Oleg Yakovlev appeared at the gate of the monastery, and inquired about arranging a brief meeting with Father Konstantin. By this time the abbot had been thoroughly briefed on Pavel's eventful day at the market, and on his astounding progress, a miraculous healing of memory and soul, he concluded. He was prepared, more or less, for other surprises related to his guest.

"I understand your generosity and that of St. Sansais has been unlimited in ensuring the recovery of Pavel Ivanovich Zyclov," Oleg said, after introducing himself. "Your Brother Anton informed my wife and I that the young man has been helpful, bless him and all who reside here. I do believe, however, that not only he but his family members would benefit by a reunion. I have come to take Pavel home to them if you would be so kind to allow me."

He cleared his throat, uncertain whether this proposal would be accepted. "I feel a bit like a thief for wanting to abscond with so worthy a person as our dear Pasha who may have his own wishes to consider," he added.

Abbot Konstantin braced himself. He had long been aware the time would come when Pavel might leave the monastery. He had deep reservations about his safety in the outside world, where simple, good-hearted people such as Pavel were vulnerable. Given the unknown extent of his memory loss, he might unknowingly subject himself to danger. The abbot also feared the recruiters might come again and take him, concerns he argued repeatedly with himself. Or perhaps in his heart, Pavel will not want to leave permanently if he chooses to take vows. The abbot lapsed into a prolonged silence.

"I fear I may have overstepped my authority as a friend of the family," the elder man said, reassessing his intention. "I did not know if Pavel had a commitment to St. Sansais, either in devotion to the faith or indebtedness for its protection. I merely hoped to reunite the young man with his family, and to discover the whereabouts of the cousins, Svetlana and Tatyana. However, no one seems to have had news of them for some time."

At last, Konstantin's soul told him he must yield his charge to this representative of the family and to the outer world, that is, if it was Pavel's desire. The gatekeeper was sent to find the longtime guest and bring him to the office. In the interval, Konstantin related the entire story of Pavel's collapse in a nearby field and his recovery at the monastery. Leaving nothing out, he hoped the knowledge would assist the family in caring for the young man appropriately until he fully regained his memory—if he ever did. Konstantin knew he was being especially protective since the recruiters had taken Dmitri, one of their own, along with workers from Konsky and the surrounding countryside.

Oleg immediately understood why the abbot had hesitated. "Ah, it is well that Pavel, a veteran of a campaign against the Axis, was spared recruitment for the collectives," he replied.

"He is a slight, seemingly frail individual with obvious musical abilities, not one well suited for the harsh demands of labor anywhere," the abbot agreed.

Pavel's brown eyes were wide and shining when he came into the office, picking bits of straw from his clothing. He did not immediately recognize Oleg Yakovlev, whom he had met a week ago, but his natural friendliness made everyone a friend.

"I invite you to accompany me to see your family if you are willing, dear Pavel Ivanovich. They would like to see you." Oleg's face lit up with pride and enjoyment in Pasha's presence. Pasha seemed to have that effect on people, the abbot noticed, becoming more apprehensive about Pavel's safety because of it. Pavel glanced eagerly at the abbot and back to Oleg.

"I have agreed to permit you to go, if this is what you wish to do," Konstantin said.

"I have not thought about such a thing. I find that I am fully occupied here," Pavel said tentatively. "My days are committed to God." In the ensuing silence, he added, "And to St. Sansais and Father Konstantin and prayer for Brother Dmitri, my teacher and benefactor, and—"

"You are quite occupied," Oleg laughed. "I wonder if you can maintain all those prayer commitments while you make a brief visit home. Then you may decide if you want to return to St. Sansais."

The abbot appeared relieved, given the uncle's consideration, though the prospect of leaving appeared to be unfathomable to Pavel. He dropped to one knee before the abbot, and tears welled in his eyes, curtailing a reply.

"I shall say thank you for all of us," Oleg said. "How can we ever convey our gratitude for your rescuing Pavel Ivanovich?" His own eyes were moist when he lifted Pasha to his feet.

"We must gather his few belongings, and advise the others that Pavel is going away to visit family." Father Konstantin reluctantly led the way down the long stone corridor towards the guest room. He had a sense that much of the gaity of the monastery would be leaving with Pavel Ivanovich.

A few days later, Father Konstantin received a telegram alerting him to meet the train at the Konsky railroad depot. Comrade Dmitri, now irretrievably crippled, was being sent back to St. Sansais Vineyards from a hospital in Moscow.

XV

Tiger

The facetiously dubbed Society of the Women in the Fields, formally known as the women's farm labor crew, met in splinter groups well after their assignment to separate farms. In ever more fiercely dedicated secret meetings, they brought their energies to bear on the problems confronting them, which, not incidentally, reflected the larger world of Soviet Russia in 1946.

"My mother suffers melancholy. In fact, my whole family sees little joy in their existence. Is there no laughter in the world anymore? What has happened to the soul of our people?" The crew huddled together on the grass in the shade of a willow tree.

"We need to do better for the young people. Poor Emilia—"

"That is what happens when religious faith is banned. Neither young nor old have anything to turn to," Ludmila said, her always busy hands restless without her knitting.

"How can one feel supported when parents are alienated from the Church and their children separated early from both the Church and their parents? The young often appear to be harnessed to the industrialization machine without a thought to their humanity."

"Try as I might to devote myself to serving the starving in the south's Black Belt, my patriotic fervor brings me no sense of grace or peace. It is an ultimately defeating position to be in."

"But my dreams tell me we desperately need to rely upon one another," Ludmila broke in again. I am haunted by the dream that occurred last spring in Konsky, a recurring nightmare about a tiger that leapt from the corner of the ceiling upon a room full of women and children. Remember, I told you then."

"A tiger? *Da*, Jessica, I mean Svetlana, raved about a tiger when she had the fever," Tatyana burst out, coddling her midsection with her arms to contain a shiver.

"'Tis the same. It seems the beast has followed us."

"O, I am so afraid for Svetlanka. I must find her before something dreadful happens," Tatyana moaned, readying to flee from the field.

An older woman next to her gently pulled her to the ground. "You will not find your cousin with the strange American name in the fields or farmhouses. Did you not know she went away? With the Captain, I am told."

The blow rippled from the youngster's stunned, unseeing eyes to her quivering chin, and down to her trembling hands lying limp in the hollow of her cotton skirt. A precarious silence followed.

"I believe there is something in Svetlana meant for survival. That is what I saw at the last farm. Do you not agree?" The woman looked hopefully around her at the sad, weary faces of those gathered there.

"Very strong, *da.* You should be proud, Tatyana," another said.

"The tiger means the men, doesn't it?" Tatyana queried.

"I think it is the power of the State. I believe we are all pawns, including the Captain. The men are powerless to defend themselves or us, just as we are powerless." An angry young woman who had spoken after the suicide continued to rage. "You will see. It will come to no good."

Ludmilla shushed the group. "Yet suffering has meaning just as Sasha said. She may be radical, but she looks for meaning in everything." The women scattered when a supervisor circled around the field in their direction.

Around the clock guard duty continued at the four new camps since the sabotage at Red Bounty *Kolkhoz*, evidence of the paranoia experienced by those in authority. In addition, mechanical breakdowns were regularly attributed to the hostility of the laborers. Even the failure of the carburetor earlier in the harvesting was questioned now, as well as the mysterious way the thresher had chewed up a conveyor belt and spewed its contents into the gear mechanisms. Loss of one grain truck and the recent breakdown of the workhorse Ford truck were reassessed in terms of sabotage. The need for half a dozen guards was now blamed on the imported field hands.

"The recruits are trying to defeat the harvesting," one official said. "They fail to demonstrate loyalty to the motherland."

"*Da*, they are contriving to side with previous landowners to disrupt the work. They want to save the crop for the people here," said another. "That is why they wrecked the truck."

"I wonder they can steal hams right from under our eyes. We have been warned. If anything happens now, it is our fault," the official concluded.

For the next few days the strategy was to expedite the harvesting before cold weather set in by feeding bundles to one threshing machine from all four sites simultaneously, rather than move the thresher from field to field, which would have idled two-thirds of the laborers. In the process of new procedures being implemented, Tatyana asked those coming and going if they had seen the mechanic, Dmitri, her last hope for finding Jessica. She became frantic when she learned Dmitri had been in a terrible accident and hospitalized during the move from the last farm. No one had seen him return to the camp from the hospital in Moscow.

Tatyana barely ate or slept for several days, imagining the worst for both Brother Dmitri and Jessica. Her stoicism, adopted earlier at Jessica's insistence, swiftly faded. Her slight figure became a parody of herself, as thin as a plucked bird. In desperation, she approached one of the officials.

Summoning all her courage, she said, "*Pozhaluysta*, sir, I would like to speak to the truck driver, Dmitri."

"The truck driver? Do not expect to find him. He was sent back to the monastery." The blunt news came unexpectedly, though she immediately felt happy for the monk.

"He was sent home from the hospital?" she pried.

"*Da, da*, go now. We have troubles enough without a cripple to care for." The attendant shooed her away with a wave of his arm.

Tatyana ran back to her team, stumbling and incoherent. "Dmitri is safe. He is back at the monastery. You didn't know he is a monk? But he is crippled." Imagined scenes of the accident and disfigurement whipped through her mind. "Brother Mitya nursed Pasha day and night. Now I have lost both he and cousin Jessica." Suddenly her sixteen years, since a birthday had passed, felt more like thirty.

"I think I shall never trust anyone again," she gulped, then wished she could take back the words. Anna must be even more distrustful than she.

"My parents lost everything except each other," Anna said. "Nationalization requires sacrifice, not the same for all, but none are spared. I am sorry for you, Tanyecha, and Jessica both. I wish I were so lucky to have close cousins."

"I shouldn't complain and cry. I would like to be like you, Anna, so beautiful and kind and brave."

"You are as you are and that is best. Do not ever wish otherwise, and never wish your life away. This may be hard, but look how strong you are. You have distinguished yourself in the fields. You will always do well, Tatyana Gilkova." Anna gave her a warm hug.

The blue Opal coup was well underway to Leningrad on the highway linking Moscow and Leningrad before Svetlana felt her fear of making a mistake begin to dissipate. Perhaps accompanying Captain Stanislov would be a reprieve from the insufferable camps. She shifted her attention to the passing countryside and towns. They had driven through Novgorod, the first large city they came to, and one known by the film *Alexander Nevsky*. A few monuments remained intact in the medieval city, and it appeared most of its early architecture had escaped the bombing.

But Svetlana was reminded that Norgorod was also vaguely linked to her parents and grandparents long ago. It had the ring of better times for her family, a suspicion that she did not share with the Captain, who seemed to be sensitive to insult by those he perceived as his "betters." She was uncertain of her family history, only that they had resided in Konsky since she was very young, and that they had lost their home in the city-to-farm relocation program. Sergey and Vera Gilkov had been obliged to become involved in Communist Party affairs and raise their daughter in the Young Pioneers and later the Red Brigade.

Between miles and miles of heavy forest and taiga lands of northern *Russ*, Svetlana witnessed the torched landscape. Massive piles of concrete rubble, tangled fences and blackened uprooted trees remained. Towns rose from beneath piles of ashes and debris. Feeble gardens struggled to thrive on the outskirts.

"You will find wreckage everywhere," Captain Stanislov said. "Despite the destruction you see, this represents a victory for us. We live. The mother country lives, bought by the carnage you do not see. We are not forced to speak German. Why mourn? It is a new day in Russia."

"Leningrad? How is Leningrad—?"

"After a 900 day siege? Streets upturned with trenches, blocks of buildings uninhabitable. Broken heating pipes exposed. But Leningrad will be rebuilt. We have infinite resources in timber and oil and minerals that the Germans did not get."

His refrains sounded very much like her mother, Svetlana thought. 'Mother Russia won the war, not the Americans' rang in her ears. The disabled veterans arriving by train in Konsky to take over jobs at Benyanske's represented a visible part of the carnage. Invisible were the lost minds like that of Pasha. Svetlana shuddered and pulled a large scarf around her shoulders.

"The road to our once proud capital city was lined with abandoned and destroyed German artillery and two T-34 tanks, a gift of the Germans," Yuri said. True, trenches and bunkers attested to defense of the city. Massive holes marked incoming mortars. In the deepening shadows of evening Svetlana saw even more disturbing sights—ragged groups of displaced persons trailing both into and out of Leningrad, as if there were nowhere to lay their heads.

The couple arrived late in the sprawling city overlain by the acrid smell of cheap petrol, smoke from factories, and inner-city heating plants whose slim towers punctured the flat skyline. The captain took her at once to a section of dense five-story concrete buildings with narrow walk-up stairs similar to workers' housing in Konsky, except that these housed thousands of workers crammed into rows of rooms. A view of the night sky and a few random lights of Leningrad gave the city a sense of mystery that lifted Svetlana from her earlier despair. His third floor apartment consisted of one room and a small bedroom, the metric space allocated Yuri by permit. Svetlana gasped at the smell of good coffee. Neatly organized shelves and a gas burner to the left were the extent of the kitchen. To the right two upholstered armless chairs faced an imported rug on the floor. A desk occupied a corner next to the dining table. The furnishings seemed much too expensive for someone of his rank, Svetlana guessed, though she had little to compare it to, but her intuition had been right. He liked nice things, liked to look good. Maybe concealing a sense of insecurity while he condemned superiority in everyone else. She shuddered and moved tentatively about the room satisfying her curiosity, unclear where to stash her drab travel bag while Captain Stanislov unpacked his belongings.

"I must return the car." he announced. "You will come with me."

He drove fast through abandoned streets and neighborhoods of similar gray concrete apartment houses amid a few business complexes. They soon arrived at a warehouse district, which was fenced and reserved for the military. A gateman checked the captain through and signed off on papers certifying the car had been returned. With that, the couple walked a few blocks and took a clanking bus with rusting paint back to his apartment.

"We will tour Leningrad. I am sure you will find the city of interest."

So exhausted that her knees quivered, Svetlana only nodded and let herself be led through the rituals of undressing and preparing for bed.

"Call me Yuri, *pozhaluysta,*" he said, now casual and at ease, a side of him that Svetlana had not experienced before.

For the first few days they stayed close to the apartment. Yuri arranged reams of paperwork on the desk and table to complete files he was required to submit prior to a deadline. Svetlana gratefully accepted the respite, finding she needed time to restore herself, mentally and physically, after the rigors and trials of the collective. Moments of guilt and self-chastisement caught her time and again, though she tried to adjust to a better life, as the captain had promised.

I could not have fought like Anna if I had tried, she repeated in defense of her leaving the camp with Captain Yuri Stanislov. Not that she wanted to admit it, but the thrill of being in Leningrad helped her overlook much of her plight, allowing her to deny complicity in the living arrangement. How else could I escape the factory and farm? Every day she questioned her motives until finally she accepted the patently obvious truth that what the captain offered was a way out.

Yuri walked her to and from small shops, often skirting idle street people whose emaciated forms convincingly proved they were unable to work, their pinched faces registering apathy. Svetlana's curious observations took in everything. She realized at once that she would not feel comfortable alone among those who appeared lost and sullen. He introduced her to several occupants of nearby apartments, but they generally maintained a distance. When his table became too loaded with papers, they ate at a nearby restaurant where they ordered light sandwiches or snacks and splurged on coffee, real beans brewed at their table in small Turkish-style pots, and topped with milk or cream and a sweetener.

This is bizarre, Svetlana mused. I am drinking real coffee while Lettina is laboring in the fields. But I cannot talk about the farm or my friends or much of anything with Yuri. Not how I feel, or who he is, or who I have become. The sense that she had become two different people persisted—she would often see a stranger in the mirror. Being abruptly cut off from her former life completed the sense of alienation from all she had known. Yuri tended to keep it that way.

"I am wondering where you came from originally," Svetlana remarked one day when they were out walking.

He looked at her sharply and replied, "Tver, not far from here. I came to Leningrad after the war."

That was all Svetlana knew of his past, and she could have guessed most of that. His evasiveness intrigued yet repelled her with its sense of risk, danger, or cover up that she failed to understand. She felt uneasy being with him because of it and because of his authority over her.

How much am I *willingly* giving for the means to get out of Konsky, she asked herself, which was immediately followed by a new thought: how much am I being exploited for *his* pleasure? Mulling this over, Svetlana found herself changing, becoming more insightful, perhaps maturing in a heated environment as did the crops of the fields. Ill advised as her choice may have been and continued to be, she sensed she had some subversive need that wanted him to want her, to approve of her. A tea at their apartment cast her in a new role, somewhat revealing of whom that new person was becoming.

Yuri introduced Grigory Ratkevich, a friend on business from Moscow visiting Leningrad with his wife, Lydia.

"We served together in Byelorussia, a campaign against all odds," Yuri said by way of explanation of his friendship with Grigory. "*Ochen priyatno*. I am happy to make your acquaintance," he said to Lydia, whom he had not met before.

The guests brought a trail of chilly autumn air inside, yet instantly warmed the room with their excitement in reuniting with the captain. Clearly, some of the adrenalin had to do with meeting Svetlana whom Yuri had introduced as "my companion" in a nod to mutual consent not lost on Svetlana. She went with it while witnessing Yuri's sociability and hearing his laughter, neither within her experience when he supervised harvesting on the *kolkhoz*.

She had thoroughly scrubbed down the apartment over the past few weeks. Beneath the dingyness of the walls, there had once been a coat of ivory paint. Earlier today she and Yuri had arranged chairs for guests and placed the samovar in readiness. A quick trip to the tea shop furnished bits of stuffed dumplings typically served with tea. Yuri's tall tea glasses with stout handles portrayed his decidedly masculine-style. While he hung coats next to the door, the guests turned to Svetlana with a rush of questions which, fortunately, she had no time to answer. Yuri interrupted to seat everyone and signal that Svetlana pour the tea. Occupied with the tea service, she felt the guests staring at her, a rather bewildering sense of being seen as attractive or a novelty, perhaps an unspoken "how did you get her?" A flattering flush of her cheeks could have been mistaken as a reflection from the crimson red silk blouse. She shifted in her chair and her black hair, now shoulder length, fell softly around her face. Her long straight legs above slim black pumps with walking heels completed the stylish look—Yuri had demonstrated good taste when he bought them.

"Will you come to Moscow now and then since you are relieved from the harvesting?" Grigory asked.

Yuri looked uncomfortable, uncertain how to answer the question. He glanced at Svetlana. "I have had no word yet where my next assignment will be."

"I wonder if anyone knows," Lydia said. "With petrol so scare, unavailable in many places, it is doubtful how the country can carry on."

"So I have heard—" Yuri started to say.

"Sources have literally dried up," her husband added. "Whether it is poor planning or the industry lagging since the war, I do not know. Travel for my department has been severely curtailed. We came by train of course."

"While you are here we must make the most of it," Yuri said, changing the subject. "I would like to tour the Winter Palace with Svetlana if you would care to join us. We could go tomorrow afternoon."

"Certainly. We would be pleased to do so. The afternoon would suit us perfectly. *Nous aurons une grande journie au musei.*"

"Have you a particular interest in the arts, Svetlana?" Lydia asked, searching for clues to the younger woman's character and past.

"The Museum will be new to me," Svetlana said quietly. "Yuri has escorted me to see parts of Leningrad though my experience is limited." Her voice sounded strangely like her mother's to her ears, a low, rich cultured resonance compatible with her fashionable looks.

"Then you find the city enchanting?" Lydia pursued.

"I can only imagine how beautiful it was before the Siege. There is much more that I would like to see, the Russian Museum, of course." Unaccustomed to social conversation, Svetlana felt like a movie star in an obscure film, and to her, all Russian movies were obscure. She turned to Yuri, her long moist lashes sheltering frightened eyes. He quickly steered the guests to a discussion of their plans. Would they be going to the Crimea this winter? And did they have plans for children now that the war was over?

Chirping like a thicket of blackbirds, the couple soon left, agreeing to meet at the Embankment entrance to the Winter Palace and proceed to tour the Hermitage. As soon as the door closed firmly behind him, Yuri moved across the room to take Jessica in his arms.

"*Ti takaya krasivaya.* You are so beautiful," he breathed. "I am so proud of you," the words drowned as he lost himself in her hair, down the nape of her neck, and deeply into her lips.

The used napkins Svetlana had gathered dropped to the floor. Not knowing what to do with her hands, her arms, her rapidly responding body, she remained still until it no longer mattered. A part of her became a woman in a romantic *Ameriskaya* film.

XVI

Lydia

The broad waters of the Great Neva reflected the subdued gray cast of the sky over Leningrad. From the Troitsky Bridge to the Fortress of Peter and Paul, the river looped capriciously past the Winter Palace and beneath the Palace Bridge. Contained within the Embankment shoreline, it lent its graceful abandon to the wide, green Admiralty where the Bronze Horseman survived the Siege to forever rear his mount in a symbol of conqueror and victory.

Svetlana first beheld the fabled Winter Palace rippling its Baroque green and ivory image in the Neva long before they met the Ratkeviches at the address, *Dvortsovaia Naberezhnaia,* 'embankment,' and the entrance on that side. Jessica caught her breath and tried not to stare like one of the forlorn cows in the pastures outside Konsky, a town that suddenly seemed wretched and obsolete. She adjusted her collar and flipped the ends of her hair so it naturally rolled under in a becoming frame for her high cheekbones and deep set eyes. The walking pumps Yuri bought for her were possibly of fine Italian leather, unknown at the boot and shoe factory she left only three months ago. They set off the long black raincoat he had also provided. Knowing she was well-dressed, her firm stride kept up with Yuri, though she felt much more like tip-toeing into the *muzei kartinnaya galiryeya* that she had never dreamed of visiting.

"Nous aurons une grande journie' an musei', we will have a great day at the museum," Lydia Ratkevicha said. She wore a short, fur-lined cape against the usual damp chill of the port city. Her heavy chestnut hair swept up in a French knot topped by a wispy black veil on a palm-sized hat gave Lydia a polished matronly look of one far older than her mid-twenties, and far better dressed than even deposed nobility of Leningrad. She paused to straighten the seams in her silk stockings.

"The rocket and smoke damage to the roof of the Winter Palace have yet to be fully repaired. Citizens maintained constant vigils on top of the building during the Siege to fight fires from incoming rockets," Grigory said. "Volunteer spotters, women known as *Blokadnitsa*, watched for bombers from there and relayed warnings."

But Svetlana barely heard him relate startlingly recent events above a squirrely buzz of excitement that pounded in her ears. The floor to ceiling white marble columns of the entrance and hallway offered a cool invitation to another age. Svetlana snugged her arm against Yuri's and gazed upward at the towering arches with a sense of awe. At last Yuri nudged her when Grigory and Lydia attempted to introduce her to the curator with whom they were well acquainted.

"Dobroye utro. Kak vas zovut? Good morning. What is your name?"

"Mehya zovut Svetlana Sergeevna Gilkova. *Mnye ochen'priyatno.* I am pleased to meet you." Since she had been with Yuri Svetlana felt it natural to conceal that she was "Jessica" to herself.

"Raisa Aleksandrovna Dobryna came to the Museum from the University of Leningrad. On loan, is it? Surely the University would not willingly allow a lead researcher to stray far. She specializes in Catherine the Great's European contributions to Russian culture, as well as the additional acquisitions by Tsars Nicholas I and II," enthused Grigory.

"On loan, yes, like a book," laughed Raisa, her serious but pleasant face lighting up. "I continue my research here, as you might imagine. However, there is much to be done to restore artworks to their proper galleries since they were secreted away by the trainload to the Urals during the Siege." Her short stature and plain middle-aged features resembled that of a farm woman rather than a university professor.

"In fact, as I recall the Gilkovs were known in social circles at one time in Saint Petersburg as Leningrad was named then."

Svetlana noticed Yuri wince and draw away from her side. She took her cue at once. "Surely it must have been the Gilhoyovs. We are often mistaken for them. A pity," she said disarmingly. "I am sure they were charming."

Raisa caught Svetlana's steady knowing look and understood that her recognition of the Gilkov name had been correct. "I am so sorry. It was likely the Gilhoyovs who entrusted the Museum with their art works and personal property for safekeeping during the war."

"Russian art, was it?" broke in Lydia.

"There were a few small works, if I remember correctly, but family treasures were generally confidentially preserved until retrieved. May I direct you to a particular exhibit? The registrar is home ill today, and I must remain here at the desk," Raisa said.

"I must see the Dutch artists. I will look for paintings that I may not have seen before," Lydia said, moving their party into the opulent marble halls through soaring, gold-gilt arches painted with intricate motifs.

"The State rooms of the Winter Palace are being restored to represent the family life of its original occupants, Peter I, his second wife, Catherine, and tsars until the fall of the Romanovs, which may relate to Raisa's research," Lydia said. Instead of taking the Jordan Staircase leading to the living quarters, she led the group toward the Grand Staircase and the galleries of the late 18th, early 19th and 20th century exhibits on the second floor. "The Provisional Government occupied much of the Palace until it was overthrown by the Bolsheviks," she explained. "At that time, the Winter Palace housed the capital of Russia. The arches you were admiring are the signature architecture of Bartolomeo Rastelli, a court architect who designed much of the Winter Palace."

This information was more than Jessica wanted to know—or remembered from her short stint in Ten-Year School. She was much too preoccupied with her family name being recognized by the curator, a notion at once thrilling and threatening. Here I am in the great city of Leningrad where my name is already known.

"I am looking for a portrait of Peter the Great," she blurted to cover her lapse in the conversation.

"His portraits would likely be in the Russian Museum and family quarters of the Winter Palace and his home at Peterhof. The statue of him, the Bronze Horseman, you doubtless saw in the *Senatskaya,* Senate Square, on the Admiralty Embankment. *Grand? Oui!* He is about to take flight it seems," Lydia said. "I saw his giant-sized riding boots in the Kremlin's Treasures of the Tsars. You must visit us in Moscow, and we will take you to the Kremlin."

Inside the gallerias, the vibrant art of Europe's foremost painters that so excited Lydia did not impress Svetlana nearly as much as the experience of connecting with someone who knew of her family. The question of Gilkov relatives living in Leningrad teased her mind. Who were they and what was their story? But even more importantly, she realized she coped with the disclosure by quick thinking and lying and got away with it. An inner sense of elation escalated until she smiled radiantly at Yuri, but immediately squelched soaring spirits in fear he'd suspect something,

He'd never guess that I just demonstrated that I can handle my affairs in this city, in this society. I learned my lessons well in the factory—evasiveness and self-preservation for myself and others, that is the way of *Rossiya.*

All else now seemed possible, or at least manageable. She overlooked Yuri's questioning glance and took his somewhat tentative arm with a new confidence. "May we see the Dutch artists," she asked, echoing Lydia in an attempt to sound casual. Yuri clung to her long after it was necessary.

Lydia escorted the foursome down dimly lit palatial passageways past the Monet gallery, and those of the Flemish and German painters, each ballroom-sized galleries. They passed sections that were closed where irreplaceable paintings were in the process of being unboxed and reinstated in their frames which were not evacuated with the paintings. A guard informed them that other works had been taken or acquired by museums in Moscow, a loss for the Winter Palace.

Eventually Lydia steered the group to the Dutch painters. Svetlana immediately recognized paintings familiar in content and style to those in her parents' and grandparents' homes when she was a child, family treasures of landscapes, peasants and animals. Their pieces had been sold or traded for bare necessities during hard times. She tried to resist looking too closely at titles and the artists' names for fear of showing her ignorance.

"Pieter Brueghel, the Elder, was highly influenced by Italian Renaissance painters, yet he depicted landscapes and life in the Low Countries, honoring his countrymen," Lydia said in her ear. "The landscapes could have been painted in the fields and villages in regions of Eastern Europe or Persia, the origins of *Russ* in its early history, in my opinion. To me, he is closer to the Russian painters, Issac Levitan and Fyodor Vasilyev than the European painters because he was so passionate about the land and its people."

Lydia's appreciation of the Dutch paintings and her willingness to share it drew Jessica into a world far from the farm collectives and boot and shoe factory, indeed from the deadening talk of post-war Russia and reminders everywhere of the Siege. In the Winter Palace, none of that existed, only the breathtaking interpretations of the natural world and its stories and drama of the human soul, all in delicate hues and glossy frames befitting royalty, paintings actually selected by the Emperors and Empresses themselves

"I am sure that is true. I understand Soviet Realism predominates while influences of the West are discredited. The notion that the poor and the old ways are worth exhibiting reminds me of a tiny print my mother prized," was all she managed to say.

"Hundreds of years old and they survive," Lydia whispered. "The oils act as a preservative. See how they have yellowed the paints. Are we not fortunate to view such work?"

With Lydia at her side, Jessica felt more at home in Leningrad than she had as a stranger and involuntary "companion" to an unpredictable man. Too much to digest at the moment, she lingered at a painting in grays and browns of a poor peasant family crowded around their simple supper beneath an icon, a lustrous painting of the Holy Mother that endowed the room and its occupants with an unnatural warm glow. It was not the icon, but the sheaf of rye tucked behind the icon that caught Jessica's attention.

"The sheaf of rye is a tradition of the country people near Konsky, honoring Poludnitsa, the goddess of harvests," Svetlana said, pleased to share her knowledge with Lydia.

"*Oui, art verite,*' naturalism is popular now," Lydia said beneath her breath. "Hardly a controversial departure from religious paintings, though the icons we skipped and the portraits of nobility in another gallery might at some time come under scrutiny. Igor Stravinski's 1930s ballet celebrating Poludnitsa brought him heavy criticism, though he rewrote it later to acclaim."

Both women skirted the fact their public upbringing had etched disdain for religion and decadent cultures in their views. Again focusing on ordinary people, Lydia tugged Svetlana's arm to come see a series of sanguine sketches on rice paper that captured the life of working people, boatswains, brick makers, and railway operators. It was the drawings of harvesters, both men and women, that gave Svetlana a chill—farm workers were honored in art yet dishonored in the field, *da*. She had time to quell instant anger while Lydia led the party to another section of the building, which afforded a view of the courtyard. Here were the French, Italian and Flemish collections preferred by the men, though Grigory and Yuri were becoming restless. Svetlana soon stepped aside for a closer look at dauby-looking paintings in vivid reds, blues, and greens dashed with a bit of yellow. Up close the strokes appeared confusing, as though the artist could not decide what to do with the paint, but when she stepped away from the paintings, sunshiny meadows, charming villages, or wave-dashed waters formed miraculously from the paint strokes.

"O, look," she said to Yuri. "These are paintings of the sea, but the style of painting is so different."

"Yes, this is a collection of French Impressionist paintings," Lydia cut in. "Grisha finds the French painters more to his liking, though more modern abstract art is discouraged in preference for our native culture. However, I hope this exhibit will remain in the Museum to show the evolution of thinking and experience of the artists, as well as their time in history."

"Lydia has become an inveterate cultural preservationist," her husband boasted. "She insists on our regular attendance at museums, operas, and symphonies."

"Not so," Lydia laughed. "If for no other reason than we must support our composers, Prokofiev and Shostakovich, who remain loyal." Dropping behind the men, she whispered to Svetlana, "Anna Akhmatova has been arrested. I heard it on the radio. Surely you have heard of her strong political views. Her poetry denounces purges of the *avant-garde*—artists like Kandinsky who left Russia and painted in France. It means crushing the Russian soul, often in exchange for vulgar pragmatism. But shush. The wrath directed at the poet will turn on us," she said with a warning look, not wanting to endanger her cultural recruit.

Svetlana nodded, and when the museum guard pointedly looked in from the hall, Lydia switched to a discussion of Prokofiev's *Fifth Symphony* that they had heard in Moscow shortly after she and Grigory were married. "It is a magnificent symphony with a voice that speaks of the glory of *Rossyia.*"

Later that evening when they were alone at the apartment, Yuri brought up the subject of the Gilkovs. "I am curious about the connection the curator made with your family, that they may have been upper class before the Revolution."

"That was an unfortunate—"

"Raisa is a professor. She does not make unfortunate mistakes." Yuri glared at Svetlana who could think of nothing that would appease him. He had been drinking with Grigory downtown after the museum tour while the women window shopped on Nevsky Prospekt, though windows displayed little other than a half dozen tins of caviar, out of reach for most residents, and Svetlana had no money. Since they came home, Yuri had poured several large shots of Stolichnaya, his last preferred bottle of vodka which he had acquired by bartering.

"Are you hiding something from me, Svetlana?"

"I am sorry to upset you—"

"Tell me or the truth will come out some other way."

Svetlana grimaced at the threat and dropped her head. "I have nothing to tell you." She dully reported what he already knew. "You saw me working in the boot and shoe factory. I worked throughout my younger years. My parents had nothing."

"And I rescued you from that fate, Svetlanka. My parents put me in communal day care at age four and later in Young Pioneers, their fervor a credit to Lenin. I barely knew them. I was raised on slogans and kasha, while my parents waved flags and held Party meetings in our apartment. When another whole family moved in with us I left. I was thirteen and on the streets. I was beaten up by thugs and starved when they robbed me of kopeks I earned doing errands. I faked my age and worked fourteen hours a day in industries to meet production goals, until I joined the Army."

The Captain paused and flexed his shoulders as if he were still heavily muscled. Tightness in his jaw competed with the pouty lips of a little boy. His usually slicked blond hair flopped in greasy strands over his pale brow.

"I know how it is without connections or rank of any kind. Count me among the first to agree that the barons, counts, and stooges of the Duma had to be defeated. Uprisings represented landless farmers, workers like me, and the poor like your parents and mine. But the Zemstro lacked power to act on behalf of the workers—call us proletariat, if you like. You are working class, Svetlana. You will not put on airs like Lydia. Or expect to shop on Nevsky Prospekt. Or hide anything from me, you hear?"

His strident voice smothered the room, an atmospheric shift altering the euphoria Sveltana experienced earlier. Clinking sounds at his desk meant he emptied his pockets of coins and the silver cigarette case he often carried. The military dress shoes stood awry where he had left them by the door. His sweaty socks left a warm ripe smell in the closed rooms.

"What I do know about you, Svetlana, is that you and I want the same things. I knew it when I first saw you at the factory, and I was sure of it when I saw you on the bus dressed like a modern girl." He paused as if fatigued. "You want a better life, not drudgery, and so do I," he repeated at last.

Increasingly fearful with the tenor and speed with which their relations were tested, Svetlana kept her aspirations to herself.

"Say something. Talk. You were able to talk to my friends." Yuri paced the cramped room, not taking time to light the cigarette he alternately waved then stuck between his lips.

"You got out of harvesting. You chose to stay with me, but underneath you think I am not good enough for you. Is that what it is, Svetlana?"

Svetlana glanced sideways for a means of escape, but there was none. Yuri always locked the door securely when he came or went. And they were on the third floor. She was sweating profusely and trapped in the apartment with a half-drunk soldier. She did not want him to hear the fear in her voice or see it in her eyes.

"*Nyet,*" she managed to reply.

Yuri has an uncanny ability to read my mind, but no. I hadn't thought that about him, though Tomenko was not good enough for Lettina. Am I trying to better myself by staying? *Da. Verité.* Thoughts swirled in her mind, defending and chastising, until tears pooled on her cheeks. Questioning everything, she wondered if her family had been upper class at one time? When a long shudder went through her body, she hoped Yuri failed to notice.

Only half attentive, he pulled himself up from the chair and poured another shot of vodka. "Maybe you need a drink."

When his back was to her while he looked for another glass, Svetlana panicked and slipped his heavy, silver-handled letter opener down behind the desk. His pride was hurt and alcohol inflamed his passions. Tense vibrations in the room told her this was no idle conversation on his part—keep a clear head Lana, she vowed. Her exploits drinking with Lettina and the girls in the park had made her feel giddy and irresponsible. Of all things, she wanted to avoid feeling out of control right now. Already reeling from holding her breath, she forced an outward calm, her eyes searching the room for other potential weapons.

Do not set him off, she cautioned herself. Moved by the resolution and a deep intake of air, she hung their coats neatly next to the door and lined up their shoes precisely as Yuri would have done. Moments ticked away, moments Svetlana marked with a leap into now familiar adulthood, well aware of the consequences of drunken conflicts, a part of every home, family, and neighborhood since she could remember. Yuri retrieved a bottle of vodka flavored with Russian wild cranberry juice he had bought for Svetlana. Cheap and common, it was typical of bootlegged brews central to lives that had lost property, purpose, and hope for the future. Attempting to swallow her fears, she dropped to her knees, fussing to tidy the fringe on the rug, as if smoothing the ragged edges of his temper.

"Sit down, Lanenka" Yuri lifted his glass. "To tomorrow. We will start over."

To Svetlana, the act of kneeling felt like a connection to humble origins, a denial of any trace of nobility in her family. But she had to get up, to place one foot after the other as precisely as she had lined up the shoes. Yuri handed her a frighteningly large glass of vodka and gulped his own. Svetlana sipped from the rim, unable to keep her teeth from chattering. Yuri watched her closely and waited. It was not long before light-headedness dissolved her inner resources and again separated her from her senses. She became a celluloid figure on screen whose feelings were fabricated in a script meant to titillate, beguiling one into believing the actors.

Red Bounty *Kolkholz* faded to a distant memory two weeks after a worker's death by hanging, a Soviet car explosion, and farm workers labeled "a mob" were sent to four separate collectives beyond Novgorod, where irritable supervisors drove them relentlessly.

At the new locations, the farms' few vintage tractors, supported by iron wheels as tall as a man's head, roared into life at dawn seven days a week. Several other tractors plus teams of horses and wagons had been requisitioned from landholders in an attempt to make short work of the harvesting. The oats were fully headed out, sun-ripened and glowing with that peculiarly autumn-bleached radiance of new straw. Lettina and the crew left their tents in the dark and began work in the fields at first light, which inched a few minutes later each day as summer waned.

One morning in the mess tent Lettina dusted the chaff from her tattered dress and took an opportunity to speak with Tomenko, whose sagging features betrayed his age and weariness.

Pressure to complete the harvesting fell on the workers' shoulders, along with blame for the delays. Officials had sent Tomenko scurrying, tool box in hand, from one broken machine or stalled engine to the next, but keeping them running without new or purloined parts from other equipment often proved futile.

"I could count the numbers of Soviet heavy equipment and vehicles produced in one year on one hand," he said.

"You have made it easier for the rest of us," she said.

"Fortunately, my parents gifted me with considerable patience. As you know, I kept the old flour mill operating in Konsky, long after milling became industrialized. The townspeople ordered their preferred grind and I delivered that kind of flour, until the flood washed the waterwheel away."

Lettina nodded, keeping one eye on the doorway. No one was allowed to linger after breakfast, but Tomenko talked at length, pleased with her affirmation and apparently relieved to have company.

"I suppose the authorities could assign me to worse," Tomenko said, helping himself to a bit more *selyodka*, pickled herring, and leaned back patting his midsection.

"The mill was built with simple working parts over a hundred years ago," he continued as if he had all day to reminisce. "Dmitri was a real mechanic and a monk at that! We hardly get along without him. He deserved better. That accident was an act of negligence."

Catching the end of Tomenko's whisper in her ear, Lettina was drawn to a commotion outside the mess tent. An official she did not recognize swung his car into the driveway. His uniform had several more strips and decorations than that of Captain Stanislov.

"He must have come from Moscow," Lettina said, and steered Tomenko to the edge of a a group of laborers. Visits from officials usually meant bad news. Gone was her casualness with Tomenko and any sense of her spontaneous carefree youthfulness.

"We must have missed a call for everyone to gather here. I become nervous with Katya here, Greita at the next farm, Anna somewhere else. None of us know exactly what happened to Svetlana and the captain, though it pains me to say his name. The authorities' means of breaking us up feels risky when something like this occurs."

In a commanding voice, the official announced, "I have been informed that the delivery of petrol for harvesting did not arrive today. Supplies are desperately needed elsewhere. None is available for the collectives until further notice." The words fell upon a silent crowd, men and women who quickly calculated what this turn of events meant to each of them personally. It was too soon to entertain a glimmer of hope.

The official walked back and forth with a halting step, his graying hair riffling in the breeze below his Red Army hat. "The remainder of the crops will be returned to the landholders for harvesting by hand and by teams of horses. You will therefore be transported to the rail station for immediate transfer back to your hometowns." Tense faces were again uplifted, weighing the official's announcement without responding, without necessarily believing what they heard, that essentially the harvest was over for them.

Impatient now with the lack of reaction to the news, good or bad, the official turned to leave before adding, "You must tear down the tents and pack up the camp as before. Trucks will arrive in two hours to remove all the supplies and transport you to the rail station. Tickets will be handed out when you check in."

Two hours. Now voices broke from the group in wary undertones, many convinced they had not been told the whole story, or even a true story, given the nature of state pronouncements. Others were openly suspicious of a coup, of sorts, by administrators of the Farm Program after the death of a worker and the explosion. Yet there was no time for theorizing or conspiracy mongering.

"We can go home," recited several women, offering shy smiles in lieu of a celebration. Rejoicing seemed tacitly forbidden. No one was quite sure what may or may not be acceptable; only that two minutes ago their lives of the past late summer and early fall months pivoted to two hours to accomplish the task before them.

"I must find Anna, Greita and Katya," stressed Lettina, biting her lip. "I wonder if we will arrive at the station from separate farms at the same time or staggered times. There is no time to plan anything."

"It seems the plans are made for us, Lettina," Sasha said.

"Yes, no, I mean—"

Sasha started for the tents with Lettina. "What do you want to do?" she inquired, recognizing Lettina's anxiety.

"I don't know, but I might not want to go home. Go home to what? Others are running the old mill." She had obviously given thought to the harvest ending, and leaving them unemployed and subject to another assignment.

Sasha bridged the gap and provided a sounding board. "I can see your point, unless you have family or commitments."

Lettina couldn't help glancing around, and not seeing Tomenko, she said, "No, no commitments."

"It is interesting that you might be exploring alternatives. Certainly we have broken free of old constraints, not always by choice. Recruitment to the farm *programme* has done that for us, yet discharge is sudden and unexpected." She gave Lettina's arm an affectionate squeeze and left to gather her belongings. "I will convey a message to the girls if I see them," she called back.

The mood of the conscripted labor force in leaving was nearly as strained as when they boarded the train for the trip north. The blunt severance meant no time for goodbyes, for seeking new or old friends, or closure with acquaintances, much less settling within oneself the sudden fact of departure. However, the now experienced crew made short work of dismantling the camp, and it was not until the collection bins for discarded items overflowed with tattered, faded work dresses and shabby shoes that someone broke into laughter.

"We are thinking the same thing!"

"We are finished!"

"It's a blessing. I am so happy to be going home." The bin resounded from a thud of discarded muck boots.

Men picked up the pace and joined in with subdued merriment of their own.

"You will miss the fields—and us," one teased. "See, the life of the farmer is a good life."

"Where is my girl—er, my partner?" asked the timid young man who had suffered burns to his face.

"Tatyana? Did I see you with Tatyana? Where is she?" Lettina felt especially responsible for looking after her, but had slipped in recent days.

"She may be on the next farm, or looking after the horses," he offered.

Lettina railed against the dispersion of the work force that caused these separations. Her friends were not on this farm, so she doggedly packed her travel bag with one spare outfit and ran to meet the truck. Her legs felt strong, even powerful, and she glanced at her sun-baked arms rounded with firm muscles, admitting the farm work had been good for her.

"I don't recall the authorities even thanked us for our service." She had spoken to anyone in general. "O, well it was our patriotic duty."

"Hopefully, it was worthwhile for the benefit of families in the drought region," someone added. Other men and women acknowledged the same hopes. The transport trucks came in, loaded the farm workers under the watchful eyes of armed guards, and went out with no more ceremony than that offered by the commanding officer.

"We're being delivered to the station like the barley and oats we harvested for other folks," one commented. "I feel as if I live for someone else."

"Live for the Spirit," interjected a woman saying her rosary. "The Spirit is more important than the day-to-day lives we live."

"Shush. Caution," warned an older man. The roar of the gigantic, aged motor effectively drowned further conversations. At the station, the assortment of displaced civilians from the farms began to think of putting the pieces of their lives together again.

Lettina leapt from the truck and rushed to a lineup of other trucks parked at the station. She spotted Anna in the crowd and they forced their way through to meet Greita and Katya, finally locating Tanya under Sasha's protective care. Heaving with relief, Lettina grabbed the small hand and held tight.

"We must talk, Tanechka," she urged. "Come here. I want to tell you something, but quickly, what do each of you plan to do now?"

"I didn't know we had a choice," Katya said.

No else one spoke until Anna said, "I must see my parents. They have worried, but Lettina, what do you have in mind? Something other than going home? Don't be crazy. We have waited for this day—"

"I want to stay here in Novgorod for now and get a job. But I must see that Tanya finds her way safely back home."

Tanya's face was stained with a trail of tears through the dust. Murmuring indistinctly, she managed to say, "I am leaving Jessica, but what can I do? She is with Captain Stanislov—."

Lettina sensed Tanya was near a breakdown and they had no time for it.

On impulse, Anna said, "I will take you back with me, then you can make your own plans if that suits you, Tanya."

"I had not considered plans other than returning to Konsky," Katya said, stalling for time to think. "We have no money, no place to go, no place to sleep. It seems foolhardy."

"We can sell our rail passes, cheap, and have money left over to get started. I have saved a little," Lettina said." The prospect of luring her friends on what may become a fruitless path raised some doubts on her part, and likely for Katya and Greita, too, but there was little time to discuss it.

"The officials have no reason to count us, or care where we go now. They are not responsible for us. Your idea is possible, Lettina," Katya reflected with growing excitement. "I would like to stay, since we are here already. Would you stay, Greita?"

"I want to but I am afraid. I have never been on my own other than staying with you at the mill."

"We can find work in Novgorod. Clean houses if necessary, but it will be our chance to do and see something different than we would in Konsky. Most of all I promised I would find Jessica." Lettina looked at Tanya, the promise sealed in her eyes.

"We have to queue up or none of this will happen," Anna said, hurrying the group to join the crush of men and women eager to pick up their tickets.

XVII

Pilgrim

Brother Dmitri had been sent back to St. Sansais after the accident on Red Bounty *Koklhoz* that rendered him unable to work. Days of despair during his convalescence preceded any significant mental or spiritual healing, until a pilgrim arrived to occupy the guest room. Dmitri had found himself sinking back into the ordered routines of the monastery only to be yanked from its cradling warmth by images burned into his mind on the collectives. Unable to sleep because of chronic pain in his knee, he willed his flagging spirits to focus on the Cross, but focus for long he could not. He repetitiously uttered the Prayer of Jesus aloud, "Lord Jesus Christ, have mercy on me" until this, too, took flight. Propping his injured leg over a soft pillow, the monk thumbed the threadbare copy of the *Philokalia* searching for the usually comforting teachings of Simeon the Theologian, but these, most of all, disturbed his unsettled mind almost to the point of rage.

"My injuries are minor compared to most," Dmitri had replied when Abbot Konstantin met him at the rail station, but he suspected his haggard face, severe pain, and general weakness told the abbot far more of the experience than he wished to divulge. He had hobbled on crutches that were much too short for his tall frame, taking care to avoid placing weight on the crushed knee, held in place by swathes of cloth. A baggy Cossack tunic lashed by a cotton belt topped his workman's loose pants, disguising how much weight the monk had lost.

"*Ya tak silro skuchal po tebe,* I missed you so much, Brother Mitya. *Vsyo pod kontrolem.* Eveything is going to be all right. *Ya blagodalyu za eto Lord Jesus. Lyubov vsyo preodoleyet.* I thank God. Love overcomes everything." Father Konstantin had welcomed Dmitri, thrice kissing him on the cheeks and talking so fast that Dmitri did not have to tell his story immediately. For that Dmitri was immensely relieved.

On the way to the rusted Moskvitch that served as taxi to and from the monastery, the abbot had continued filling the hollow space between them, "You will be pleased to know that the harvesting is finished here, and the vines nicely put to bed for the winter. We are blessed in many ways, though we mourn our losses—principally your health and wholeness, and Pavel's leaving—"

"Pavel left?" Brother Dmitri halted his slow progress to the car. "I am saddened to hear of it. He left on his own?"

Surprised at Dmitri's reaction, the abbot remarked, "As I recall, you found the young guest quite trying."

"Trying, *da,* and worthy."

"A friend of the family came to take him home for a visit with his family. I believe Pavel understood that he was welcome to return if he so desired." Father Konstantin wished to placate the monk who had suffered too much already.

Lost in his reflections, Dmitri mumbled, "Pavel Ivanovich Zyclov has a good mind for the deeper teachings and an open heart. To all appearances he was committed to the spiritual path."

Konstantin laughed. "I believe that under your supervision, he was nurtured as if under the care of a mother hen. You taught him well. We may be confident that the Lord is leading him by the hand if only we could see it."

Now, several weeks later, the aftermath of the precipitous and tragic events of the communal harvesting continued to overwhelm Dmitri's considerable reserves. Respite from a harsh and chaotic world that he had sought at the monastery once before again became his only goal, an opportunity to devote himself to a life of contemplation and freedom from the demands and intrusions of the outside world. But the trauma he witnessed and experienced personally in the outside world tormented his innermost being. Dmitri shrank ever more into himself. He often did not hear the bells calling the monks for Matins or meals. Brother Anton took it upon himself to be at Dmitri's side, keep him involved in affairs of the monastery and reunite him with the healing presence of the Brothers. But incidentally, it was the pilgrim who began to bring Dmitri out of his shell.

"I have chanced upon the most wonderful stories in my wanderings that give me great joy, and I wish to share them with you," the old man said, accompanying Dmitri toward his room. Whereas Dmitri limped haltingly on crutches as they moved down the corridor, the pilgrim's legs had a strong, springy bounce despite his scarecrow appearance.

"Is not a pilgrimage outlawed under the regime? Wanderers are considered wastrels, and a blight on the nation these days," growled Dmitri, irritated by this latest intrusion.

The pilgrim was not to be dissuaded from telling his stories. Throwing back his head he laughed, showing gapping spaces among his yellow teeth. His long white hair trailed well past his shoulders. "Ah, my first story is that I was indeed a wastrel under the Tsars' debauched reigns, which led me to much suffering. Now I own nothing but a Bible and this rucksack, and very often I have no ruck! So you see, I must continue on my pilgrimage regardless of the ban on pilgrims. The wolves will find me faster in the forest than the patrols, ha," he laughed happily at himself and his cleverness. "Besides, the woods are full of legions of the dispossessed. There is hardly room to breathe!" He cackled uproariously like a man with his tankard and too much vodka.

The pilgrim leapt ahead to open the cell door for Brother Dmitri who negotiated his crutches inside with the pilgrim following unbidden right behind.

Windbag, groaned Dmitri, as he painfully eased himself onto his cot. Swelling in the injured knee had subsided somewhat, and the fiery inflammation that had kept him in the hospital had been reduced to small red spots that remained extremely tender. Brother Anton applied poultices from garden herbs, giving Dmitri a measure of relief and a slight hope for improvement. As a result, the retaining wrap was bound less securely now, allowing him to walk, but the joint was far from being properly healed, a prospect the surgeon doubted would occur.

"Let me tell you of a most remarkable teaching by a well-known *skhimnik* in Kiev, whom I sought on one of my many journeys. He was a true and compassionate ascetic who recognized at once that all my deprivations had not brought me peace of mind nor a joyous spirit."

Obviously the pilgrim broadcast his story wherever he went and so, too, Dmitri resigned himself to become an audience, confined as he was to his cot.

"I had lived in the forest eating roots and what little bread was given me, and I prayed continuously for forgiveness for my wastrel ways, which I had no regret leaving behind. Then I made my confession thinking that I would henceforth leave with lightness of heart and an even lighter spirit. But the wise teacher challenged me by asking, 'Do you love God?' And I spouted my platitudes affirming my endless devotion, but the *skhimnik* advised me to examine my conscience in light of my present difficulties. I went away deflated, crushed by his assumption that, first, he had the nerve to question whether I loved God, and secondly, that my pilgrimages, fasts and devotionals had not given me peace of mind and a joyous heart.

"I immediately began another pilgrimage, on these legs that you see, with the destination less important than my examination of conscience, asking myself, 'Do you love God?'"

The pilgrim paused to reflect on the long circuitous path that had apparently brought him back to the Spirit. Brother Dmitri was now awake and alert. The pointed inquiry by the mystic touched upon the very difficulty he had been confronting without resolution.

"If I loved God I would continuously say His name in prayer," continued the pilgrim, "and my joy would fulfill my soul's longing. I would know by the Word of God that He is always with us, which would bring me great peace. My heart would then be willing to keep all of His commandments and to live wholly in his Light so that I need not mind all the other things in life."

"And trust? How do you come to trust God?" Brother Dmitri ventured to ask, uncomfortably shifting his bony frame. He was aware the tinge in his voice conveyed a state akin to disbelief. His recent plunge into despair over the godless events on the farm *programme* had thoroughly taken possession of his outlook.

"Trust? You must ask your good Reverend Abbot, who would surely tell you to trust in the Providence of God," the pilgrim said airily, as if speaking to a child.

Fully chastised now that he had exposed his broken soul, Brother Dmitri confessed, "The abbot is so kind to me that I do not feel challenged. I needed your story to encourage me, to help me double my efforts to connect with the Spirit and a God who is lost to me. I am grateful, pilgrim. You may go."

A long night of fireflies, crickets, and the cry of a far away night hawk found Brother Dmitri still awake on his cot. Do I love God? he repeated over and over searching for an affirmative in his heart, yet the image of the body bag plagued him. I do not love a God who allows the suffering of children and young people of His creation, who allows bombs to drop on villagers' homes where mothers are giving birth or nursing their babies, a God who allows the exploitation of women. Becoming more agitated, he added all the horrors of war. I defy a loving God to explain all the persecutions by the regime which I abhor. Indeed I have lost my trust, perhaps even my faith.

By dawn Dmitri's knee burned like fire, the inflammation in need of Anton's medicinal herbs. The raging battle between Brother Dmitri and an unseen, unresponsive God had played out in one scenario after another until the monk became limp from exertion and pain. He raised his bloodshot eyes in time to see the happy pilgrim jauntily walking down the corridor with his rucksack on his back.

Windbag, Dmitri said again, this time without conviction. He momentarily wished that, had he the ability to walk, he could go with the pilgrim.

Novgorod, as seen from a rise, lay in a sea of yellow-greens and golds where church domes reached for the warm afternoon sun. Avenues of placid trees among tall apartment buildings stood out along streets of splintered tree trunks and piles of rubble not yet cleared from the bombing. Lettina, Katya and Greita viewed the vast stretches of burned forests and farm land tracing the railroad bed that curved into the city. Their train had been idled at the pass because of a separation of the aged track, a frequent occurrence amid the shambles left behind from the invasion.

"The others are going south and here we are going the opposite direction." Lettina said, while they waited beside the tracks for a repair crew.

"*Ya boyus'*, I am afraid," Greita plucking absently at the frayed edges of her print blouse. "The city looks very beautiful but so large. What shall we do?"

Katya tucked Greita's small hand comfortably under her own arm. "Our fearless leader will provide," she teased, turning to Lettina.

"I suspect you are ingenious yourself," Lettina retorted, "but we will not discuss that little triumph. I do believe the explosion caused the removal of Captain Stanislov, and led to the termination of harvesting, despite the official excuse of a shortage of petrol."

With no acknowledgment of her conjectures, Lettina continued. "Somehow I will inquire about the captain in hopes of finding Jessica. I cannot get her off my mind—I am more concerned about her than for myself. I will survive. I do not know about her." She wiped tears on the sleeve of her shirt and turned away. Katya and Greita shifted also, allowing Lettina, who never cried, a private moment.

Their mission to find jobs and a place to live as well as locate Jessica seemed daunting on top of other unknowns. The girls again boarded the train agreeing that at some point they needed to get permits to live in the city. In Novgorod, they found Russian train stations were remarkably similar, a welcome discovery when they took their first steps into a strange city. "We might have to come back to the station and sit up all night if we fail to find a place to stay. We could say we are going out in the morning if we have to," Lettina suggested, seeking solutions before problems actually occurred.

She was generally familiar with the history of Novgorod. The city belonged to the Kiev Oblast centuries ago, dating back to Norse occupation under Prince Rurik. Hundreds of churches and cathedrals were built over time, of which only a few survived the recent German occupation. The girls passed shambles of monuments and civic rubble next to the soaring architecture of the Cathedral of Sophia and St. Nicholas Cathedral, both of which had survived while indiscriminate bombing took out whole sections of industry and homes. Yet a semblance of life carried on. Buses and trams were operating. Long lines of shoppers on the streets waited for any kind of food or goods to become available. Hundreds of shops that formerly served the upper and middle classes were closed.

On advice of helpful people downtown, the girls made their way to Nizhnyi, the poor section of Novgorod. Here crowds milled about a dank People's Market, a vast warehouse housing vendors. The guttural languages of Georgians contrasted with the higher pitched Asian of colorfully dressed Uzbeks and Tazhiks. The hopeful asked *skol ka stoit?*, how much is it and haggled, but many walked away empty-handed.

"See, we know where to go already," Lettina said. "We can find low cost food, and probably the *chernyy rynok*, black market." Making her own decisions left her as high as she was in Konsky when the girls acquired Turkish coffee or vodka and partied until the last drop. She wished heartily for both.

"Shhh, be careful what you say. The *NKVD* are everywhere in the cities," whispered Katya.

The smell of hot food drew the girls to a pleasant Ukrainian vendor who cooked kasha on a small brazier at her stall.

"Are you always here? What time does the market open? How can you live selling for so little?" they asked at once.

The woman laughed, "Which is better? '*Cheap happiness or noble suffering?*'" she quoted from Dostoyevsky's *Underground Notes*, a quote as known as a proverb, though the woman was likely illiterate. "You will find we all suffer. There is nothing, no work nor money, but we get by," she added, while serving overly generous portions on small tin plates.

Katya stared intently at her, marveling at the good humor from one in desperate straits, and responded in kind. "'*One can be poor but honorable*,' according to the *Notes*," she said. She had seen this phenomenon among the women at Konsky's flour mill and again in the farm collectives. The contradiction between their good spirits and depressing conditions, prompted her to blurt, "How do you stay so happy?"

The woman's merry round face lit up, revealing missing lower front teeth. "My children are alive, God provides," she said simply. Yet a shadow drifted over the pale blue eyes searching the girls' faces. "My husband was killed not far from here defending the city. I must go on. What else can I do?"

"I am sorry," Lettina said, softly respecting the loss and hardships alluded to by this enduring woman who crouched over her brazier. A flower print scarf wound around her head and knotted in back, a hand woven wool shawl and long full skirt linked her to peasants of centuries before. It was said their nature tended to be happy, Lettina recalled from stories she had heard of the old days, though that history may have been revised in her early schooling. Thinking of schooling, she turned to Greita.

"You are a teacher. You have more advanced education than either of us. Surely you can get a position translating or teaching. I doubt if we will find many cleaning jobs or manual work since unemployment is widespread and money scarce for services."

Greita brightened at the prospect but shrugged, unsure or unwilling Lettina couldn't tell.

"We can try tomorrow." Lettina led the girls in search of accommodations for the night, not as difficult as they expected in this damaged and seemingly forgotten section of the city. Placards in the windows of private homes stated Guest House, or Boarders Welcome, or Cheap Rooms. Lettina fingered the few roubles left in her pocket after paying for the kasha, knowing that several more were sown inside her clothing for emergencies only. They took a room in what was at one time a spacious mansion, though the rooms had been carved into small apartments and separate bedrooms. The toilet was down the hall.

Bursting with the need to seek information, Lettina soon left the room and approached the older gentleman who owned the home.

"Do you know where I might find Captain Stanislov, supervisor of harvests on the *kolkhoz*?" Showing her sunburned forearms and calloused hands, she added, "I believe he has another assignment for us."

"*Da, da*, the harvest to feed the starving in the South. I have heard of it. You must be proud." His wizened features showed no emotion with the words, alerting Lettina that he had no passion for the sacrifice. This was confirmed when he said, "Now *we* shall starve without the grain. There will be no bread for us this winter and a cold winter it will be in Novgorod."

He carefully placed her payment for rent in a small tin box and slid it behind books on a shelf.

"The captain,—" urged Lettina.

"They are all the same, the soldiers. They take and take. I do not know where he lives." He finished abruptly as if he had said too much.

XVIII

Yuri

Two weeks after they arrived in Leningrad, Captain Yuri Stanislov paced the small apartment, ranting that he had expected immediate reassignment and none had been forthcoming. Several times he had dressed with care, a clean shave and spit-polished shoes, to visit the offices of Army headquarters in Leningrad. He considered these offices provincial since Moscow made all major decisions; nevertheless, he had previously received orders from the local Department of Internal Affairs, which required the military to administer the farm *programme* in response to the drought disaster. Every morning Svetlana heard an earful of his opinions about their slothful procedures.

"I worked hard to get where I am, Svetlana. You would be astounded if you knew of our campaigns. Poland and the Balkans fell as our troops seized the capitals of Lithuania, Latvia, Estonia. By raw manpower and superior numbers we brought these countries into the Republic.

"So you see, I did not rise in the ranks by shirking my duty. I—we who fought our way through Germany and the northern states expected a certain gratitude if not honor, after our conquests. To advance, I need to know what my next duty will be." With that even Yuri became tight-lipped rather than complain.

Lacking definite orders, Yuri lingered at the table, his usually starched cotton shirt wrinkled, sleeves rolled up to his elbows. He chain-smoked and cursed the department for pandering to insiders, those with half his ability who received twice the promotions, and the absurdity of the military serving under a civilian agricultural agency despite the charitable cause.

"Our country survived the last five centuries because we depended upon our farms—farms run by *mirs*, the *obshchina*, who directed the serfs—yet now agencies fail to plan for enough petrol to complete the harvesting. If the story of shortage is true, it reflects poorly on me since the farm *programme* was under my supervision." Even his small, usually precise mustache with its lack of symmetry registered disapproval.

"It is a setback, but not a permanent one," he added. "We are *odinakoviye*, alike, Svetlana. You want more out of life like Grigory and Lydia Ratkevich. They travel by train from Moscow to Leningrad on business, but stay for parties and the symphony. We toured the museum. Am I not helping you, Svetlana? You cannot fool me with that stare of a dumb goat."

"I do understand you want a new assignment. I wish they would hurry with the summons. *Da*, we want to better our lives, but—"

"But what?"

A half-suppressed retort that shocked even Jessica escaped her lips. "You dare not treat me like--like a goat!"

"You are complaining? If I had left you in the fields, you would be dead. If I had left you on the farm, you would be back at Benyanske's stitching boots, or recruited for a worse *programme*. Then where would you be?"

Svetlana saw her fantasies tumbling like amber beads scattering across the rough floor of her parents' *izba* when she was four. Her small hands had flown over her mouth.

"That amber necklace is all I have," her mother had said in a voice Svetlana did not recognize, as if the person who stood over her aghast had lost a piece of herself, of her past, a link to a time unknown to Svetlana.

"I—I'll pick them up, *Mama*," she had cried, crouching on the floor and scrambling under the table and in dark corners. Svetlana never saw the necklace again. Perhaps it had been sold for food.

A surge of nervousness aggravated a rash she kept hidden. The increasing stress of waiting with him for a summons had stimulated her nervous condition, causing a rash that she noticed had now spread beyond her sleeves.

"I am helping you, Svetlana, get that in your head. With luck we will both live comfortably, perhaps in a larger apartment near Nevsky Prospekt."

Svetlana knew she could not reassure Yuri one way or the other when he became belligerent. He sat hunched over with elbows on his knees, eyes cast on the fine rug he admitted having traded collectibles for. She sensed his thoughts were now on a trajectory of his own ambitions. Or more likely, on his insecurities.

The eczema that crawled up her neck and studded the undersides of her forearms itched until Jessica could ignore it no longer. Her fingernails rasped over the dry scaly patches.

"You are repulsive," Yuri said, "Get rid of that scabby stuff." He produced an ointment from the bedroom.

"I had eczema before when—when--I started work in the factory. It went away."

Yuri refused to look at her while he rifled through his desk drawers, sorting and tucking away items that Jessica could not see. The ointment, a mixture of lanolin, lavender oil, and petroleum, smelled fragrant but failed to mitigate the problem overnight. They had barely spoken in the meantime. Yuri pushed the two armless maroon leather chairs together, and tossed her several Army blankets and a pillow to sleep on that night.

"I do not want to get it," he said. Yuri began to take long walks alone, his mood deepening.

"I need to wash my hair," Svetlana excused herself one time when he went out, though he had not asked her to walk with him, and on another occasion, she said, "I will mend my dress," to cover her relief that he was out of the apartment. The cost of the impasse was her unchecked splotches of eczema and increasing claustrophobia when he locked the door from the outside.

"I feel like a dumb goat to put up with this," Svetlana stammered each time the door closed, her lips forbidding a string of expletives.

A few days later Grigory and Lydia stopped by to invite Yuri and Svetlana to a dinner party at the apartment they maintained in Leningrad. Svetlana woodenly took his hat and her cape, instantly signaling her discomfort to the guests.

"Come see many of our old friends," Grigory urged Yuri, filling in a gap in the conversation. "And meet a few who have no affiliation with the military. They are primarily social acquaintances, the opera, and so on," he said, generally dropping names but evidently thought better of it with the tension in the room. His short stature and smooth boyish cheeks contrasted with the sense of importance that he managed to portray, as if he perpetually had a long list of celebrated figures in his circle, ascribing him a more impressive appearance.

"You would be surprised how the theater and concerts have flourished in Moscow in recent months. Subject matter has been circumscribed, to be sure, but a lively scene exists in the capital nevertheless. *La ville est grand avec l'art et la museque.* We are pleased to find Leningrad has also begun to recover and resume—"

"It never stopped, even during the shelling, so they tell me. You and I were on the march in Germany at the time," Yuri cut in, his roving eye on Svetlana rather than his guests or attending to the conversation.

"Svetlana, find the box of chocolates I bought last week," visibly relieved when she stepped out of sight.

"*Verite'*, 'tis so," Grigory said, reaffirming the contributions of Shostakovich whose *Seventh Symphony* was performed by the Leningrad Symphony Orchestra during the Siege. The composer has an uncanny ability to appeal to the masses, while trumpeting the glory of the state and remaining in favor," he added. Dropping his voice, he added, "He has a future with films, I understand, likely because he chose to remain in the motherland."

"A composer with a future. Certainly we have seen writers and poets flee. Does one really have a future in this country?" Yuri again paced the small room, waving his arms to emphasize his discontent. Grigory rolled and unrolled the end of his tie, flashing a glance at Lydia that Yuri was best suited to being on the march, a trait she understood from the stories Grigory had told her. Unoccupied, Yuri was like a caged animal.

The chocolates, if they existed, were not on the kitchen shelf or in the bedroom. Svetlana pulled her chair near Lydia's, who realized at once that no woman would want to be seen at a social gathering with the rosy spread of eczema on her neck and arms. Besides, Svetlana's puffy eyes looked as though she had been robbed of the little she possessed, her youthful delight vastly altered from the person she had been at the museum.

"Svetlana, are you feeling all right?" Lydia asked, while the men were talking. "I can bring you naphthalan for that rash. It is an oil."

Jessica's mouth became dry, unable to assemble a non-committal response; in reality, she checked her panic and tried not to scream out all the pain and fear she felt to one of the only two women she had met in Leningrad. Emotions rolled across her face despite her attempt to appear hospitable. The rumpled dress, faded from exposure to sun and wind on the farm, further emphasized her distress.

"Would you like coffee?" Jessica managed to offer. "Yuri made fresh—"

"We really must be going. I assume you would not want to come."

Jessica signaled she could not talk, and Lydia covered for her by resorting to her usual one-sided conversation. "There will be gatherings once or twice a week from now on. Yuri, you two really must join us. We find them most enlightening, and we keep up with the times this way. We intend to support efforts to return to a civil society, if not be in the vanguard of the movement. I believe we can best serve in that capacity. Grisha feels entirely in agreement."

Grigory nodded vigorously and replaced the new felt hat over his thinning brown hair.

"I wonder if I should resume life as a civilian as long as I am on an unofficial sabbatical," Yuri said. "You seem to be thriving."

"I am actually stationed in an administrative position with the Guards. We have had a bit of slack time. Our mission is changing. We shall see." Grigory downplayed his own position, perhaps in consideration of Yuri's uncertain situation, perhaps covering a sense of jeopardy similar to Yuri's. "I understand our newly established Party control in Ukraine and Poland may draw our troops for enforcement. Deportations and imprisonments are ongoing, though the countries and their populations have been beaten into the ground, as you know."

"The Poles always protest. What is new? They refuse to be governed." Yuri's disgust brought the conversation to a close. After the guests left, he again unburdened his impatience about the hiatus on the only person present, Svetlana Gilkova. "Here I am doing nothing while the Ratkevichs freely enjoy themselves, whether his story is true or not. It's a devil of a situation."

"Surely you will hear tomorrow," Svetlana said, knowing he became infuriated when she did not answer. She set out two coffee cups to distract him.

"Nevermind. You think I would take you anywhere looking like that? You would embarrass me in front of my friends."

The piercing insults did not go unheeded, but Svetlana replied levelly, "I would have liked to attend the dinner. Lydia said the events are enlightening."

"Lydia talks too much. She would have you thinking pretentious thoughts."

"You could buy me a dress suitable for the city."

Yuri cocked his head, his eyes roving head to toe of the once modern girl with swinging black hair in a crimson red silk blouse, who had become a dowdy, sharp-tongued *Russki* housewife. He cut short a spiteful response.

"Get ready for tomorrow. We will find a dress to make you presentable."

The next day they left the apartment to shop, not at the few boutiques on Nevsky Prospect, the center of the city, but at РЫНОК НАРОДОВ, the People's Market, several miles distant from the neighborhood where Yuri lived. They walked one way and planned to return by bus. Yuri carefully allocated his funds by nature, if not by uncertainty of future employment. His faux-bourgeoisie lifestyle in an apartment with a view, a woman, drinks, imported coffee, and an affinity for collecting handcrafted silver objects apparently required considerable upkeep.

Jessica relished the chance to be outdoors, inhaling a moist breeze deeply imbued with the scent of the Baltic Sea, a crisp Arctic freshness that made her snug her heavy scarf around her chest. The sense of open space between the damaged, mostly abandoned concrete apartments provided relief from the confinement she endured with the captain, though an uncharacteristic silence held sway over the city. A few people, mostly elderly, nodded at the couple, though many wandered aimlessly as if they had forgotten or misplaced something, their faces vacant—the future too hard to endure, the past so alive it stole their thoughts. Broken streets forced pedestrians to walk with caution around great craggy potholes. Yuri and Svetlana balanced on temporary board bridges over trenches dug by the city's defenders. Mountains of demolished building debris, tree roots, and trash had been heaped on empty lots or former city parks. Residents had become scavengers on the streets where they lived, survivors still uncertain of survival. Boarded-up windows on pockmarked buildings reminded Svetlana of rural Konsky that bore the brunt of German invasions and retreats.

"Millions of defenders are buried all over the city, most dying of starvation within the three years of the Siege. The cemetery is—"

"Please, I cannot bear to think of it. I was only fifteen when it began. Can we be free of all that today?"

"There is no money for reconstruction. Work is done by *zeks*." Yuri leaned close to her ear and mouthed, "Leningrad is not favored by our leader. He could have rescued its citizens from the Siege much sooner had he brought our units back from the campaign in the Baltics." Aloud he said, "You know from experience we must first feed the people. Our war is yet to be won in terms of recovery. Nature has been less than helpful in the South. Everyone is asked to sacrifice to get through the coming winter, you understand?"

Was that Yuri's story to cover his attacks on the State? Svetlana questioned his tone. It sounded like the mouthpiece the farm workers heard day and night during the harvest. She wondered if he secretly feared reprisal for the tragic events on the collectives. He and Grigory both seemed to be waiting, for advancements or demotions, she dared not guess.

Either way, she held her always sensitive stomach, the sense of starved corpses on the streets where she stood a vivid image, the near dead burying the dead during bitterly cold winters, made worse by little or no heating fuel. Ghosts seemed to rise from the pavement, the silence reigning over human efforts that also dared rise, to rebuild. Yet Yuri did not seem like one to sacrifice; in fact, the opposite was true. He liked to maintain appearances. His charitable statements seemed an attempt to defend himself and his actions, that he was a friend of the State like the Ratkevichs. Both Yuri and Svetlana recognized his friends' active social life and patronage of cultural events set them apart.

She felt like an outsider looking in at a world she had only glimpsed in the movies, and those heavily censored to elevate the image of the common man. Yet her fashion eye observed that Lydia had casually slipped off a new cape and straightened the seam in her silk stockings as if these were too ordinary to mention. She wanted to say, but did not, that the Ratkevichs can afford to put on dinner parties and buy Grigory a new hat.

"You wonder about their expensive tastes," Yuri continued in that disconcerting manner of reading her mind. "*Alors,* they were married not long ago, and they celebrate while others scrabble to get by. Either she has money or they shop at a market in Moscow similar to the one we are going to today." He stubbed out a cigarette on a broken iron railing of a once stunning mansion that now appeared to be a convalescent hospital.

It occurred to Svetlana that Yuri might change his mind about buying her a new dress after this discussion about money. He never seemed to tire of admiring her in the crimson red silk blouse and slim black skirt she wore today. She knew he was unlikely to spend lavishly, even for her. In addition, the Ratkevichs' lives were such a contrast to the wretchedness of her own: unmarried, lacking resources, and unsafe, this last a telling postscript to several sleepless nights on the chairs in which she endlessly reassessed her situation. But no alternatives arose for the very reasons she found herself in the predicament in the first place.

The People's Market, a trade center Svetlana suspected was in concert with черный рынок, the black market, was housed on the ground floor of an abandoned factory, notable only for its absence of uniformed guards or police. Evidently condoned if not sanctioned, the market attracted a crowd that flowed through its wide opening, a former shipping dock. The shoppers spoke in subdued tones with friends and neighbors, and hard times were evident in the dearth of produce and goods. Stall after stall of empty shelves and foul-smelling rubbish formed one side of the cavernous room. On the other side, old women hawked the culls of their gardens, soft cabbages with limp outer leaves, onions already beginning to mold, and small lumpy potatoes unfit for the shelves of grocers.

Yuri took Jessica's arm and expertly steered her through the aisles, hardly looking left or right until they came to a section exhibiting tangled radios and parts.

"I need a radio with better over-the-wire reception. Perhaps one has come out I'm not aware of." He separated battery-operated from electric radios, wartime walkie-talkies from military headsets, and bulky Delcos from Red Army metal sets. He lingered so long Svetlana circled to shelves of broken Victrolas and junked antiques. Distracted from the radios, Yuri followed her and thumbed through odds and ends on the shelves of collectibles, reading inscriptions on the backs as if he were knowledgable. Svetlana examined the dirty, hand-woven Eastern rugs that lined the end wall, remembering her father had traded goods from Asia. At last, Yuri directed her to tables piled high with women's wear.

In dismay, Svetlana looked at the previously owned garments, seeing a reflection of sacrifices her parents had made when they sold or traded everything they owned for a bit of food.

"I--I--cannot," she started to say.

"There." Yuri pointed to a clothes rack behind the women who appeared to be excited about the prospect of making a sale to these well-dressed buyers. They fussed over the rack and produced several well-designed gowns. "No, no, a dress," he demanded, pointing to a rack of finely tailored women's two-piece wool suits and knee-length linen day dresses with wide lace trim. The women fluttered about to please the captain, who chewed on his lower lip, now impatient to make the purchase and leave as quickly as possible.

"This collection came from a prominent—"

"I don't care about the rich bitches," Yuri said.

A saleswoman about Svetlana's age looked sympathetic, and offered a slim unadorned black dress with long sleeves, a high collar held in place by an ivory brooch and accented by a gaily-colored silk scarf.

"That one," Yuri said, already reaching in his pocket and offering something other than roubles for the dress. Svetlana could not see the transaction, but the exchange appeared to satisfy both Yuri and the woman. She smiled and wrapped the dress in a few sheets of the *Izvesta*. Yuri rolled the package and carried it like a newspaper. Svetlana glimpsed headlines blaring Soviet charges of United States interference in Iran. *"Deal fails to give USSR oil field. New tensions loom between former Allies.*

They hastened through the Market and out the back door, drifting through narrow, canal-lined streets of what must have been the old city and emerged at a bus line. *New tensions loom*…Svetlana dismissed her dream of going to America out of hand. It would never happen if new tensions now loomed.

XIX

Fantasia

At the next bus stop, Yuri motioned Svetlana to get off at an unpretentious barbershop with dark closed curtains. They entered a raspy weathered door into the quiet charm of a salon. A graying older gentleman bowed and stiffly led them to an inner room. Gas lights flickered with multiple reflections in mirrors revealing two modern women stylists, distinctive in *Rossiya* for their hair separated in side parts and held in place by combs.

"The aged rosette wallpaper is so elegant," Svetlana exclaimed to Yuri who looked pleased with himself. The gentleman was obviously Yuri's barber.

"This is the closest thing to home I remember," Yuri whispered." The barber's total acceptance kindled a warmth in Yuri that Svetlana had not witnessed, a heart-felt relationship apparently surprising even him. Without a word he handed her over to an eager young woman in an above-the-knee skirt. He took a chair in the outer room, though the door remained open.

"*A ya Svetlana.*" At once she felt at home in the realm of beauty and fashion. The clearly delighted stylist offered her arm and Svetlana floated into the back room, again in touch with her benefactress and mentor, Madame Marsolet, the core of her experience, the epitome of her fashion design dreams. She overheard the host offer Yuri tea and shift his chair next to Yuri's.

"What do you make of this peace time?" the host asked. "A few more women are seeking services of the salon, though I am unsure how long we can stay in business."

"Our troops coming from the Front hoped for peace and rest," Yuri said. "We were promised better lives after our victories. I was one of them. Between you and me, trainloads of prisoners are being sent east to labor camps, not just insurgents from border states," he confided, "but our own people," alluding to reinstatement of pre-war oppression and crackdowns. "Here is a newspaper. See for yourself."

Svetlana heard the barber rattling the newspaper the dress had been wrapped in. "*Allied Countries Threaten Russia over Middle East Oil*. We have sickness and hunger enough without fearing another war," he muttered.

Yuri seemed to be shuffling his feet back and forth or crossing and uncrossing his legs, nervous about everything these days, uncertain about his fate after the abrupt end to the harvesting. He was usually closed mouth about his affairs, and Svetlana knew from experience that the walls may have ears. The men fell silent, a pervasive sense of dread hovering in the outer room.

In the softly scented inner room, the hairdressers, one a little older than Svetlana and the other possibly her mother, spoke to each other in French, but switched to Russian to communicate with Svetlana.

"Like yours," Svetlana said, pointing to the women's short bobbed hair. She tossed her own shoulder-length hair, feeling the weight of days at the farm when no one tended to their appearance. "*Pozhaluysta*, a modern cut." Svetlana felt she had again stepped into the mysterious realm of the shopkeepers, Madame and Monsieur Marsolet. Their attention to the innermost dreams of a twenty-year-old and the magic of fashion had transformed her world to this day. She had a sense of celebrating her birthday at last, long after it had been cruelly usurped by the recruiters in Konsky, unconsciously giving Yuri a pass for being one of them.

Madame and Monsieur had seen something in me that made me believe in myself, she mused, although others have tried to rob me of it nearly every day since. Aloud she said almost shyly, "You look very fashionable. Is it allowed in Leningrad?"

The stylists giggled as if it were a joke shared by women like themselves. "Dress like a *babuska* in public, *ma cherie*," the older woman whispered, laughing again as if progressive women in the city were in a conspiracy, a mood that infected Svetlana. She laughed with them.

"My friends are not concerned about fashion, but it is very important to me. Neither the peasant style or housewife look appeal to me, and certainly not the blue and white uniforms or lead-gray jumpsuits the factory and aircraft workers wear. They are as similar to one another as worker bees." She could not continue knowing she'd likely become a factory worker again.

The dim interior and firm snips of the scissors allowed Jessica to submit herself entirely to the joy of being thoroughly cared for by the well-versed beauticians, whose oval faces and shining eyes looking back at her in the mirror were sparkling and beautiful. With each clip of the fallen tresses, Svetlana felt more like the Jessica she knew as herself.

At last, admiring the cut in the mirror, she nearly cried, "O, *ya lyublyu eto*! I love it!" and warmly kissed each woman on both cheeks. "A conspiracy of women, *da,* I can do this," she affirmed, knowing the women did not understand what she meant. She wondered if she dared do business in this cunning manner if she pursued fashion designing. They showed her off with pride to Yuri and the proprietor.

"*Choodyesno!* You look marvelous!" Yuri said. A small smile tricked the corners of his wide stern lips when he paid generously in roubles for the service.

Swept up in the thrill of open admiration by men, even by the tottery old proprietor, Svetlana's fantasies flew above the crowd in the rickety bus they rode home to a world of stunningly dressed stage figures, whose smart quips and appraising eyes ultimately led to love. Black and white films merged into those in chroma, the scenes all topsy-turvy, but a vision of long lovely legs in black mesh stockings left a tantalizing goal for her next acquisition. She turned up her collar as if to hide her evolving self from prying eyes, those who might be inclined to take it all away from her. Their trip back to Yuri's apartment was over before she realized it.

Inside the apartment he closed the door and Svetlana heard the familiar click of the lock. He slowly removed his uniform and hat, and placed them on the coat rack.

"*Ti takaya krasivaya.* You are so beautiful," he said, his voice throaty and measured as it had been when he first approached her on the farm. Running the back of his fingers along her high cheekbone, words seemed to force themselves from his heart. "You are the best thing that ever happened to me, Svetlana. I want you to know that."

His light blue eyes hinted of a humility she never expected to see in him, a look that threw her off. "*Ya khochu, chtobee my vsegda byli vmeste.* I wish we would always be together," he said.

She saw him swallow hard, his jaw tight with emotion. She could not look at the tenderness in his eyes, as if the captain might be embarrassed to be so readable. No words, no thoughts, no reaching out occurred to her. Yet it felt like a scene inspired by her fantasies of romantic movies, until Yuri handed her the crushed newspaper-wrapped dress. The reality of her present situation struck her. Svetlana sat down hard on one of the maroon leather chairs, the parcel in her lap. Her legs had given out in the confusion of Yuri's admission. His tenderness triggered fear, incompatible with her earlier bold yearnings. Vaguely dizzy, she reminded herself to pay attention, breathe.

Yuri went to the cupboard and set out glasses and several flavors of vodka. He appeared absent minded, pouring his drink and lighting a cigarette as though he put the shopping trip behind him. Jessica used the excuse to hang the new black dress in the bedroom and gather her thoughts, to calm what felt like an irrational impulse to flee—Yuri had bought her a dress, Yuri had been tender, why?

He turned on the radio, but did not eat though Jessica set out a tray of pickled herring, sliced rye bread and hard cheese.

"The static garbles the news just when I need to know what is going on." He fiddled with the knob and jerked the antenna. "I'll try to find a more recent model next time at the Market. You cannot trust the sellers there. They get in cheap loot that has been raided for parts. Anyway, most of the broadcasts report production is up when it is dismally falling behind."

Svetlana knew his criticism included farm *programme* predictions and failures, as well the shortcomings of the military to adjust to peacetime occupations. The elusive new assignment was always on his mind. His brooding intensified. Being injudicious about his remarks meant he was increasingly worried about decisions at the higher levels of the Red Army, which was subject only to the unpredictable and often crushing control of the Ruler.

Empty bottles began to accumulate on the dining table as afternoon hours dragged on. By evening, Yuri recklessly searched bottom shelves for additional stores of liquor. He stripped off the stiffly starched shirt and pants he had worn to the market, and changed into his undershirt and loose cotton pants of a day laborer. Overheated with the drinks and inflamed thoughts, he went to the windows and drew the shades.

"There's going to be a storm," he said to Svetlana, attempting to explain his actions. Svetlana pulled into herself, wary and distant, willing her thoughts to dwell one at a time upon Pasha, Lettina, Tanya and Anna. She tried to imagine what each might be doing or thinking. Pasha is recovering in the monastery, I am sure he will have recovered by the time I return. We will be so happy. Surely the abbot surrounds him with prayers enough for all of us who fail to do so. God, if there is a God, take care of Pasha. She slipped easily into prayer for each person, imitating her mother, or perhaps Tanya, the cousin she'd left behind. But I know Anna has taken her safely home. O, I wish I were home with them.

"Where is the letter opener?" Yuri fruitlessly sifted a stack of unopened mail on his desk. "It is supposed to be here. Here," he indicated pointing to other silver objects on the desk and sputtering at Svetlana.

"It must be there. I have not seen it. Did you look behind—?"

He yanked the desk forward and a distinct drop meant the opener had fallen to the floor. Fumbling in the crevice he grasped it and began stabbing at one letter after another.

"There is nothing here. Not a summons to appear for a new position, nothing about a new assignment." His eyes balefully searched the room, the letter opener still in his hand. A roar pounded in Svetlana's ears, her growing terror abetted by thunder of the storm outside. She breathed only when Yuri slit open a carton of crackers from a shelf in the kitchen.

Hoping food would sober him up, she thought coffee might help, too, but before she could make a suggestion, Yuri belched, his voice thick. "I don't know why I keep you. I can't afford you anyway."

He turned fully toward her revealing blond hairs on his chest above an undershirt now stained yellowish and brownish from the drinks. "You must bring me bad luck. See, I get nothing." He pointed to the ripped letters on the desk. He brushed the box of crackers off the shelf, and strode across the room towards Svetlana whose bloodless face met his florid countenance.

"The women at the farms, they caused me problems. They broke the machinery and set fire to the car. As supervisor I could not tolerate mob insurrection. It would give me a bad name, even if I had not wanted the cursed, low-ranking position in the first place." He saw Svetlana's wordless mouth open and close, her dark eyes unflinching.

"Sabotage the reports said. Sabotage so the laborers would get sent home. Well, *Shlyukhi byli otpravleny domoy vse ravno , chto teper'so mnoy?* The whores were sent home and now what for me? And you were one of the mob. The women blew up the damn car. Tell me about that, Svetlana. You know about that. Women talk, I'm sure." Before Svetlana could form a *nyet* with her frozen lips, he added, "And one girl took her own life. Would you take your own life, Svetlana? Tell me," he demanded, bending his foul 90-proof breath near her face. "Tell me!"

"You know I was in the house during that time—"

He hesitated, sweat beaded beneath his nostrils, leaving droplets among the tar-tinged hairs of his mustache.

Svetlana rose, elaborately balancing herself beside one of the armless chairs and steadying her voice at the same time. "The girls were taken—the men raped the girl who died."

O, Bozhe, chto ya sdelal? O God, what have I done? I accused him and his officers of rape and murder.

Her long legs tensed for flight, her mind aware there was no escape. Rain came, slashing the windowpanes in an insistent drumming, heralding a cool freshness outside that contrasted with the deteriorating, perfidious atmosphere in the room. She willed herself to appear un-defensive, her hand resting lightly on the slim outline of a maroon chair, conscious only of the calculated poses of an actress in a harrowing plot, the letter opener out of reach in the kitchen. An increasing sense of abstraction left her merging with figures she so often identified with—a play of expressions across Ingrid Bergman's face in reply to Humphrey Bogart, Jessica Tandy's containment in *The Seventh Cross* with Spencer Tracy—the Jessica of American films sewing boot leather by day, tolerated only by forbidden dreams of amorous alliances in glamorous fashions—*Fantasia*, the sense of being enfolded in Stokowski's wickedly enchanting score in the Mickey Mouse film. Her lips twitched in a one-sided smile, a sense of being elsewhere, knowing her story, her drama, ended with the heroine being trapped.

Seeing herself playing the part of victim, she no longer felt able to change the course of action when Yuri stepped closer. Until his fist struck the left side of her face, cracking the cheekbone and edges of several back teeth, she was absent from her body.

Jessica of the movies again became Svetlana. She leaned over and spit blood on the imported rug. Rising, her youthful face dissolved into the hardened features of many Russian women on the streets of Leningrad.

"You are like my mother when you look at me that way. See what you caused?" Yuri retreated to the bedroom, toting the last bottle in the apartment, a cheap vodka-cranberry flavor he had bought for Svetlana. A last glare over his shoulder at her composed a score as if to music, the crushing end of his dreams for better times together, the reflexive blow meant to crush "the mob," if only by an immediate target.

The score, as it were, resounded in dizzying flashes inside Svetlana's head, followed by a creeping blackness. She barely straightened the matched pair of chairs and laid down without benefit of blanket or pillow. When she finally slept toward morning she dreamed that the sun came up in the west and it set in the west.

XX

Raisa

Morning light revealed a profile of Leningrad beneath a heavy atmosphere left over from the night's storm. A discreet tap at the door brought Captain Yuri Stanislov to his feet. He plunged across the front room, awakening Svetlana. She squeezed open her matted left eye in time to glimpse a young messenger place an official envelope in Yuri's hand. Pausing a moment, the messenger waited for a gratuity, but seeing the recipient was fully engrossed in the letter, he did not wait long.

"It is the summons," Yuri mumbled. The words slurred over dry lips that awkwardly tendered a half-smoked cigarette. He started to say "Make some coffee," but thought better of it after a glance at Svetlana. Tossing the envelope on his desk, he made it himself, making a statement of sorts by clattering the cups and utensils. Twice he snatched up the letter to reread the contents before stuffing it back in the envelope and dropping it on his desk.

The ten minutes of fussing before he went into the bathroom dragged for Svetlana; any slight movement sent streaks of pain from her jaw. A headache like she'd never had before compelled her to hold very still where she lay. Barely touching the hot swollen side of her face, she tentatively assessed the damage. Her lips pursed into a bloody pout expressing her dogged refusal to endure any more.

He might try to hurt me again before he leaves, *O, Bozhe, chto ya sdelal, chto ya sdelal?* What have I done, he will hate me. But I will—I will get out of here—

The apartment soon smelled of fresh coffee made hot and strong. Yuri poured his own cup and paced the two small rooms, fuming over a wrinkle in his best shirt and a small stain on the trousers of his uniform. Purposefully, he did not look at Svetlana. She struggled to sit upright and rotate her head, an attempt to loosen her stiff neck that felt jammed into her shoulders. Yuri slurped his coffee, trailing dribbles over the formerly immaculate floor. Fresh brown stains blended with those of the now brownish blood in the rug.

"It is the summons, Svetlana. I must report to headquarters." His voice sounded forced, dispirited. "It had better be good news—for me—for us," overlooking last night's assault.

She heard it as a reckless gamble on good fortune or another fist to the jaw. Either way it would fail to pacify her.

"I expect respect from you, Svetlana. Be careful what you say next time." He strode toward the door but turned back to retrieve the envelope. "*Vy stavite vashi rozovyye sis'ki oni prodvigayut menya.* You bet your pink tits they are promoting me." At last his gaze shifted to Svetlana whose blunt wounded stare met his. "You have come a long way, Svetlana of the Boot and Shoe factory. Remember, I said I could help you if you let me, but you lie about my officers."

Lie? Her mind worked slowly to formulate a safe response, but there was only one, and Yuri would beat her senseless if she told the truth—or looked like a dumb goat. The truth was he knows the girl hung herself because she was raped. He cannot bear to hear it because he was supervisor.

She refused to answer; what could she say? Her head hurt. Her jaw throbbed. Pains stabbed her cheek and eye. The coffee burbled in the pot once more then joined the leaden silence of the apartment. Yuri's hand grasped and released the door handle as if he hadn't finished the accusations, or perhaps he needed to make amends and failed to find means of expressing himself. Otherwise, the two remained like pathetic wooden figures on a stage, unspoken words weaving their short past into an unreadable present. The maddening lack of response escalated Yuri's insecurities, precursor to one of his threats. Svetlana unconsciously shrank from him, hands behind her clutching at air, finding only threads of frayed clothing.

"We can start over if you stick with me, Svetochka." He jangled keys in his pocket, his words thick, sticky. "I will get a promotion. They owe it to me."

The earnestness, the endearment, a momentary hint of the ambitious young man she had known reminded Svetlana he had another side, a tender side he had revealed just this afternoon and had already forgotten. She dismissed the promises with a flutter of her fingers. At once Yuri's temper flared. With flashing eyes and blanched lips, he snarled something she did not hear. Cowed, she ducked. She heard him furiously open the door and step out, turning the key to lock the door from outside. Svetlana lifted her head and uttered a long sigh of relief at the sound of the click.

"*Slava bogu, on ushel.* Merciful God, he is gone. He's *p'yan v stelku*, still so drunk he could have hit me again, *svoloch'*, the bastard," she shuddered. A glance around the apartment told the story of the last twenty-four hours; drained bottles lay on the table and floor, rugs were scuffed and furniture awry. Heat flaring under the copper coffee maker was too high, tingeing the brew with a scalded odor.

Svetlana slowly took stock of her situation. It's not like Yuri to mess up his apartment. He never leaves the burner on, never drips coffee on the floor, never sets his cup on his desktop, and never goes out in less than a perfect uniform. The scene suited her plan perfectly.

Not Svetlana of yesterday, but Jessica of today, allowed her head to clear. Commotion in the apartment building resumed with weekday routines. Rapid steps down from the fourth and fifth floors meant tenants hurried to work. Sharp commands sent children off to school in their blue and white uniforms, their book bags slung over bony shoulders. Distant grinding of engines switching tracks at one of Leningrad's terminals signaled urgency for one to be up and out.

The autumn sun, unusual for the typically overcast port city, found its way into the east window, creating long patterns across her still form, upright on the armless chairs that had been her bed. Slowly she rose; one piercing eye surveyed the disheveled room, while a course of action coalesced in her mind. Every last detail of the escape plan crystallized as if she had written it in an instruction manual overnight. Charged with a fury all her own, Jessica experienced an evolving confidence that bent her life in ways she'd never imagined. She swore that a beating would never happen again. Mechanically, she set about securing her future; a future that had yet to take shape. An image from the story of her mother and father fleeing the Bolsheviks flashed through her mind—they had little choice about their future, she recalled. I don't really know their story, which must be my story, too. I never understood why my mother was so angry. Now I am fleeing—I will never submit to Yuri again—I must get out of here to save my life.

"I am a *zek*, a prisoner, for the last time."

She dared not think otherwise.

First withdrawing her scant collection of clothing from Yuri's bedroom, she avoided glancing at the bed. "The bed of compromises, not promises, nothing in it for me, the dirty *ublyudok*, the bastard. Like Anna, I take away only bitterness"—the trauma of the *kolkhoz* returned with a rush, the officers taking the girls, the explosion, the suicide, and finally Yuri's insistence, "I can help you," when he only helped himself.

Bozhe, it's like the filthy old miller helping himself to Lettina when he had a wife. Perhaps Lettina cared for him anyway. And what has become of them, scattered or home?

"I feel—," but thinking of friends and home triggered jerky sobs that set off racking pain from temple to jaw. Fearful of Yuri returning, she stifled the tears. She had no time. Shoving aside the forbidding paraphernalia of a military man, she stripped the few dresses off hangers, driven by the danger of her present situation.

"A better life? What is better in this? Left beaten and alone," she cried aloud. "He didn't want me. He only wanted to look good. *Bah*. Any cursed brass dame from the streets could do that. Why me?"

Her lips trembled, mushing the words, but the dialogue continued inside. Because I let myself. I had to get away from--from it all. Like

Lettina, I wanted a man. A sequence of events rolled like worn movie tape in her mind: robbed of her birthday, packed like cattle in a rail car, beaten down by work, heat and fatigue. Starved on rations and solicited by an official who forced her into servicing him with sex. That was Yuri, the bastard. Her hand involuntarily swept the bad movie past her face. She struggled to set aside any idea that she was at fault for the beating, that she need not justify her current actions. But she had to hurry. The dresses lay in a heap on the floor, two pair of shoes set aside.

O, *Chort voz 'mi!* these clothes aren't going on as I planned." She twisted her arms through armholes above her head and pulled the dresses down, layering them one over another, adding a loose faded farm dress last. Remaining were her black skirt and silk scarves that she tucked inside the front of her top dress. Buoyed now by a rush of blood beneath the burgeoning purple bruise that smarted, she searched for any more of her belongings. The wretched, thin canvas bag she had packed for the harvest *programme* remained. She stuffed it into her bosom, too.

Moments later without hesitation, she removed the coffee pot and turned the gas burner on high heat. Methodically, she layered pieces of bread over the flame until they were black crackling crusts rolling with smoke.

"Ah, keep smoking, baby," Jessica exclaimed. She fished the charcoal off the stove into a metal tray, and placed it on the front window sill. A breeze fanned the smoldering charcoal into fantastical swirls of blackened air.

Quickly slipping into the black raincoat, she looked around thinking there was something else. *Da!* She pounced on the black pumps with the rubber walking heels, the first thing Yuri had given her, expensive pumps that he had bartered. Pausing a moment, she considered keeping them. They were comfortable and flattering and evoked their tour of the Winter Palace, but she threw them on the burner. By the time she swept the silver letter opener and cigarette case into her pocket and rummaged in desk drawers for additional collectibles, a dense, acrid smoke from the burning rubber rolled in clouds from the stove into the sitting and dining area. Hurriedly tying a blue print dishtowel over her head *baba yaga* style, she opened the window wider and screamed, now without pretense, "Fire. Fire. *Pomogite mne! pomogite mne!*. Help me! Help me!"

Jessica choked straining to take short breaths, the smoke unbearable, but her mind worked like the largest, heavy-duty leather sewing machine at the Benyanske Boot and Shoe factory, chomp, chomping through the toughest cowhide. She had one last gesture to make. Scooping a smoking, curled pump from the burner into a pan, she dumped the sizzling hot remains on the firm cushions of the armless maroon chairs that had been her bier, so to speak. I know, I know, they will smolder, she told herself, but all the same his precious furnishings will be ruined. So much the better.

Bending low to the floor and edging toward the front door with a handkerchief over her nose and mouth, Jessica swore *"Chort voz'mi!,"* as running feet paused at Yuri's door, fists pounding. *"Nyet*, it dare not be Yuri!" She crouched, waiting for the key to turn.

Stout shoulders crashed against the door, stripping the lock from the door frame. A blast of air fed the tortured flames behind her until they became dancing demons. Just in time, an old woman with very large breasts hobbled out, bent over an umbrella for a cane and became lost in the crowd.

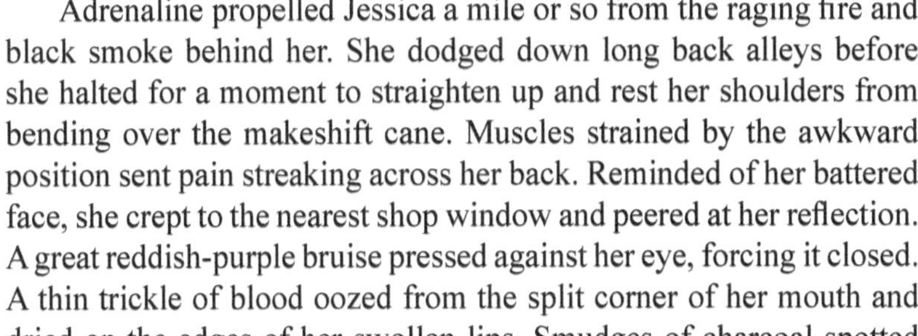

Adrenaline propelled Jessica a mile or so from the raging fire and black smoke behind her. She dodged down long back alleys before she halted for a moment to straighten up and rest her shoulders from bending over the makeshift cane. Muscles strained by the awkward position sent pain streaking across her back. Reminded of her battered face, she crept to the nearest shop window and peered at her reflection. A great reddish-purple bruise pressed against her eye, forcing it closed. A thin trickle of blood oozed from the split corner of her mouth and dried on the edges of her swollen lips. Smudges of charcoal spotted the dishtowel and blackened her hands and cheeks, all permeated with the odor of burned rubber. The welts that spread along her jaw made her ear ache.

I hardly recognize myself, but by the grace of God, I am alive, *no Bogom ya zhiv*, I might not be if I had stayed. In a full-length window she noticed the heavy old factory shoes she had been so glad to relinquish only a few weeks ago. They now felt like friends, cohorts making an escape with her. She heard herself utter a strangled gurgle that passed for a laugh. Almost giddy, she said, "If only Lettina were here to laugh with me."

She bent again in her disguise and cautioned herself to think, to carry out the next step of her carefully devised plan that had kept her awake most of the night. She reached inside the top layers of dresses and removed a small envelope. Proceeding down a major avenue, she saw a young man on a bicycle.

"Garcon, s'il vous plait prende un message?" she called, remembering French was frequently spoken in Leningrad. With a furtive glance around, the young man whispered, *"Rooskie* preferred in the streets, Madame. It is safer."

"I must have this letter delivered to the curator at the Winter Palace Museum. Place it in her hands, and only hers. No one else, *vy ponimayete meniya*? Do you understand me?" Jessica said in Russian. He looked carefully at the address, and at the earnest young woman dressed like a hag. He understood the disguise when he saw her pulpy face and black eye.

"Of course, I shall hurry. I am sorry," he indicated her injury and started to get back on his bicycle. Jessica stopped him and slipped the silver-handled letter opener into his hand.

"I will be at the Warsaw Station waiting for a reply."

"Find a door at the south end away from the main entrance. Wait inside or out."

"Yes, yes, go now. Poŝ*peshite, pozhaluysta*, hurry please."

She watched the young man streak away on his bicycle until he rounded a corner, sensing that he formed a lifeline between her and Raisa, between her and the likelihood of perishing in the city. Moving slowly away from the major avenue, Jessica avoided familiar streets where she and Yuri had walked, and joined a crowd of commuters heading toward the rail station. It felt right to ask Raisa to help her, comforting, as if leaning on a strong, resourceful woman like Agata Illyinicha.

She cast about for anyone who might have seen her. *I am disguised yet I must stay out of sight. I have the rest of the day, hours and hours, to wait. How did I get into this mess in the first place? I --I will be hunted like an animal,* she gasped, pounding her fist to her heart as if at first thought of it. *Arson, theft, fleeing without papers, and whatever charges Yuri will invent. I'll be arrested instantly if they recognize me.*

O, Raisa, I need you, she implored privately, clinging to hopes of a miracle that the note she had written at Yuri's desk would reach its destination. *You are the only person who can help me in Leningrad. I couldn't find Grigory and Lydia even if I knew how to contact them, and they are going back to Moscow.*

Hunted! She forced her feet away from the crowd. Crouched over the cane, she walked unsteadily, distancing herself forever from the scene of the fire, from Yuri, now a likely pursuer. Hastening down unknown back streets and alleys, she attempted to maintain a sense of direction. *I am one of them,* she admitted when brushing shoulders with gaunt, foul-smelling men and women who shuffled through broken neighborhoods as if life began for them somewhere else. Signatures of the 900 day Siege were present everywhere, most of all in these hollow-eyed faces whose grief and loss claimed what little spark that remained of the unfed, unwell living.

Shaking off the gloom before it engulfed her, Jessica stalked along, tapping her cane firmly around shattered concrete walls and walks, markedly deterring wayward advances from vodka-inflamed derelicts and disabled beggars. Realizing that she was lucky, she snapped out of a downward spiral of despair. Only she in this deathly morass had a future.

Only I can make choices. Ah, if Lettina and Katya and Greta could see me now, so chic, so bizarre, yah, so alone. In that moment she again saw herself as Jessica. A tingling sense of purpose overpowered caution until the enormity of her plight drowned a rising spirit.

Unbridled thoughts filtered through her rambling mind: this is worse than being sent to the *kolkhoz*.

I am a fugitive, one of the lawless in the streets soon sought by NKVD. Right now I can only hope and pray, but I don't know if I can pray or whether it is allowed, even inside of us. If only I could pray with confidence like Agata or Sasha, that prayer would make a difference but I don't know if it does. I should have gone to church like Tanya. *O khorosho, slishkom pozdno.* O well, too late now. I have surely broken every law there is.

Walking and shedding tears, she tried to ignore her heels rubbed raw by the heavy leather shoes, refusing to line them with paper as the beggars did. Jessica groaned and stretched her aching back. The dishtowel head-covering fell back on her shoulders. Her haircut, so stunning yesterday, was now tangled, the natural curl partially stuck in dried blood.

It was still early, before noon, when she passed a display of musical instruments behind stout iron bars in the narrow window of a pawn shop. On impulse, she turned and opened the door, setting off a string of small bells that jangled crazily to the back room. Speckles of dust hung in light that filtered among the jumble of glassware, books, and hat stands, several holding men's fur hats. Old shoes, caught in the shadows of the cramped aisles, betrayed the history of courts under the tsars, military life, and working men and women. Stacks of cookware and Tiffany-style lamps occupied long tables. Dimly lit upper shelves displayed nested Russian dolls from thumb size to a foot tall in joyous primary colors of folk art. Imitation Fabergé eggs girded with lace or gems filled a glass case behind the counter, a mockery of genuine, hand-painted Ukrainian eggs held in the Kremlin beside rare jewels of antiquity. Wares appeared at once expensive and shoddy, detritus of another time, now chipped and layered in a film of dust. A figure appeared from a back room.

"Please, *ser*, may I see the violin." Jessica pointed to the window. She hardly recognized her own voice; it wavered between that of the girl who gaily window shopped with Lettina and the old woman who now stood in her shoes.

The shopkeeper moved up the aisle on a crutch, a pant leg cut away and tucked to the stump where he was missing a lower leg. Scowling at the disturbance, he shoved aside a hand-decorated folk zither and lifted the violin from its ancient but sturdy open case.

"You will find no finer violin anywhere. This one was brought in by a musician, a member of the Leningrad Symphony. He was widely known, having performed in the Moscow Symphony, and at the Marinsky Theatre. It was his misfortune to part with it, but he and his family faced starvation like so many others. The Siege forced these terrible decisions. I do not know what has become of him. Why do you want this?"

"O, I do not want it for myself. I was thinking of my cousin Pasha. He would dearly love to have a violin." Her hands ran over the smooth red-mahogany surface, marred only by sweat of the previous owner.

"And he cannot buy it?"

"He—he may not remember he was a musician before the war. And his finger tips were frozen. I do not know if he can play, but I'm sure it would help him recall his past." Her thoughts wandered astray and the shopkeeper lifted the violin from her hands.

"We cannot have it smelling like burned rubber. You were in a fire?"

"*Da.* Worse. So I am leaving the country." The words came out unexpectedly, sounding strange, foreign to her ears. She supposed he would not report her; he had obviously suffered much himself, probably a veteran. But she would have to be more careful after this.

Jessica had written to Raisa,

*"I must leave the country. Please help me. I will be at the
Warsaw Station at five o'clock.
           Svetlana Sergeevna Gilkova."*

Even unspoken in her mind, her plan sounded like eerie echoes of another time and place.

The shopkeeper nodded his head, motioning toward the black eye and old hag disguise. "Unfortunately, violence is a frequent occurrence these days. I wish I could be of help to you."

Jessica met his sympathetic gaze and said simply, "I–uh—I am alone in Leningrad, but I have contacts," not naming either Raisa or the boy on the bike. At second glance she found the shopkeeper was about thirty with smooth skin, thick brown hair and beard. She felt herself wanting to tell him everything, what happened to her, her plans, her desperation, but she paused and sighed, "Maybe I can return someday and buy the violin for him."

A profound sense of the reality of being alone in Leningrad with no money deepened. When she turned to leave the shop, she stopped and pulled the silver cigarette case from her pocket. "I would like to sell this," she said.

"A cigarette case, is it?" The shopkeeper held it in the light to examine a small insignia on the back. While he appraised it, Jessica studied him, sensing his intuitiveness about human nature, as well as a world of experience in dealing with people and their often treasured belongings.

His gruffness was surely a cover, Jessica noted. His fine deep eyes like Abbot Konstantin's had squiggly laugh lines at the corners. She had met so few men, none so kind and attractive to her. She felt herself absurdly leaning toward him in her wretched disguise. Embarrassed, she looked down as if studying the amber pendants on the counter.

"This case is from the Anatoly Rasputin family, a collector's piece. Someone had a sharp eye." The proprietor weighed the silver in his palm before setting it on a shelf with dozens of other cigarette cases. "We get all kinds from discredited families of nobility, some genuine, some cheap imitations." At last he handed Jessica a handful of roubles and a number of kopeks, none of which she took time to count.

"There comes another," the shopkeeper said, when a well-dressed woman of about forty entered to the cacophony of bells. The woman glanced about and instantly assessed Jessica's appearance with a knowing but shamed expression. Jessica slipped out before the woman stated her business, the shame still with her, both having been visited by misfortunes.

O Bozhe moy! why the misery and sorrow? Jessica thought, acknowledging that each item of personal property in the shop represented someone's sad story. The Rasputin case was one of the few collectibles Yuri had prized, strangely since the Tsaress' chosen healer was the antithesis of the Red Army soldier that Yuri represented.

Jessica wandered in a wasteland, a section of Leningrad Yuri had avoided showing her on their bus or walking tours. Pillars of once grand buildings lined streets devoid of hustle of townsfolk or children. Upper stories of entire blocks of offices, apartments and shops had caved in as a consequence of two and a half years of shelling. Subsequent fires razed the area leaving charred remnants of store signs clinging helplessly above remaining doorframes. A small engraved slab of granite proclaimed сапожник, cobbler, from its repository in a pile of stones, as if they were tombstones to the unknown dead in unmarked graves, the city their final resting place. Jessica turned away fearing she might see toys, clothing, or even bones of the lost uncovered by workmen.

I can always find work making boots and shoes, she realized, after spotting the sign. She hastened on past the constant roar of lorries backing into cleared spaces to haul away the salvage and debris. The scene reminded her of rickety old GAZ trucks loading grain and racing to train stations with shipments to the South.

Removal of the destruction had barely begun, though the Siege ended two years ago. Workmen in baggy khaki pants separated usable bricks and concrete slabs from the heaps of mortar and twisted iron scraps, their backs as bent as the iron, movements as heavy and conversation as sparse. Jessica had a sense their spirits, too, were imbued with melancholy that knit citizens of the city together like the mortar they now cleaned up.

A human being cannot live with what occurred here. Yuri said the Army could have stayed to defend Leningrad. *Da*, Leningrad was not favored by the Ruler. Troops were sent to the Ukraine, Poland and the Baltics instead. Scuffling through the trash of torn newspapers and broken bottles along the wrecked streets, Jessica found discarded *samzidats,* the handbills and bulletins of dissidents, some expressing the same sentiments as Yuri. She quickly gathered that many of the intelligentsia and political opponents had gone underground and were still active, others going into exile. Is it only in Leningrad, rather than in villages like Konsky? I believed in duty, though my parents never became loyal. But the farm *programme* was cruel. Yuri and his Army are cruel. Benyanske's suffocates me. I simply cannot force myself to go back.

She half-stumbled, following signs toward the Warsaw Rail Station. Poignant images of films intruded upon her outer reality—not *The Foundling,* an abandoned American girl acted by Mary Pickford, but passionate dramas of daring women, broken promises and deceit. Deceit is my story. Yuri promised to help me, *bah*! I am worse off— my story may end in death.

Passersby often looked a second time at the youthful profile beneath the old hag garb.

"Do you need a doctor for that bruise?" one asked.

"Come home with me, honey," a derelict begged, reaching for her sleeve.

Jessica pulled the headscarf forward to conceal her face and hurried on. I may become a *szheleznodorozhnaya stantsiya shlyukha,* a train station whore.

Weaving from hunger and exhaustion, she remained barely conscious of her surroundings until she neared the station. The once ornamental Gothic architecture of the massive building had long ago been stripped of amenities. Red banners hanging above the street paid cursory homage to the vitality of the Soviet rail system. Jessica found a bench outside the south end to wait. The wet windy storm that had passed through in the night left startling blue sky overhead and a musty earthy smell beneath her feet. A young twig springing from a Norway maple stump waved its few autumn reddish-gold leaves, signaling that its roots were alive and thrived. Jessica dozed, warmed in the coat and many layers of clothing, but awoke with alarm.

What if Yuri looks for me here? If not here, he will find me in Konsky or at my parents, or he might remember I mentioned the Gillhoyovs and try to hunt them down, but that was a fictional name. Yet I cannot leave without papers. The *politsiya* will search for me once Yuri finds the fire—I have no choice—I must leave the country if

I have to crawl through forests in the Baltics to Poland. The prospect of exile roiled her stomach.

"I may have thrown my life away today," she murmured. Becoming careless about her disguise, she panicked and hurried into the squalid lobby as fast as the cumbersome outfit would permit and studied the wall map, squinting with her one good eye at the network of fine lines. The station, one of many in Leningrad, primarily served as a transportation corridor between Leningrad, Pskov, and Warsaw, Poland. Spider webs of other lines branched in different directions that appeared confusing, especially since she did not know her destination. She located a lesser line branching from the main line southwest to Konsky. A country spur served villages due west along Russia's border with European countries.

The routes were obscure but she could still be spotted, jailed, or shot. Dry heaves wracked her body, urging her to make a decision, yet a plan failed to coalesce in her mind. Her earlier raging fury now ran cold. With icy fingers she itched what felt like eczema on her upper arms. She went out to the south entrance, frantically searching the crowd for Raisa, a low moan escaping her dry lips. Trains pulled into the station and departed, giving her a sense of the time, as well as an increasing urgency to make decisions, form a plan, and go into hiding for the long term.

Raisa, please come. Hurry, hurry. *Bystreye bystreye.* She may not come. She may not have received the message—do I remember what she looked like? We met only once. She will never recognize me in this garb. I must have money to get out of the country, or I am stranded here—O why did I start the fire?—*lah*, I am stupid.

Arson! *Ya ne mogu byt' zhaderzhana.* I cannot get arrested. Jessica pressed her palms to her stomach to quell its churning.

"I really don't know what to do. If I get caught I will be exiled to Siberia." She daubed the dampness from the purplish swelling below her left eye with the end of the dishtowel. "My life now depends on Raisa! If she doesn't come by six o'clock, I'll board when workers rush on the train just to get out of Leningrad.

"But Yuri is cunning. He will search this station before Raisa gets here—*bah*! How could I have acted otherwise? Yuri would have kept me locked in, maybe killed me in a drunken rage."

The internal argument confirmed she had made a wise decision, radical as it was, unconscionable really. "I beg, Holy Father if you are like Abbot Konstantin, if you pay any mind to your people, *pozhaluysta*, protect all other Gilkovs from becoming implicated in my scheme." The sense of an entity hearing me would be a comfort, though I'd test a glimmer of faith side-by-side in the light with atheism. Pray like my mother to no avail? Or protest acts of God like Anna Ahkmatov?

On and on she tussled with imploring God, denying delusions of religion, and reinstating even more far-fetched beliefs. Pasha would be healed. Tanya protected. A river of *nyets* followed to drown hopes while she embraced then discarded one after the other until she cried, the salty tears stinging her bruise.

The port of Leningrad was a terminus north, luring Jessica to see the world, to become a fashion designer. *Da*, that would be worth all these endless hours of waiting for word from Raisa. Red and yellow locomotives thundered into the station, whistles reverberated off concrete walls, and engines backed out on battered side rails to turn around. Arrivals and departures occurred irregularly, as if schedules were mere inconveniences. Dreaming her dreams and clinging to her last hope, Jessica scanned the crowd for Raisa one minute and Yuri the next. Every uniformed security guard wearing a red star looked like Yuri. With each lurching fear, the pallor of Jessica's features became whiter, contrasting with the purple blotch that blacked her eye on the left side of her face. At last she heard the young messenger who had been searching for her.

"*Madame, Madame*, I have a message for you."

Jessica hailed him with the huge, folded umbrella then rushed forward unlike the bent old woman she purported to be. He handed her a medium-sized, hefty packet.

"O, you cannot know how happy I am to see you! I almost gave up hopes that anyone would come to my rescue. How did you find her? What did she say? This package—you managed to deliver it safely to me. Here I want to—," she reached into her pocket.

"I have been well rewarded, Madame. I urge caution in carrying valuables on the streets. Perhaps you can find transportation immediately." He patted his bag containing the silver letter opener and rode away with a cheery wave, a bright spot in her otherwise desperate day.

"*Spasibo*," Jessica called after him, at the same time examining the packet in true *Russki* fashion to see if it had been tampered with. She stripped the intact seals on the parcel and ripped the outer wrapping. Aghast at the thought of being robbed at the very moment she'd made contact with the only person who could help her, she fled some distance before unfolding the note. Suddenly chilled to the bone with fear of the contents, she scanned Raisa's message.

"Go at once to the port. It is safer. Take an old steamer across to Stockholm. Your papers are all in order. The Gilkovs died in the Siege, therefore your identity is protected. They left the enclosed personal items for safekeeping during the war."

She gave her sister's address and signed *R*. A handful of roubles were in the packet along with a sealed green velvet pouch that felt to Jessica like jewelry. Trembling and weak in the knees with relief, she tucked the packet safely between her breasts under the burden of clothing. Now hyper-vigilant about her surroundings, she walked briskly as she reread the message until she memorized Raisa's commands. Reserving only the strange-sounding address in Stockholm, she let the note with the "R" fall like snow in minute pinches of torn paper along her route.

To the port. My destination!

Without letting her disguise hamper her, she hurried to the nearest bus stop and inquired about the correct route to the port. A driver motioned her toward a bus and she was soon in and seated. The sequence of Raisa's orders revolved like a phonograph record in her mind—no image followed the thought of going out of the country. Words barely registered the significance of what that meant. It sounded so far, so impossible, so permanent. Motion picture scenes of travel applied to the lives of others, not to hers. Only the note from Madame

Marsolet seemed real at this moment: *"We must leave the country."*

Jessica knew instantly that she would never have conceived of such an idea otherwise, nor of chasing a reality in fashion design herself. No one else had understood her yearnings or elevated her with approval, or given her a such a priceless gift as the crimson red silk blouse and black gabardine skirt. Tears again burned the bruise inching up under her left eye.

By now a typical autumn drizzle turned everything gray except the flamboyant reds of maple saplings among stumps of large old trees that had been cut for firewood. The runoff slapped underneath the aged bus in a steady sing-song of "Go, stay, go go, go, stay." Caught in an ambivalent state, Jessica barely noticed the trees, streets or canals until they drove at length along the Neva, passing Admiralty Square, where she recognized the Bronze Horseman "in flight," as Lydia described him.

The unexpectedness of this leg of her journey brought her to a standstill when she left the bus at the vast tumultuous port. The song of the bus continued to play on her nerves, creating an uncertainty that mushroomed into full-blown anxiety. The girl from Konsky looked about uncomprehending where she was or what she had to do. She had been looking back, not forward for the past few hours, except for the bizarre accompaniment of Yuri's old oversized umbrella, which somehow felt comforting. Her inland experience was about to end. Her thoughts scattered like wharf rats, her impulses ran rampantly as a wild child's. She sank down on a bench on one of the docks and stared in a trance at the immensity of the dark, lapping sea beyond. The day that seemed like many days all in one left her feeling weak and dazed. The moving water with its dense murky odor made her nauseous, but there was nothing in her stomach to heave.

"I must do this, this one last step." Jessica braced herself. "I will do what I wish for the first time in my life. *Blagodareniye Bogu,* thanks be to God who has delivered me safely here, as cousin Tanya would say."

She straightened and exhaled. Indulging one last impulse, she laid down the dishtowel for someone else's use, and on second thought, left the umbrella with it. Unfettered with the disguise, she buttoned the raincoat securely around the precious belongings hidden beneath, and resolutely walked upright to the nearest window labeled билетная касса, a ticket office.

"The steamer to Stockholm." She handed over her papers as if she did this every day.

A tired officer barely raised his head to view her, but his brief glance did not fail to notice the battered side of her face. Hunching over the papers, he took his time examining them.

"I see farm *programme* documentation along with your passport papers," he noted.

"*Da.*"

"I have relatives in the South." He stamped the papers and shoved them back with a ticket. Jessica swallowed the lump in her throat and managed a brief lop-sided smile.

"Get in that line for the next checkpoint before departure."

"Where?"

"Down four docks." The officer waved her away while several guards eyed her. Jessica did not know if they were questioning the bulky farm clothing, her bruises, or uncertain whether they were flirting with her because of her modern hair style.

"*Lah,* stupid of me to include the farm identification. I could have been detained if they thought I was escaping the *kolkhoz. Vot tak tak,* whew. I may not be so lucky next time—I cannot be detained for any reason." She slipped the farm card from her papers and examined the exit visa and passport. There in beautiful calligraphy were the Gilkovs' patronymic names and a list of relatives she had never heard of. But she had no time for genealogy. Thumbing through pages emblazoned with the seal of the Interior Ministry she found her name and a current date. It will be enough thanks to Raisa, Svetlana breathed, and stepped into line.

Long queues strung along the dock from the checkpoint. Passengers swapped valises from hand to hand to rest their arms while staring at an ornate clock above the weathered gray building. She joined the throng, attempting to act normally so as not to attract attention. Armed military guards patrolled outside as well as inside the warehouse-like offices for civilian staff. The young men reminded her of Yuri when he was a recruiter in Konsky, hard eyes, distant expressions, uncompromising attitudes, driven for their own ends, she supposed. Again her legs threatened to give way as if Yuri might grab her this last moment before departure, and turn her in to the guards. She swayed and an older woman, who reminded Jessica of Sasha, grasped her arm. Jessica's battered woman's appearance was no disguise, the gross injury an honest statement of an all too often experience of *Russki* women. Few words were exchanged, only a silent acknowledgment "*My mozhem prevzoyti eto*, we can transcend this."

Blasts of steam obliterated the view of the clock by the time the woman and Jessica checked through. It may have been the haste to board all passengers that the Gilkov papers were summarily passed. The women separated, the older woman urging Jessica to get something to eat. Lacking time and any evidence of food vendors, Jessica rushed to hand her ticket to the steward and walked the bridge onto a steamer flying a flag she did not recognize. Within moments, it was underway.

She gripped the rail and found herself in a world of mysterious channels and islands that comprised the mouth of the Neva River. The Peter and Paul Fortress faded behind them under slanting rays of the late evening sun. Breakers rolled from beneath dozens of other vessels, crashed against the steamer, and spun away in crested black waves.

Rocking like a cradle, the sturdy *Arctic Plover* sat low in the water as if burdened with all the cares of its human cargo. Straight into northwesterly winds, it plowed its way into the Gulf of Finland, an open expanse of water tipping over the horizon in every direction. Jessica's head felt like a furry ball as it did when she, Lettina and Anna drank a half-gallon of black market Bordeaux. No more decisions, no more thinking of Yuri or fears of prison camp in Siberia.

"I am out of the country," she said half aloud. Hot tears streamed down her smudged, bruised face to blend with the chilled misty rain of the Gulf on her way to the Baltic Sea.

XXI

Exile

As autumn eased into later sunrises and earlier sundowns, cooler temperatures extended across the motherland, and relative quiet prevailed at St. Sansais Monastery in Kursk Oblast. Brother Dmitri balanced on the edge of his cot and unwrapped the *onoochi,* the long strips of linen peasants used instead of stockings. His injured knee angled in an unnatural manner, the prognosis for recovery consistent with the physician's assessment of "irreparable." Yet the elder monk's thoughts leapt unbidden elsewhere, provoked by the pilgrim's visit.

"I believe in God more than in my own life." He saw himself in his boyhood days, a gangly youth with fine, blow-away yellow hair, wearing the coarse pants of the Polish workers. He had been suddenly visited by an overwhelming presence. And it was the Spirit whose brilliance overtook even the sun, its fingers riffled the leaves of the plants, and it spoke in whispers from the stones. A static electricity stood the hairs on his head on end, and a kind of buzzing filtered through the marrow of his bones. He knew then without a doubt the path he would take, indeed could not refuse what felt like a calling.

Remembering, he murmured, "I believe. I do believe, though it flies in the face of all I have seen." Feeling faint now, the images came without a thread of enlightenment: the radiant sunflowers in the fields outside Gdansk, Pavel's suffering loss of his mind and fingertips, a young girl hanging from a tree, an official's car in flames. Abbot Konstantin arrived at Dmitri's cell in time to prevent the monk from collapsing over the edge of his cot.

"The pilgrim—" Dmitri managed to say, attempting to rise.

"A devout and learned one," the abbot motioned Dmitri to lie back on his cot. "A pilgrim has the privilege of harboring profound theological questions without practical application to the living. A handout of bread or alms provide him for another day. Fortunately, the living adapt teachings to their everyday lives to find inspiration and comfort. I doubt if the pilgrim referred to our sustaining belief in Thor, God of Thunder, or Janus, protector of the gateways, nor a favorite of our land, Poludnitsa, Goddess of the Harvest. The pilgrim plucks cherries, while the people preserve traditions dear to the Old Believers. Their lives are hard but their faith is great."

Konstantin paused to tuck a small pillow under Dmitri's head and rewrap the *onoochi* to immobilize the fractured knee. "I am most sorry for the injury to your person, as well as outside disruptions to your prayer life, both regrettable sacrifices indeed."

Dmitri raised his head to protest. "I have brought agony and despair to St. Sansais with me."

"To your credit, Brother, and a blessing to all of us who must share the suffering." Frowns written over Abbot Konstantin's usually merry outlook betrayed his deep concern and grief. At last he admitted, "I wonder myself what the meaning of pain and suffering could possibly be."

"I care not for relief from suffering or sacrifice myself, good Reverend Father. It is only for others that I worry, my dear nieces and nephews in Gdansk, and the young women who came here on behalf of Pavel Ivanovich, and for their safety in the hands of—"

Abbot Konstantin kneaded his fingers together in front of him and said, "I fear I will speak lightly, perhaps giving unwelcome advice to one who constantly enlightens me, however, you may take this as you please." After a momentary pause in which Dmitri remained silent, the abbot's teaching poured seamlessly into the room.

"Ask the Almighty Lord that your sacrifice on the collective be given up for the safety of those you cherish. Pray for the healing of souls, especially those who persecute. If given the grace to heal spiritually, the meaning of suffering becomes boundless. And if you are weary beyond words, allow the Gospel to lie within your room. The Spirit will be retained therein and carry on, on your behalf."

"A teaching from St. John Chrysostom," finished Pavel who slipped in the door. He had heard Dmitri mention his name while he waited outside for an audience with the abbot.

"Brother Dmitri, you read those words of the great mystic to me night after night when I was lost. I have returned to St. Sansais because I cannot live, except for the prayer and sacrifice you taught me." Pavel's round brown eyes opened into the astounding depths of an innocent soul, one magnified in beauty and devotion.

"*Da*," breathed Konstantin, again humbled by the honesty of spirit and forthrightness of the two monks before him. "Your homecoming is most welcome and timely, Pavel Ivanovich. With your gift of pure love and joy in the Lord, you would do well anywhere in the world, but here you will fortify all of us with your gift. As you can see, Brother Dmitri suffered a terrible accident on the farm. The damage is irreversible and the images he carries even more painful. Unable to heal them, we must rely on the words you just heard and also those of St. John Karpathisky who tells us 'the Spirit maintains one when one's own strength fails.'"

Grasping the extent of Brother Dmitri's crippled limb, Pavel fell on his knees in thankfulness for the elder monk's nursing him through the difficult days and nights of his recovery.

"No sacrifice I can make would be enough to express my gratitude. My relatives assured me the monastery rescued me from a field, my hands and feet frozen and my memory lost," he said, hands pressed together in prayer, his undyed homespun tunic and trousers draping softly around him.

"It is I who have benefited one thousand times over," Brother Dmitri replied, his deep voice muffled in his cowl while emotions swept away what little strength he retained. Dark eyebrows, mustache, and pepper-streaked beard hid his face while gray overtook the dark hair that had once been like a sunlit aura.

"It was you who taught me continual prayer," Pavel said, rising to his feet, "and prayer rises within me like strains of music that gladden my heart. I once played the violin, hence I hear music in my mind, and it seems as though the whole world sings with prayer."

"Even now?" Dmitri asked incredulously.

"Even now. Only more so."

Speechless, Abbot Konstantin wondered if any more surprises might surface today, or if such purity of heart existed anywhere else in the world. Pavel remembered, or his relatives helped him recall that he once played the violin. "Did you play the violin when you visited your family?" he inquired.

"I did not. There was no violin to be had. I believe it had been sold for food, though they did not want to tell me so. They have endured great hardship." He unconsciously massaged the stubs of his finger tips.

"It seems so," the abbot agreed, "but I do believe the recovery of your memory and healing of your Spirit is a miracle we have been privileged to witness, Brother Pavel." Under his breath he added, "if only Brother Dmitri could be so healed."

Pavel flushed, a smile widening in pleasure at the abbot's recognizing him as a "Brother." His joy appeared boundless.

Anchoring the Spirit in good works, Abbot Konstantin mentioned offhandedly, "I believe that Brother Dmitri could benefit from assistance in navigating about the garden and vineyard these days."

"*Da, da*, Reverend *starets*. I shall be here forever. It is my most earnest desire to become an oblate at St. Sansais if you will accept me."

Konstantin could not resist a deep heartwarming laugh at Pavel's eagerness. "We welcome you. Brother Anton and Vessaly will as well. St. Sansais is blessed to have regained two steadfast members with so much to offer the world."

"To offer the world, *ser*?" Dmitri asked, "or to God?"

"The Lord does not require our offerings because He has all he needs, but even a minute sacrifice this second, this day, this week, or this month lessens the pain in the world. Lord Jesus the Christ offered Himself as a means of demonstrating compassion for loved ones, for those who suffer injustice and those oppressed."

The words fell on a prolonged silence, not because they were misunderstood, but because the command was so clear. And so immense and essential that Dmitri immediately glimpsed a way forward for himself.

"I can do nothing else," he admitted. "I was unable to protect women on the collectives. With all my strength, I was unable to save others during the invasions of my country, or at this time when abominable repatriations are uprooting native Poles of Russian and German descent.

"Alas, I am in exile. I am crippled. I am only a Pole inspired by a Polish poet in my youth. I came to believe not only in our mysterious destiny of compassion and faith, but that we must *"lift ourselves... and aim at higher and higher thresholds ...of consciousness..."* ah, our poet Czeslaw Milosz.

"Compassion I do understand. I find it healing me as you speak. Perhaps it will heal others." Tears moistened Dmitri's heavy lids. He shifted his spent body on his hard bed and sighed, though the injured leg quivered with pain.

Part III

"Russia—land where my heart is buried deep." Pushkin

XXII

Lera

The Baltic Sea, rising under a saturated mist, felt rough to Jessica as if an uncertain earth constantly shifted beneath her. The *Arctic Plover*, a sturdy black-hulled steamer trimmed in the white and gold of its namesake, transported a hundred and twenty passengers in a comfortable lounge and cargo in its hold. Jessica craned her neck to peer through windows at passing freighters and ships bearing colorful flags of far off lands. These jockeyed with the workhorses of the seas, noisy tugboats towing unwieldy barges often linked together like a train.

Jessica had never before been off land other than a youthful fling on a tacky raft that nearly sent the three girls over the millrace in Konsky. Her present unease contrasted with the social occasion enjoyed by passengers who chatted with strangers, smoked, and frequented the onboard saloon. Yet once the initial thrill of the shrouded horizon-less sea subsided, Jessica found it a slow passage with more than sufficient time to arouse all her childhood fears—fear of abandonment, of storms, the dark, the unknown. In her weakened condition, the unknown in particular loomed over her.

At last she collapsed into a forward aisle seat among the comforting presence of elderly women, a few couples who were obviously tourists, and a cluster of young male stewards. The young men cast sidelong glances at Jessica, while they passed around a pack of Chesterfields and a bottle of vodka, plainly forestalling onboard duties.

"You need a drink," one steward said to Jessica, extending the bottle. A mixture of teasing laughter and honest concern flickered over his open Danish face as he walked toward her.

Jessica ducked her head, not wanting to reveal her battered features but tempted to respond, to talk with him, to tell her story to any living soul, and this one so brash and charming. She yearned to put her hand on his arm to regain a sense of security, at least be assured she would survive this trip, this dream to leave the country. She determined to smile, though the naked truth of her exile was becoming more apparent every second the boat chugged away from the motherland. So distant from family, even on this first night at sea. Being half way between Raisa Dobrynova and her sister in Stockholm, Jessica's lifeline seemed dependent upon two imaginary characters in a film, yet they held her future in their hands. How will this movie end she wondered, not for the first time, and extended her hand for the steward's drink.

"*Nyet, nyet,* no vodka. Crackers help the stomach." The thick voice of a motherly Ukrainian woman in the next seat interrupted any glimmer of a potential tryst, now or ever. The woman immediately dug in an enormous hand-woven tapestry bag through what must have been provisions for crossing the Atlantic. Jessica reluctantly sank back in her seat only to see the swaggering rear ends of the men disappear.

Later, musing about the steward with a sense of loss, loss for all the years she and Lettina and Anna had grown up without boyfriends, she realized it wasn't so everywhere. She began to assess a social milieu foreign to that of her previous experience.

Verité, vast numbers of Russian men like Pasha were lost in the war, but this young man is about my age. He has the whole world and a bright future before him. He is likely free of the sacrifices we endure in *Rossiya.* Or maybe that is what I wish for myself. Toying with the fantasy became an engaging project that occupied Jessica while she nibbled soda crackers. The woman introduced her husband, dressed in a dark wool suit that barely buttoned across his middle. Their eagerly related tales of adventures on the Baltic Sea countered the settling effects of the crackers. At last, Jessica gathered her nerves and stood up. Clutching the backs of seats, she attempted to initiate her sea feet.

Many passengers slept as the steamer settled in a steady drumming over the waves. Others wrestled foreign language newspapers into relatively steady positions in order to read the contents written in Swedish, Dutch or German, but she read only those written in Cyrillic. Several people referred her to a *smorgasbord* in the cabin, but the smell of pickled fish, sausages and piquant cheeses nearly sent Jessica running for the rails.

"I will try black rye bread with sweet butter later," she said. The disconcerting reality that she had no plans beyond finding Raisa's sister competed with her persistent hunger alternating with nausea. She inched her way about the steamer, surprised to find tactile pleasure handling the brass knobs and smooth rails. Drawn to inhale damp air of the sea, she escaped dense cigarette smoke inside. The endless rolling Baltic mirrored the indefiniteness of her life, its blue-gray vitality merged into hazy cloudbanks on every side.

To pass the time she tried to guess whether couples, young or old, were married or not. With a sixth sense about their relationships, Jessica listened for the genuineness she had witnessed between Grigory and Lydia, and conversely, for the shallow façade she had established with Yuri. Her fingers unconsciously touched her cheek and jaw, painful to the touch. Yuri—the fire—the disguise and flight from Leningrad, all painful. Considering the shock at the termination of her first and only relationship, she found that the couples on the boat appeared loving. Or do only lovers travel? Too exhausting a study to analyze, she knew only that her loneliness was markedly amplified by their togetherness.

The next morning the pallor of early snowcaps on high granite peaks pierced overcast skies. Low-hanging clouds seemed to be scuttled by the forward motion of a myriad of seafaring craft, while the steamer thrust its way north up a winding fjord, threading a route past daunting islands towards Stockholm.

Scandinavia! At last!

Jessica had alternately slept on the steamer's benches and walked the deck throughout the night when gusty winds permitted. Reviewing whole chapters of her life, the dismal prospects of her youth, and the past months' life-numbing abuses, she found herself catapulted into a startling, unanticipated foreign world.

"Whatever else happens I have this moment! I am standing here as if I flew up on a perch to get a better view and I see myself."

Her bird's eye view saw a thin, fairly tall woman weaving among dark forms on deck, a pulpy left cheek distorting the symmetry of her face. Tears glistened in her eyes and slid over the lacerated edges of the bruises, stinging like dozens of hornets. Yet erect, wide shoulders hinted at defiance. The sturdy oxfords defined her as a solid Russian woman. *Da*!

I have become my mother, but a victim? *Nyet*, I'll not mourn my lost life, or live out my years in anger and defeat in an *izba*—I did what she never attempted to do. I left the country.

The view from above faded. Jessica turned her attention to her journey.

The mythical Baltic Sea!

The Baltics anchored one end of western Russia's border trade, the Crimea the other, according to her father's stories, though at one time the whole region comprised Prussia from which *Russ* was born. The stories he retold countless times created the beautiful images impressed upon a young girl's mind.

"The well-known trader, Sergey Fedorovich Gilkov!" It sounds so decadent, so upper class yet not how I've known my parents. They seem alive only in lost memories that continue to sting, and *Mat* whips herself with the stings. *O Boshi moy*, I cannot live on my father's stories forever, but did I trade my family and friends and homeland for a lark? The sea irretrievably cuts me off.

Banishing a lurking homesickness, Jessica finally admitted, "I had no choice," and that she was too far away to grapple with the circumstances of family and friends in *Rossiya*.

A strange warmish breeze uplifted her hair, enticing her back to the present, to the task of releasing her past. She strained to see the headlands or catch a glimpse of river valleys sheltering proverbial steep-roofed farmhouses with white shutters, but more often she saw an immense city blanketing hilly terrain along inland waters, sheltered by a garland of islands from the sea. Outward bound freighters bearing enormous loads of birch and linden logs sailed toward foreign markets.

The *Arctic Plover* passed monuments, a castle, a stunning palace, and the impressive architecture of city buildings, all molded to the islands' granite features and framed by Bay Riddarfjarden. A church-like tower on one island, topped by a splendid golden ball and three golden crowns, caught the first pink rays of dawn and sent reflections skittering down the increasingly placid waterways to a vast, stunningly beautiful harbor. The spires of Gothic churches rose above banks of fir, black in the shadows along waterways.

Soon the powerful vibrations of the steamer engine maneuvered the boat against a dock, shutting down with a shudder next to the famed Strandvagen, a wide boulevard framing the city of Stockholm. Jessica trailed disembarking passengers, her unsteady legs matching the shaky confidence she summoned to leave the steamer, her only connection to her country, for what felt like the New World. She stepped from the boat to the busy boulevard with a sense of severing her past. Still feeling the motion of the sea, it seemed she was caught in a cast of characters on a wavy screen in Konsky's dim theater, the scene alien to her experience and countenanced only because it was imaginary.

Lydia had regaled her with tales of operas in Moscow and Leningrad, tragedies that so brilliantly reflected the lives of the people that the composers became famed at home and abroad.

"Operas did not usually end well, that was the beauty of them," she had said. The long-running *Sleeping Beauty Ballet* drew audiences as diverse as auto manufacturers, old women who swept the walks, and proprietors of haberdasheries to free public entertainment.

The reflection snapped her into the present which was ripe with potential and only threatened by the shoe-maker's girlish tendency to escape reality. She dismissed the ways she tended to avoid confronting her own quirks, and paced the boulevard until she regained her land feet. An adrenalin-arousing urgency to determine what would happen next prompted her to follow the sweet smell of bakery goodies that drifted along the waterfront. Jessica stepped into a queue at the *Kaffe och Bageri*. its lace curtains offering a warm, homey feeling. Breaking her long, involuntary fast, she soon ate her first meal out of the country.

Anonymous, alone with her crimes of passion, yet with a first real sense of security, she shed the long damp raincoat and held the cup of steaming coffee in both hands, coffee so hot and strong and tantalizing it brought a smile to her face before she took a sip, before she sampled the warm moist slab of cardamom bread.

"So heavenly, the spice so exotic," she said to the shop owner, who understood Russian and changed a limited amount of Jessica's roubles to krona. Tension between her shoulders began to fade. In the ambiance of the café, she experienced her first modicum of contentment since she had boarded the train in Konsky to help harvest on the collectives months ago. At last fortified by generous second and third cups of *kaffe,* she felt restored enough to proceed with what felt like an impulsive and often perilous plan. Yet she found it difficult to focus, her mind dazed by events of the last two days and lack of sleep. Bewildered that she had escaped Yuri's rage, the fire, and harrowing events of emigrating, she glanced down at her old hag apparel, padded at her breasts with other clothing, betraying one cost of survival. The clingy odor of burned rubber was another. Her hand ran over her hollow stomach, the familiar gauntness now part of a skeletal form she inhabited beneath the disguise.

"You are so beautiful," Yuri had said when he claimed her body. Jessica startled and stroked the hollow again, a momentary panic thrusting her from her seat. At least I am not with child, his child. A burst of relief sent her back into the street. The need to reclaim her person, to forget Yuri's uninvited embraces made her move on."

"I must find Raisa's sister," she stammered to herself over and over again.

The boulevard had no lack of transportation if one knew where they were going. For Jessica it meant accosting numerous cab and bus drivers, inquiring if they could take her to Riddarholmen and the address Raisa had given. Shrugs, blank stares and indifference greeted her entreaties. Acknowledging her wretched appearance, she did not doubt their reluctance to deal with her. She rushed back to the water's edge to ask the boatmen without success, her jaw quivering from pain and anxiety.

"*Da, da*, not far past Gamla Stan," a kindly pedestrian intervened in Russian. "There, take that bus and show the driver the address. It is Old Town," he added.

"So it was not that other drivers did not know the address, but that they did not understand what I was saying," Jessica replied, somewhat mollified. "International travel may present more difficulties than I anticipated." First among first encounters was the landscape, the rugged coast dense with population. Her homeland was flatland taiga smothered in damp dark forest for a thousand miles seemingly in every direction. Sparse population huddled in major cities, those a thousand miles from each other. "*O Boshi moy*," she breathed again, steeling herself for subsequent encounters.

After frequent stops and several changes, the bus driver motioned that she get off at a stop in a residential neighborhood, closely packed houses, cinnamon-colored in the morning sun. Tall, late season chrysanthemums struck bobbing shadows on walks and walls among dried plants and leaves in overgrown flowerbeds. Jessica soon approached a three-story stucco apartment building and found the bell near the correct number. The door itself presented a feeling of security, the sense of a sanctuary, just in time to squelch the absurdity of her approaching a stranger in a strange land. Hardwood gleamed under fresh varnish over bright tole-painted flowers in reds, greens and yellows there and on the window shutters. A heavy Norse latch of wrought iron seemed to say at once "come in" and "stay out." Before she could decide if it was bolted against visitors, Raisa's sister answered her knock.

"O, I am so glad to see you. I am Svetlana Sergeevna Gilkova from—"

"Welcome, Svetlana from Leningrad. I am Lera," she interrupted, pressing Jessica's cold trembling hand between large warm palms. "Raisa let me know. I was expecting you," she said in a foreign-sounding Russian.

At ease at once, Jessica's glance took in Lera's fashionable brown, two-piece linen suit accented with a string of pearls, and her briefcase, closed with a shell-inlaid snap. Not a sign of workers' dowdy dresses or comrade uniforms had she yet seen. The woman standing so erect and confident before her seemed to represent all that Jessica could desire for herself. She straightened her shoulders, attempting to adopt Lera's stance as a means of acquiring the same sense of presence. She also had the feeling that Lera missed nothing assessing her, including the baggy dresses showing beneath the black raincoat.

"Come in, I am about to leave for work, but I have a moment. You have sailed overnight." Lera's smile was as warm as Raisa's and just as comforting. Otherwise the sisters appeared to have little in common.

"I want you to stay and rest from your travels. I will come home early. Fruit and cheese are in the kitchen. I am sorry to have to rush out, but I must catch the bus at the corner. Please, make yourself at home here." Lera quietly closed the door and Jessica heard the latch lock.

"Safe at last," Jessica breathed, and dropped into the nearest comfortable chair. Succumbing to lack of sleep the last two days and nights, she slept until Lera came home.

In the kitchen Lera seemed like an ordinary Russian housewife whose only concern was for her guest. The pearls she had worn with the brown suit lay on a side table, to Jessica a disconcerting carelessness—she recalled breaking the string of amber beads her mother considered priceless. Lera's classy briefcase dropped in the entry beneath her coat seemed as casual, a lifestyle a continent away from that of the Soviet Socialist Republic.

After formalities and Jessica's abbreviated tale of leaving Leningrad, Lera moved closer to examine the bruise on the cracked cheekbone that had swollen and spread over Jessica's eyelid, puffing her face and disjointed jaw.

"I left a man who struck me—"

Lera raised an eyebrow, patted Jessica's shoulder, and encouraged her to talk.

Hesitant to bring up her fury and despair that drove her among whores and beggars frequenting the rail station, Jessica pushed herself back from the table. Her eyes explored the room and furnishings, escaping for a moment in a glimpse of the ease in which Lera lived among plain but modern furnishings, glass cabinets, magazines in a sculpted wood rack, and a vase of wildflowers. An image of her old apartment with the broken chair and Tanya's bedroom in a closet made Lera's home appear even more astonishing.

"I—I—made some poor decisions," she began, her voice distant and hard, her look saying it will never happen again. Lera picked up the dishes, leaving Jessica space to compose herself.

"I met Raisa at the Winter Palace. She recognized my name, Gilkova. I tried to cover up, but my companion, Captain Yuri Stanislov, suspected we were hiding something," Jessica stammered. "He was angry when we returned to his apartment and accused me of lying. He drank heavily—you know the rest. Raisa was the only person I knew in Leningrad. She understood immediately. She took great risk in securing papers and sending a message to me. I shall be forever grateful. Yuri would surely have had me arrested."

"My sister sees many women in similar circumstances at the University. She is well attuned to their misfortunes. I must say, she has experienced profound losses of her own." Lera did not elaborate, sparing Jessica further sorrow, and Jessica did not pry as her own defenses slowly ebbed. "What do you want to do now?"

Shifting from her story, Jessica now had a chance to look ahead, to express what felt like childish dreams to an accepting soul, to forge in her mind what the next step would be. Assembling parts of her fantasy felt like opening doors on rusty hinges. Not so long ago, but what seemed like her deep past, Jessica saw herself as a worker, an image of herself not so different from the few men in the workforce. Valued only as long as she kept her head down over the machines like the other women did. Cracks had begun in that perception. Service as a *kolkhoznitsa* ruptured that ideal. So did a twentieth birthday and a red crimson silk blouse.

"To answer your question, I want to go to America." Jessica's chin quivered at the surprising, previously unspoken, even unconscious words.

"To America! Many of us want to go to America! Not only to see but to pay tribute," Lera said, visibly humbled.

"The Allies, *da*. You would know more than I do. In Kursk Province we were caught in the midst of back and forth of all consuming battles on the Western Front." Jessica paused. "I often imagine myself studying fashion design in New York City. Formerly, it was a silly notion. But now, for me it would be a better life in America. My parents and grandparents have known only suffering since the Revolution."

"Ah, yes, a better life. The wish of so many, though most despair of attaining it. Perhaps you will find it." Lera poured milk into tall glasses.

"I see you have trouble chewing *knackerelrod*." The crisp thin oat cakes she served were hard for Jessica to eat.

"Thank you. My teeth and jaw hurt." Jessica marveled at the woman's brightly painted fingernails, seldom seen in the Soviet Union. It spurred Jessica's resolve—freedom would be worth it to have nail polish. "It seems everyone would want to come to Sweden. You--your country seems to be so safe and offers so much more."

"You cannot imagine the influx of refugees to Sweden during the war. Our country remained neutral, though it became a pass-through state for military and supply lines. I work in an immigration office. Deportations from Estonia alone clogged the ships and trains. Those of Swedish descent were forced out by the German invasion of '41, despite many families having lived in Estonia for generations. Then three years later, a mass exile and deportation of Estonian landholders occurred after the Soviet occupation. These were Swedish families repatriated after the Germans left, if not killed or sent to prison. Farms of the landholders were turned into Russian collectives. From your recent experience, you know how that turned out."

"*Da*, I do know. I am sorry to bring up such still raw experiences."

"Raw, yet we refuse to dwell on the past. In fact, to many who suffered most, the past does not exist. The human mind is able to cope only by looking forward."

"O, that describes my cousin Pasha perfectly. He lost his mind at the end of the war. A monastery took him in. A kindly abbot and the Brothers saved him. How I wish to see him again!" Tears pooled in the corners of her eyes.

"It is often difficult to leave one's country and loved ones."

Pulled between loyalties to her cousins, friends, and her very country of birth, Jessica seemed to freeze. The shock of a pending launch to America set off a new litany of questions.

"What am I doing? Perhaps I need to think about going into exile, what that means. I am forfeiting all ties to my family and friends."

Lera's smile indulged Jessica's youthful reaction and doubt. "You are a refugee from violence, but I understand you needed to leave the country to pursue your ambitions."

Jessica scrambled to check runaway fears. She needed time to reexamine her dreams, to test them against Lera's good sense and experience with people leaving the country. Lera would unlikely be swayed by a twenty-year-old's yearnings.

Disregarding Jessica's abrupt rethinking her decision, Lera asked, "How can I help you?" The strained look of her brow and eyes betrayed the compassion she likely brought to and from processing immigration papers. Yet she maintained a reserved tone and outlook, so much like Madame Marsolet, Jessica realized, wanting to become like these independent women who had unexpectedly, maybe undeservedly, appeared in her life. Again she was astonished that Raisa had been positioned to help her get out of the country, and Lera not only encouraged her fantasies, but asked how she could help. A sigh emerged from deep in her soul. True, she wanted to become immersed in the world of style. To look stylish always made her feel better. Even a little belt or the colorful scarf lifted her spirits, gave life zest.

Caught up in the magic of the moment, Jessica hastened to explain her immediate plans. "Raisa has made it possible for me to travel. I believe I have what I need. My papers are in order, and she made sure I could pay my way. Her note suggested I ask you what to do next."

"If you are determined to sail to America, I suggest you take a passenger liner to Amsterdam, and inquire there about an international ship bound for the United States. I am sure you will find people to assist you."

"America! O, I am so excited I could start tonight—"

"*Nyet*. I could not allow it." Lera had a deep infectious laugh showing straight white teeth, so different from Raisa whose plain, unpretentiousness set her apart only by the intellect she demonstrated. "You will stay here for the night. We have lovely baths."

Biting her lip, Jessica realized with embarrassment that she smelled of burned rubber. "How could I forget. I am so accustomed to--to--the horrible odor."

"It is pretty bad."

"I started a fire—I burned the shoes Yuri gave me."

"You are a plucky girl. You acted desperately." Lera was still chuckling when she directed Jessica to the bath and bed.

XXIII

Lettina

The late evening sunset in Stockholm, Sweden, created chiaroscuro patterns of hillside gardens ringed by silhouettes of elms.

"So lovely. So tempting to stay in Sweden, not so far from Russia—but---but I cannot go home," Jessica murmured over the last cup of coffee. She hung her red blouse and skirt to air on the revolving clothesline outside her window, the outfit occasioning renewed sentiment, a statement of who she was, a woman going abroad. After hesitating, she also aired the dress Yuri had purchased. The black dress reminds me of Yuri, but so does my red blouse—what can I do? I don't have a nice suit like Lera's. I'll have to make the best of the travel clothes I have. She fingered the brooch that came with the dress, feeling its elegance, and shook out the gypsy-style silk scarf, unable to cease feeling the stories behind each.

The colors remind me of the paper Madame Marsolet wrapped my blouse and skirt in. I may still have bits of it in my bag. I wonder if I can find her. I am sure they went to Paris—or America. One thought skipped to another. Yuri said Lydia Ratkevich would have me thinking wild thoughts. Why not? I could stopover in Paris.

Jessica half-laughed and began to deal with the odor in her black raincoat. It required a thorough scrubbing in Lera's utility sink before she lounged in a spa-like, free standing bathtub on legs. At last, rose-scented suds gently lapped back and forth over her body, erasing not only the odor but much of the memory of it.

She was still asleep the next morning when Lera left for the immigration office. She reluctantly rolled from under the duvet and assessed her image in the mirror, rediscovering the wizardry of the women at the hair salon. Her clean, newly styled hair fell into a natural swinging bob that flattered her wide face. She explored an array of Lera's expensive toiletries such as she had never seen, and chose a light cream and powder to diminish the appearance of the bruise. A radical dark red lipstick set off the black dress.

After lingering a moment to savor the result, she jammed her belongings in two bags, one a spacious, lightweight bag Lera had given her, and the other the old canvas tote from her harvest days. She wrote a note of appreciation to Lera, the Cyrillic letters waltzing over the paper as tension rose with the need to face the outside world. By the time she left to find a passenger liner, she had a distinct sensation of moving from one station in life to another. Raisa and Lera had befriended her, rescued her, and she had tasted the extraordinary comfort of an ordinary, middle class way of life.

At the harbor, she tossed her old bag into the nearest trash bin, discarding the two faded dresses she had worn at the factory and later in the fields, a farewell that felt like a ritual. Jessica smiled, flashing red lipstick that caught the eye of several dockworkers. Her only regret? That Lera had not seen her stylishly dressed, that she had not had the opportunity to show Lera how she saw herself.

Later on the dock, she again passed through checkpoints and bought passage on a sleek passenger liner, the *Baltic Express* flying the Swedish blue and yellow flag, according to Lera's recommendation. She found a comfortable seat by a window and crossed her legs, the silk and wool blend of the slim black dress draping softly just below her knees. Once settled onboard, an irrational calm settled over her as if the notion of going to America had crystallized in her mind. She had been initiated to the sea on her previous crossing; this second trip, though longer, posed a less daunting challenge. Nevertheless, tightness in her jaws aggravated the injury from Yuri's fist. Shamed,

Jessica kept the left side of her bruised face toward the wall but soon fell into fitful dreams of Yuri chasing her, threatening her with arrest. Her screams in the dream jolted her awake.

Sweating out these inner storms, Jessica recalled a previous dream in which she said very clearly, "I am going where the sun rises in the west and sets in the west." Why did the dream tell me that? America is west or east of Russia, but we call America the "West". She wondered if there was something prophetic about the "sun setting in the west," whether it boded good or ill for her. She shrugged yet the bizarre notion seemed like a footnote to recent events.

Shifting her focus to the other passengers, she noticed a few were fashionably dressed, and tended to acknowledge her stylishness with appreciative nods, but most were weary laborers lost in their own concerns. Those with a great deal of luggage appeared to be emigrants seeking a better life just as she did. "Emigrant?" It sounds strange. I do not see myself as one, Jessica discovered. If not that, what? A criminal wanted for arson and theft? A fugitive in exile? Fear shadowed her face. *Da.* a refugee from violence, Lera said. But Yuri will find me if it takes the rest of his life. I can never go back.

Afraid others would notice her near panic, she forced herself out of her seat to the railing, which she clung to with both hands, lost in conjectures of worst case scenarios until the ship edged next to a dock. Jessica startled when doors opened and closed behind her, almost feeling Yuri's hand on her shoulder. However, it was only a stop. Amsterdam was hours away.

"I shall become mad," she murmured. Her shadow beckoned far below in the backwaters behind the ship. No one heard her monologue. The dizzying thought of falling quietly into the wake nudged her consciousness, magnified her plight: Yuri and the Red Army will search for me, first in Leningrad then the railways and in Konsky. *O Bozhe moy*, then the ports—surely the ports. They will find my papers! They will lead to Raisa and her sister and me. O, I wish, I wish I had never left the farm, a terrible selfish mistake.

The joy of her miraculous trip dissolved into a nightmare. She wanted to flee once again, but had nowhere to go. The notion of tumbling into the sea seemed the only solution. A hollow groan escaped her lips, only to be lost in the steady drift of the liner and the turbulence below. Her dark eyes flashed wildly about. Only when Jessica caught herself and shook off the insidious voices in her head did she release her death grip from the rail. Trembling, she eventually pulled herself together, banished the hail of doubts and turned back inside.

For the next twelve hours she spun in one universe then another; one made real by the stinging pain in her jaw, the other a fantasy long fed by American celluloid and tenderly nourished by Jessica's passion for *haute couture*. She was drawn to the West as surely as the setting sun, yet pulled back by all she had ever known. Her dress lent glamour to her slender form, yet her feet were encased in sturdy oxfords stitched by worn out women in the Benyanske's National Boot and Shoe factory. The earlier sense of finding who she was behind the clothes became blurred, if not obscured.

I need Lettina, she cried at last into her handkerchief. Sobs kept all but the most concerned passengers away from her. To those she simply said, "I want to go home."

Lettina discovered that hundreds of girls, possibly thousands, wandered Novgorod day and night seeking food, lodging and work. She paid cheap rent for herself, Greita and Katya, pleasing the homeowners so much they gave the girls what they could spare for breakfast, bracing beetroot coffee accompanied by black bread flavored with molasses and caraway seeds. The elderly couple seemed starved for conversation. He was a history and philosophy professor at the university. She worked at a bookstore, but their minds generally turned to the scarcity of rations, even bread with reduced kilograms per person.

Among young people on the streets, they more frequently heard "you think this is bad, try Moscow." Men, long unemployed or discharged from the service, fared no better. Bodies of those who drank themselves to death or starved had become a common sight on downtown streets despite war's end over a year ago.

Lettina approached a uniformed young man and asked, "*Pozhaluysta*, where might I find Captain Stanislov? I served in a farm *programme* under his supervision until recently."

He swore and walked away. Another said, "You will not find captains here, ma'am. You will find them in *khorosheye mesto*, nice places in Moscow or Leningrad." Lettina heard this repeated often enough to convince her that searching for Jessica in Novgorod was futile.

"We must go to Leningrad. Captain Stanislov will more likely be there. If not, he could be stationed in Moscow or on another collective. We must find a better way to locate Jessica, *bistro*, quickly."

Greita reacted with immediate resistance. "That may be foolish, Lettina. I know you mean well, but it is difficult enough to live here. Leningrad is vast and much poorer after the Siege. What would we do there?" She shifted toward Katya, looking for confirmation, as if the two of them could withstand Lettina's urging to join the mission that drove her.

Lettina waited, searching each cautious face, and let the matter lie. She had made up her mind. She would do whatever it took to find Jessica. Katya and Greita could make their own way, besides their love affair annoyed her, reminding Lettina of the loss of her own. She found that men in Novgorod had not looked twice at any of the girls. Perhaps their frayed farm dresses told a familiar story, one as hapless as their own. Civilian men appeared to consist of depressed veterans lost in their own pasts, and unruly youths stealing everything they could get their hands on. What's the use? she concluded.

At last Katya broke the silence. "If Greita can get a position in the schools, I think she and I should stay here. I know how upset you are, and I feel badly about Jessica, but is it possible to find her?"

"Is it possible?" Lettina exploded, clenching her fists. "Is it possible to leave her to her fate? I will not abandon her now or ever. She may be in danger with the captain." Her voice cracked and broke, the loyalty so like Lettina.

"We will walk with you to the station," Katya offered.

"We must inquire at schools along the way, or we will be in serious trouble here," Greita said. They had depended largely on Lettina's savings the last few days.

The Moscow to Leningrad train rattled over worn and twisted tracks from Novgorod to Leningrad. Lettina's broad shoulders slumped, betraying her sense of isolation. She had honed a watchful eye for pickpockets in Novgorod; now she scanned fellow passengers as if everyone were suspect, fearing her few belongings would be stolen. Strange, I have never been alone on my own like this, she mused.

Tired and nervous, she arrived at Nikolaevsky Station southeast of Nevsky Prospekt anxious to find Jessica, yet she first had to become familiar with the city. Leningrad seemed to have a refined character compared to Novgorod. Her outlook brightened when she found factories where she could work, freeing her to set about her original purpose, finding Jessica. She inquired where she would find government offices or military offices in charge of the farm harvests.

"You want to work on a farm? We have farm *programmes* a plenty for you," one official assured her.

Lettina escaped before they drafted her and thwarted her plans.

"Captain Stanislov? Why would I know him?" Or "Why do you want to know?" others replied. Discouraged, hungry and exhausted from walking all day, Lettina followed a group of indigent older women to a flophouse and fell asleep on a military cot similar to those on the farm collectives.

Morning in the port city brought tangy, crisp smells of the sea, the clamor of the harbor, and inspiration of a new day. Lettina leapt out of bed and found herself on a street of vendors, one selling warm *kuckenbread* she absolutely could not resist. Sitting on the dirty stone steps of a bombed-out building, she savored it in small bites, leaving a buttery smear on her lips.

Fortified, Lettina asked in earnest for clues where she might find Captain Yuri Stanislov as a means of finding Jessica.

"Are you one of his women?" asked an agent at an office.

"I would not be asking if I were you, miss," another said.

Her fears for Jessica escalated; if only I could telephone someone or send a letter, she moaned, but both were out of the question, given the restricted use of telephones and her lack of money or knowing who to call. Determined in the meantime to acquaint herself with Leningrad, she sought a familiar *Russki* heritage, the traditional Church of the Savior on the Spilled Blood, the epitome of Russian medieval architecture and art, preserved as a cultural treasure during the rise of the USSR. She found it in the heart of the city on Griboedov Canal. Five green, red and yellow onion domes towered above imaginative folk-like windows, and doors mounted among ringed bands of rainbow colors around the building.

Breathtaking to view from a distance, Lettina at once grasped its significance as a monument to Alexander II of Imperial Russia, who had been assassinated on the site. The Church had been constructed over the blood-stained cobblestones, which could be viewed inside. She dared to enter, trailing people who may have been Old Believers: there was no way of knowing within whom or where spirituality versus disbelief resided in 1946.

The interior, radiant in sunlight slanting through narrow windows, struck Lettina as too dazzling for words. Unaccustomed to holy edifices of any kind, she stood as if blinded by the wealth of mosaics of biblical scenes. Tiles of the finest gold, lapis lazuli and cardinal reds lined the walls and inside the central onion dome in a myriad of shimmering colors. Preserved as evidence of national pride, the Church of the Savior, however, bore evidence of recent use as a morgue and warehouse.

Leaving with a sense of Leningrad's dual personality, its romance and grandeur along with its gruesomeness, she sought out Nevsky Prospekt, the street of tsars and nobles, where palaces competed to share space along the busy walkway. The boulevard celebrated Peter the Great's stunning achievement of building the city on swamps. Lettina followed the street toward the foghorns and blasts from barges to the Neva River, her boundless energy overcoming any reticence she might have about being alone. She asked at a window if any positions were available.

"Go over there. Ask them." An overworked seaman pointed the way to a string of offices.

"Today, *da*, tomorrow we do not know. *Nekotoryye dni ochen' khorosho, nekotoryye ne,* some days are very good, some not. He examined her identification papers, and sent her on an errand. "Take these papers to that shipping dock in the brick building just off the water and bring back stamped papers."

Skipping like a school girl, Lettina carried messages back and forth all day and collected her small pay, enough to live on for a few days if she was careful. This meant she would be free to tour the renowned Winter Palace, known even in Konsky as the Hermitage. The next day she walked in the Museum door, free to the public, thanks to the Party. Even her voice became subdued in the palace.

"I cannot believe such beauty exists," she said. "I could get lost in here forever," but with security guards monitoring every room, she did not get lost. However, she found the European art made less of an impression on her than the old, traditional style of the Church of the Spilled Blood. In her exuberance, Lettina spoke to the hatcheck women, elders sweeping floors, and the few tourists like herself. On her way out of the Museum, she asked a receptionist if anyone knew how she might locate Captain Yuri Stanislov, whom she believed lived in Leningrad.

In the ensuing silence, women at the desk glanced at each other. Lettina tensed, her large hands grasping as if she could save Jessica from whatever terrible event had happened.

"What happened to Jessica? I mean Svetlana Sergeevna Gilkova?"

"Was there an American woman named Jessica involved?"

"*Nyet, nyet,* Svetlana and I are friends from Konsky, Kursk Province. The Captain took her away."

"I think you need to speak with the curator."

Soon a short, sturdy woman stepped between Lettina and women at the desk. "Did I overhear your friend is Svetlana Gilkova?" Raisa interrupted. "I met her here at the Museum."

Lettina's mouth opened but no words came. She had a distinct feeling of standing forlorn as a farm worker out of her element in the

Palace of the Emperors, where affairs of the state formerly decided the fate of peoples of the motherland and appeared to do so now. Jessica's life would have been as nothing, not even a postscript then—or now, in an age of disappearances ascribed to the Ruler and the military under his command. With outstretched arms, her hands open in supplication for one last hope for Jessica, Lettina waited for Raisa to explain.

"I believe that your friend, Jessica Svetlana, left Leningrad for Stockholm. From there she intended to travel to America."

The *Baltic Express,* an efficient marine diesel-driven ship, the modern alternative to steam power, exuded confidence Jessica sorely needed. Jessica followed the ship's course on a smudged map taped to the wall. How does one find their way across the sea from the labyrinth of islands around Stockholm to the deep port situated on a manmade contrivance, the North Sea Canal? Yet even the northwest gale-like winds of late autumn favored the heavy craft and she lost track of the time, alternately dozing and dreaming. Black waves reflecting glowering skies kicked angrily around the stately liner while it turned away from land masses and jutting islands, and struck out across the sea toward an endless array of canals surrounding the international city of Amsterdam. She traced the River Amstel to connecting canals now resting out of the storm's path. Through swollen eyes Jessica observed the waterways that appeared to be a quixotic puzzle, much like her own life.

In Amsterdam, masts and towers, broad decks and chiseled smoke stacks of a variety of ships broke the horizon in a tangle of dark geometric patterns. Jessica gave one last glance at a map of the city's concentric canal system making up the *Grachtengordel.* Peter the Great had found inspiration here for establishing the capital of *Russ* on the swamps, where he gained the seaport of St. Petersburg, later called Leningrad, the first sprawling metropolis she had encountered, and now she was about to land in another.

"It's not so bad. You can always ask the *gedmeente,* the local authorities, if you need help. Many of them speak Russian." A clean shaven steward grinned in a familiar but welcome sign of attention. He offered an arm and led her to the rail to watch the liner navigate among anchored vessels in a dizzying number of ports of the vast harbor system.

"You seem to have little work on the ship," Jessica couldn't help saying, covering the silence between them.

The steward threw back his head and laughed. "Why should I and miss moments like this?" He squeezed her arm. Jessica blushed; his warm appraising glance left her as unbalanced as one of the buoys tossed by the waves in the harbor.

"I must warn you, do not venture into de *Wallen*, in the oldest part of town. It is not a place for a nice girl like you, but you might enjoy the *Westerstraat Markt* or any of the dozens of open air markets."

"Amsterdam seems to have a great deal more activity than Leningrad. I found it terribly battered and recovery burdensome considering the weakened state of the workers. I wish—"

"So do I, but you will find Amsterdam an ancient trading port and template for your Petersburg centuries ago." The steward gave her slim cold hand an extra squeeze and released it when he felt obliged to assist passengers. Jessica disembarked alone in Amsterdam.

She mulled over the steward's flirtations in the afterglow of their few moments, which carried her along the wharf with an energetic stream of humanity, a strange assortment of well-to-do businessmen among a crowd that appeared to be struggling immigrants such as herself. Bare-waisted longshoremen labored to load and unload ships, while a surprising number of young women in fine hats and silk stockings with crooked seams appeared to be waiting for loved ones to disembark.

Jessica felt herself shrinking, disappearing into insignificance similar to that she experienced on the production line in the boot and shoe factory. Knowing her face was tear-streaked and the once bright scarf hung limp as a dead fish, she wished she were safely back in Lera's spa-like bath in Stockholm soaking in hot water, lathering with rose-scented body wash, not thinking or running or scheming, just feeling mellow, even a little drunk—an image of the steward's smile inspired even more wishes.

But here the rumpled suits of those ahead of her and the constant whimpering of small children meant they were all together among strangers, unshaved, unwashed, each with unspoken destinations unless it was to the nearest *koffiehaus*. Jessica stepped quickly into a line at a money exchange office sheltered behind iron bars. Nazi retaliation after the war had reduced the former neutral Netherlands to one of the most damaged European nations. The rebuilding of destroyed dams, dikes, bridges and industrial centers had badly inflated the Dutch guilders Jessica now had in hand.

The heady aroma of great urns of coffee melded the diversity of travelers into one driving force—break the fast with a deliciously savory molten liquid, freshly imported she hoped, in the trade center of Amsterdam. She found a spacious, popular café on a side street next to souvenir shops with trinkets and postcards, and flower shops with bins of rust-colored chrysanthemums, all symbols of rising spirits after the Hunger Winter of 1944 to 1945. Yuri had spoken of deprivations on his campaign north through the Baltics, yet Amsterdam was supposedly the hardest hit city because transport of food and goods were limited by massive destruction of waterways. Without comparing the hardships to the 900 Day Siege of Leningrad, she recognized a familiar layer of weariness and loss beneath the sense of celebration among citizens strolling the streets of Amsterdam.

Standing half submerged in the hazy unconscious of sleeplessness and post-trauma fatigue, Jessica's vacant stare ran a film in reverse from the *Baltic Express* to the *Arctic Plover* that spirited her out of the country, back to her birthday in Konsky. Back to the wretched apartment which in retrospect felt secure. Back where comrades did what they were told, worked in the factories, and picked up the pieces after the war. Life according to Five-Year Plans was predictable in Konsky, and dull.

A constant nagging hunger lured her back to the present. Displays of *amended taartjes* and *kringler* pastries competed with truffles for attention until the sight of elegant, ringed coffee cakes, *napfkuchen* on tiered glass shelves fully awakened her senses. Adjusting the slim dress, she felt the hollowness of her stomach from a fast to avoid sea sickness.

"I'll have—I need a slice of the tall yellow one filled with raisins and almonds," she said, pointing to the one in the case. The clerk appeared to speak many languages, but probably not Russian. Before the young woman returned with her order, Jessica's eye caught a bank of international newspapers along the opposite wall. Block Cyrillic letters headlined the prominent *Komsomolskaya Pravda* tabloid at the top of the rack. Drawn to news of the world, any news outside Russia, her eyes sought the story.

Stunned, she looked again and stumbled out of her place at the counter. She peered around other customers for a better view of the paper. With her battered left eye partially closed, she tilted her head to scan the front page with her right eye. Unmistakably, she read the headline that wavered in her vision across the rumpled newsprint.

"*Nyet,* the farm *programme* dare not follow me. I am out of the country!"

SOVIET HARVEST FEEDS
DROUGHT-STRICKEN IN SOUTH

Investigation of Farm Program Finds Neglect

Edging past large men absorbed in their newspapers, she pressed her weakened body through the crowd towards the news racks and slipped the paper from its bracket. Swiftly scanning the front page, she skipped over accolades recognizable as Soviet propaganda. The number of metric tons of grain shipped to the Black Belt, a region curling across southern Russia, was likely exaggerated. The remainder of the article she could have written herself, except for the conclusion.

> *Death of a woman laborer and destruction of vehicles and machinery at Red Bounty Kolkholz in Smolensk Province led authorities to terminate an additional late harvest intended for the drought region---*

Why, it doesn't say anything about lack of petrol. Yuri said they ran out of petrol for the program. That is why it ended. That is why he went back to Leningrad. That is why he was waiting for a new assignment. Jessica paused, disbelieving the reports or the journalism. This is absurd. He expected to be promoted, in fact, he felt he had earned a higher rank. That's why he waited for a summons for his next assignment. But I am finding excuses—she turned to the back page to read the rest of the article.

> *An investigation initiated by Red Army headquarters in Moscow, which contracted with the Farm Drought Rescue Program, found neglect on the part of one of their supervisors, Captain Yuri Stanislov of Leningrad, who was in charge of harvesting at a collective located some distance outside Novgorod.*
>
> *The kolkholzniks under Captain Stanislov's command, reportedly revolted and sabotaged machinery, as well as caused an explosion in an Army vehicle. An investigation found Captain Stanislov, a veteran of campaigns on the Front and through the Baltics, derelict in his duty to honorably and efficiently complete the grain harvest designated for life-saving distribution in southern Russia.*
>
> *After due deliberations, Captain Stanislov has been dishonorably discharged from the Red Army and sentenced to thirty years in Siberia for negligence...*

Jessica could read no more. The newspaper hung limp in her hands, her jaw dropped as if a torrent of protests, *"nyet, nyet,* it is impossible," would rush forth of their own accord, yet only a kind of mewing emerged, compressed horror, disbelief and, *da,* belief.

"Miss, oh, Miss, your order." The young woman leaned far over the counter extending a small plate mounded with the warm yellow coffee cake. Other customers stepped aside for her to reach the counter. Eyes turned toward the frail, distraught woman who was clearly shocked by the news in the paper she held in trembling hands.

Little by little the impact of the report began to sink in. *"O Bozhe moy*," she cried, clutching the paper to her breast. The young boy in short pants tending the news racks held out his hand for payment. Her eyes passed over without seeing him. She read the news article again, her finger following it word for word—the praises heaped upon the Central Committee for its generosity and commitment to the Relief Program, the Ruler's stern admonition, "Comrades must meet the goals set by the Committee. Comrades must sacrifice for the common good…" Jessica felt the penetrating sun of late summer boring into her skin as if she were again in the fields; the still form of Emilia, the young *kolkholznikita*, hanging from the tree swam before her eyes, also other imagined images of the explosion in the night and fingers of fire edging across dried grass of the camp.

Ripples of fear surged through her gaunt empty stomach. She needed to sit down. Staggered by her own naiveté, her association with Yuri, her defense of him just now—it was not the petrol, it was Yuri, the rapes, the negligence. I would have been scooped up and exiled with him had I stayed. He would accuse me of the fire and explosion. "See, she is a fire-starter. She set fire to the official car."

Nearly faint with shock, Jessica grasped for the familiar: Lettina, Tanechka, where are you? Yet the dialogue, the reflections, the awareness continued unabated. He blamed the lack of petrol for his own failings. His waiting for a new assignment was a sham—that explains his drinking. It wasn't about me. He must have feared a reprisal—he was not unaware of blame and punishment meted out by the authorities. Yuri was many things but he was not naïve like me. But surely he would never have expected exile and hard labor for thirty years.

"Ma'am, ma'am, your order."

Surrounded by customers, Jessica quickly assessed the impact on her current situation. She was not an accessory, she had not been detained, and Yuri no longer pursued her—she thrust the paper back to the newsboy. *Bal 'shoye spasibo* and shouldered her way out the door. The bakery clerk set the plate of *napfkucken* aside.

On the waterfront, one dock blurred into another before Jessica's unseeing eyes. Seagulls swooped and squawked unnervingly low overhead. She circled mindlessly past great piles of ropes, anchors, shipping containers, and stalwart men carrying an endless number of crates onboard waiting ships. Some dock workers carried immense bags of laundry on their heads and over their shoulders. Others rolled dollies bearing trunks aboard passenger ships, while tractors shuttled pallets of metal or wooden packing boxes onto barges.

Amid the commotion and clanging, American music blared from a radio. Jessica stopped her headlong pacing to listen, recognizing a Charleston from a *Zeigfield Follies* film, the tune piercing her conjectures about Yuri, and the sudden improbable end to his pursuit. Her feet short-circuited the turmoil in her mind, drumming the beat on the dock timbers, her heavy oxfords now lighter. She wanted to dance a few steps she knew of the Charleston.

Yuri is gone, sent to the gulag, so terrible, but he cannot follow me.

The Charleston sounded louder, beckoning her footsteps toward its source as if it held answers to questions she had yet to ask. The thin, scratchy music blared from a speaker at a shoeshine stand. It switched to the Camptown Races, *"doo da, doo da"* that reverberated in her ears.

Whew. I will search for Madame and Monsieur Marsolet in Paris. Or join a fashion house in New York and meet someone and fall in love, but I'd have to learn to speak English—*"doo da, doo da."* The harvest ruined Yuri. It will me if I let it, just as the Rebellion ruined my parents.

Wiping her brow, Jessica stood on the dock like one of the unclaimed stacks of cargo. The American folk song became a senseless pounding in her ears. Her limbs hung helplessly, leaden weights that lost the memory of how to respond, immobile as if waiting for a rumbling lift to heave her aboard the nearest nondescript boat to anywhere or nowhere. She held her breath so long that a gasp of air went straight to her head.

I can go to New York—or I can go home.

Her steps automatically retraced the way back to a familiar wharf. She spotted the *Baltic Express*, the passenger liner from Stockholm she had arrived on. Her heart jumped—a link to what or where she did not take time to consider. Hurrying along, she turned toward the ticket office. Not until she reached the window out of breath did she decide which it would be.

"To Leningrad," she said lightly.

XXIV

Jessica

The passenger liner was not scheduled to return to Leningrad until the next day. Jessica had her ticket in hand, her decision made, her mind wiped as free of Yuri's pursuit as if the tide had come in and gone out. First she needed to find something to eat. She walked in the opposite direction of the *koffiehius* and its bank of newspapers, still shaken by the shock she had experienced there. She bought a sandwich at a waterfront window and ate it on her way down the street. Churches, cathedrals, and buildings in delightful warm reds and oranges lined the banks of the river, casting glowing reflections in the river and canals. Gulls screeched overhead and daring pigeons barely hopped aside as she walked.

Twenty-four hours in Amsterdam! The undulating rhythm of the mammoth trading center touched something in her bones, her trader-father's legacy, a hint of Eastern spices and Western minerals reaching centuries back to ancient times that the steward had mentioned. A pull to explore off streets and markets propelled Jessica to assume a role as a trader herself. Deep down it felt like honoring her father, his life, living his unfinished story. She fingered articles inside her pocket that meant she had something of value to trade. Free of Yuri, except for his silver collection, she could suddenly relate to the emerging energy and excitement palpable in the streets.

"I love the city," Jessica said in Russian to a stranger beside her who pointed out the canals that Germany had bombed in retaliation for the Netherland's neutrality, and shook her head. But Jessica inhaled the invigorating cool air spiked with scent of the sea, overlooking that it was tinged with motor car exhaust and decay of the damaged waterways. Amsterdam's freshly washed, frank solidity beckoned Jessica for further exploration of privately-owned merchant businesses that drew her into the city's concentric circles, each contoured by historic canals. The narrow streets of Negen Straatjes reminded her she had walked with Yuri in Leningrad, where they had observed signs of shortages in state-owned shops that read *No Meat. No Milk*. She had seen the likeness of Stravinsky on a concert billboard, where leaflets for *The Rites of Spring* were pressed into hands of passersby. Yuri had cursed the wretchedness of the poor. Yuri—Yuri, how long until he no longer walks with me, Jessica shuddered.

Still sensing Yuri's unseen presence over her shoulder and abiding by the steward's warning, Jessica avoided the busiest thoroughfares served by electric trams and scouted out little shops on the side streets. Shops, still closed due to the worsened economy, displayed modern sleek Danish furnishings next door to velvet-curtained shops featuring new and old traditional French Provincial décor. Either were certainly out of reach of anyone Jessica had known in her twenty years before or after the war.

"I saw a dining set similar to that one in Leningrad," she mentioned to a young woman who had paused to adjust her bicycle. "In the Winter Palace, *da*! It was so beautiful in a room with a Tiffany chandelier!"

The young woman continued adjusting her bicycle, allowing only a brief glance at the Russian-speaking tourist. Embarrassed, Jessica hurried on wishing she had not tried to impress anyone with her recent cultural experiences or share the fun of window shopping. "It feels flat when we cannot understand each other. Lettina, I wish you were here."

On a corner she stopped, amused with the irony of discovering a display of sienna explorer maps featuring a flat world in a bookstore window. The copies of ancient navigational maps showed badly distorted landmasses, but Jessica paused to locate the harbors she knew. Leningrad, Stockholm and Amsterdam originated in indentations to the far north, but outlines of continents were cumbersome and features were strange. Her finger traced a line on the sparkling clean window glass to what would be known as America, but the fuzzy contours of the continent held little relation to the geography she knew.

New York harbor did not exist for the mapmakers, and it might as well not exist for me, she mused. This map is scary, like an omen; that is how close I came to emigrating to America. O well, I'm not going to New York. I needn't locate it nor dream of studying fashion design abroad.

When the proprietor stepped out the door Jessica laughed. "I wanted to see how far it is to New York." He shook his head in wonderment at tourists these days, yet the letdown was evident in her face.

But the vitality of Amsterdam whooshed in the grayish air from the North Atlantic. Small brave bursts of commerce harkened back to better times. The United State's Marshal Plan supplied money that now aided reconstruction. People seemed to grasp for relief, reclaim their country, adjust their priorities and reward themselves in some small way. Hopeful mint-fresh signs in bold red and white advertised toasters and Hoover vacuum cleaners, modest-sized refrigerators, stoves and hot plates to suit the ordinary citizen's pocketbook. Vendors at long tables hawked a variety of makes and models of radios including American brands such as Philco, Westinghouse and RCA. Awed by the sight, Jessica realized radios existed here by the hundreds as if everyone should buy one or more, in contrast to the rarity of individual ownership she had experienced in Russia.

"How did I get here and who am I?" she wondered and checked her reflection in a window. A modern woman traveler with a stylish bob and a nasty bruise gazed back at her. Tinges of fatigue lay in translucent hollows beneath her eyes, yet she had to smile.

"You have come a long ways, Svetlana of the Boot and Shoe factory," and her reflection laughed back.

"Ah," Jessica breathed, finding a bench in a linear park along a canal, where the amazingly warm Gulf Stream lifted her hair and wandered over her face with a gentle caress. Dried grass crunched under her feet, yet late summer roses and marigolds maintained bold colors. She sat down and kicked off the sturdy leather shoes with a wry smile. Love-hate, or hate-love, that is how I feel about my shoes, but with this dress, I must have new pumps.

The thought was like a dinner bell on the farm; all she needed as a woman, as a fashion enthusiast, as a suddenly free, twenty-year-old diehard shopper was to have a goal. A sense of purpose prompted Jessica to hurry back into the stream of shoppers. She wandered cobblestone streets with boarded up windows, and skirted drifters in dirty, ragged clothes who shuffled among the crowd. Dutch, German and French cafés with posted menus on their doors tempted her to stay an extra day, but she had already purchased a return ticket to Leningrad.

Open air markets that the steward had referred to were everywhere, but Jessica whispered to herself, "I know what I want," nervous that when she made a wish it seemed to come true. Nevertheless, when she found a sandwich board sign at a pawn shop, she turned immediately and entered. Unlike the small single proprietor shop in Leningrad where she saw the violin, this one, the AMSTERDAM INTERNATIONAL TRADE CENTER, spread behind several boarded-up storefronts. Inside, grassroots entrepreneurs angled to meet current demands for the post-war exchange of goods in a fervor of capitalist opportunism.

While her eyes adjusted to the dimly lit interior, Jessica bypassed stalls of cheap dresses, all suggesting ties to Yuri that made her cringe. Manufactured boots and shoes, household goods, and castoff military wear were also deterrents. Without hesitation, she went to a section of glass-topped display cases. Serious middle-aged men and women behind the counters, most wearing glasses, assessed individual items for owners and handed them back to make their decision. Jessica observed that most sellers accepted the offered price.

She slid into a long line of a remarkably mixed group of age and ethnic individuals waiting to sell their valuables. Street urchins with cocky attitudes made fun of shy youngsters, whose families appeared to be hawking their belongings for the inflated guilders. Humility showed in downcast eyes and pursed lips. Tightly grasping her bag in the likely presence of pickpockets, Jessica nudged her way up the line behind a self-assured, older gentleman in a moth-eaten green jacket. He nodded politely then regained the vacant stare of others who shared the same humbling circumstances.

But a Follies dance tune still echoed in Jessica's ears. A current of excitement rippled beneath the splotchy bruise on her face. She pulled the collectible she intended to sell from her pocket, a two and a half-inch high, silver Chinese pheasant from Yuri's desk drawer. Its eyes were insets of tiny emerald-green jewels and others formed the startling green ring-neck that distinguished the pheasant. Its alert head and long silver tail feathers lent beauty to the heavy piece.

Perfect, Jessica breathed. Yuri had good taste. The woman buyer at the counter held it up and turned it this way and that in the light, a slight smile indicating she was pleased with the piece. It assessed at more than Jessica would have guessed. She never knew its origin or whether the jewels were real. It was enough to know that she had sufficient funds for shopping and travel expenses. Suddenly all the windows in Amsterdam's portside shopping district were enchanting to rurally born Svetlana Gilkova, but a showcase of Italian pumps turned her head.

"Tanya should see these," she murmured with awe. "She would appreciate the supremely soft leather and craftsmanship. And the colors—black, natural, green, red!"

"I would like to try the red pumps with the toe out and the heel strap, *pozhaluysta*," she said to the shopkeeper, a gentleman with thin graying hair, who wore a pinstripe suit.

"The sling heel is the latest fashion, Madame," he replied in good Russian, retrieving her size from a long glass case not unlike Swiss Chocolate or Italian gelato cases she had seen in other shops, giving an immediate sense of their exclusiveness, even an exotic, delicious, incomparable treat. And she meant to treat herself.

"Yes, that one," Jessica assured him, so excited she did not notice him frowning at the yellowish-blue bruise under her eye. Or was it at the ugly oxfords she now wore, or at her plain dress surely lacking in style? However, once she slid her slim feet into the soft pumps, there was no turning back. Retreat from the spell of the shop was impossible. Jessica paid an exorbitant price to be able to place the precious new shoes in her bag, pleased that Yuri's silver collectible had financed this fling.

And I still have enough roubles left to get home, she thought, entirely satisfied with that decision as well.

XXV

Countess

Shorter days of autumn were closing in on the far northern countries along the 60 degree latitude of Leningrad. Just over 2,000 miles of mostly tundra and ice from the North Pole, the city was located one-third of the distance to the equator. A sense of urgency was in the air. Harvesting is over. Prepare for the legendary winter to set in. Jessica found that returning from her abbreviated international tour aroused far less scrutiny than leaving the country. She was soon back on the docks of the Neva River across from Vasilyevsky Island, an extension of the City of Leningrad and a short way from a palace in which she had found a benefactor, Raisa Dobryna.

Despite a threatening chill in the port's overcast weather, Jessica folded the coat and black dress Yuri had given her into her small bag, and wore the red silk blouse and black gabardine skirt that so became her. She wished she had red lipstick and nail polish like Lera wore in Stockholm. The modern look of Anna Akhmatova, the controversial *Russki* poet, was all the rage in Leningrad.

A photograph of the poet appeared on posters advertising readings that attracted literary types and dissidents. Akhmatova had deep-set eyes and straight black hair, bobbed to turn under on the ends, though she was presently older than the image on the photograph. Jessica instantly felt an affinity with her. Yet Lydia had begged caution when introducing Jessica, whom she knew as Svetlana, to Akhmatova's poetry. The day they toured the Winter Palace Lydia had whispered, "She is thought to be spying for the British. She has been arrested a number of times. Her poetry is banned. Her son is in prison because of it."

Jessica later saw posted *samzidats* that railed against crackdowns on those opposing the Party. She had a new appreciation for Akhmatova's courageous and modern poetry as well…

> *"a hundred million voices shout through*
> *my tortured mouth…."*

The poem, protesting purges and persecutions in the 1930s, also spoke for those who suffered the Siege of Leningrad and subsequent persecutions.

"In a sense, she speaks for me, all of us women." Jessica gathered her reflections as she walked across the Palace Bridge, assimilating the statement of sorts about her own voice, her sentiments regarding a world discovered, won, lost, and rediscovered. At rare moments, she wondered how she could be so happy after having been so wretchedly sad, yet she acknowledged that how she looked affected her mood and sense of who she was.

Her spirits soared at times like this when she appeared fashionable, touching an as yet unfulfilled yearning. She was tempted to take the steps two at a time upstairs to the Winter Palace, except she feared damaging her red sling-back pumps. At the main entrance, the registrar informed Jessica that the curator, Raisa Dobryna, was not in today. She was teaching at the University where she did research.

"I understand. It was unlikely I would find her without advance notice, but I took a chance since I am traveling through Leningrad. I would like to leave an envelope for her if you would see that Raisa receives it the minute she comes in."

Jessica stepped aside and wrote a letter, words wanting to overflow the page to this one woman she knew in Leningrad, the single soul who had recognized her family name.

Rayechka.

I am so grateful for your kindness when I was in need, and for your saving the Gilkov family treasures. News re: my situation came to me in Amsterdam, therefore, I am free to return home. Enclosed please find repayment of the money you generously gave me when I was desperate. You have a kind and generous sister, also.

Yours,
Svetlana Sergeevna Gilkova.

She sealed the envelope, and slipped the surprised woman a more than adequate number of roubles, doubly reminding her to see that the letter was delivered.

Jessica practically waltzed out of the museum with the sense she had put past life-threatening days to rest. A slightly bizarre image of a conqueror coming home, perhaps from the Alexandre Nevsky film, crossed her mind. She almost burst out laughing. That was a film she had disparaged. If anything, I have made a conquest within myself. "I am twenty" sang in her head. I conducted my own affairs. I believe I can achieve even more worthy goals.

The notion stayed with her for the long train trip to Konsky. Her mind, seemingly of its own accord, played first one scenario of independence then another. At last she dozed, the rocking motion of the train mimicking the *Baltic Express* rolling on the North Atlantic Drift, propelled by strong westerly winds toward the motherland. Dreamily she recalled the travel adventure—the *skerries*, islets off the towering Langfielden mountains of the coast of Norway, steep and dark in dreary weather, yet resplendent under scattered bits of sun. The mountains contrasted sharply with the flat Jutland Peninsula that formed Denmark. It seemed like a world tour, Jessica mused. Sights and sounds cascaded one over the other, only one remaining in tight focus—the steward in the white uniform of the passenger liner, whose warm hand she still felt holding hers.

Agata Illyinicha was the first to see Jessica when she returned to Konsky.

"Svetlana, I heard you had gone to America!" Agata nearly dropped her handbag. "Tatyana was distraught, as you can imagine. Lettina came to the factory only a few days ago with news you had gone out of the country, yet here you are. Rumors do fly."

Jessica beamed at Agata and a couple with three small children who bore a resemblance to her, round, cheery faces under wispy hair. Jessica greeted them as if they were her family.

"Agata befriended me at the factory," she explained to the woman who appeared to be Agata's sister.

"I came to the station to meet them,"Agata said. "They are escaping from the South before winter sets in. The drought has driven out those with means. Those remaining will likely endure famine similar to that of the '30s. I insisted they all come." A small child toddled over to take Agata's hand.

"You look beautiful, Svetlana. I must admit seeing you is startling after Lettina spread the word you had emigrated. And finding you in these handsome clothes is also unexpected. But something terrible must have happened." Agata's usual care-taking tendencies prompted her to peer at Jessica's face, discerning the not yet faded bruise from cheekbone to jaw bordered by unhealed lacerations.

Jessica waved off the subject and embraced the motherly figure before dashing off.

"You looked after my family as well as your own, *spasibo*." Jessica wondered how they would all live in Agata's two bedroom apartment or acquire a permit to live in another flat, but knowing Agata, the rooms would be filled with laughter.

Jessica discovered that Tanya boarded with friends of her parents. In consideration of others who might also find her clothing startling, she pulled the black raincoat over her blouse and skirt, and put on the old leather oxfords. The plain heavy shoes had essentially mapped the course she had taken from Konsky on her birthday to the farm collectives, to Leningrad, and from there to Stockholm and Amsterdam. Upstaged by the red Italian pumps from Amsterdam, the oxfords had returned to Russia in the travel bag Lera had provided in Stockholm.

Jessica met Tanya at Benyanske's wearing shoes made in the factory amid mixed sentiments about them.

"I couldn't wait to see you, Tanechka, so I came here." The shoes forgotten, Jessica seized her cousin and kissed her first on one cheek then the other. "I did not mean to surprise you so much!"

Tanya had yet to utter a word, her round eyes searching Jessica's face, her questioning stare asking, Why did you go? Why did you come back? What happened? She pointed to the evident battering.

"And you, Tanya, are you all right? And how is it to be back at the factory? Is old Boris still superintendent?" The torrent of questions served to reconnect them without need for answers.

"The Captain? Did he—?" Tanya was yet to be reassured.

"In a roundabout way, I let myself go along with him, that is all I can say."

"I knew he was bad—I was so afraid for you, Lana. Then Lettina said you had gone to America—"

"I am home, Cousin. You may put your worries to rest. I will talk to Lettina."

"The factory is busy. They need you to stitch boots. Will you come back to work? " Tanya gave up trying to fill in the gaps between Jessica's story and hers.

"Tanya, I do not know. If I have to, I will do such work again, but we will see. My life has been a mixed up series of—I don't know what to call them, disasters or miracles, but somehow I am back here. I truly have not had time to think or to see my parents."

"I wrote what I knew to them, that you went away with the Captain."

"Enough. I'll go right now to set their minds at ease." She gave Tanya an extra squeeze. "You are so strong," she teased. "We survived the harvesting, didn't we? O, I have something for you."

Jessica slipped a small packet of brilliantly colored thread from the Netherlands into Tanya's hand. "For your traditional folk designs. You are the designer in the family! Thank you again for the beautiful blouse you gave me for my birthday."

Tanya's radiant face meant a gift from cousin Jessica was even more special than the thread, though she still looked perplexed, as if Jessica had gone away one person and come back another. In the ensuing hours, Jessica also felt herself living in two worlds, two-faced like the god Janus, who was capable of looking at both the past and future. She had to admit it was astonishing to her as well as to Tanya. She had peopled one world with Lera and the steward and the Marsolets, all of whom she prized, that lived abroad. The other world spun with her dear family and friends in *Russ*.

Darkness had long settled over the quiet countryside with its dilapidated bridges, rambling streams, and stretches of charred forest surrounding ruins of burned homes and small farms. Jessica had found a driver to take her to a village of weathered frame homes, some with thatched roofs, lining both sides of a dirt road. Jessica paid for the ride and knocked on her parents' door. A hesitation inside suggested they might be afraid. Jessica called out, "It is me, Svetlana! Please, may I come in?"

She heard a match strike and a spurt of flame lit a kerosene lantern. I know that routine by heart, Jessica reminded herself, a routine unchanged for as long as I can remember. Like peasants, so sad compared to what I saw in Stockholm and Amsterdam. But how do I know? It seems I saw so little yet took in so much. I cannot believe that I crossed the Baltic Sea and part of the North Atlantic and walked the streets in foreign lands and ate *piroski*. Konsky had given me one story. My six months away gave me exposure to another. It seems like a movie in my head, she concluded, an epic film without the Knights, only me. And I am so tired.

The wavering light approached the window. " Svetlana?" Her father's low rough voice sounded uncertain.

"Pozhaluysta, dorogoy otets, please, dear Father, open the door." Jessica picked up her bag.

His shuffling steps stopped while he unbolted the door. "Is that you come home, *moy rebenok?* my baby?" He held the lantern aloft and peered into the dark.

Jessica slipped in and threw herself choking with sobs on his broad chest. Vera appeared behind her husband like a shadow in her nightgown, her tidy white hair well brushed and flowing from beneath a lacey old night cap. Not being a fool, the bruise told her the story at once.

"It has been too much for her, Sergey," Vera said. "Here, set her down for tea." Her own head was bowed, her shoulders hunched from work and sorrow, and more work to overcome the sorrow. Knobby fingers fumbled to light the fire and put on the kettle. She set out a round loaf of black bread she had made that afternoon. The smell of warm fennel and caraway seeds baked into the rye flour made Jessica weep all the more between gushes of a confession.

"*Mama*, you would not have been pleased with your daughter, the choices I made, *ya proshu proshcheniya*, I am sorry. I thought of you and how much you can bear, but I was more willful than strong. I became twenty years old and it gave me ideas, dreams like those in American movies you disapprove of—"

"Svetlana, you are home. We will not talk of dreams and movies. You have been struck and you never apologize for that. Let me soothe the bruise with a cream." She pulled a housecoat around her slim body and bustled about. Jessica knew she handled things better if she kept busy. They had not touched or shared an embrace, a normalcy Jessica expected from long years of her mother's melancholy. Her own impatience with the poverty and the grip the past had on her parents had also distanced Jessica.

Sergey Fedorovich lit a large candle and set it on the table. The room began to warm with the fire blazing in the blue-tiled Russian wall stove. The first thing Jessica noticed when the light reached their little corner table was a sheaf of rye tucked behind the icon, a reminder of the celebration of Poludnitsa, Goddess of the Harvest, the harvest that had beaten but not defeated Jessica on the farm collectives. She found her mind flitting disconcertingly from her past trauma to the present familiar yet unfamiliar reunion at home. Fatigue hung heavily over her lids.

"I left the country," she blurted. "I set sail for America."

The looks on the abruptly awakened faces of her parents told her the statement failed to register. There were too many gaps, too much of her story unrevealed, too many improbabilities. Her confession sounded like lies, a means of distraction or denial. Everyone lies. Jessica realized it would take time for them to comprehend. Jessica tried to soften the blow of their daughter almost permanently leaving the country.

"It was not intentional, at first. My fantasies led me in deeper and deeper," she admitted, half laughing, half crying, her youthful voice rising and falling in the dark room. "I am like you, Vera. It was you I heard in my mind that I should be proud of my country, *Rossiya Matushka*, Mother Russia. I--I--I don't know that I am proud, but I am too Russian to leave." She recalled the photograph of Anna Akhmatova she had seen and smiled. Anna was also too Russian to leave.

"*Russia—land where my heart is buried deep*." Her father quoted Pushkin as effortlessly as pronouncing the inevitable proverbs, as if exile in the village's *izba* had so deprived him of mental stimulation that he lost the power of independent thought and speech.

But Jessica's stories came out, partly backwards from Amsterdam to Leningrad, to the train and home, where the story of Agata's starving relatives from the South reminded her to tell of the harvest on the *kolkhoz* and of one girl hanging herself. The almost petrified faces of Sergey and Vera betrayed that they were caught in their own stories, rather than hers. Their eyes turned back in time, sensing the horrors she endured through their own experiences.

"The bruise, Lana, the bruise." Her father's fist curled and uncurled until he hid it under the table. Only then did she tell of the Captain and the days amounting to captivity.

"But I allowed myself to accompany him to Leningrad, to my shame. I--I believed him when he rescued me from the farms and promised me a better life. I did not repeat the tragic story of Emilia, nor did I want to, even in the most desperate moments. I lived, but in a sense, I chose an alliance dishonoring myself and our family."

Stillness moved in like a fog and settled its presence in the dark corners, squirreling its way into the storytelling scene. Dry linden leaves of overhanging branches scraped the roof and window sills, punctuating the solemnity of the moment.

"Quite the opposite," Vera declared at last. "You are a Gilkov." Glancing at Sergey, she twirled a lone ring on her thin finger. "We have not told you our own story, Sveta, because it would only make you unhappy." She paused, possibly reconsidering, then began.

"In 1927, ten years after the Revolution, we escaped the persecution of landholders like us by subterfuge, lying, and forged papers," she said. "We even stole horses to gallop away from Novgorod in the night to avoid being arrested. Your father was caught, tortured, and beaten before our estate was taken by force and nationalized as a collective."

Her voice, once rich and mellow, quivered with fear even now when she relived details of their exodus. "You were a tiny baby. I carried you in a breadbasket for safety until we came to Konsky. Your father excelled in the trading business, and we enjoyed a few good years, but even here the reformers found us. We were drafted into the *programme* for several years when you were very young. After that we were banished to this village where we found this hovel. Did we fight back? O *da*. Did we die? *Nyet*."

She pulled her robe closely around her shoulders as if the telling cost her every ounce of warmth and strength in her body. Their stories, both her father's and mother's, came out throughout the night, falling upon Jessica's senses like bricks dropped one at a time.

"We, too, are tied to the motherland. I cannot help it. It is who I am." Her father's heavy brows knitted in concentration. He lit a stub of a cigarette from the ashtray, exhaling the smoke with a deep sigh.

"Is it shameful, Lana, for us? For you?" Vera continued. "I think not. My father, your grandfather, Count Basil survived under the tsars and fought against the Revolution—"

"Count, did you say, *Mama*?" Jessica cried; her bleary eyes blinked and blinked again, doubting what she thought she heard.

"My father, Count Basil was shamed for his wealth by the idealists. The nobility was shamed, banned, or shot. He was imprisoned until they needed him to defend Leningrad during the Siege." Jessica had never heard her mother's voice so full of pain and bitterness. She had never spoken so openly of her family.

"And they died in the Siege," Jessica added.

"*Da*, after all the suffering, to die like that."

"And you spared me knowledge of the downfall and death of my grandparents because they were of the nobility."

Vera Basilevna Gilkova's frail, shrunken body appeared to cave in, as if the revelation left her with nothing to tend—her last kettle to boil had spilled, her final injury to soothe snatched from her. She reached across the table to place her hand on Sergey's arm.

"Jessica," she said absently, before she caught herself. "Your beauty, Lana, the beating, your recognizable name. You have experienced the brutality because of the Gilkovs' noble blood on your father's side."

Unable to piece the threads of her mother's disclosures together so quickly, Jessica listened attentively, catching herself frowning like her father. "My name was recognized by a woman at the Winter Palace. She provided me with identity papers and passport under the name Svetlana Gilkova. Apparently, her title as Countess had been concealed at that time. I did not know this story."

"Svetlana, *vy mozhete obvinit' menya , mne ne vazhno*, you may blame me, I care not for that. *Verite*, I covered up and lied to you about my family all your life."

"You covered the family's downfall and what you considered shame, *Mama,* and the suffering they and you experienced. Now your daughter admits to being shamed in a different but coercive situation."

"Vera, is this necessary? What is happening? I say *ne trogay problemu, poka problema ne trogayet tebya,* let sleeping dogs lie. We have suffered enough." Sergey snuffed out the light in the kerosene lantern.

"Is it too late to be a proud Russian family, to be too Russian to leave the country, Sergey? I imagine Svetlana would think not." Vera had to have the last word. Jessica noticed the slightest spark in her eyes, even in the dim light.

"I brought you some of your mother's, my grandmother's, belongings," Jessica said abruptly, remembering the packet Raisa had given her. She withdrew the brown paper tied with string from her bag and placed it in her mother's hands. It felt like a memorial to the passing of generations and time.

"The packet was given to me by an agent at the Museum in Leningrad," she said with a shrug, not wanting suspicion directed at the curator or herself.

It was five o'clock in the morning, the sun barely sifting through the trees, when the reunited Gilkovs bent over the table to examine the contents. Vera slowly unfastened the drawstring of the enclosed green velveteen bag. The jewelry flowed onto the bare wooden table with tinkles and chimes, the tones assembling in musical variations. Candlelight reflected off myriads of rainbow hues of diamonds, rubies, and emeralds.

"*All breathes of Russ, the Russ of old*!" Sergey again fell back on the words of Pushkin for lack of his own. How exquisite an expression of how he'd felt for decades about the "old" motherland, one that brought cheer to the faces around the flickering light.

Gasping soundless "O, Os," Vera looked like a small child yearning to reach for the shining objects, yet afraid to touch them, holding back as if the beautiful creations would break, or *pouf,* disappear. Her thin hands fluttered about, the worn ring loosely revolving on her bony finger.

Jessica wished she could wilt away and leave Vera to her memories and jewelry, aware this transparent display of emotion exposed her mother, amounting to another shaming of the woman who had lost everything except her husband. Embarrassed for her, Jessica tried to look away to preserve the dignity her mother had long maintained, yet in surveying the dark interior of the family home, she saw a house with no plumbing, no electricity, and no chance of improvement without money. She forced herself back to their story, obviously much more long-suffering and degrading than hers.

"O Sveta, my mother wanted me to have her gold ring with this amethyst when you were born. I was afraid it would be stolen like the valuables of all the nobility, so I did not accept it," Vera said, her voice quaking. "We had not told you she married into nobility—it would have been too dangerous for you to know, *vy ponimayete?* It was safer to be unknown and have nothing. They had to leave the modest wealth they had accumulated in the Museum for safe-keeping. *Bah,* do you think we live better since the Revolution? Not for us. How can one live like human beings stripped of title and position?"

"So they hid the jewelry not only from the Germans during the Siege, but from the idealists after the Revolution."

"We have had no peace, this insurgency, that invasion, the dictator's persecutions and executions," Sergey's voice, heavy with defiance. "What are parents to leave their children? A future of working in a boot and shoe factory? I am sorry, Svetlana, but it was the best we could do for you." He paused, moving the candle near Vera.

"*Pozhaluysta,* Verochka. See what Svetlana has brought. Think no more of the past. *You cannot break a wall with your forehead.*"

Jessica expected her father's proverbs and her mother's fury. Reminded of the luxuries that were her birthright, Vera had worked up a good head of steam. Her family had been robbed of everything down to a kopek, she had often said, and she had acted it out in dozens of ways all of Jessica's life, the depression, the bitterness, the withdrawal from social life, even from her daughter.

Sergey turned to Jessica. "There are a great deal of valuables here, *moya doch'*. Gold rings, silver pendants, and finely-wrought necklaces with precious gems. What—?"

"I want you to move back into Konsky and become a merchant trader again, *pozhaluysta*, Father. Apply to the authorities for a little place with an apartment above, so we can all live there. We may have to give *vzyatka,* bribe one or two local officials to get the papers, but I know how to barter and exchange—O, *Bozhe, moy*, I will tell you that story another day. We can be happy now." Her words blurred from sleeplessness and relief that seemed born of the ages.

"I will open a small consignment boutique with fine fashions to help other women. Maybe they, too, have dreams. And I will buy a violin for Pasha." The details drifted about untethered for the moment, but quieted the questions that were sure to come from Sergey and Vera. Vera led her daughter, like a small child, to a sleeping platform above the ancient stove. Before she blew out the candle, her aged hands caressed the green velveteen bag and snuggled it safely behind the icon and sheaf of rye.

On the weekend, Jessica met Tanya early, intending to spend the day with her. "How are you managing at the factory these days? I know you preferred working in the fields."

"I will leave the factory if there is a place for me elsewhere. I trust in whatever comes." Tanya had grown taller and her former round face had become more mature. She spoke matter-of-factly, evidence she had taken a leap into adulthood.

"Cousin, if you mean you trust God, look at what happened to us and our parents and everyone I know. It is a sin, a crying shame what we've all gone through. *Nyet*, it was often criminal."

"But Jesus the Lord brought you safely back to us. I knew He would."

Tanya's tender smile reminded Jessica of Agata's, radiating from an inner calmness that had first drawn Jessica to the mystical. She changed the subject in consideration of Tanya's enduring faith, or more likely, because of her own ambivalence about it.

"Speaking of God, shall we visit the monastery today? Surely Pasha has recovered. The Brothers could not be more compassionate. Abbot Konstantin has likely been lenient about his staying there. We must go! I cannot wait to see Pasha!"

Tanya stared at her as if breaching a chasm that seemed all too obvious. Only reluctantly did she explain. "You haven't heard? St. Sansais Monastery has been nationalized. The State changed the name to Central Kursk Vineyards. They have taken Abbot Konstantin away. No one knows where."

Before she finished speaking, Jessica screamed and cursed. "Trust God when God lets that kind soul be taken away? Tanya, how can you accept that? O Kostya! Kostya! He saved cousin Pasha. I would die for him! Tell me, but do not tell me, were Pasha and Dmitri taken away?" Jessica wrung her hands, then placed them over her ears. "They" were everywhere, behind reinstatement of persecutions which Yuri had alluded to. Perhaps coming for her, too.

"Our dear poet Anna Akhmatova wrote *The Last Toast.*

'*—I raise my glass—to God's not saving us!*'

I'm sorry, Tanya, but she speaks for me, and for many of us. Her son was taken away. She stood in line for him at the prison for a year, unable to get his release. She and her work have been condemned yet still she writes in Leningrad."

"Jessica, there is more. Listen to me." Tanya shook Jessica's arm to get her attention. "Pasha is at the vineyard with Dmitri. Dmitri is head vintner. The others are there producing wines as before. Surely they maintain their secret community just as other orders do. Dmitri looks very much like he did at the farm, except for being crippled."

Dumbly, Jessica gaped at the news, her knees nearly buckling as if she were again under the thumb of the authorities. A woeful voice emerged from somewhere deep inside. "Crippled? Dmitri is crippled? I did not know."

Where was I when it happened— allowing myself to be taken to Leningrad? Aloud, she said, "I can never forgive myself for not helping him in some way."

"It is the suffering. That is the way of Russia. *Eto normal'no*, the old people say. It is a sacrifice we must bear."

"I don't want to hear it," Jessica fumed. "Why? Suffering has no meaning. Sacrifice has no meaning. It is all a lie to keep us down like all the other lies we hear."

Tanya appeared so crushed that Jessica relented. "Perhaps it has no meaning—outside of—outside of giving it up for someone else, as Sasha told us many times."

She sat down hard on a bench, weary eyes staring at her feet, recalling how fervently she had prayed throughout her odyssey, a desperate running supplication for protection for herself, Lettina, and Pasha. Her pleas for redemption were even more fervent for forgiveness—selfishly yearning for a better life, and breaking every law there was.

When Tanya ventured to sit next to her, Jessica sensed strength and reserves that Tanya had acquired as a result of their separate ordeals and by growing up. In a way Tanya seemed to possess Agata's serenity and Sasha's assurance in her already steadfast nature. Jessica had flirted with and denounced both at critical moments of the past year.

At last Jessica said, "I wonder if Sasha is right. You and I, the women in the fields, we experienced one assault after another on our bodies and senses. And, Tanya, I felt the Siege of Leningrad as if I'd been there. You cannot imagine the haunted look of poor gaunt survivors who appeared to have lost their families, their home and jobs, all but the last thread of their lives. It is not so everywhere. I found hope and a sense of peace, even joy on my travels out of the country. How can we accept suffering as our own *zavtra*?"

The whole weight of the past six months bore down upon her, clouding the clarity she wished to have gained. The heart rendering turmoil she had experienced, and the racking pain of victims of the Siege, the war, and the persecutions pierced her sense of a godly beneficence.

"*Nyet*, Cousin, yet what am I to believe when even the abbot and Dmitri could not be saved from suffering? Surely persecutions and imprisonment and forced labor, in the name of Mother Russia, cannot be accepted as normal. It is the tiger, I think."

Tanya startled and swung herself around to look sharply into Jessica's eyes, her knuckles gripping the bench turned white. "Jessica, don't go away from us again, not like Pasha!"

"O Tanechka, do not fear I'm going out of my mind, I have defeated the tiger once. I know we can do it again."

A burst of sparrows chattered overhead and swooped to elude a raven. The odor of stale tobacco reeked from damp butts of Chesterfields crushed on the sidewalk. Swirls of late autumn leaves huddled in clumps against the drab concrete factory building of Benyanske's National Boots and Shoes. Jessica took Tanya's hand as a deepening chill crept into the wind, hinting of a snowstorm sweeping across the country.

An entry in the black leather-bound book of donations at the Winter Palace State Museum, located near the mouth of the Neva River in Leningrad, USSR, noted:

"Jewelry, property of Countess Svetlana Baronova, held for safekeeping during the war, was returned to the Gilkov family, according to the Countess' instructions, November 15, 1946.

Signed, Raisa Aleksandrovna Dobryna, Curator

Acknowledgments

The inspiration for *Jessica of Russ* occurred many years ago when I first read *The Way of a Pilgrim*, and *The Pilgrim Continues His Way*, translated from the Russian by R.M. French. The ancient mystical traditions eventually led me to the monastic mysticism of Mount Athos in Greece, a journey that has been personally rich and rewarding.

While researching this novel I found that books, acquaintances and opportunities arose which shed light on how conflicts existing within the Russian State impacted individuals and their faiths. It was a great privilege to meet Irina Kochetkova who kindly shared insights into Soviet life and assisted me with Russian names and phrases, as well as introduced me to the Eastern Orthodox Church. I credit Ingeborg Van Zanten, international cultural facilitator, for drawing together writers of diverse backgrounds, including those who have lived under Communist rule. I also fondly remember a former professor at Montana State University, Dr. Titus Kurtichanov, who radiated so much joy in teaching Russian literature.

A wealth of resources including the book *1946* by Victor Sebestyen jumped off the library shelf in perfect timing. Sigrid Rausing's *Everything is Wonderful!* is a living story of Estonians' experience of farm collectivization after Russian annexation of Estonia. *Natasha's Dance* and *The Whisperers* by Orlando Figes mirror the spectrum of cultural life and influences from the Romanovs through dissolution of USSR. Solzhenitzn wrote his impassioned reflections on the war years, heavily supporting the faith and values of his countrymen. Edward Rutherford's *Russka* will forever live in memory as the country's history dating as far back as a tribe originating on the River Rus. (See Selected Bibliography).

My gratitude also for the editors, including my daughter, Jeanne Elpel, and Margie Peterson, as well as the many authors and others who consented to review the book. The novel became a reality due to the creativity and digital talents of layout and designers, Linda Griffith and my son, Thomas Elpel.

It was not by chance that I came to write a novel set in Russia. WWII left a lasting impression on my seven or eight-year-old mind by the transients who stopped at our home on old US Highway 10 in southwestern Montana. Their shoes were often wrapped in rags and the men usually so weak they could barely eat the plate of scrambled eggs and homemade bread my mother gave them. Whether veterans or other castoffs of wartime, we witnessed the hardship they endured walking the long lonely highway across our remote state.

The suffering I find in Russian history and literature likewise resonates in my consciousness with a sense of social justice that forms a thread through all of my writing. Deep down I acknowledge the suffering and sacrifices of these men and women, as well as those who suffer oppression and displacement in the past and present.

— JE

Selected Bibliography

Akhmatova, Anna.　　*Requiem*, a poem, 1953

Daniels, Robert V.　　*Red October, The Bolshevik Revolutions of 1917*, 1967

Doerr, Anthony.　　*All the Light We Cannot See*, 2014

Figes, Orlando.　　*Natasha's Dance*, a Cultural History of Russia, 2002

Figes, Orlando.　　*The Whisperers*, 2007

French, R.M.　　(translation). *The Way of a Pilgrim and The Pilgrim Continues His Way*, 5th printing, 1965

Himelstein, Linda.　　*The King of Vodka, The Story of Pyitr Smirnov*, 2009

Kelly, Catriona.　　*An Anthology of Russian Women's Writing, 1777 - 1992*, 1994

Kelly, Catriona.　　*St. Petersburg, Shadows of the Past*, 2014

LaFeber Walter.　　*America, Russia, and the Cold War, 1945 – 1990*, 1991

Meier, Andrew.　　*Black Earth, A Journey Through Russia After the Fall*, 2003

Milosz, Czeslaw.　　*To Begin Where I Am, Selected Essays*, 2001

Neville, Peter.　　*Russia, A Traveler's History of Russia*, 5th Edition, 2006

Otto, Rudolf.　　*The Idea of the Holy*, 2nd Edition, 1950

Peskov, Vasily.　　*Lost in the Taiga*, 1992

Pushkin, Aleksandr,
trans. Johnston, Charles.   *Eugene Onegin*, 1977

Rausing, Sigred.   *Everything is Wonderful!*, 2014

Rutherfurd, Edward.   *Russka, The Novel of Russia*, 1991

Sebestyen, Victor.   *1946, The Making of the Modern World*, 2014

Slezkine, Yuri.   *How to Parent Like a Bolshevik*, (New York Times), 2017

Smith, Hedrick.   *The Russians*, 1976

Solomon, Volkov.   *St. Petersburg, a Cultural History*, 1995

Solzhenitsyn, Alekandr.   *The Russian Question at the End of the Twentieth Century*, 1995

Valantasis Richard, Ed.   *Religions of Late Antiquity in Practice*, 2000

Zubkova, Elena.   *Russia After the War, 1945 – 1957*, 1998

About the Author

Jan Elpel, Psy.D., is the author of historical novels set in Montana Territory, *Berrigan's Ride, Healers of Big Butte,* and *Heirloom China.* Her novels, including *Jessica of Russ*, were influenced by her international travel and studies in the classics, psychology, philosophy and religion. She is a Montana native and lives in Bozeman, Montana, where she enjoys writing, backcountry horse riding, and oil painting.